A HOUSE
DIVIDED

A HOUSE DIVIDED

JOHN CORLEY

TATE PUBLISHING & Enterprises

Published by Tate Publishing & Enterprises, LLC
127 E. Trade Center Terrace | Mustang, Oklahoma 73064 USA
1.888.361.9473 | www.tatepublishing.com

Tate Publishing is committed to excellence in the publishing industry. The company reflects the philosophy established by the founders, based on Psalm 68:11,
"The Lord gave the word and great was the company of those who published it."

Book design copyright © 2011 by Tate Publishing, LLC. All rights reserved.
Cover design by Kristen Verser
Interior design by Sarah Kirchen

Published in the United States of America

ISBN: 978-1-61777-032-6
1. Fiction / Historical
2. Fiction / War & Military
11.02.22

I dedicate this book to the cherished memory of my late wife, Joyce. This beautiful woman, by a life well lived, left me a better man and the world a better place. I miss her every day.

ACKNOWLEDGMENTS

To my cousin, Karen Powe. I must give full credit for bringing my book from a lonely file on my computer to the printed page. Without her mentoring, editing, and proofreading, this book would still be just that—a lonely, unfinished file. I also wish to thank my special friend, Janet Rossidivito, and my friends Merlin Orr, Marie Doolittle, Carl Carlan, and Rhea Gilbert for taking the time to read my book and encourage me to seek publication.

TABLE OF CONTENTS

BOOK THREE

BOOK FOUR

BOOK FIVE

PROLOGUE

It had finally come to it! Until now, it had just been an intellectual exercise. But now, now it was real. I nudged Betsy back into
the oak tree's shadow. Even as we moved back, the great man
came into view.

As he approached his magnificent home overlooking nineteenth-century Washington, I suddenly felt fainthearted. If anything had been out of the ordinary—anything at all—I might
have chucked the whole thing. Nothing was, though. Everything
was as it had been for the last week. Anyway, to wait another day
would finish it for me. I might just as well go back to Louisa's
and ponder my future—a future living out a life in the past.

No, I couldn't quit now. The America I had left behind
was in mortal danger of losing what was left of its hard-earned
birthright. I could not and I would not stand back and let that
happen. To allow Benjamin Clay to prevail would destroy me as
surely as he would destroy America.

I watched the general dismount and greet the servant taking
his horse. He wasn't a general, though, not any more a general
than I was John Kelly of this century. He was Colonel Lee of
the US Army. The general title would come later. He didn't look
much like the fabled grandee of the Army of Northern Virginia

either. No steel-gray uniform; he was in street clothes. And no gray beard—except for a mustache, he was clean-shaven with black hair just beginning to show flecks of silver. The difference in years, rank, and army, though, couldn't change who he was and what he represented to the history I had long since left behind.

Betsy snorted and swished her tail as Lee entered into the secret darkness of his home. My biggest challenge had been to master horseback riding. As if she were tired of all the surveillance and waiting around, she actually cooperated in negotiating the winding path toward Lee's house.

I managed to dismount and tether her without making a fool of myself. She nickered softly as the sun's pale-golden glow seemed to morph into a peculiar bright grayness. I untied the small haversack from the saddle and, with trembling legs and fearful heart, walked to the door.

I knocked softly and waited. For an eternity, it seemed. Just as I started to knock again, the door swung open, and a pleasant but authoritative voice greeted me and asked whom I wanted. It was a middle-aged black woman.

I must have hesitated because, with a smile of genial condescension, she repeated her question. "Who are you here to see, sir?" she asked while subtly placing her not inconsiderable girth between the hallway's dusky confines and myself.

As I fumbled for my card, I blurted out my single, well-rehearsed sentence. "Colonel Kelly to see Colonel Lee."

Now it was her turn to be flustered. She knew I wasn't a Lee family relative, nor did she recognize me as one of Lee's extensive circle of friends who frequented Arlington House. She probably assumed, despite my well-cut and fashionable suit, that I was a peddler or tradesman—someone who, at the Lee mansion, was beneath even her own limited station in life. Gathering herself together, she politely invited me in and offered to take my coat and hat. I gave her my hat but kept my coat. At this point, my fears evaporated. Maybe it was because of the deference replacing the amused contempt in her face. Maybe it was like an actor with opening night jitters: once stepping onto the stage, the days of rehearsal and memorizing take charge. Whatever it was, I was infused with confidence.

As she left to see if Lee was available, she glanced at my card. With a barely audible gasp, she stopped, turned her head to look at me, and then, looking back at the card, left with an indistinguishable mutter and a swirl of her dress.

Once she was gone, I had time to look around. It looked substantially as it had on my last visit more than a century in the future. It was homier: a family lived and loved here. It wasn't very tidy either, though the floors were polished and the drapes were clean and pressed. But the most pronounced difference was that it was alive with activity—a family's activity of pleasurable, familiar noises instead of the transient bustle and whispered voyeurism of tourists eavesdropping into the past.

So far everything had gone well enough. I was in Lee's home, and judging by the time it was taking for the woman to return, he was not going to have me peremptorily shown the door. I had been sure my business card would be a matter of special curiosity to him. Even though calling cards among the officer corps of the era were *de rigueur*, my picture in vivid color would be sure to attract his attention. He could make what he wanted of the telephone number and e-mail address printed there. I could take comfort in the fact that he could hardly pick up the telephone to call the police to have me carted off.

After a few minutes, she returned and announced that Colonel Lee would be honored to see me. As she beckoned me toward Lee's office, I was aware of interest and curiosity on her face. She was a dowdy woman, but a factotum with a quietly competent look. I couldn't help but reflect on what my presence here might mean to her and those like her. As she ushered me into a rather smallish room, Lee rose from his desk with his hand outstretched. The persona of the man shaking my hand almost overwhelmed me. I couldn't afford to let it affect me today, though. Today I had to shine. Everything depended on how I presented myself to this man and how he responded to my Alice in Wonderland tale.

I wasn't dealing with just any man. I was face-to-face with a man of truly heroic proportions—a man whose campaigns and battlefield skills would be studied in military schools around the world. But beyond that, I could see how and why Robert E. Lee, the man, would transcend his legendary exploits as a soldier. While his eyes showed a hint of the speculative curiosity I had counted on to gain entry, the rest of his demeanor demanded my attention: polite but correct, friendly but distant. A leader he certainly was, but perhaps not so much the charismatic sort. Instead, his was a natural dignity—a presence that at once drew people to him but, at the same time, marked a boundary not to cross. Tens of thousands of men would see in this one man the embodiment of the archetypal Southern gentleman born to lead and equally obligated to serve—an American paladin! One did not easily get close to this man. I struggled to maintain my composure.

He said, "I am Robert Lee, sir, and it is my pleasure to make your acquaintance. Please take this chair. May I offer you refreshments?"

A double shot of Wild Turkey came to mind. I was already feeling the need for a bit of the liquid courage I once depended on so terribly much.

"Yes, please. That would be most enjoyable," I heard myself say.

As I settled into the straight-backed chair, he went to the door to speak to someone in the hallway. A few seconds later, a young woman entered and looked at Lee expectantly. I recognized her as Mildred, his youngest daughter. She was young—really little more than a girl—slight, and perhaps not the prettiest of the Lee girls but with a vivacious insouciance born of the special place she occupied in Lee's heart. Fiercely loyal to her father, she, like all the Lee girls, was destined never to marry. She remained with her parents until their deaths. She would also become the most fiercely partisan of Robert and Mary Lee's daughters during and after the South's struggle for independence.

His face showed the affection a father always has for a favorite child as he asked her for two glasses of cool lemonade. And when I stood up, she showed she knew it too because she said, "Father, where are your manners? Aren't you going to introduce me to the gentleman?"

With a look of fatherly exasperation, he made the introductions and gently reminded her that we had business to discuss. She just smiled and said she would bring the lemonade directly. I knew Mildred—or "Precious Life," as her father called her—was the most precocious of the Lee girls and was more apt to take liberties with her father's admonitions.

After she left, we engaged in idle talk, as men who have in common the profession of arms will do. Underneath the harmless chitchat, though, I knew he was sizing me up. In this day's army, he would personally know, or know of, every single senior officer. And he would know I was not one of them. Did he think I was an impostor or maybe a politically connected dilettante? Either way, his estimation and respect for me was suffering. I was certain that as soon as the lemonade arrived, he wouldn't spend much more time with me. I would have to give the best briefing of my life.

I wasn't disappointed! No sooner had Mildred returned with the lemonade, and Lee firmly ushered her out the door, than he said, "Now sir, what is your business with me?" He still spoke politely but in a tone that took me back to other times and to other places.

It was the voice of a man born to the uniform. How many times had I heard it? Not often, but enough times to know it when I heard it! It was more than that, though. In spite of his renowned and well-deserved humility, this was a man possessed of the calm assurance that he would be heard and heeded.

Mustering what was left of my newfound confidence, I said, "Colonel Lee, the name and title on the card you have on your desk are entirely genuine, as is my picture." I went on. "I am here to discuss military matters of profound importance to you and to our country."

Was that a slight bit of hesitation I saw on his face?

He picked up the card and said, "Oh yes. Your *carte de visite*. The picture; it is most interesting. No, it's more than interesting. I was unaware they could introduce color so vivid into portraiture images. Or that such a picture could be transferred onto regular paper. Is it a new process? If so, it is remarkable what they have done and an exceptional likeness, I might add. How on earth did they ever make it so small? Where did you have it done?"

Eager to keep the slight advantage I had gained, I continued. "Colonel Lee, I will be glad to tell you where I had it done. But first, with your permission, I would like to show you something even more significant." Not waiting for an answer, I pulled a book out of my bag. Getting up, I offered it to him. Just as I had rehearsed dozens of times, I opened it to the tabbed page and said, "Do you happen to know today's date?"

He took the book and responded automatically, "Yes, of course. October the sixteenth."

He began to read and almost immediately stiffened. He read a few more seconds before retrieving from his desk what I supposed would be his still unsent letter to his son, Rooney. The letter he had started yesterday, October 15, 1859.

A quick comparison of the book and the letter followed, during which I closely observed his face. Amazement and confusion were quickly replaced by barely suppressed outrage and finally by denial. He was reading what was impossible to be reading. His nineteenth-century mind couldn't accept what he was seeing. There were too many unanswerable questions, too much to cope with in such a short time.

I had planned this moment. I had put myself in his place and had tried to imagine what he would think when he realized what he was looking at. I had rehearsed and rehearsed, going over it time after time. I had tried to anticipate every eventuality in his response.

Without finishing, he abruptly closed the book and looked at the cover. It was the famous photograph by Matthew Brady taken shortly after Appomattox. An image, in spite of the profound difference in appearance, he couldn't fail to recognize as an older, much-changed Robert Lee.

I continued to watch him closely so I could observe his reaction. I needed to gauge how this inexplicable and impossible book affected him.

He pushed himself away from the book as if it were a poisonous snake from his garden. His face turned pasty white, and he started trembling uncontrollably. Well, why not? Not only had I presented him with a situation that defied the impossible,

I was the messenger of his own mortality. I had shown him his twilight years. This vigorous man in the flower of his prime had just seen the man he would become. Did he detect the look of steely defiance and ineffable sadness on his self-to-be?

Still shaken, he could only utter a strangled, "Who are you?"

I had cracked Lee's legendary self-control. Even so, he was behaving with more equanimity than I had anticipated. He was quickly pulling himself together.

"Who are you, sir?" he repeated, standing and towering over me in a paroxysm of consternation. "How and why have you come in possession of my personal letters? What does all this mean? Who sent you? Explain yourself!"

The force of his anger chastened me. I needed to be heedful of his demands, but it wasn't quite time to reveal my origins. I had to build a mountain of evidence, build it until the truth would be undeniable. "Colonel Lee, if you will grant me fifteen minutes, I give you my word that all your questions will be answered."

Not waiting for his reply, I pulled out my watch. He was the first man of his century to see this marvel of the electronic age. I had preset fifteen minutes on the stopwatch function. He looked at it briefly with no visible sign of emotion and returned his eyes to me.

"Go on," he said as he finally sat down.

Bingo! I had him. It was just a matter of making my case now.

Nodding, I pressed the stopwatch button and handed it to him. Drawn by the unnatural ping sound, his eyes widened as he saw the seconds count down in the digital format familiar to hundreds of millions of denizens of the next century.

Drawing his attention back to me, I said, "Colonel Lee, in the next few minutes, I promise to stretch the limits of your imagination. Telling this to anyone else would label me a charlatan or insane—or both. But you aren't anyone else. You are Robert Lee, future general and commander of your country's army. When I have finished, the evidence I will have presented will be ineluctable. It will be up to you what you choose to do with it."

He reacted only slightly to this pronouncement of his future. Other than a barely perceptible straightening of his posture and a hardening of his penetrating gaze, you would have thought I had done nothing more than mention the weather.

I reached into my bag and pulled out my next gimmick. I laid it on the desk in front of him.

"I suspect, sir," I said, "that you will recognize this, even if it is like nothing you have ever seen." It was my Beretta. I was betting the soldier's mind would take over at what was most obviously a tool of his trade.

I was right.

Almost involuntarily, he reached over and picked it up. He handled it as a soldier would: feeling its heft, keeping it pointed away from either of us, running his hand lovingly over the smooth charcoal-gray barrel. I knew he would want to test the hammer and trigger pull, so I took it from him and showed him the magazine was out and the chamber was empty. Not that he would know what a magazine was. I could see he recognized my instinctive response for what it was: a fellow soldier's innate respect for the weaponry of war. I detected a subtle change in his face, and I felt we had established a bond that I hoped would serve me well the next few minutes.

As he sighted the pistol and tested the trigger and hammer, he said, "Very impressive. Must be dreadfully inaccurate, though, and only one shot at such a small caliber. Perhaps sufficient for self-defense, but other than that I'm afraid it has very little practical use. Excellent workmanship, though. In fact, superior to anything I have ever seen. Why, it's Italian—a Beretta! I wasn't aware they manufactured pistols such as this. Especially this caliber! And how again, please, did you expose the chamber?"

"You are entirely correct. It is a small caliber," I said. As I showed him again how the lever on the side of the frame pushed forward to pop the barrel and chamber up, I assured him, "I must tell you, though, that it is extremely lethal and is much more than just a well-made, one-shot pistol. It will fire as fast as you can pull the trigger—up to eight rounds. At your convenience, I can give you a very convincing demonstration."

"Colonel Kelly," he said, "I suspect you may be able to do exactly that, although it is beyond my comprehension how it could be so. As for all these clever objects you have here, I am perfectly mystified. But what I am ready to hear from you now is this: Where have you come from, and why are you here? And how could you possibly know of what future successes I might be blessed?"

Before I could answer, he continued. "You have presented a paradox. You showed me something that can't be yet something I see with my own eyes." He said this as he tapped the book.

For the last time, I reached into my bag of tricks and pulled out a small, wallet-sized calendar and a folded map. As I laid them in front of him, I said, "Colonel, I am from here." I pointed my finger to North Carolina. "I was born in Texas and later moved to Fayetteville. But more importantly, this is the date I left North Carolina and came to Virginia."

He really didn't react as I thought he would. In fact, he didn't react at all. Then I realized what it was. The calendar itself intrigued him. It was made of plastic; something he had never seen. I was about to again point out the date when his hand began to tremble as if he had suddenly been stricken with a seizure.

This was it! He was as ready as he ever would be.

"Yes, Colonel Lee. The date is correct, and that explains how I have a book with all your letters, personal and professional. That is how I come to have these other items too. And that, General Lee, is why I know how history will record your achievements. I am from a different time—a time yet unseen by you or your generation. But it is a time, nonetheless, as real as the calendar in your hand."

I had sold insurance for a while after retirement. One of the first things, and hardest things, was to know just when to shut up. The maxim was: "Make your presentation, close, and then say nothing. The first guy who talks, loses."

So that's what I did.

BOOK ONE

CHAPTER 1

My world changed forever that cold winter afternoon in the waning days of the twentieth-century.

It had actually started several months earlier at a faculty social function; I just didn't know it then. An inconsequential gathering of academia would become a most unlikely setting for the first act of a preposterous science-fiction movie. I would be a costar in an epic production, and my partner in equal billing would be an American icon, a legend now dead for more than a century.

It was there, at the beginning of the school year, that I met Margaret. It was the kind of event no one really wanted to attend, except me. It was my first year as a faculty member, and I was lonely.

My status was only technically as a full member of the faculty. As a PhD candidate waiting approval of my dissertation, I had been offered a position contingent on my work being favorably received. The dean, Randolph Connors, had taken a personal interest in my research and me. I hadn't much doubt that my dissertation on the very first battle of the Civil War, Manassas, would be accepted. Likewise, I was sure of the success of my dissertation defense. I had years of experience giving briefings, and I had fully immersed myself in my topic: the Civil War. It had been a particular interest of mine since I was a lad in school. I fully expected to be St. Lauren University's newest full-time faculty member well before the school year was over.

I knew I was the subject of a certain amount of faculty speculation. I had come to St. Lauren three years earlier as a recent widower. I had been a career army officer, and my last assignment was at nearby Fort Bragg. Moving around from post to post, with overseas assignments every few years, we had no place we could call home. So after retiring we had just stayed in the area. With our circle of friends and with the familiar trappings of army life all around us, we took the path of least resistance and made Fayetteville our home.

When Caroline died, I had kicked around on the edge for a year before pulling myself together. We had had fifteen wonderful years together, and the void her death left was intolerable. Our lives had revolved around one another. As a couple, I hadn't realized how we had truly become one. Not until that faded, golden fall morning when the flame flickered and slowly but inevitably went dark.

What happened the following year is an old, familiar story. I became a worry for family and friends and a problem for myself. I sank deeper and deeper into self-pity as I isolated myself from life. Booze and cigarettes made me unbearable to everybody who dared to help. My son and Caroline's daughter both reached out, but they had lives of their own, with their own families, careers, and responsibilities. I just wanted to be left alone. I was resentful that life had to go on. Friends gave up on me in rapid succession too. I did all I could to turn them all away.

Then one morning, a few days before the year's anniversary of her death, I awoke with a worse hangover than usual. Grabbing a cigarette on the way to the bathroom and just on the verge of gagging my guts out at the porcelain throne, I glanced at my reflection in the mirror. Staring back was no one I dared recognize. I jerked my eyes away and back toward the now-inviting maw of the toilet bowl. I couldn't bear to look at that ghastly specter. But something, some force outside of my own self, pulled me along. Slowly and reluctantly, I brought my eyes up to meet that stranger's gaze. They say that the man in the mirror tells no lies.

In that instant, I looked deep into my soul, and I saw with absolute and dreadful clarity what I was doing to myself. And I knew with utter conviction that I was staring at death. I was on the way to being just a sad and unpleasant memory to my friends and family.

There was no place to hide. If there is a judgment day here on earth, this was it. Those accusing eyes were relentless. Every dark and twisted place in my mind was subjected to the unforgiving glare of a bright, silvery noonday sun. I was laid bare. I saw for the first time what I had become—a drunken, burnt-out bum. I had turned into someone that Caroline would never have tolerated. I had defiled our home, and, worst of all, I had defiled her memory.

But that apparition promised salvation too. Like turning over a large rock and watching the crawly things slither away, months of self-pity and neglect began to peel away. During that lifetime of a few seconds, my psyche was renewed. I finally laid Caroline to rest. I looked at her in my mind's eye and told her I was going to be all right—that her memory would always be cherished and that to honor that memory, I would not let her down ever again.

Slowly at first, then with increasing confidence, I transformed my physical self too. Soon I was back among the living. My long ordeal was over.

It was about this time I attended a reunion of one of the military organizations with which I had once been affiliated. I went only because it was being held in Fayetteville and it would be something to do. There, I ran into an old comrade in arms, Ambrose McBride. I hadn't seen Ambrose in more than fifteen years, and if not for his nametag, I would have never recognized him. A full beard hid his face now. I was fascinated to learn that he, after retiring from military service, had gone on to earn a PhD in American history and through research, publication, and perseverance had advanced to the rank of full professor. He was teaching at St. Lauren, a private university about thirty miles away, and living there with his wife, Mary.

I had minored in history and had maintained a keen interest in it. Caroline used to say that I simply preferred the past to the present, which I had always denied. She had been right, of course, as always. So when Ambrose invited me to visit the history department, it worked to rekindle a long, dormant academic curiosity. Within a month of my visit, I applied for admission as a graduate student in American history.

That's how I met Margaret. I had seen her around campus and even had exchanged greetings with her on occasion, but that was about all. She was a full professor in applied physics, and I was a lowly graduate student, so I had little opportunity to do more than admire her. In truth, at the time I had been glad to do no more than that.

I had to admit, though, that she had all the right curves in all the right places, and I liked the way her auburn hair gleamed in the sunlight. She was very attractive, and I was very lonely. And I had finally completed my dissertation.

That late summer afternoon started out well and ended up even better. I spotted her right after arriving, but I spent the next twenty minutes or so circulating while working up the nerve to approach her.

Before I had figured out a smooth way to introduce myself and think of something witty to say, she walked over to me and said, "Hi there. I'm Margaret Benning, and you are to be the latest addition to our history department."

I had been talking to one of the other graduate students, so I excused myself to greet her.

Wearing heels, she was just short of my height of five feet seven inches. Her lustrous, dark brown hair, with just a hint of copper, was done up in a small bun at the nape of her slender, graceful neck. She had deep brown eyes that projected warmth and sincerity. Her full lips were parted in a sensuous smile. What struck me the most, though, was her poise. She projected awareness of her worth as a person and a scientist, and yet she was utterly feminine. This was a woman unafraid to risk friendly overtures.

I set my cup of coffee down, took her hand, and said the only thing that came to mind. "How do you do, Dr. Benning? I am John Kelly, and I sure hope I'm accepted. I was afraid I wouldn't get the chance to meet you."

"Me too," she said, "and that's why I decided not to take any chances. And please, call me Margaret. You needn't worry about getting on. I understand your doctoral submission is a brilliant piece of work. But let's not talk shop. I want to learn more about the mystery man on campus. I've heard so many stories about you that a person wouldn't know what to believe.

"Let's see," she went on, "which is the real you: the soldier of fortune, the international jet setter, or maybe the disinherited son of a mafia chieftain? The staff and faculty gals are all a twitter about you, so I thought I'd find out for myself."

I knew that there had been quite a bit of speculation about me early on, but I thought that had abated by now. And I had never heard any of that stuff before. I started to give her a serious reply when I noticed her eyes. They signaled loud and clear that she was laughing inside.

So I just laughed and said, "Don't tell another living soul, but I'm here on a special mission for the Klingon Empire. If you reveal that to anyone, I'll have to warp you to Zylon Two, our penal colony."

She had an infectious laugh that started us both giggling.

"I guess I can't pull the wool over your eyes, so I'll just have to admit that I have been dying to meet you."

They say the way to a man's heart is through his stomach, but a little good old-fashioned stroking of the ego will do just as well.

Of course, I knew I was an old fool. She was at least ten years my junior and an established scientist with an exciting and promising career ahead of her. I was in my fifties, with my best years long vanished. It had been a long time—much too long—since I had responded to a woman in this way.

It didn't hurt she was wearing a dress that showed off her legs to the best advantage. She was lissome, and the swell of her breasts just a few inches from my hand was impressive. I released her hand, hoping my appraisal hadn't been too obvious.

"There's not much to know, and anyway, on this campus, everybody soon knows everything about everybody else. I wonder how we ever get anything done."

Laughing, she agreed and asked, "How did you ever come up with that fresh perspective about Bull Run—or Manassas, as Southerners call it? By the way, I'm sort of a history buff myself. Sometimes history is important in my work." She gave me a little smile and quickly changed the subject, and then we spent several minutes chatting about ourselves. I did manage to find out she was in her forties and single.

I learned precious little else, though, and she said nothing further about her work. I had already heard, via campus gossip, that she had come here from MIT as a tenured professor. Nobody could quite figure out why. Even though St. Lauren had a nationally recognized record of academic achievement in the liberal arts tradition, it could hardly be called a step up. I wasn't sure if she had classes or just worked in her lab.

But she learned plenty about me. I couldn't stop talking about myself. I talked about growing up in the South, my military service, and my interest in the Civil War. She seemed interested because she maintained eye contact and encouraged me with questions and comments. I was vaguely aware I was talking too much.

Finally realizing I was acting like a love-struck teenager, I stopped long enough to say to her, "Listen to me. You would think I had never talked to a woman before. In about five minutes, I've covered my entire life with someone I just met. Let's talk about you for a while."

Resting her hand on my arm, she just smiled and said, "You're much more interesting than me, and besides, we can talk about me next time. Actually you are the first career soldier I can remember ever talking to. Was it difficult to make the transition from that structured environment to the abysmally loose discipline here?"

I didn't know how she did it, but she managed to keep me blathering on, even when I knew I was being vamped. I loved it, so off I went again.

We had been talking about twenty minutes when she looked over my shoulder and said, "Looks like Dean Connors is heading this way with something on his mind. Guess I'm going to lose you for now. I'm having such a good time too. Maybe we can talk again sometime soon."

Couldn't be clearer than that! "How about I give you a call this weekend, and maybe we can meet for lunch next week."

She just smiled as she greeted him. "Hello, Dean Connors. I'm afraid I've been monopolizing John. You look like you two have business to discuss, and I really need to see Linda about some new circuitry I ordered."

Linda Huff was the school financial manager.

"Now, Margaret, there's no reason to rush off. I'm just doing my duty by mingling with everyone. Must say, though, you two are a couple I would rather chat with than old Bindle."

I glanced over in the direction he was looking to see the familiar tall figure, with the wavy, snow-white hair, dominating a conversation with two faculty members who hadn't been quick enough to avoid him.

She laughed at his remark. I wondered if she noticed his reference to us as a couple.

"Really, Dean Connors, I have to talk to her or it will just get lost in the shuffle, and I'm already running behind schedule." She turned to me with a mischievous smile. "I'm so happy we had a chance to meet, John. I'm looking forward to seeing you again."

Before I could answer, she was off—a woman with a mission.

Connors chuckled appreciatively, "Ah, if only I were twenty years younger. Better yet, thirty years younger. She seems to have her eye on you, John. And you can probably relax now. You can't hold your stomach in forever, you know."

As I let my breath and gut out, I was embarrassed to realize that I had been doing just that. Preening like a schoolboy. I was even more chagrined that it was so obvious.

I managed a self-conscious laugh and said, "Well, she's easy to talk to and good-looking too. I didn't get the chance to ask about her work. What is her project? Who in the world is funding whatever it is? If what I've heard is anywhere close to the truth, there is a lot of money going into it."

For just a heartbeat, it seemed his eyes narrowed ever so slightly and his well-tanned complexion took on an unhealthy, yellowish hue. And then it was gone. It happened so fast I figured it must have been my imagination.

He laughed easily. "You'll have to find that out yourself, John. I really don't know. As for her benefactor, you know how that works. That will just have to remain a big secret."

I decided to talk about something else. Dean Connors had been a friend and mentor to me. He had taken me under his wing and guided me through the lengthy and confusing labyrinth of doctoral studies. I was smart enough to realize that much of my success so far was due to his interest in me. And now, as a novice faculty member, he was still mentoring me and guiding me through academic land mines. He had been and was a friend to me. There was no way I intended to put him on the spot.

After a few minutes, he excused himself and headed off to see the head of the English department. I was on my own for a while, so I had time to ponder his reaction to my question about Margaret's project. It seemed strange he wouldn't know anything about it. All that money coming into such a school as ours didn't sound quite right to me. In fact, Ambrose had told me that the physics lab was state of the art and brand new.

Then I noticed Margaret across the room in animated conversation with someone, and my thoughts turned back to her. There was no denying it; I wanted to spend some time with her. Dinner would be nice, maybe in a quiet little restaurant someplace. Wonder what she saw in me? Maybe my availability, or maybe she was just bored. Well, she did say she was a history buff. And I was a history PhD, or soon would be.

I must have been thinking out loud because I heard a familiar voice.

"You are going to make an excellent professor, young man, talking to yourself like that."

Startled, I turned around to see old Bindle looking at me, or more like appraising me.

"You seem to be enjoying the party, Colonel Kelly," he said. "Let's see if you still like them after a few years of the grind."

He had used my old military rank, probably because he didn't quite know what else to call me. After all, I wasn't a professor yet, and no longer was I just a graduate student.

"Yes, Dr. Bindle, I have been enjoying the party. Socializing isn't something I've had much time for these last couple of years. You should know. You played a big part in my lack of a social life." I said this jokingly, referring to his demand for perfection in my graduate studies.

"You were the ideal student," he said. "Wish all my upper-level classes could have someone like you, and Ambrose too. There are far too many professional academicians around to suit my taste. They act as if they know everything when—it's been my experience—they don't know much at all. Except about their area of expertise and then only through the lens of their own education and inclinations. You two are different; although I fear Ambrose has been at it too long. He's becoming like the rest of us."

I laughed. "Nobody can accuse you of being in that category, Professor."

"No, they can't," he acknowledged. "At least they don't to my face. I know what they say behind my back, though. 'Gigantic bore,' 'old fool,' or 'incorrigible curmudgeon' ought to be about right. And when I have their attention, they're too busy trying to figure out a way to get away to bother about prolonging the conversation."

He was undoubtedly right about that. He was difficult and demanding—an irascible old man. In fact, he was very similar to many fine senior military officers I had worked for. They may have been difficult, but you always knew exactly where they stood. And that, for a soldier at least, makes everything else a lot easier.

With a sudden flash of an intuition that I wasn't normally blessed with, I asked him, "You must have been a soldier at one time."

"Yes, I was."

Such a short answer was unusual enough for him, so I decided to change the subject. Probably was a period in his life too painful to recall.

Before I had a chance to say anything, he surprised me by asking, "John, how is your schedule in the evening this next week or so? I want to invite you to my place for dinner. I'm a pretty good cook, if I do say so myself."

"I would be honored, Professor Bindle," I replied. In truth, I was immediately apprehensive. Our relationship had always been one of student and teacher. It was an arrangement that I could deal with. I really didn't want to complicate things with a more personal relationship. Plus, I would rather spend what available time I might have on more pleasurable things. Things like dinner with Margaret.

"Fine. Well, that's it then! Let me know a day that is most convenient, and I'll give you directions to my place.

"Have to toddle on, you know. Find somebody that I can watch squirm as they try and find an excuse to get away." As he started to turn away, he looked back at me and said quietly, "You watch your step now."

And then he was gone, leaving me to ponder that cryptic warning.

The familiar drive home was alive with new sights and scenes. The remains of a sultry summer day were alive with new possibilities and new vistas. I felt energized in a way that I had all but forgotten. I knew what it was: it was the promise of a new beginning to life. Margaret—I let the name linger in my mind, savoring the silent sound of it—had swept me off my feet. Who knew what it all meant? What I did know for sure was that right now I felt good, and for now, that was good enough.

I recognized that the exhilaration of the present would eventually be compelled to submit to the nostalgia of the past. Thinking of Caroline, I felt like a Judas. For now, though, I turned my back on the permanence of the past and greedily grasped the possibility of the future.

With that one-sided contest decided, I turned my attention to replaying the events of the afternoon. Margaret's overture had taken my breath away. I had hardly known how to respond, and I suspected that I had sounded overwhelmed. I had been, of course. And the way I rambled on left me worrying if I had come off like someone on his first date.

The lengthening shadows were fading into night as I neared the outer limits of the city proper. The late summer day was just about at an end. And so too was my preoccupation with pondering the uncertainties of boy meets girl, boy wonders what in the hell is going on.

And what was I to make of Bindle's invitation for dinner? Presumably he had something on his mind. Was it connected to his parting admonition? Was it friendly advice to an obviously infatuated colleague, or was it something else? Maybe it was just a warning to not be too inquisitive about the mystery project over in the physics lab. Was that it?

To break the mood, I flicked on the radio to my favorite station. Public radio often drove me up the wall with their political commentary, but the music was good. Classical music thrilled the soul, warmed the heart, and calmed the emotions, but the mellow feeling quickly evaporated with the first news item.

"The president sparked certain controversy today by announcing that he was nominating General Benjamin Clay as his next chairman of the Joint Chiefs of Staff. In a speech to the Foreign Journalists Association, President Odets noted that the allegations against Clay were not proven and, in any case, were not relevant. General Clay had been accused of involvement in and subsequent cover-up of the cheating scandal at West Point several years ago. His critics have noted that, while his military credentials are indeed impressive, his public comments over the years set the tone for such ethical lapses as occurred at the military academy. Virginia Senator Lee Jackson, a member of the president's own party, is Clay's most outspoken critic. Jackson pointed out last year that General Clay has consistently maintained that America's security interests are best served by an officer corps willing to adopt a more modern, pragmatic approach to warfare and that any and all means leading to victory are ultimately validated by winning. That has been interpreted by many, including Jackson, as advocating an abandonment of what Clay considers an archaic code of honor for one that stresses results on the battlefield. Senator Jackson is chairman of the Senate

Armed Forces Committee and is expected to use his committee chairmanship to kill the nomination."

Coming around the bend to home, I stabbed at the off button. It was a perfect way to spoil an evening. I hadn't known Benjamin Clay personally, but I had known of him and what he stood for. For my generation of officers, Clay was representative of the new breed of military leaders. For Clay and his adherents, the most dearly held precept was not honor but success. For them, success was the only standard of measurement. I feared Clay's view was well on the way to becoming official national policy. *National policy without a soul represented on the battlefield by an officer corps without honor could only produce war without limits.* War was hideous, but without some rules of conduct, it became truly monstrous. What it did to our fighting men was even worse. It coarsened and brutalized the spirit. Everything sacrificed on the altar of expediency.

It's a changed world we lived in now, a world with different values and expectations. "Guess I'm still living in the past," I grumbled as I drove into the garage.

I went inside to my familiar surroundings and back into my established and safe life. Except it all seemed a little less settled now.

CHAPTER 2

The sun was just beginning to sift through the blinds when I finally roused myself. In spite of last night's news about General Clay, I awoke from the best sleep I had had in a long time. Most mornings I jumped up pretty quick. Military habits, long cultivated, weren't that easily abandoned. I had wasted too much of my life sprawled out in bed that nightmarish year of wallowing in self-pity and self-indulgence. What a difference a day made, though.

I could smell my coffee, already brewed and beckoning from the kitchen, but it didn't seem so important this morning. Languishing in my warm cocoon, I wondered if Margaret was an early or late riser. Would she still be in bed this beautiful morning? Would she be thinking good thoughts too? Would I play a part in those thoughts?

My little fantasies weren't moving the day along, so I reluctantly crawled out of bed.

"Get a grip, John," I said. "Get back in the real world." The likelihood was that she was long since up and around and probably working differential equations or whatever physicists do in their spare time. And if she thought of me at all, it was probably with justifiable amusement. I wished I had acted a little more my age yesterday.

I flicked on the TV and stepped outside to get the paper. Not much news except for a report of another one of the area's interminable hurricanes. Hurricane Beth had been upgraded from a tropical storm yesterday and was on the usual path straight toward the Carolinas. There was nothing much to worry about for now.

I resolved to call Margaret as soon as I had showered, shaved, and made myself presentable. I had a lot of chores to do and some errands to run, but I needed to call her first, before I chickened out. Although she had made it perfectly clear she was interested and, unless I had totally misread her, was fully expecting me to call, I still had a king-size case of fear of rejection.

I needed to call Bindle too. I really didn't want to get involved with him on any other basis than academic matters, but I couldn't afford to offend him. And it wasn't like I was so busy or anything like that. It was more of a fear that it would become a regular thing that might be difficult to extricate myself from later. As things eventually turned out, I needn't have worried!

After finishing my ablutions, I called Bindle, and we settled on tomorrow evening. And then, half hoping she wouldn't be home, I dialed Margaret's number. She answered on the second ring with a cheerful voice. Apparently not a late riser on the weekends! Good!

"Hello, Margaret. This is John, John Kelly. How are you this morning? I hope I haven't caught you at a bad time."

"Oh hi, John. No, you didn't, not at all. I've just been sitting here, pounding away at the computer for the last hour with plenty of things to do piling up on me. I'm so glad you called. If you hadn't, I was going to have to work up my nerve to call you later today."

"Talking with you yesterday was the high point of my day. In fact, the high point of the week."

I could have said it was the high point of the last two years.

She laughed and said, "I'm glad you didn't wait; this way I'm able to hang on to what's left of my dignity. But I really do hope we can get to know each other."

Laughing with her, I said, "I'm taking you off the hook this time, Margaret. Consider this an official and formal call for a date. Would you like to go out some evening the next week or so?"

"I'd love to, John. In fact, if it's not too presumptuous, are you busy tonight? I hate to put you on the spot at such short notice, but I have a short meeting today in the Triangle, and I'll be coming home through Fayetteville. What with the school year starting up and a seminar in Boston next weekend, tonight seems like the perfect time. If you have something already planned for tonight, I definitely understand, and we can do it whenever it's a good time for you."

She obviously didn't know my situation here. With the social life of a cactus on the Rio Grande, an insurance salesman calling at dinnertime would be an improvement for me. Anyway, even if I had had an engagement of some kind—say dinner at the White House—it would be no contest.

"Margaret, I don't know how to tell you this, but other than dinner at Paul Bindle's tomorrow, my social calendar is about the same as it usually is; it's just waiting to get filled in. If you come back on US 401, rather than the interstate, you'll pass about a mile from my house. We could drive together to a good restaurant instead of one of the chains. It's a nice drive on a day like this."

With a bubbly little laugh, she said, "What a wonderful idea. I'll be leaving there about five o'clock, so that will give us more time together." I gave her directions, and we chatted a few more minutes before we said our good-byes. The Triangle, the high-tech area of the Raleigh area, was about a two-hour drive for her.

I had to clean up the house and take care of the lawn. A good first impression was what I wanted. I also needed to pick a nice place that would be right for the occasion. I fretted over what she might like to eat and what I should wear.

I reluctantly finished my coffee and cigarette and started to work, but a little black cloud of apprehension was threatening to ruin the day just when good things seemed to be happening.

With the same edgy stillness as before a summer rain, it dogged me, casting a yellow pall of uneasiness over my already nervous anticipation. It was Margaret, of course, and why she seemed so interested in me. Even in my prime, I had to depend on myself to do the heavy lifting to establish a relationship. Maybe it was my lucky day. I decided just to let the evening play itself out.

The day was interminably long, and I did every chore I could think of to make it pass faster, but it didn't help much. I even started a book I had long intended to read but had been putting off. I felt like a kid lying in bed, waiting for Christmas morning. Only it wasn't Christmas morning. It was a warm, lazy Saturday afternoon, and I wasn't a kid anymore. I was a lonely, past-middle-age man.

Finally it was close enough to six o'clock for me to feel like I wasn't jumping the gun by too much. By the time I finished showering, shaving, and changing clothes, I still had time to kill, so I sat out on the back porch with another cigarette and a weak bourbon and water. I hadn't been sitting, enjoying nature, more than twenty minutes when I heard the sound of vintage MG pulling into the driveway. I sauntered as casually as I could around the side to the driveway.

There she was! She had just gotten out of the little red MG that she buzzed around campus. She was leaning over the side of the top-down car, getting her handbag out of the backseat. She was quite a sight in a clingy, silvery-gray pantsuit that hugged her hips. I stopped to admire the view until she stood up and turned around.

Caught in the act and feeling guilty, I hurried over to her hoping my ogling hadn't been too obvious. "Hello. I see you found your way here all right. Didn't have any trouble, I hope. Here, let me give you a hand."

She smiled what seemed the most beautiful smile I had ever seen—perfect, white teeth delightfully framed by full and sensuous lips. Then my eyes were drawn down to her breasts and how they strained to escape her fitted jacket. God, she looked hot. Conscious that I was practically drooling, I managed to tear my eyes away before I made a complete ass of myself.

Handing me her attaché, she laughed. "Why, John Kelly! I do believe you're blushing. I know I look a mess. It's what I get for having the top down, but it was just too nice a day to pass up."

She had caught me staring and had deftly taken me off the hook. Before I could stammer some inane reply, she said, "I really need to find your bathroom. It's been a long drive, and I drank too much coffee today."

I led her into the house and pointed the way to the bathroom. She was back in about five minutes, looking less wind-tousled but with the same exuberant smile on her face.

"You have a beautiful home, John. It's not at all what I expected. I'd pictured you in a much smaller place, more like an apartment. You should see my place. I think all of it would fit in your living room. And look at your yard. You obviously put a lot of work into it. Do you like to putter around outside a lot?"

"I do, but it seems my time is mine less and less now. Would you like a drink?"

"No, thanks. Not now. Those meetings always leave me worn out and hungry. In fact, I'm famished."

This was it. This was the start of our first date. This was what I had been anticipating all day. I asked her if she was going to put the top up on her car, or if she wanted to put it in the garage while we were out. I wasn't too surprised when she asked me if I minded her driving.

"No way do I mind, Margaret. In fact, I'll enjoy it. I haven't ridden in one in years. Is it stock, or have you jazzed it up? It should be about a nineteen seventy model, or maybe a sixty-nine."

"Very good. I'm impressed. It's a nineteen seventy. You sound like a fan, or maybe you have one yourself tucked away somewhere."

"Yes, I did. I spent too much money on it and too much time under it. Loved it, though! I often wish I hadn't sold it. This brings back fond memories."

She was well down the street before she asked where we were going to eat and how to get there. I gave her directions and settled in to enjoy the drive.

"In answer to your question," she said, "I've fixed it up a bit. Most of the work I did myself, if you can believe that."

She said the last part somewhat defiantly, as if she expected me to disapprove or to just not believe her. I believed her all right—no one could fake knowledge of the mysteries of British sport cars. Plus, I had noticed the ease with which she glided effortlessly through the gears and kept the little tiger hugging the road. She certainly knew how to handle it, if nothing else.

"It's obvious to me, Margaret, that you know how to drive this beauty, and I know for a certainty that not many college professors could afford to drive one without being able to work on it themselves. It seems like you beefed up the suspension a bit too."

I could tell my acknowledgement of her work and driving prowess pleased her. Good! It never hurt to score a few points.

It didn't take long to get to the restaurant I had finally settled on. It was a small German place a few miles south of town. It was nestled in a wooded area, with a stream running past the deck in the back.

I had made reservations for eight o'clock. Betting that the mosquitoes and other pests wouldn't detract from what I hoped would be a romantic evening, I had taken a chance and asked for seating on the back deck. It was a sultry evening. Margaret slipped out of her jacket and revealed a camisole top she was wearing underneath. Her bare arms were soft and creamy-looking, belying an otherwise athletic appearance. I had to restrain the urge to reach out and touch her.

After ordering, we chatted awhile about school and her car before the waiter brought our dinner. It was delicious and plentiful. Margaret had a healthy appetite; I marveled that she was able to stay so slim. I was in miserable shape myself, and I always tended to resent those that made physical fitness a religion. Maybe she just had a high metabolism. I didn't know what I'd do if she suggested a quick five-mile run after dinner.

Midway through the meal, she paused and looked at me and asked, "John, as a historian, I know you must have to deal with the realization that there are some things in your chosen field that you can never know. With all the previous research, and with all the possibilities of further discoveries, there are practical limits to what you can know. How does the certainty of that knowledge affect you?"

She was looking at me intently but with a faint smile. I noticed that the tip of her tongue was working against her upper lip. I felt as if she was willing me to respond with some feeling. It seemed an innocuous question, but it was more than that. It wasn't just idle chitchat, and I could see that a superficial response would disappoint her.

"Margaret, every day—every single day—my field thumbs its nose at me. History is recorded by events and dates—the media of exchange for society's measure of history. It's where the historian's frame of reference is too. But even if I were to know all the particulars about all the events of history, I will still be faced with the *why* of things. And the why, like as not, is obscured not only by the passage of time and paucity of extant records but by the intricacies of the human mind, the frailties of man, and the petty little motives that make us cover up what is inimical to us and to embellish those things that put us in a good light.

"That is the other great curse besetting historians. Not only do we have to contend with the lack of archives and the veracity of those we do have, but we also have to be especially careful to present our conclusions in an absolutely objective manner. Being a Southerner, I have to work hard to not let my heritage influence my Civil War research, teaching, and writings. My military training helps me in that regard. But I still have to discipline myself to let the facts—and the facts alone—determine the outcome."

Then she asked me, "I know you are Southern to the bone, so have you ever wished the outcome had been different in eighteen sixty-five, or do you see it all simply as a terrible tragedy that, in the end, turned out for the best?"

All Southern lads had, at one time or another, easily answered that question, and while the answer became more equivocal as the years slipped away into adulthood, the question was always there.

I must have hesitated because she exclaimed with a laugh, "I think you just answered my question!"

"Not really," I said. "It's a serious question for a Southerner, especially for a Southern historian, and maybe even more so for a soldier pledged to uphold and defend the Constitution, as I once was. Even in my most patriotic moment, I can't escape from the awareness that my people did their best to have a country of their own. They expended the blood of their finest to realize their dream of corporate liberty and, in the end, were forced to swear allegiance to a country they didn't care to belong to.

"Plus, it turned out to be the beginning of the end for the federalism our founders created, as well as a refutation of the principles of the Declaration of Independence. The Fourteenth Amendment, one of the post-war amendments, pretty well scuttled the principle of separation of powers embodied in the Tenth Amendment.

"But finally, in the end, I have to conclude it probably did turn out for the best, at least for America as a world power. It would be a far different and less secure planet Earth than it is now if not for the economic and military might of a united America. And it did rid the continent of the sin of slavery.

"So yes! I suppose it did turn out for the best," I repeated. I really preferred talking about something else. I was proud of my heritage, but I just didn't want to tar myself with the brush of extremism in her eyes. In an effort to get away from such potential controversy, I added what I hoped would be a bit of humor. "Yes, it did turn out for the best, but I am glad we whipped up on them for as long as we did."

She sighed, almost imperceptibly, as if she had been holding her breath. And then her face broke out in that wonderful smile again. She reached over and rested her hand lightly on my wrist in a spontaneous gesture of understanding. I could feel the warmth of her touch and smell the fragrance of her perfume. It was an intimate interlude, and just for a second, I could imagine our hearts beating in perfect rhythm.

It was an idyllic moment, not even spoiled by the telltale warmth of a full-fledged blush suffusing my face.

Against a backdrop of clattering dishes and muted conversation, I could hear the crickets chirping and the occasional croak of frogs. Its quiet pace interrupted by small fish splashing in the water, the creek moved sluggishly by the railing.

She said softly, "Maybe we aren't supposed to know certain things. What then? Or just knowing for its own sake is the goal, for all I know. But the revelation of why would only tell us that. It wouldn't change the facts of the matter one little bit. Actions, or lack thereof, and all the resultant consequences would still be immutable. You can look back through that door, but that's all you can do. I don't always feel—"

Her voice trailed away as she looked off into the swampy darkness with a pensive expression on her face. What an odd way to describe the study of history—looking back through a door.

I had refrained from asking her direct questions about her work, and I was reluctant to change the tempo in any way. But the conversation demanded that I at least show some interest in her work.

"Margaret, I have to admit I know very little about your field, but I am interested in you and those things that are part of you. I'd be pleased to be your sounding board, but only if you wish."

With what seemed to be real regret, she replied, "Well, I can't do that, as much as I would like to. I don't talk about it to anyone at anytime. I hope you don't take offense."

I hadn't expected her to blab secrets to me, but I was surprised by her intensity. I tried to set her mind at ease. "Don't worry about it a bit. I'm not offended at all. Secrets are a burden to have. They inhibit and encumber. I still possess information that has long since lost its relevance and need for secrecy. But they're still there, rattling around in my brain."

She clapped her hands together in delight and said, "Ah, yes. You do understand! I had completely forgotten. As a soldier, you would have had more than your share of secret information. I feel better already."

She went on. "Let me just say this about one of the dilemmas I'm wrestling with. It's essentially just a measurement problem. I can measure easily in a digital format. And of course, I can get a certain degree of accuracy. That's guaranteed every time. It's easily recorded and duplicated for future trials. But that degree of accuracy is just not enough for my work. The sheer discreteness of digital measurements works to limit how close I can measure. Analog measurement gives me exactly the preciseness I need and that I must have. But there is no way to retain and record it. Or I should say, there is no way to exactly retain it for later use."

She had a hopeful, expectant look on her face. She really wanted me to understand the problem. I didn't want to disappoint her, so I turned my dinner knife parallel between us and said, "Yeah, I see what you mean. If I measured this knife with an analog measuring device, such as a ruler, it would give me an absolutely exact measurement of how long it is. The problem is that while it gives me the exact measurement, my senses are limited in how precisely I can receive and record that information. There just isn't any way to read that exactness and, consequently, no way to exactly record it for later use.

"But, if the length of the knife is what we want to retain for later use, knowing the exact measurement isn't necessary at all. Just pick it up, put it in your pocket, and use it when you need it. There's no need to measure it each time. Just as you don't check the accuracy of the measurements on a ruler each time you use it, treat the knife the same."

She seemed lost in a world of her own for a few seconds after I finished. And then, again came the pleased smile. "Just so. Well, we both have our problems, and, as you said, if it were easy, there wouldn't be any need for us. Everything would already have been done a long time ago. We can both look forward to continued improvements and discoveries as we go along. For that we should be grateful."

She had just adroitly changed the subject.

Since her work was off limits, the conversation turned to more personal things. I asked about her family and childhood. Once again she was reticent, so I reminded her of her promise yesterday that the next time we could talk about her instead of me.

She relented and told me she had been born rather late in her parents' lives. Her father had been a chemist, and her mother had been a music teacher. Her dad had died three years ago, and her mother a year later. Margaret was an only child and, from the beginning, had been more interested in science than anything else, although she had learned to play the piano at an early age. She spent most of her childhood around adults, usually her parents' friends and colleagues.

"Piano must have been more important than I ever thought it could be," she said, "because sometimes at home, when I'm stumped or just when I'm in a lousy mood, I'll sit down and play, and before long the world seems a little better than it did before."

She laughed a little embarrassedly, as though she had revealed too much about herself, and then she turned the conversation away from herself again. "Do you play a musical instrument, John?"

"No, I don't. That was to be one of my retirement goals, though. It just never happened. I guess because it wasn't that high on my priority list. I really don't have any musical ability anyway. Caroline always encouraged—"

I lapsed into an awkward silence and looked away.

Once again Margaret did the absolute right thing. She reached over and touched my cheek. She forced me to look into her eyes and told me, "Never mind, John. I knew that you had lost your wife a few years ago. I saw her picture in your living room. She was a lovely woman."

She seemed to have a way of putting me at ease. "Thanks, Margaret. It just slipped out. Wow, I really know how to impress a date, don't I?"

"Well, John, it would have had to come up sometime. She was part of your life. Just like your military service is part of your makeup, so is Caroline. It would make me wonder if six months from now you had never mentioned her. I do hope you don't feel like you have spoiled the evening because you haven't.

"By the way, you mentioned dinner with Professor Bindle. I didn't think he socialized that much. I don't think anyone even knows where he lives. I'll be interested in hearing all about it."

She had very easily changed the subject again.

We had finished our meal by this time. Hoping to prolong the evening, I asked her if she would like dessert.

"That's about my limit tonight, John. German food is just too filling. Maybe when we get back to your place you'll give me a cup of coffee before I have to head back to Laurinburg."

In spite of the fact that she had made it perfectly clear that she hoped our relationship would grow, there was no question in my mind that when we left for my place that that was as far as it would go tonight. I was glad, I guessed. Everything was too perfect tonight.

On the way home, she demonstrated the same efficiency behind the wheel as before. I could tell she enjoyed driving, but it made me feel like the old codger I was. Too soon we were pulling into my driveway. She had a good sense of direction too. She remembered how to get back without having to ask.

Inside, I fixed us both a cup of instant coffee, and we settled in on the back deck. The weather was warm and lazy, and we could hear the trickling of the creek that ran through my property. We didn't say much, just some light conversation. We were both testing the water, as two people who are interested in one another will do, and yet there was a pleasant comfort level between us that was relaxing. It was a perfect finale for a perfect evening. Finally, she broke the mood.

"I've had a wonderful time, John, but I guess it's time to be heading home. I'm glad we decided to meet tonight."

I stood up and gathered the cups and said, "Me too, Margaret. And I might as well just tell you straight out that I would like to see you again. I want to spend some time with you, to get to know you better."

Holding the door open for me as I carried the cups, she took my arm and turned me to face her. Her kiss was warm and for, ever so brief a time, clinging. I was too surprised to respond. I couldn't have anyway without dropping the dishes. Somehow I got through the door.

I put the cups down and said, "I'm going to take that as a yes."

"You'd better, John. Will you call me tomorrow?"

"Of course. Are you going to be around most of the day?"

"I should be, but just keep trying if I'm not. I might run over to the lab."

I got her briefcase, and she gathered up her purse. I walked out to the car with her. She gave me a light kiss on the cheek and a final wave before roaring off around the corner.

The day was ending, but I felt my life was just beginning.

CHAPTER 3

"My, aren't you the chipper one today. You're lit up like a Christmas tree. It hurts my eyes just to look at you. What gives?"

"Top of the morning to you, Ambrose," I replied. "And a lovely morning it is too."

It was Monday morning, and maybe I was lit up a bit. I felt good and ready for the world. The afterglow of Margaret's kiss Saturday night lingered on. Yesterday had been the same way. I was newly energized, and I didn't want to lose the sensation.

"Come on, John. I don't even recognize you today. You've been up to something, that's for sure. You look like the proverbial cat that swallowed the canary. Not that seeing you this way isn't good. In my way of thinking, you need to enjoy life more. Get out and fool around with some of the available gals around town.

"Ha! That's it, of course. You found a honey, didn't you? I knew something was up as soon as you came in with that goofy Irish brogue. You'll never get that right, you know."

He had lapsed into his quite natural accent. And he was right; I could never duplicate it. He was right in his guess too. Before I had a chance to put him off, he pounced.

"It's Benning, isn't it? You were sniffing around her the other night at the party. Mary was right. She said the two of you were all alone in your own little world."

"Now hold on, Ambrose," I protested. "Don't jump to conclusions. We just talked about school stuff. Turns out she has an interest in history. That's all."

He squinted at me with a suspicious look and said, "That's all, you say. She is interested in history, my ass. I'd say she has an interest in a certain history teacher, although why, I don't know. I know a lot about history too. She's never cornered me at a party to discuss history. In fact she's not said ten words to me since she's been here."

"You have a way too active imagination," I retorted. "You obviously have too much time on your hands."

As if on cue, the telephone rang. He picked it up and muttered, "Professor McBride."

"Yes, he's here. You don't say. Uh-huh, I'll make sure he gets the message. Thanks, Penny."

He had a puckish grin on his face as he said with relish, "Seems Professor Benning would like you to call at your convenience. Maybe I should go get a cup of coffee so you two can have some privacy."

His emphasis on her last name and reference to privacy was infuriating. I had been caught, and I knew it. He loved every minute of it. Not much I could say except, "Don't be silly, Ambrose. I have nothing to hide. I'll call her back later. I have some work I need to get done first."

"Yeah, right. That's why you're blushing. Oh go ahead and call. You know you want to. I won't be listening."

As graciously as I could manage, I said, "Well, give me the phone then. You're making mountains out of mouse turds again, as usual."

I grabbed the phone and started to dial before realizing I hadn't the slightest notion of her work number. By now, much to Ambrose's enjoyment, I was completely discombobulated. While I looked up her number, he was making little effort to hide his amusement.

To my overwhelming relief, there was no answer. I slammed the receiver down and pretended to ignore my friend. Hard to do, though, since he was now making no pretense at all. Finally I had to join in. We both had a good laugh at my expense before I told him that Margaret and I had gone out to dinner Saturday night. There was really no reason to make a big secret out of it. We were both available, and there wasn't any faculty regulation about that sort of thing.

I told him too about dinner with Bindle. He expressed considerable surprise and wondered what it was all about.

"What the hell is going on? I've been here for years, and he's never asked me for dinner. Neither have any foxy physics professors either, for that matter. I imagine that that old fellow is pretty interesting."

The rest of the morning was busy enough that we both soon forgot the time. Ambrose finally checked his watch and said he had better hurry since he had a couple of stops on the way home for lunch. When he had the time, he tried to eat at home with Mary. It was going to give me a chance to call Margaret.

It was about 11:00 when I gave her office a call. She answered right away.

"Hi, John. I just wanted to see how you are doing. I've been thinking about Saturday night and how much I enjoyed our time together. How is your day going?"

I hastened to let her know that I too had been thinking about our date. "Actually," I said, emboldened by her admission, "I've been thinking more about our next date. Maybe we could discuss it over lunch today."

"Well, that's really why I called," she said tentatively. "I thought it would be a nice day to eat outside while the weather is still so nice. I made a picnic lunch, and I took the liberty to make enough for two. It was a spur-of-the-moment decision this morning."

"That's a terrific idea, Margaret. And it's such a nice day. Where did you have in mind? What about down at the lake?"

St. Lauren's campus was nestled in a wooded area with an abundance of nice places to picnic. While the lake was not as private as I would have liked, it would be more so than the school's small quadrangle. Once classes started, any kind of privacy would be completely out of the question.

We agreed to meet at the picnic tables a hundred feet or so off the road. I hurriedly put away my work and headed out the door in time to see her on her bicycle across campus.

I was halfway there when she caught up with me, waving merrily as she headed down the hill. It was pretty steep, but she kept her balance and rolled out of sight, heading for the picnic tables. I wondered how well she would do going up the hill on the way back. I bet myself she had the legs for it.

Instead of following the path around to the lake, I cut through the wooded area in the direction of the picnic tables. I didn't know what was on my mind, but for some reason I avoided making any noise as I slipped through the trees.

When I got to the picnic area, she had already spread a cloth and was busy setting the table. Since her back was to me, I walked quietly to within about six feet of her before clearing my throat to let her know I was there. Even at that, I startled her so much that she let out a little involuntary cry before recovering with a frown on her face.

"How on earth did you do that?" she demanded, shaking her finger at me and laughing a nervous little giggle. "How did you get so close with me not hearing you?"

"Must have been the tennis shoes," I said lamely. I didn't mention that it once had been my stock in trade. She had been spooked, that was for sure.

There was that smile again. "That's what you used to do a long time ago, isn't it?"

I acknowledged it by apologizing for sneaking up on her like that.

She already had lunch laid out, so we sat down to enjoy it and each other's company. She had prepared a pasta salad that was just perfect for a late summer afternoon. With her portable radio playing softly, I wasn't in any mood to end the lunch. It was an ideal setting for a man and woman getting to know each other.

"How was the command performance last night, John? I would bet almost anything that Paul Bindle is an excellent cook."

"He's that and more," I said. "He is a character from beginning to end. He fixed a great meal, with my entire year of fat now taken care of. He has a charming old house with a kitchen equipped like a luxury liner's galley. He talked my ear off, but that was no surprise. What was surprising was what he wanted to talk about. It was military talk all evening."

"That should have been interesting," she said. "Right down your alley. Sounds like you had a good time. I must say, though, I never thought of Bindle as a soldier or even being remotely interested in the military. He seems so patrician and academic."

"I did have a good time, Margaret. Actually he does have a government service background. From what I can tell, it was pretty high-level stuff during the Cold War, CIA kind of things maybe. James Bond comes to mind. But let me tell you the kicker. He's written a new book, and he wants me to read it and give him my impressions. It's on American military history and doctrine. And that's not all. He wants me to do the introduction. What do you think about that?"

"You're kidding me! I'm extremely impressed. That's quite an honor. It should look terrific to your doctorate committee. I know you are excited about that. I had no idea I was seeing such an up-and-coming guy. Whoops. I think I just said too much."

With that, I plunged ahead with absolute abandon. "No, you didn't say too much, and I do like to hear it. I think you've got that much figured out by now, though. You mentioned a Boston trip coming up this weekend. I'll be glad when you return."

"I usually go three or four times a year, if nothing else than for progress reviews. This meeting will be a lot more than that, though. I have some loose ends I'm going to take care of."

I told her about Ambrose's morning observations and how he had caught me red-handed in my little deception. She had a thoughtful, faraway look in her eyes. Once again I saw her parted lips with the pink tip of her tongue working the upper lip. I couldn't take my eyes off her. Like in a dream, her eyes turned slowly to meet mine, and before I could look away, our eyes met. For a heartbeat we were swept up and into that special awareness reserved for lovers.

Too soon the magic passed, and I nervously laughed. "I must have been daydreaming; kind of lost track of myself. I sure like the pasta salad, Margaret. This time of year, I can't get enough of it."

She laughed too and agreed. The rest of lunch consisted of pleasant conversation and nice background music. I tried to keep my mind on the present and just go with the flow of the day. The music fading off into the hourly news signaled the end of our little picnic. As we gathered up the dishes, it seemed that she was as reluctant to finish up as I was. She was taking her time repacking things and was acting kind of fidgety.

"John, what's your schedule like today?"

"Not much, really," I replied. "I'm just doing the usual stuff. Getting ready for new classes. What about yours?"

"Nothing that's pressing." She took a deep breath before continuing. "I'd like to talk to you, if you have the time."

There was a hopeful tone in her voice. Like she needed to get an unpleasant task out of the way but wasn't looking forward to it. My heart sank! It was going to be a kiss off.

"My trip to Boston next weekend is more than just business. Oh hell, John. I'm involved with someone." Her face was composed now, but her eyes exposed her anguish.

"John, I'm terribly sorry for not telling you sooner. I know I should have, but everything was so perfect. I never imagined we would hit it off so well this quickly. Please forgive me. It just never seemed to be quite the time."

"I wish you had told me sooner, Margaret. But what's done is done. Maybe we should be heading back now."

I started to get up.

"I haven't explained myself very well," she said. "I'm going to Boston for my seminar, all right, but also to break off the relationship. Hell! Let me just get it off my chest. I've been having an affair with a married man. He's the Director of Security as well as the federal liaison of my project. It's a sorry story. There's no way to say it without it sounding sordid and cheap. In fact that's exactly what it is: cheap and sordid.

"I'm committed to my seminar," she said. "I wish he wasn't going to be there, but he will. Otherwise I would just call and do it the coward's way. Thank you, John, for listening to me and all my true confessions. I guess you're right; we're about finished here. It's time to be getting back."

Before she could get up, I impulsively reached over and covered her hand with mine.

"So now I know. I'm glad you told me. But that's not the end of it for me, Margaret. If you want, I'll be here when you get back to pick up where we left off ten minutes ago. Wherever that was."

"I know where we were, John. Except that now I don't know what you think of me. Am I the person you thought I was?"

She looked so vulnerable. And utterly desirable! I wanted to take her in my arms and carry her back into the woods. I didn't have to say anything; it must have been obvious to her. Her breathing had quickened, and her eyes had that faraway look again.

But just then the radio began blaring the sound everyone in hurricane alley is so familiar with. The spell was broken. We both laughed self-consciously and listened to the long-expected news that Beth had turned toward the Carolina coast and was expected to make landfall later in the week.

I think I fell in love with her right then and there. We had entered a new phase of our relationship. One that perhaps couldn't be called a romance yet, but one that was stronger than it had been before lunch.

We gathered up the picnic things and, engaging in small talk about the hurricane, headed up the hill and back toward the campus. As we topped the crest, she gave me a quick kiss goodbye, asked me to call her tonight, and hopped on her bicycle and pedaled on ahead.

The rest of the day was uneventful, except for Ambrose's behavior. He managed to contain himself for about five minutes before asking how we enjoyed our little picnic. I don't know how he found out. I just brazened it out. I knew that was the best way to keep a lid on him.

"Hell, Ambrose," I said, "you think I'm crazy or something. We didn't eat anything. We spent the whole time rutting like sexed-up rabbits. The picnic was just a prop for our little tryst."

He was in the middle of a swallow of coffee that he ended up spluttering all over his shirt and his desk. After regaining his composure, we both had a good laugh, and that was the extent of his ribbing for the day.

It was almost three when we decided to call it a day. There was a lot of work to do around the house, and by this time our efforts to communicate with staff and colleagues were met with more and more ringing phones. Most everyone was feeling the urgency of Beth and was heading for home.

I didn't have any idea how hurricanes affected Margaret, so about eight o'clock I called to see how she was faring. Hurricanes were awesome, with their immense potential for death and destruction. It had always frightened Caroline more than it had me. She was always the smarter of the two of us.

"Hello, Margaret. It's John. Are you battened down for the duration?"

"Hi, John. I'm glad you called. Yes, I've taken all the precautions I can. The car is safely tucked away in the garage, which I'm glad I have. How about you? Are you ready for it?"

"About as much as I'm going to be for this one. I don't think it's going to be that much of a problem for us this time. Are you worried?"

"Not yet really," she said. "Maybe I should be. If it does come, I'll probably be scared to death, though. Just talking to you makes me feel safer already. What makes you think it won't hit us?"

I laughed. "I wish I could tell you it's a special talent I have, but it's not. All in all, though, I'm usually right about hurricanes. Tornadoes, now that's a whole different thing. In any event I would never recommend that anyone follow my lead. But I was worried about you; it's kind of a new feeling for me."

"John, you are just the nicest man I know. It's been a long time since I've felt that anybody really cared enough to worry about me."

I heard bitterness as she said it.

"I'm so aggravated with myself," she said, reading my thoughts, "just thinking how I let myself get involved like I did. It was like I forgot everything I was ever taught, every Sunday school class I ever attended. I'm just plain disgusted with myself. I'm sorry, John. I'm sure this is the last thing you want to talk about."

"Well, Margaret, I would be lying if I said it didn't bother me to think about it. But I care for you a lot. If it's helpful to talk, go ahead."

"I'll just say this then. While I'm not looking forward to the actual face-to-face meeting, I am eager to end it. And I want to get the weekend over with as quickly and cleanly as possible and to hurry back home."

There was a tentative sound to her voice that melted me on the spot. I wanted so much to tell her exactly how I felt, except I wasn't sure myself. Was I in love or just lonely and horny? I instinctively knew, though, that now was not the time to be telling her anything heavy.

I merely said, "Margaret, I will be here, and I hope you'll call me the minute you get home. In fact that reminds me, do you need a ride to the airport Friday? I will be happy, more than happy, to take you and pick you up."

"Yes, yes! That would be wonderful. I really don't like to leave my car at the airport overnight. It's just too tempting. Besides, you're the first person I want to see when I get off the airplane."

"I'm putting you first on my priority list, too, Margaret," I replied. "Hopefully Beth will blow over before tomorrow. You can never tell, though. Another one can be forming and heading our way before the first one is long gone. In fact there is another one forming out in the South Atlantic now."

"Well, I'll leave it to you, Mr. Hurricane Expert."

After hanging up, I checked the weather again, and since it wasn't quite bedtime, I decided to go online and see if I had any messages. I hadn't checked my e-mail in several days. I normally checked about twice a day, but my new social life and the hurricane had seriously cut into my time and my interest. I usually had a message every week or so from Darla, Caroline's daughter, and from my son, Robert.

Sure enough, along with about half a dozen messages from friends around the country, there was one from each. Darla's was the usual chatty message about what was happening with her family, and Robert's was an update on his latest assignment overseas. Both mentioned my lack of a social life. I knew they had my best interests at heart, but I decided it was too early to mention my new romance.

I read through the other messages quickly and decided to put off answering them until tomorrow.

With that, my day was done.

CHAPTER 4

Picking Margaret up Friday morning was no problem. The last few days had been generally routine and uneventful, and Beth appeared to have run its course. I stayed pretty busy with a few late registration chores, but it was a slow week, even at that. The coming weekend would allow plenty of time to batten the house down, if needed. But if taking her to the airport was a breeze; picking her up Sunday became a gale-force wind.

Just before leaving for her apartment, she called to ask if I could pick her up at the lab instead. "My lab assistant is going to stop for me on his way in so I won't have to leave my car there, and I'll have my bags with me."

I was grateful to drive along and enjoy the countryside and radio news. The news was the usual recapitulation of the previous day's events. I normally caught all the news the night before, but last night I had spent my time reading Bindle's book. It was an easy read, for a scholarly work. Paul was a superb writer, and he knew his subject exceptionally well. It was provocative, though.

Just then a news item caught my attention, and my mind immediately switched from idle musing to focused attention.

"Senator Jackson, in an apparent effort to ward off confrontation with the president over his expected nomination of General Benjamin Clay to the Joint Chiefs, suggested in an interview yesterday that General Benjamin Clay would be more ideally suited for the president's selection of the next supreme allied commander of NATO. Jackson's suggestion is seen by many as an olive branch to the White House in an effort to defuse the squabble. The president's political enemies in his own party have yet to comment publicly. And the Democrats seem content to let the Republicans fight it out without any help from them."

The rest of the news faded into the background. There was no question Clay's credentials were no less than perfect. He was a bona fide war hero with combat injuries that would have incapacitated a lesser man. He had proven his courage beyond even what his worst critics could question. His personal life was likewise impeccable and indicated not the smallest hint of scandal. He was smart too. But in spite of all those attributes, I believed his appointment as Joint Chiefs Chairman would inevitably corrupt the American military. I hoped Senator Jackson would prevail and not give into political pressure. I resolved right then to send him a supporting e-mail. Hopefully others would do the same, but that was unlikely. After recent foreign policy debacles, and an increasing tempo of terrorist attacks against American interests around the world, the mood of the country had shifted. America wanted a hero, and it wanted winners. Clay filled the bill on both counts.

I tried to put it out of my mind, but it kept nagging me until I pulled into the lab parking lot, where my dark mood instantly evaporated. I was getting out of the car when Margaret came out the door. "John, one of your most endearing qualities is your dependability."

The drive to the airport took about an hour. It was an hour that passed all too quickly. As we were driving down the airport parkway, she said, "John, you know I have feelings for you. Every time I see you, they just grow. I think I know my own self, my own mind, but am I fooling myself and you too? I've spent a lot of time thinking about the possibilities.

"And then there's you. It's not just me. It's you too. And I have this unfinished business to take care of. How do you feel about that, and do you want to complicate your life with someone who obviously doesn't have it all together?"

My reply was about the smartest thing I had said or done up to then. "When you get back, we will have had time to give it a lot of thought. We can talk about it, then."

After getting her bags into the terminal, I gave her a light kiss on the cheek and told her to have a good trip and that I would be thinking about her. We waved good-bye through the terminal window as I drove away.

The rest of the day went by fast. My class load wasn't very heavy, and I had taught the core curricula classes before as a teaching assistant anyway. All that remained was to get all the little inquiring minds into the classroom next week and to see what kind of secondary education they had been exposed to.

It was easy to blame the kids, but it wasn't so much their fault as it was a NEA-driven education system that no longer found relevant the people, events, and times that shaped our national character. The mindset seemed to be that the past was just that: the past. All that went before is immaterial to today's needs. It was the same with that essential of communication, the ability to express oneself clearly and concisely. The kids' grammar reflected the educational doctrine that their abilities were not near as important as their self-esteem.

Still, most of the young people were bright and eager to learn, if not always so eager for the demands I made of them. As always, there would be a few that were indifferent to anything but whatever was gratifying to them. Others were naturally inquisitive and had open, quick minds.

The vast majority had to be brought along at just the right pace. Too much and you lost them; too little and they quickly became bored. But I loved it all.

By the time I was ready to leave for the weekend, the campus had pretty well cleared out. Next week it would be humming with the curious and awed murmurs of the incoming freshmen and the excited chatter of the returning students. There would be the hustle and bustle of faculty and staff running from one place to another, trying to establish order out of chaos.

By the time I got home, the bright, sunny day was fast disappearing, along with the summer heat. Gathering cumulus clouds and a storm-driven haze produced an eerie cast against the western horizon.

After an early supper, I drove down to the grocery store to pick up some canned goods and to stop and top off the tank with gas. For the inevitable power outage, there were plenty of candles and lanterns and sufficient batteries stored away at the house.

After that, I settled in with a bourbon and water, cigarettes, and Bindle's book. I was anxious to get into the meat of it to see where he was taking it. His research was thoroughly documented, and so far his conclusions seemed well grounded.

Oddly there were several chapters on the Civil War. Of particular interest was an entire chapter devoted to Robert E. Lee. I was seriously interested by now, but I got up to take a break before reading further.

It was just about time for the weather report on the hurricane—or Clyde, as I now knew it was named. Just about then, the phone rang, and I gladly put what I had been reading and my building interest out of mind.

"Hello, John. It's me, Margaret. I hope I didn't catch you at a bad time."

"Are you kidding? I'm always glad to hear your voice. Besides, I needed a break from Bindle's book. How was the flight? Were there any delays or lost luggage?"

"The flight was fine, just the usual hassle. I'm registered for the seminar and all settled. I've been watching the weather channel for news of Clyde. Looks like you were right about Beth, Mr. Weatherman. What's your prognosis for this one? I'm hoping I won't have any trouble getting back."

"I don't have as good a feeling about this one, Margaret," I answered. "I've already stocked up on my canned goods, and I've filled the car. I've been meaning to get a generator for several years now; after one comes through, though, the urgency passes, and I always put it off. Then I always regret it when the next one comes through."

"Aren't we all like that, John? No telling where the human race would be now if we tended to today's business today instead of tomorrow. Or better yet, if we took care of today's messes yesterday."

I had to think about that one for a second. What a strange thought!

"John, my presentation tomorrow is awfully important to me. Just in the past week I've made major progress. It might even turn out to be a real breakthrough. I know I must be sounding uptight, and I am. This is so important to me and to my work. I don't think I'll be able to relax until it's over. And I really want to hurry home and start back to work on it.

"I was in a big rut, John. Until we met, that is. You helped me get my mind off other, more distracting problems. That's true. But it's much, much more than that. You gave me an idea. Or I should say, you cut through all my scientific crap and, inadvertently maybe, supplied me with a commonsense approach to what until then had been an intractable problem. It was the crux of my part of the project. Maybe a more theoretical physicist than I would have thought of it too. I don't know. I just know that I didn't, and you did."

I didn't have the slightest idea of what she was talking about. I knew little enough about science as it was, and I knew even less about her work. Although I was pleased at her obvious excitement and for her successes, what I really wanted to hear about was her progress in her personal affairs. Finally, when I had just about given up on it, she told me that she wasn't staying at her usual hotel at the site of the seminar.

"I don't care for the drive back and forth in the infamous Boston traffic, but I thought it would be best all around to stay here. Plus, it's convenient to the airport."

That buoyed me some. It seemed that she was saying that she and whoever he was had previous arrangements where they would stay for their assignations.

I told her I was excited for her progress. "I'm anxious to hear all about how this old, obscure historian could have helped the soon-to-be-world-famous scientist in her Nobel Prize winning work. And I'll be glad when you get back. Hopefully Clyde won't cause a hitch in your travel plans."

We said our good-byes, and I reluctantly picked Bindle's book up again. I decided to try and watch the tube for weather reports while reading. I started out with his Lee chapter while keeping an eye on Clyde's progress toward the coast. It did look like Fayetteville would soon have a date with him. The best estimates were landfall around Southport, just north of Myrtle Beach, sometime Monday.

By the time I had read the Lee chapter, it was near midnight, and I wasn't in a good mood. I was worried about Margaret, and not just about her getting back on time. I wished she had been a little more informative about her progress, or lack thereof, with ending the relationship with what's his name. I wished she had told me something. Still, what could I do? I'd shot my best shot. The rest was up to her.

My real discomfort, though, was with what I had been reading for the last several hours. It had taken a while for me to conclude that the book was a study of the erosion of the profession of arms. To see it documented all in one place was disheartening. Bindle described, in compelling detail, policy decisions that slowly but surely undermined the moral precepts long held dear by generations of officers and replaced those precepts with a form of military relativism.

It was little wonder that the casual acceptance of a style of military doctrine best characterized by slash and burn without restraint was now mainstream thought in the higher levels of the military community. It was the sound philosophy of "no substitute for victory" taken to a perverted extreme.

The Lee chapter was Paul's counterpoint to his other Civil War chapters. Without taking sides in the conflict itself, he had devoted those chapters to the formulation and implementation of the war policies of both the Confederacy and the United States. The war aims were vastly different, of course. Nevertheless, it was instructive to note how the national policies designed to realize those goals were equally different. For the one, it was existential. With no territorial ambitions and desirous only of having a country of their own, little more than homeland defense was all that was thought necessary. For the other, like any empire trying to maintain territorial sovereignty, it was compelled to invade, to go on the offensive. The men selected by their peoples to achieve their respective policies reflected those differences.

Bindle's theme was based almost entirely on the premise that the blight of total war originated with the American Civil War, that the Lincoln administration's execution of the war had demonstrated the first use of a planned and coordinated campaign unencumbered by moral restraints in pursuit of national goals, and that that policy was the precursor of today's military ethic. Other warlords in antiquity had waged war against a country's human infrastructure too. But the United States had been the first modern democracy to institutionalize it, to make it national policy, and to carry it out with strategic aims in mind. For President Lincoln's United States, maintaining the Union was an end justifying whatever means.

I well knew that efforts of most Civil War historians today were geared to rationalization of the Union cause and the methods used to preserve it at any and all costs. It seemed to be a knee-jerk reaction and could be seen easily in histories of the war years and, even more so, in biographies of leading figures of the time. I knew it particularly well in regards to Lee. For the first hundred years following the war, he remained the central figure of the war, on both sides. His genius on the battlefield and his personal honor had kept him immune from the same demonizing that befell most of the other Southern leaders. Lately, though, he too had become the target of the self-anointed elite. The only real tool needed was a clever pen and a willingness to compromise principles.

It had been a long day, and I was bone tired. Too much reading and too much thinking had worked me up into a real snit, so I decided to call it a night. I hoped to be able to get some sleep tonight, but I wasn't optimistic.

With that thought in mind, I decided to have another drink and fire off a supporting e-mail message to Senator Jackson before getting the coffee pot ready for tomorrow morning.

Nursing my drink, I also sent a message to my kids, hinting at an improved social life. I wasn't quite ready to go any further with it just yet or to give too many details. The truth was that there wasn't anything firm to tell anyway. It could all just be wishful thinking on my part, and if things didn't turn out, it would be less embarrassing to have to explain.

Drifting off to sleep later, I thought again about Margaret's praise for my contribution to her project. I assumed it was my comments about measurements that she was referring to. It didn't seem all that big a deal.

What I couldn't have ever imagined was just how important it would become to me much, much later!

CHAPTER 5

It must have been the change in the wind. One minute I was sound asleep, and the next all my senses were in overdrive, straining to identify the break in the house's nocturnal rhythm. It was the feeling of something not right; a subliminal aware-ness of a sound so alien that it startles one awake like no alarm ever could. Sometimes a pinecone would fall on the roof or a car headlight reflecting off the windowpanes would rouse me from a deep sleep. But it would be a known clank in the night, and it would soon usher me back off into slumber. Not this time, though! I shivered, despite the warmth of the night, and realized that the hair on my arms had risen. My breathing quickened. Something was wrong!

Lifting my pistol out of the nightstand, I got up and quietly moved through the house, pausing at each shadow and doorway. Nothing at every turn or at each creak of the house—nothing but the electricity of raised hackles. Finally, feeling like a fool but satisfied that nothing was amiss in the house, my breathing returned to normal. I could feel the adrenaline's aftereffects slow me down and leave behind its own peculiar hangover.

The microwave oven's digital clock was flashing, signifying a power interruption sometimes during the night. But instead of the usual 12:00, though, it was rapidly blinking 11:55. Then 11:54, and it quickly accelerated back through the hours. It just kept going faster and faster—the damned thing was totally whacked out! The unnaturalness of it so unnerved me I impulsively reached around and pulled the plug.

That done, and purposely avoiding the beckoning display on the coffee pot, I hurried into the living room. The old-fashioned wall clock indicated a little past three. That felt about right, so it was probably just a power-surge hiccup caused by LORD only knew what. Whatever the cause, it had pretty well screwed up my night, as well as the microwave. The house was eerily still. The wind was muted and steady. I peered out the bedroom window and toward the streetlight a couple of doors down. Its harsh shadows seemed to vibrate in tune with the arcing current pulsing across the filaments. The tree branches were unnaturally iridescent as the lambent reflection of the full moon struggled to survive the artificial glare.

It was all too weird and creepy. Shaking my head, I headed back to bed while I still had a chance to get some sleep.

The next morning, the wind was starting to blow debris into the yard as Clyde began to make its presence felt. I was worried about Margaret getting back today, if it kept on its current heading and speed. I wanted her back here and out of the geographic area of what's his name too. I really didn't want to know his name, but it was awkward referring to him anonymously like that.

The day was an uneventful one until Margaret's call late morning. To my relief, her voice was light and cheerful, just like the first night we met. Only a little over a week ago! So much had happened and was still happening in such a brief flash of time.

She chattered on and on about how her part in the conference had gone exceptionally well. And she mentioned that she had taken care of the other matter with not much problem. I was happy to hear that, of course, but I was really happy that she was able to get away today. She expected to be at the Fayetteville airport mid-afternoon.

It was soon time to shower and get ready for the drive to the airport. I went around to the side door to gather up my earlier purchases. One of the rolls of tape had fallen out and rolled under the front passenger seat. Bending over to retrieve it, I noticed a piece of folded paper wedged against the seat frame. I dropped it in the sack with the other things and forgot about it.

Inside, I checked the telephone recorder and fixed lunch. Drink in hand and smoking a cigarette, it was prepared in all of ten minutes and consumed in just a few more. *Ah, the life of a bachelor.*

After showering, there was nothing to do but read more of Paul's book until time to go. As much as Margaret had been consuming my emotions, now this was asserting its place too. Just as I hoped it would in the highest levels of government.

His indictment of our national security apparatus would make a splash across the spectrum. I had no doubts at all about that. The military community, of course, would be in an uproar. No less would the political sphere be blathering about it. The academic world would be awash in weighty and pedantic pronouncements, and it would be the subject of many a Sunday morning talk show, with all the attendant experts to lend their opinion.

By now I just didn't feel like reading anymore, so I flicked on the television to catch the weather report. But even before I could find the channel, the phone rang.

It was Margaret.

"John, I'm so glad I caught you before you left. I'm in Raleigh, and they just canceled my flight into Fayetteville. Seems like Clyde is moving faster than they all anticipated, but you probably already knew that."

"You can never predict those things, as volatile as they are. Just hold tight there, Margaret. It'll take me about two hours to get there, depending on the traffic."

"Oh, John, I hate to be such a bother, putting you out like this. Why don't you just let me see if I can get a bus? That's such a long drive for you. Or I can just stay over and see what develops tomorrow."

"Don't be silly, Margaret. I'll pick you up curbside at the baggage claims area. Look for me in a little less than two hours."

"You're such a dear, John. Thanks."

I was on my way to the car when, for some reason, I thought of the piece of paper I had found earlier this afternoon. I rummaged around until I found it and stuffed it in my shirt pocket. In less than five minutes I was on US 401 with the backdrop of threatening clouds in the rearview mirror.

The wind had picked up quite a bit, but instead of gusts, it had leveled out to a steady fifteen to twenty knots. I was in a hurry to get there beyond just wanting to see Margaret. There was the real possibility that the four-hour round trip would put us at some risk from Clyde on the way back. At the very least, I would have to worry about the trip back from her apartment.

Ahead, the cirrus-flecked skies were in marked contrast to the gloomy, turbulence-driven storm clouds I was leaving behind. As I sped along an empty highway, I felt a peculiar angst.

As so often was the case, I couldn't even identify the feeling, let alone what it was I was concerned about.

It was in that state of mind that the events of last night intruded on my thoughts. It had been unusual for me to wake up with that absolute certainty that something was very, very wrong, only to find out that nothing at all was out of the ordinary. Most times I would lie quietly in the darkness, a dark full of nighttime whispering sounds, listening for a repeat of a noise that didn't belong. On rare occasions I would be concerned enough to prowl through the house with the same shiver of prescience. And the same primal circling of the wagon's reaction! Well, it had been nothing last night. Nothing, except that crazy microwave!

The wind change had seemed to be the only answer to the strangeness of last night. But it just didn't seem right. Maybe that was what was bothering me. Something that wasn't right, something out of sync.

Then I remembered the piece of paper in my pocket. At the first traffic light, I fished for my glasses to read the small type. As I read it, it reminded me of Margaret's strange comment Friday night about doing today's chores yesterday. It read:

The door to the past is a strange door. It swings open, and things pass through it, but they pass in one direction only. No man can return across that threshold, though he can look down still and see the green light waver in the waterweeds.

Loren Eiseley, American Anthropologist

What in the world? I had heard something like that recently. Where did I hear it? It sounded pithy and profound, like something ancient philosophers would have been pondering over for years on end. No one but Margaret and I had been in the car for the longest time. Maybe it was hers.

Just then a weather bulletin blared out the latest on Hurricane Clyde. And it wasn't very good. High winds were whipping up the water off Charleston, a little south where earlier estimates had placed it making land. I couldn't quite visualize the track they were describing in relation to home, but it was going to be near enough, in any case. And St. Lauren was south of Fayetteville, so I really had no idea what was going on, except that the quicker I picked up Margaret and got on the road south, the better.

Finally, the exit to the airport lay just ahead. Ten minutes later, after wading through the piles of cars picking up other passengers, there she was! Like a beacon, I picked her out of the mob and pulled up to the curb. She was standing as calm as the eye of the hurricane soon enough to make itself known. While others were frantically craning their heads first one way and then the other, she stood with a serene and confident look on her face. The sea of humanity, with anxious faces and impatient eyes all around her, was in such contrast to her little island of tranquility. She seemed, indeed, like the captain of her fate.

Still, was that relief on her face when she recognized the car and gave me a cheerful wave? Five minutes later, after wending our way through the waiting and honking cars, we were cruising down the interstate on the way to home and safety. I hoped.

To my complete surprise, considering her previous reticence about the subject of most interest to me, Margaret, after the greetings and usual stuff about the flight, took me off the hook. I didn't have to dither around in my mind about risking sounding like a lovesick calf. But what she related to me just about knocked me out of my socks.

"He was violently angry. I should have just called him and told him it was off, but I felt like that wasn't the right way to do something like that. We were in the lounge at lunchtime, and he made such a scene. John, it was truly an example of Dr. Jekyll turning into Mr. Hyde. Even his physical demeanor changed. I was so mad, embarrassed, and thankful, all at the same time. Thankful we were there and not someplace more private. And even more thankful that I know what he's like now. John, I used to think I loved him and that he was a kind, gentle, and loving man. I just don't know about my good judgment anymore. How could I have been so completely fooled?"

There wasn't anything for me to say, so I just waited until she got it all off her chest. I had envisioned all sorts of scenarios of the encounter, but nothing like what she had to tell me. She obviously had taken an emotional beating at his hands. I soon found out that more than just emotions were involved.

"I know you'll listen to me talk, John. You're a good man, and I know you care. Just tell me to stop when I start repeating myself. I would never have imagined that he—Ken is his name—could have behaved like he did. There were threats. Threats! I would never have believed it of him or anyone else, for that matter. It was like another personality emerged from someone I thought I knew so well."

"What kind of threats, Margaret?" I asked quietly. I had intended to just listen, but the question was out before I knew it. It was the soldier in me. I told her I was sorry for butting in and to go on.

For a brief second, she seemed taken aback at my tone. But she quickly assured me, "No, that's all right, John. I need to tell somebody, and you are the only person I would ever talk to about it anyway. Besides, you have every right to put your two cents in. And I know, not just because I'm burdening you with it, but also because I know how you feel about me. It makes me feel good; I don't mind telling you.

"Well, the threats weren't specific, but there was no doubt that he intended to intimidate me. It scared me. Not the threats themselves. I mean, he was just mad and jealous. He wanted to know who the other man was. Like there had to be somebody else, of course. As if someone like me would be so desperate she would never break off a relationship unless she had another one lined up. It was so insulting, which is exactly the way he meant it. *Ooh!* I'm so pissed off. Can you believe how little he thought of me that he would say that?

"Anyway, I don't take the threats seriously. Well, maybe a little. How can I know what he might do anyway? I would never have thought any of this stuff about him until yesterday, so I guess I can't say it was only the jealousy of a spurned suitor. It was right out of soap operas, John. Things like telling me I'll be sorry. And job-related stuff, like my project grant might be in jeopardy. Oh, and he insinuated that it was only because of his recommendation that I'm even on the project."

She stopped and, with a little contented smile, continued. "That's when it all came bubbling up at once. I wasn't too nice about it either. I don't think he ever knew what hit him. I won't repeat what I said to him, but suffice to say that his vanity will take a long time to recover. And that was it. I haven't seen him since. That asshole! Sorry. I'm not feeling too ladylike about the whole thing.

"Well, that's about it. Except that everyone in the lounge had to have seen and heard it all. They can think what they want; I don't care. But he'll have to live with it, since most of them are his colleagues at MIT. What a jerk!"

I took my time responding to her. I really didn't quite know what to say, except some meaningless platitude. Finally I just said that I was sorry that she had had to go through all that, especially under the circumstances.

It must have been the right thing because she reached over and touched my arm in a gesture of thanks. I knew then that I was ever so close to professing my love for her. I didn't, but she must have sensed something because she said the one thing that I wanted to hear all weekend.

"I'm glad I'm back where I belong. And I'm glad it's with you."

The warm, comfortable glow of affection given and received mellowed me like I hadn't felt in years. The skies ahead to the east and south were threatening and dark, and the wind was coming now in a steadier and ever-increasing flow. But there was no hurricane big enough to mar the warm feeling I had. All I could see was the promise of love, intimacy, and companionship. Off to our right, the western sky cast its vivid purples and oranges from the sun dropping toward the horizon. I thought it was as beautiful as I had ever seen it.

It wasn't until we were ten miles out of Fayetteville that, as much as I hated to break the mood, I decided we needed to find out what was going on with Clyde. It wasn't like I couldn't see what was happening. Our immediate front was getting darker and darker. The rain, which had been coming in with the wind gusts, was now pelting the car with a vengeance.

We came in on the middle of the latest weather advisory. It sounded like it would be about an hour to touchdown, with no immediate fix on the hurricane's most likely path. It looked like we were going to catch moderately high winds, at the very least. If that were all it was, I would consider us lucky.

Margaret had been relatively calm for someone who had never been through one as intense as this one was shaping up to be. Now concern was in her voice and on her face. I had done my best to interpret the weather reports for her and tell her that her area seemed to be away from the worst part of the storm.

I decided it wasn't too late to suggest turning around and finding a motel, but she beat me to it, with a pleasant twist.

"John, I really don't like the idea of you bringing me home and then turning around and going back into all that mess. I'd feel so bad, guilty, if I let you do that. I wouldn't be able to sleep tonight, and with the possibility of the telephone lines down, I would worry myself sick. It's not much, but the sofa converts to a bed that you're welcome to use. I have to believe that classes next week are going to be terribly disrupted.

"Stay at my place tonight. For my sake, please? I know you are reluctant to do it, and I know why. I love you for that. I feel the same way too. Right now, though, the important thing is safety, not to mention my peace of mind. Besides, I'd feel better having someone around who's been through these things before. There. That ought to appeal to your male protective instincts."

I had to laugh with her at that. She was right: it did make me feel good to feel like I could comfort her when she was scared or worried. So I conceded the point and agreed to stay, only if she wouldn't go to any trouble.

By this time, we were in her neighborhood. Through the dark, my headlights picked up signs the wind had already been at work. Blown debris and unsecured trash can lids and the like were scattered throughout the area. I followed Margaret's directions and pulled into a parking pad off the street. It was an old Victorian house. The only way to know it was apartments was when the headlights picked up a small, discrete sign that said "Wisteria Apartments." We grabbed the bags, and I followed her to the veranda and waited while she unlocked a side door that led into her apartment. We had run through the light rain, laughing all the way. We were like kids running through the lawn sprinkler. Except that we weren't kids. She definitely wasn't. Her breasts, straining against her light beige blouse, were rising and falling from our brief exertion. Raindrops had spotted the sheer material.

She caught enough of my appraisal because she laughed and said, "Just look at me. I'm such a mess. I'll be right back. Why don't you flick on the weather while I do a quick change? Do you need a towel? I may have something around here that you can put on, if you'd like."

I demurred on that offer. I intended to keep my clothes on and my dignity intact.

Her apartment was small and snug. A baby grand piano took up about a quarter of the living room. The rest was furnished in dark antique furniture highlighted with silver and sparkling crystal. There were concessions to comfort too. A large, over-stuffed sofa, with plenty of throw pillows, faced the TV on the opposite wall.

I turned on the weather channel while she changed. I tried not to think about it, but images of her in her bedroom kept poking their way into my thoughts. God, I hoped she'd come out wrapped from neck to ankle in full body armor. Tonight was going to be a pleasant hardship for me. Well, I was just going to have to suck it up. I hoped it would be just as difficult for her, but what man knows anything about how women deal with those things?

While I was waiting, I could faintly hear her telephone recorder from the bedroom with her messages that had come in while she was gone. The messages were background chatter and, in any case, meaningless to me. My ears perked up at a vaguely familiar voice. It was the message that identified the voice for me.

"...in an accident this morning. They were on the way to church. I'm leaving here in just a few minutes and, depending how bad it turns out to be, should be gone at least three days. I want to get on the road now, but I'll call as soon as I can after getting there. I ran the test last night or early this morning actually, and it does look like we were right about atmospheric conditions. There was displacement with skewed results. But the retro timers worked perfectly, just as we calculated. I worked it all up, and it's in the safe. Sorry to be leaving you like this. Mom's number is on your desk in case you need me. I need to get going now, Professor Benning. Good-bye."

It was her assistant, Warren. I knew she would have preferred I hadn't been privy to her professional affairs, but there wasn't anything I could do about it now.

By the time she came out, thankfully in loose jeans and a baggy cotton shirt, I was engrossed in the volatile weather situation. Even that costume looked good on her. This was going to be a long night!

She asked about the progress of the storm. I told her I had learned that Clyde was on land and acting in an unpredictable way. Just like they almost always did. The only worrisome thing was that it wasn't heading north up the coast but seemed to be aiming itself in a more northwesterly direction. That meant that we could get more winds than I originally thought.

Margaret didn't seem overly concerned about the advancing hurricane as she disappeared into the small kitchen and busied herself putting together something for us to eat leaving me to monitor the storm situation.

I felt like it would be neat sharing little kitchen chores with her, but I was preoccupied with the weather graphics on the tube. They weren't making any calls, but I had a feeling things were going to get much worse in a few hours.

Margaret called from the kitchen. "John, this old building has shutters on the windows. Would you mind closing them for me, please? The handles are right on the inside of the screens."

The ones in her room were old and cantankerous, so it took a few minutes. I could see that a studio-type bed was her barest concession for a bedroom. Most of the room was full of books, papers, and computer equipment. It was Margaret the physicist's room here. The bathroom, though, reflected her softer side, with frilly matching towels and washcloths neatly arranged and little bottles and tubes of mysterious potions and balms. I detected a trace of the fragrance she wore. I lingered for a few seconds, surrounded by the aura of her personal and intimate place, until, feeling like the voyeur I was, I went back to the living room to report everything secure.

She had spread a tablecloth over the plush oriental carpet that covered the floor and thrown down two of the pillows from the sofa. She came out of the kitchen with cloth napkins, bone china plates, and sterling flatware. Asking me to open the wine and cut the bread, she proceeded to light some candles and turn off the overhead light. The TV was left on, with the volume turned down low. By the time I got back with the bread, she had a large platter on the tablecloth. It looked like a big salad, but not mixed together. Margaret said I should serve myself, so I took a leaf or two of lettuce, loaded up on the cheese, ham, tuna, and salami, and added a healthy helping of tomatoes and green peppers.

Not even the weather could distract me for long from enjoying the evening. The wind howling outside accentuated the coziness I felt here in the flickering candlelight with wine warming my insides. I even managed to persuade her to play the piano for me. With the TV barely audible, she played a couple of short etudes and then "Chopsticks" before laughing and remarking how she had let her music play second fiddle to her work.

About eleven o'clock, after one final check of the weather, she said she'd about had it for the day. We gathered up the remains of our picnic. She gave me a hand in pulling out the bed from the sofa; sheets and pillows were stored in a special compartment of the big, matching ottoman. She managed to rustle up a toothbrush and towels for me. Then she gave me a light peck on the lips. I thought it was a perfect ending for the day. I was about ready to turn in myself.

Then, the telephone rang.

She stiffened, with a look of dread on her face; I think she knew who it was, as did I. She hurried off into her room to pick it up. I knew it had to be that guy, Ken. I didn't even like to say his name. It afforded him a personality and a legitimacy that I didn't care for. Maybe I'd just call him *asshole*.

Now would be a good time for the telephone lines to go down with the storm.

It came to me that I wished I was back home and that I didn't know about any of this stuff. I was getting jealous and, I had to admit, distraught, thinking about how their relationship might have been. I knew I needed to grow up and scratch those things from my mind. That was the past; this was the now. As far as I knew, she might have the same reservations about me.

Surprisingly, sleep came easy. I drifted off to the mournful wail of Clyde's passing on the way to its own past. The trees, swaying in the storm, creaked their tortured protests. I faintly heard someone's alarm tugging them awake to do something about the insistent rattling of rain against the building. Now persistent, it came louder and louder. Why wouldn't they just turn it off? Someone was calling out for assistance too.

I awoke slowly, reluctant to leave the arms of sleep and my distant thoughts.

"John! John!"

It was Margaret! Now I was fully alert. For the briefest of seconds, I thought that she was coming to my bed. She would be in a soft-white, flowing negligee, and we would—

No, it wasn't that at all. Her voice was hesitant and timorous, not the soft, provocative siren of seduction. She needed my help. She was scared.

"Just a sec, Margaret," I called as I stumbled out of bed and into my trousers. I stepped into the hallway to see her standing at her bedroom door. With the light behind her, I couldn't see her face. But her voice and stance revealed her distress and anxiety. My protective instincts took over, and I hurried over and took her in my arms. "It's all right, Margaret. Everything's fine. I don't think there's any danger now. The wind is already starting to die down."

"It's not that, John. Just hold me for a minute. I'm sorry I'm bothering you like this, but I'm scared, and I have to talk. I just had no idea he would be anything like this." Her voice was calm, but I sensed the timbre of fear in her words.

It wasn't the storm that had so frightened her, but asshole, the ex-boyfriend. That was the alarm I had heard—the telephone ringing.

She pulled away too soon and said, "He called again, and at this hour, can you believe? That was him before bed. I had told him it was over and never to call again, and I thought he got it. But no! As soon as I answered this time, he said, 'I know he's there, you little whore, and you'll be sorry,' and I just hung up. I didn't know what else to do. Oh, John, I'm so sorry you're part of this now. I didn't want it to be this way."

I didn't know what to say, so I just pulled her close to me and stroked her back and neck, murmuring what comforting words I could muster. All the while my mind was racing. This went beyond a jealous and spurned lover acting out. This was a man with, presumably, a head on his shoulders. He was married. Did he have children? Did his wife know or suspect his straying from the connubial bed? Did he have any idea the risk to his reputation, his work, and his livelihood with this kind of behavior? Was he horribly unbalanced or just childishly immature?

I had to know more about that, but first, I needed to make this all right for her. I suggested we have a cup of tea and talk it out. But she resisted my lead to the kitchen and instead clung to me with an urgency that transmitted its feeling directly to my core. Time and space slowed and narrowed until only the two of us stood in the universe. Her body tempo and rhythm quickened, and, at the same time, fear's tension and uncertainty melted into a soft and satiny pull.

I knew her eyes would have that faraway look I had seen before. In the hollow of her neck—her secret place—the barest trace of perfume merged with her own special blend of woman's eternal scent. I could feel her warm breath against my bare chest. I cupped her chin, lifted her head, and gently kissed her cheek. And then our lips joined in a demanding explosion of need. Rational thought was gone; only feeling remained. And it swept us both in its inevitable path. Like the hurricane outside, it would not, could not, be denied.

I picked her up and carried her to her bed, kicking the door shut on the way, shutting us off from the rest of the world. The wind and fury outside faded to a distant throb of background music.

With her head on the pillow, I looked down at her with an all-consuming wonder at the mystery and power of love and need. I remained transfixed, with the imprint of our moment seared into my being, until she drew me to her with the yielding strength of physical desire and anticipation.

And finally, shrieking wind and driving rain ceded the ascendancy of our union and faded into the night.

CHAPTER 6

It was getting late in the day to be around the campus now that classes were out for Christmas break, but I was picking Margaret up, and she was working late again. Yet another one of her tests today. She still hadn't told me much about what was going on over there, but I had figured out enough to know that it was truly revolutionary work. And she was getting more and more upbeat about it.

Pausing for a minute, my thoughts sneaked back to the past. The lonely and empty times of a few short months ago were now a distant memory. Caroline's imprint on my life was like an old eight-mm home movie: flickering, grainy film and poor lighting that slowly but surely fades into the lingering, warm glow of love long past. It was like fondly recalling the happy days of summer as a young boy—gone forever, but never lost. Sometimes I missed her in ways I couldn't even begin to explain, though.

I shook my head and smiled at the recollection of Hurricane Clyde and of the night it brought Margaret and me together. We had never looked back after that. There was no more worry about things moving too fast.

The rest of that weekend had been a little short of the perfect love story, though. Clean up and minor damage repair denied us the indolent, playful luxury of enjoying and exploring the next morning. It didn't help any that the power had gone out as the winds, thankfully sparing the apartment, had snapped utility poles north of town. Clyde had done fearsome damage all along its wayward path.

It wasn't long before things got back to normal.

Early in the term, I had decided to try a new approach with one of my classes by exposing them to life in the period they were studying. American history pre-1860 appealed to fewer and fewer people nowadays, but the kids seemed to get a big kick out of the period clothes, implements, and money. So the demonstration had gone over quite well.

I opened the safe and transferred the coins and currency to my old, leather valise. I had long since taken the clothes and other artifacts back to the various museums and private collectors I had borrowed them from. But the money had been Caroline's inheritance from her father, who had been an avid collector. With school break here, it was time to get it all back home.

And the Beretta! It had become my traveling companion now for almost three months. Never had I thought I would be carrying again, but for now it was an insurance policy.

I stuck it in the valise, along with the box of .22 long rifles, buckled up the worn, leather straps, and checked my desk drawers one last time before leaving. Then I remembered one of my reference texts, and it too ended up in the now-bulging and heavy valise. I had used it for the introduction to Bindle's book.

The book had hit the streets less than a month ago, and the establishment reaction had been predictable. I was pleased that it got good play from the public too. It seemed to strike at the heart of the citizenry's love affair with their army, which, in spite of the decades-long experiment with a military they had less and less connection to, was curiously abiding. I had thought it would fade into obscurity when the pundits moved on to something else, but it hadn't.

It had been something to see for St. Lauren too. Suddenly people all around the country knew who we were. TV crews had been out to tape an interview with Paul and anyone who had the faintest connection with him. I had declined my chance for the simple reason that it was Paul's day in the spotlight and that I was a bit camera shy. Plus, I really didn't like to put myself at the mercy of editing crews who often tailored the tape to achieve the result they wanted. But the book and my introduction to it had put me on the academic and journalistic map. And the whole episode had sealed my doctorate candidacy too. I had already been notified, and now the formality of investiture was all that was left to make it official.

I headed across the nearly deserted mall to Margaret's lab. Everything was peaceful now. The damage from Clyde was mostly repaired, and, other than the still-raw earth where trees had been uprooted, one would never know how close a call it had been for St. Lauren. We had been lucky enough in that Clyde was the worst of the lot. None of the season's other hurricanes caused any further problems.

A convertible full of homeward-bound jocks sped by the other side of the quadrangle, beeping their horn. *Damn fool kids.* Still, I could remember the day, not that long ago, when I would have thought nothing about doing the same. And I hadn't even had the excuse of youth. I did feel younger now—younger than I had in years. It was easy to see that that was Margaret's influence. Having someone who cared for you, and who found you attractive and interesting, had that effect on people. But I was getting older.

Could I keep up? It was a question I often asked myself. While I was in better physical shape than most men my age, there was no question that I was slowing down. Too many ciga-rettes and not enough exercise. And my reactions weren't all they should be. If I ever needed reminding of that sad fact, all I had to do was recall my slow response one late September night.

I had been on the way home from Margaret's and not really paying that much attention to the road. I had traveled the nar-row country road so many times I could almost drive it in my sleep. I hardly paid any attention to the two cars gaining on me from behind. And when one of them started to pass, I obligingly slowed and moved to the farthest part of the lane.

As he went around, the other car's lights switched to bright, and the front car's brake lights came on. I instinctively hit the brakes and swerved to my left to get around him, but he moved with me. At the same time, I sensed the headlights behind me looming larger and brighter. I was practically standing on the brakes. In that split second, I realized what was happening. I was being neatly boxed in. There was nothing to my right or left but an embankment and steep incline, and the car behind me was straddling the highway marker. The one in front, still slowing, was seconds away from coming to a full stop crossways on the road. Howling brakes and the smell of rubber protesting against asphalt assaulted the quiet countryside.

Something clicked! Strobe-light images of dense jungle, the whining of turbines, the staccato drumbeats of chopper blades, and the acrid stench of burning rubber and flesh! Everything around me was in vivid slow motion, but my mind was stroking at warp speed.

There wasn't another headlight on the highway, and no houses were around. It was pitch-dark, and I was alone and unarmed. The car behind me was lagging now, and I knew that meant he was ready to block me when the one in front skidded to a full stop almost perpendicular to me. It was a smooth operation. I didn't have much of a chance.

But then the car in front—it was an old, battered pickup—momentarily rocked while the driver completed his maneuver. I could see him swing the steering wheel around to correct the vehicle's top-heavy tendencies. Another second and he would have it under control, and I'd be trapped.

It wasn't near enough, but it was all I had.

While keeping my left foot gently on the brake pedal to keep the brake lights on, I hit the accelerator while shifting down to the lowest gear. I aimed the car at his left rear bumper and readied myself for the worst. My minivan, wretchedly under-torqued, could muster only the most sluggish acceleration. In that short distance, it couldn't build up any speed at all. It wasn't going to work! The driver looked back at me incredulously as I crept toward his rear bumper.

At the last minute, the old bus gave a fit and start and surged forward. It was just enough. My left front bumper caught him just as, like a pendulum, he was starting another sway away from me. The impact was surprisingly light but multiplied its direction of sway.

As I crept past him, it slowly began tipping over. And then I was around him, and it all was fading in the distance. In the rearview mirror, I saw, with satisfaction, the rear car smash into the underside and push it around on its side. And then I was gone around a curve and speeding for home.

It seemed that mine was the second incident along that stretch of road in the past week. The first had not turned out so favorably, though. But that had done it for me. I started carrying my Beretta and soon applied for a permit to carry.

Puffing from the exertion of carrying the old portmanteau, I made it up the steps to the lab and paused to catch my breath before ringing the buzzer. In the fading light of the winter after-noon, Christmas decorations in office and dormitory windows across the mall were just visible. It reminded me I needed to buy a tree and do some decorating myself.

The ROTC building was close enough from the steps to see the drill hall through the windows. As it always did, it took me back through the years. So many times I had longed for my old life—well ordered and hierarchical—where everyone knew their jobs, what was expected of them, and their places in the giant pecking order. It was a structured existence, not for everyone. But you had goals in life that you could feel were worthwhile—goals that justified the sacrifices of months and years of depriva-tion and loneliness.

But I had loved it all. I had the sneaking suspicion that was what had kept me soldiering long after the doubts and cyni-cism had set in. It had only been in the last years of my career that I began to question the quality of the mortar and bricks upon which I had built my edifice of self-esteem. Then the sin of uncritical complacency was replaced by an equally dangerous arrogance, a belief that I could make a difference in what I saw as a military establishment beset by corrupting influences and careerism.

The green machine doesn't always look kindly on such hubris, so it didn't take very long for me to get the word that my world, the only world I knew, had left me behind. An old and trusted friend had flown down from the Pentagon for a meet-ing at corps headquarters. He had called to arrange lunch at the Officers' Club, but had made it clear it was just to be the two of us—no Caroline or any of our mutual friends.

I had known Carl a long, long time. I had been in the year group just behind him, so he was always a step ahead. And then he was two steps ahead, and before I knew it, he had three stars on his shoulder. But we had stayed in touch, and it had never bothered me to lag behind him. That was the army way. I had always been proud of his accomplishments.

That day he put it to me straight. I was increasingly being seen, not as a team player, but as a maverick—a problem. I was going no further. There would be no general's stars in my future. I could hang on until mandatory retirement at a small outpost out of the mainstream. Or I could start the paperwork for retirement. It was the day that all career officers know comes sooner or later. There would be no more challenging assignments and no more recognition. I could mark time or get the hell out.

So I did. I started the process the next day, and in three months I was just a faint memory to my army.

And now I could only dream about past glories. No more the exultation of challenges met, no more the respect of peers and subordinates, no more the camaraderie of those sharing common danger. I would never again experience the thrill and satisfaction of leadership, the quickening of the pulse during a pass in review, or listening to "Taps's" melancholy refrain. Now it was Benjamin Clay's army, indeed, his entire military establishment. After Senator Jackson's near-fatal freak accident, the temporary chairman of the committee wasted no time and called a vote on Clay's nomination. It passed easily.

The buzzer buzzed back at me, and I walked in to Matgaret's building. Wes, the day guard, greeted me and waved me down the hall to her office as he hurried off down the hallway to my left. "She's in her office, Dr. Kelly. Go ahead and sign in and go on back. I've got to turn on the night security system."

I signed in, and after hanging up my jacket, I headed for her office at the end of the corridor. I noticed right away the red light midway down the hall. I had never seen it on before. As I neared, it started blinking, and I could hear the beginning of a low whine slowly building in intensity.

The whine gradually turned into a muffled roar—a noise much like a subway going underground. The building rattled, and it seemed as if the entire structure would lift off from its foundation.

I'll never know exactly why I did what I did next. I wasn't supposed to ever go anyplace but her office. She had made that perfectly clear months ago. But perversely, I did it anyway. I opened the heavy door into brightness in startling contrast to the dimly lit hallway.

Squinting, I leaned forward and stepped into the room. There, slightly to the right, was Margaret and Warren facing my direction. Both were wearing earphones and were in some kind of harness; they were staring intently at a bank of controls and dials. Inside, the noise was much louder now. I could feel the hair on my head and arms being tugged by a cold and odd-smelling draft. And already it was steadily increasing from gentle to brisk, then suddenly beyond. I stared, transfixed, at the center of the space between myself and where they stood.

It was a small, arched atrium with what appeared to be a gallon-size cardboard container sitting on a platform. There was something totally weird about it. It was as if it was surrounded by static—but static I could see!

Suddenly I knew I had to get out of this area. Something was happening or about to happen that I wasn't supposed to see or even know about. Hoping to get away before they looked up, I started my turn to take the one step back through the door and out of their line of sight.

Too late!

As I turned, Margaret's face contorted in a soundless shout of denial. In the next blink of an eye, in a single compressed instant of inevitability and helplessness, Warren's hand shoved forward, and Margaret's eyes dropped down to the center of the chamber. The roar reached a crescendo that nearly dropped me in pain. That same hurricane swooshing grabbed at my valise, nearly spinning me back around toward the deafening sound. Tugging it back to my body ever so slowly, as if slogging through some viscous slime, I struggled for balance toward the door and away from the howling dervish sucking me back into the room. I could see my right foot just breaking the plane of the doorway and a flash and...

BOOK TWO

CHAPTER 7

Vortices of wildly gyrating motion, and universes of warped images, unearthly colors, and cacophonous sounds! Eternities of kaleidoscopes suddenly disappearing into nothingness! Surrounds of sensory overload collapsing in a heartbeat of infinite void!

Then I felt cold—lovely cold. I was alive! But was it the chill of the tomb? *Cogito ergo sum!* Life then, not death! Awareness—it was the sweet symptom of life. I rejoiced at God's gift of rational thought.

I was lying facedown in the soft dirt and decayed leaves of a heavily wooded area. I heard frantic sounds of someone, or something, running headlong through a forest. It was remindful of long, forgotten trials in a distant past. I could hear the labored, short gasps of panicked exertion, even as the noise grew fainter.

I began to notice my surroundings, and in doing so, it started to trickle back: a beckoning red light, a furious whirlwind, and a misty amnesia. Finally, there was a roar of sound and senses. And cold—a cold so completely through and through that I wondered if I could ever bear to experience it again.

What had happened? Where was I? Where had I been? I had been in the laboratory—Margaret's laboratory. That was it!

It came flooding back in waves of memory and awareness. I had gone to pick her up at the end of the day and instead had ended up in a forest somewhere. The lab and the school were nowhere in sight. Had there been an explosion that flung me into the woods several hundred yards from her building? Was she okay? Maybe a freak storm had sucked me out of the building. I was grasping at straws to explain things. To just explain anything!

There had been nothing but sanity one second and insanity the next. Almost from the instant I had walked through the door there was little that made sense; everything from that point on was outlandishly impossible. It had to be Margaret's project. This was too unreal to have been a freak accident or a trick of nature. What kind of project, though? It seemed more like science fiction than science. I had been in her lab, and then, all of a sudden, I wasn't. What other explanation could it be?

Her project—was it a device that moved things through space? From one place to another? Had I had stumbled into her...her transporter? Had she beamed me somewhere? It was just too much to think about.

There was an archway. The noise of a freight train was bearing down on me. They were behind a console of some kind, Margaret and Warren. I had tried to get out. Then everything had happened all at once. Now I was out of the lab and outside somewhere.

Paul had been right in his guess that something more than met the eye was going on in her lab.

None of that mattered now. What did matter was where I was and how far I had been moved. Or displaced.

The heat of a summerlike day warmed my chilled bones. That alone told me that I had to be way south of Fayetteville. That was one hell of a machine!

I began to notice familiar forest sounds. The rustling of a light wind through the trees and the beautiful, full-throated scolding of a wren put me at least on this planet Earth. I could hear the gurgling sound of a nearby stream or brook. There was also a trace of ozone smell, like after an electrical storm.

Slowly I got up and, still wary, gingerly walked over to a fallen tree. Lying on the ground was a curious-looking shotgun. Then I noticed it was actually a very old flintlock musket; a black powder enthusiast's not very well taken care of toy. Whoever had left so quickly had probably dropped it in their panic. I must have materialized out of nowhere to cause him to drop it and run away. Next to it was my briefcase. Strangely it lent a touch of reality to all that had happened. I picked it up, remembering the pistol I now carried. That comforted me too.

I thought of my cell phone. Of course, the obvious answer to all my questions. I rummaged through the bag while desperately trying to recall the last time I had charged it. Not for the last time I gave thanks for the circumstances that led me to bring some essentials home from my office. I pulled it out and flipped on the power. Relief followed by disappointment—it was fully charged, but there was absolutely no signal. It was like I was on the moon.

I leaned back against a tree and tried to take stock of my surroundings. I appeared to be in a typical undeveloped, wooded area. I couldn't be very close to built-up areas because there was none of the familiar sounds of traffic or other evidence of human activity. Who knew how far the damned transporter, or whatever it was, had flung me? It would be nice to be somewhere in the vicinity of the university, but it didn't seem likely.

"Mister! Mister! You all right?"

I must have drifted off. I felt like I had a bad case of jet lag. I opened my eyes to see a concerned face looking down at me. It belonged to a young fellow of maybe fourteen. He was looking at me warily but with more curiosity than fear.

"You all right, Mister?" he repeated. "You sure don't look so good. Where'd you come from? You 'bout scared the wits out of me."

I didn't know exactly where I was, but I knew damned well I was at least in America. The boy's drawl was music to my ears. It confirmed I was in the Deep South, probably southern Florida or maybe Texas, even though the notion was simply too implausible to take seriously. The whole idea staggered me. I needed to get back and tell Margaret what had happened and that it worked beyond her wildest imagination.

The boy was wearing what looked like some kind of homespun trousers held up by suspenders. His shirt was patched, and the elbows were covered with fresh mud. He probably was the one I heard scrambling through the woods.

"I'm fine, boy. I just got sort of lost and was taking a nap. What's your name?"

"Tom, Thomas Jefferson Biggers," he said, chest filling with pride.

In spite of my predicament, I couldn't help but smile. "I guess you know who Thomas Jefferson was, by the looks of it," I said. "You live around here? And why aren't you in school?"

"Of course I know who Tom Jefferson was. I was named after him. My momma taught me that. School's out now. Crops are coming in. Which way you heading? The turnpike is up that way," he said, pointing over his shoulder.

"There's a whole raft of wagons going that way on the turnpike," he continued. "Or you can come on down to the junction, close to where I live, and maybe catch the train into Alexandria. It doesn't come through until tomorrow, though, or maybe not until the next day. It breaks down a lot."

What was he talking about? Alexandria? Alexandria, Virginia? Hell, that couldn't be. That just wasn't possible. The chill settled into my bones again. This wasn't December in Virginia. If anything it would be colder in Virginia than back home. Maybe there was another Alexandria, somewhere like Alabama. The boy had one hell of an accent.

He had said the train breaks down often. And wagons? What kind of clothes was the lad wearing? Was I in the mountains of Appalachia or something? I tried to concentrate on what all these things meant, but the boy interrupted my train of thought with the first of what I was soon to find out were lots of comments and questions.

"My momma takes in travelers. I bet you can stay with us. Don't know what we're having for supper tonight, but it's always good. Least ways nobody ever complains. We have three rooms, but only two are empty on account of the man that stayed last night decided to stay another day. He's stayed with us before, so I guess he likes it well enough."

He said the last with a contemptuous toss of his head. His nostrils flared, and his voice had a tone of disdain.

"Say, Mister, how did you sneak up so close to me a while ago? Are you some kind of Indian or something? You don't look like no Indian. Say, what kind of clothes you wearin'? "

What kind of clothes was I wearing? He ought to see how goofy his were!

"No, Tom." I managed to laugh. "You ever heard of an Indian letting somebody sneak up on them like you just did? I was taking a nap on this downed tree, and I must have fallen off. Sorry I scared you. Do you and your mom live in town? You said she takes in travelers. Do ya'll have a motel? What railroad is it that goes to Alexandria?"

I was hoping that my questions would result in some answers, but the boy's mind wasn't on answers—it was on more questions.

"Ha, you think I was scared," he said. "You just surprised me is all. Where'd you come from, Mister? What's a motel? You talk kind of funny. You're not from around here, are you? I bet you jumped the train yesterday. Where's your horse?"

"Tom, I can't remember the last time I rode a horse or jumped a train," I laughed nervously. "Where'd you get that old flintlock musket?"

What in the hell was he talking about? The first spidery wisps of apprehension infiltrated my reasoning processes, delicately hindering rational thought. That scrap of paper with the curious quote, what had it said? It was terribly important, but I couldn't concentrate. The warning signal of something terribly amiss, some dreadful mistake, persistently demanded attention. I struggled to nip an incipient panic in the bud. Nevertheless, it was there, spreading a sticky and surprisingly strong web behind it.

I committed myself to controlling my fear and focusing on this one boy who happened to be my sole touch with reality, such as it was. But he kept pestering me with questions. I was going to have to take charge of this one-sided conversation.

"You ask a lot of questions for such a young fellow. Do you want to sit here and talk all day, or do you want to show me the way to your house? I'm getting hungry, and if you want to talk, you are going to have to talk on the way."

We started down the hill, with Tom providing nonstop commentary on just about everything. My mind was only partly on what he was saying until, like a thunderbolt from the skies, he shattered the flimsy, clinging uncertainty.

"We live real close to the junction, so you can probably catch the Orange and Alexandria tomorrow all right, Mister. I'm fifteen now, and when I'm sixteen, I'm going to catch that train. My mom said I could then."

The spider's gossamer web turned into steel cables, binding me forever to what was my first tentative acknowledgment of what had been lurking in my mind's shadowy recesses! The Orange and Alexandria! That was the pre-Civil War railroad between the Washington area and central Virginia. It was long since gone. By now I was pretty sure about where I was. But I hadn't considered the most unlikely question of all—when was I? Could I actually be thinking something so utterly impossible to believe?

Images of digital time racing backward that strange night! Margaret's assistant, Warren, relating test results that same night. What was it he said? The retro timers worked? What were retro timers? Timers for what?

Everything in my life experience shrieked out at me, "You are not of this time place!"

That quote! What had it said? Something about the past? That was it! She had made a time machine, a fucking time machine, and I wasn't here anymore. Except I was here, it just wasn't the same here—or the same when either.

I took a chance and said of the tracks, "That's the Manassas Gap tracks, isn't it?" It really wasn't much of a guess. That was all it could be here in this location and with the track's weird gauge.

"Yes, sir. That's the Gap line. It meets up with the Orange and Alexandria at the junction. It comes all the way from the Shenandoah, and maybe even farther away, far as I know. It's not due here for two days. My mom said it takes the Orange and Alexandria about two hours to get to Alexandria from here. I don't give a hoot if I ever see Washington. I want to go to Richmond or maybe Texas. Why are you going to Washington? Have you ever been to Texas, Mister?"

So I was near Manassas Junction. I was where two amateur armies clashed, brother against brother, to determine the fate of the nation. Now I knew where I was all right, but when I was, that was the more important question.

I couldn't wait any longer; I had to know. "Tom, I've lost track of time. What's the date? What day is it?"

"All I know is that it's Tuesday. We went to church day before yesterday."

That didn't help much, except that it wasn't the day of the week where I was before.

Then it dawned on me: Margaret must know by now what had happened. At least she had to know that I had disappeared. I thought she had seen her machine vaporize me, or whatever the hell it did. Then a further thought struck me: did she even know that her device transcended time, as well as space? Einstein had postulated the relationship between the two, so I had to believe that a physicist would at least consider it a possibility.

In any event, I was walking away from the only point of reference she had—the physical location of where I had just landed. That sudden realization caused me to stop short.

"What's the matter, Mister? It's only a little farther."

I had to get back to where we had just come from! It was my only chance to return to my life. I was in a world that had long since passed from the scene. I looked at Tom; this young fellow, full of the vitality of youth, was the living dead. I shuddered at the thought; a thought made more frightening considering my problematic existence here.

Where I had landed was my only link to Margaret and her machine. I could go back there, but I couldn't stay indefinitely, waiting for her to retrieve me. If nothing else, I would have to find food and shelter. Gut instinct beckoned me back, but rational thought insisted that it was impractical. Then, with a chill,

I thought of that damned quote again. Just what exactly had it said? I couldn't remember, but it continued to haunt me.

I caught up with the boy and asked, "Do you think you can find your way back there tomorrow? I lost my hat someplace."

"I go up there all the time, Mister. I can take you back any time. You want to go back and look for it now? It won't take any time at all."

With that, we headed back the way we had come. I tried to concentrate on landmarks while, at the same time, thinking of something to do that would be helpful. Finally I came up with an idea. Ostensibly looking for the fictitious hat, I scouted around the location where Tom had said I first appeared. I soon found what I was looking for: a good-sized tree limb lying in the leaves. Out of Tom's sight, I carved my initials and "1850?" in the soft wood; it was my best wild-ass guess of the proximate time frame. I had just enough room to etch out "Manassas." If Margaret could zap something back to her time, it might provide her with enough information to know where I was and that I didn't know yet when I was.

I shouted to Tom that it wasn't around and went back to where I had left him. As we headed for his home, I casually tossed the limb close to where I had fallen into this century. And for the first time, I considered the ramifications of my footprints on events here. It wouldn't be the last time!

On the walk back, he continued to talk about any number of things and to ask questions.

I ignored most of his questions and just tried to encourage him to keep talking. It wasn't very demanding. He had something to say about everything and everybody. He never seemed to notice that I seldom answered his questions. Kid was probably going to grow up to be a lawyer.

Then I remembered. If this were the 1850s, he would soon be caught up in the war that was to ravage this land. Manassas would be particularly hard-hit. Two major battles would be fought here, and while the Confederacy would win both, this countryside would be occupied by federal armies for most of the war. Their rule would not be particularly benign. The landscape would show the effects of that occupation for decades; the effect on the families would be with them until the day they died. That gave me another clue to the date. My new now had to be before the war, or all this pastoral terrain would still be battle-scarred.

Tom would end up being a soldier. I had no doubt where his loyalties would lie. He wouldn't be spared the horrors that visited almost every Southerner in the years to come. If he managed to survive at all, that is.

He jolted me out of my reverie and back into the present.

"We're almost there, Mister. Say, you never told me your name."

We were approaching a moderately large house on the edge of a small copse. I thought it was probably atypical for the area and time. We were coming up from the left rear of the house. To the front was a large field cut in two by the tracks that we had been paralleling. Off past the house a bit, farther southeast, I could see what was probably the rail junction. It was here that elements of Confederate General Joe Johnston's troops disembarked to reinforce Beauregard's army in the first major battle of the war.

Tom's house should survive intact the fighting in that battle, but for the better part of the war, everyone in this area would be at the mercy of occupying armies. I had seen post-battle pictures of the area, and it hadn't fared well. How Tom and his mother fared was a terrible unknown.

"Tom, do you have any brothers and sisters?"

"No, sir. I would have had an older sister, but she died before I was born. Then my dad died, so I guess I won't ever have any now." It was the first sign of anything but the youthful optimism he had displayed in the hour or so since we met.

"My name is John Kelly, Tom. I sure am glad we met. Are you certain your mother can take another guest?"

"Yes, sir. We have the rooms, and Mom always has more than enough food on account she has to make enough for the hands. Our niggers are the best fed in the state."

He gestured over his shoulder, and looking back I could see three men working in the field across the track. It was disturbing to hear him refer to men that way. The word had a harsh, uncompromising quality to it. I shouldn't have been discombobulated, but I was. It reminded me that here I was in a different world—one that was no friend to the black man. I had heard it many times before. Indeed, I had used it more times than I liked to admit. Nevertheless, it had become unacceptable, and its casual use disconcerted me. It made me feel especially uncomfortable to hear it out of Tom's young mouth.

By this time, we were walking up to the front door. It was set back from the steps by a rather large porch—one that would have been more in place on a more prosperous-looking house.

"Thomas, is that you? Be sure and wipe your feet. Did you get anything?"

As we came into the small foyer, I could hear kitchen noises down the hall, off to the right. From what I could see in the dimness, as my eyes slowly adjusted from the bright sunlight, the house was neat and orderly.

"Tom, come on back here. I need you to fetch me some water."

"I didn't get anything, Momma. But I brought us a roomer I found out in the woods. He was sleeping up on that little hill by Flat Run."

She came around the corner, brandishing a large stirring spoon in her hands and a disapproving look in her eyes. It looked more like a paddle to me. It was obvious she wasn't too keen on Tom bringing home someone he found sleeping in the woods. I straightened my shoulders as well as I could and gripped my bag tighter. I wished that I had at least tried to comb my hair. I hoped I didn't look too disreputable.

The formidable expression she had on her face softened as she saw that I at least had a shirt on my back and looked well fed, if not prosperous. She waved the spoon in her hands as if she didn't know quite what to do with it. Finally she just let it fall to her side as she slowly approached me with a questioning smile on her face.

She was a pleasant-looking woman of perhaps thirty-five. She had a trim build and was about three inches shorter than me. That made her just a bit shorter than Tom. She wore some kind of dress of a reddish color that reached nearly to the floor. So strange! Pictures and descriptions out of history books couldn't prepare one for the real thing. It was positively a preternatural experience, except that it wasn't outside of nature; it only seemed that way. I felt like I had awakened from a dream about a surreal world, only to find out the dream was real but the dreamer wasn't—a sort of solipsism in reverse.

She brushed ineffectively at specks of flour on her dress and then made that eternal feminine gesture of patting her hair in place. There was nothing to pat back in place, except perhaps a few strands over her temple that had come loose from the tight curls.

"This here is Mr. Kelly, Mom. He's on his way to...where'd you say you were going, Mr. Kelly? We have room, don't we, Mom?"

"Hello, Mr. Kelly. I'm Louisa Biggers, Tom's mother. Yes, we have two rooms available. I ask a quarter of a dollar a day in silver, if you have it. Supper comes with the room. If you get up early enough, you can have breakfast too. Are you planning to leave on tomorrow's train into Alexandria? It's supposed to get here sometime between two and three o'clock; it seldom does, though. If you're going down to Gordonsville, it comes through the junction right after nine o'clock in the morning. Coming back from Alexandria, it's almost always on time."

"Ma'am, if it comes every day, I would like to rest up a day or two before finishing my trip. That is, if it isn't an inconvenience to you."

"Oh, heavens no, Mr. Kelly. Tell the truth, we don't get as many guests as I would surely like. I want to warn you now, though, that I don't allow taking the LORD's name in vain under my roof. I don't believe in the devil's brew either. I hope you aren't a drinker. It's all right if you smoke, just don't burn the house down.

"Now if I haven't scared you off, Mr. Kelly, I'm pleased to welcome you to our home."

"Mrs. Biggers, I don't drink much, and any case I have none with me, and you sound like a woman who won't be serving any with supper," I said with what I hoped was enough humor to make her laugh.

She rewarded me with a chuckle and a faint smile. "Indeed, I won't, Mr. Kelly."

"I do smoke, but I don't have much with me, and I promise that you'll not hear language not fit for a lady."

"Well, it's settled then," she said. "Tom, take Mr. Kelly up to the room with your grandfather's bed. Then show him the necessary. After you're done, fill up the jug for the room and fetch him a fresh towel."

She turned to me and said, "We eat supper at seven o'clock, so you'll have time to rest and clean up. We serve plain fare, Mr. Kelly, but there's always enough for everybody. My goodness, that's a handsome shirt. And your trousers; I don't think I've ever seen such material. What is it, if you don't mind my asking? I've never seen anything like it before. Is that your bag?"

"Yes, ma'am," I said, thinking fast. "It's what we wear where I came from." I wondered what she would have said if I had showed up in my normal wear, a coat and tie. Which reminded me: I knew it was customary in middle-class families to wear a coat to dinner. Mine was still hanging in Margaret's lab and, in any event, would have engendered even more comments since it was a modern, lightweight windbreaker. I apologized for not having a coat for supper, explaining that mine had gotten lost, along with my hat.

For the first time, I found something good in my situation. If today had been a class day, I would have been wearing attire harder to explain. Thankfully the circumstances of my class had provided me with some means of survival. I had Caroline's money, though precious little else.

"I think we have an old frock coat from Thomas's grandfather, if you don't mind the old style. I reckon it should fit you well enough until you can find your own."

I could tell she would have liked me to reveal just where it was I did come from. Other than the woods, that is. I think she was satisfied that I wasn't a Yankee. My accent, while hardened by modern life, still had enough of a drawl to let her know I was from somewhere south of the Mason-Dixon Line.

After leaving my bag upstairs, we went back downstairs and out in the back, where Tom pointed out the facilities. I had surely used worse. Off to the other side of the back, and closer to the house, was the well. Beyond the outhouse, maybe a hundred yards away, were two small buildings. I guessed they were the slave quarters. The barn and stable were even with the house and facing the tracks.

I couldn't stay here indefinitely, if for no other reason than my limited supply of money would eventually run out. Assuming Margaret could get me back—a mighty big assumption—and if it would turn out to take time, then I needed someplace to stay. Everything hinged on us establishing some kind of communication. I had to assume she would figure out what happened and that she would make every effort to rescue me. It was all very, very confusing.

The whole thing exhausted me, so I told Tom I would be down in time for supper.

"Don't be late, Mr. Kelly. That's one thing that gets Ma all riled up. If you aren't sitting down when we bless our food, you just don't get to eat. I'll come up and get you in plenty of time. Maybe tomorrow you want to go hunting with me? I'm a pretty good shot. I'd got me a deer if you hadn't snuck up on me like you did. Still don't know how you did that."

"I told you, Tom," I lied. "I was napping, and I fell off that tree. I'm just glad you didn't shoot me. What were you hunting?"

I felt bad lying to him. I knew my life here was going to be one deception after another, but it didn't feel so good to deceive the boy deliberately. Mostly I could just ignore his questions, and he would go on to some other topic. The best thing I could do was to keep it simple and go with the flow.

I went upstairs to get a little rest. Tom knocked a few minutes later with my towel and water. After slipping off my shoes,

I laid down to mull things over. I had a lot of things to think about.

I planned to stay at least two nights here while waiting for Margaret to bring me home. And anyway, I had no place else to go for now.

Tomorrow I would go back to the place where I landed and see what might happen. I had little expectation that tomorrow I would be back in Margaret's arms, but hope springs eternal. And just maybe the tree limb would be gone and replaced by some kind of instructions on where and when to be for the ride home.

I needed different clothes too. If I were going to be here for any length of time, I would have to look like I belonged. My explanation to Tom and Louisa had been weak, and I could tell they were curious. It might do around here for a little while, but eventually somebody would wonder and start asking questions I couldn't answer. Or maybe no one would even care.

The next thing I heard was the sound of Tom knocking on my door. I must have fallen asleep again. Apparently the experience I had been through had taken its toll.

He gave me an old frock coat that looked like it had just come out of a trunk. I hurriedly splashed water on my face, dried up, and put the coat on. The fit wasn't perfect, and it had a kind of musty smell. For better or worse, I left my room, closing the door behind me.

Downstairs, I pointed myself toward where I heard the clatter of dishes and the buzz of conversation. It turned out to be the large kitchen, which opened into the dining area. Louisa and a handsome black woman were heaping piles of food on platters and into serving bowls. The delightful aroma made me almost faint with hunger. Time travel obviously whetted one's appetite. Tom motioned me to one end of the table. There were four settings, presumably one for the other boarder. Before I could ask where he was, he came around the corner and announced his presence with a slight cough. He hurried over to the chair to my right and, sticking out his hand, introduced himself with an accent that could have never come from Virginia.

"How do you do, sir? I am Lucius P. Toomey," he said with what I knew to be that almost musical way of speaking peculiar to the bayous around New Orleans.

He was dressed for dinner in middle-class attire. His waistcoat couldn't hide the beginnings of a middle-age paunch, although he seemed to be only in his early thirties. His hair was a reddish-blond color, and he had a not-very-impressive mustache and beard covering a face that had received too much sun. I figured him for either a traveling salesman or a low to middle-ranking civil servant of some kind. I was sure he would find a way to let me know.

I took his hand and introduced myself. His grip was surprisingly firm, and his hand was cool and dry. His shrewd eyes quickly sized me up, and, apparently satisfied I was not of much consequence, he turned his attention to Louisa, who was just sitting down. I was just glad he didn't say something about my clothes. I doubted that he had missed it, though.

"Ah, Mrs. Biggers, another scrumptious and fulsome repast, my nose tells me."

"You're just hungry, Mr. Toomey," she said as the black woman brought one final plate of food to the table.

"Mary, did you make sure the boys have enough? Tomorrow is another long day in the fields."

"Oh yes, Miss Louisa. We fixed a powerful heap of food tonight. And I got plenty set aside for myself too. Not that I need it, as round as I am. Now you'll just enjoy your food with some pleasant conversation. Don't you worry any about all the mess. I'll be back to take care of things. Maybe you can play the piano tonight for your guests. I just love to hear you play them hymns."

"Well, maybe, Mary. Our guests may be tired and ready to retire after supper." She turned to me and said, "Will you please honor the LORD for all he has provided us, Mr. Kelly?"

I took a chance on her religious inclination and said an appropriate prayer over the food. I knew Virginia was still largely Episcopalian, but the evangelical spirit that had swept through the country was particularly strong in the agrarian South.

"Amen. Mr. Kelly, that was the kind of praise to the LORD my late husband, Joseph, would have approved of, and I do too. Everyone, please, help yourselves. Tom, pass the bacon over to Mr. Kelly."

Supper was a pleasant enough affair. Toomey was a lively and voluble conversationalist, expressing views on a variety of subjects. Tom would answer when spoken to, but it was apparent he didn't particularly care for their boarder. Louisa's responses to Toomey were polite, yet restrained. There seemed to be an undercurrent of unspoken tension in the room.

Finally, after ignoring me for much of the time, he squinted at me with vulpine eyes and said, "And Mr. Kelly, an Irish name I do believe, yet no brogue. In fact, you have a remarkably neutral voice. Almost as if you were from nowhere, certainly no offense intended. Where have your travels brought you from?"

He, of course, did intend offense, but I knew I was going to have to establish my identity eventually, so I took the bull by the horns and plunged ahead with as much truth in my cover story as I could.

"I'm originally from Texas, Mr. Toomey. However, you are right; one could say I am from nowhere. I've traveled all my life, all across this great country. Most recently I have been residing in North Carolina. I do believe, though, your voice readily identifies your origins. I am familiar with the state of Louisiana, from where I would wager you hail. Quite possibly Baton Rouge."

"Quite so, sir. Quite so. Like you, though, I no longer live in the land of my birth. I live in Richmond now. My position takes me throughout the state of Virginia. I am employed by a consortium of Virginia railroad companies to inspect the tracks and rolling stock. What did you say your line of work is?"

Before I could frame an answer, Tom interjected his enthusiasm and questions into the conversation.

"I knew it all along," he said. "See, mother, I told you Mr. Kelly was from Texas. I'm going to go as soon as I can. I want to fight Indians. I'll bet you killed a lot of 'em, Mr. Kelly. And Mexicans too! Oh, how glorious." He was fairly squirming in his seat with excitement.

I wondered what Tom would say if I told him my great-grandmother was a full-blood Cherokee.

Louisa hushed him with a gentle admonishment. "Thomas, remember where we are. I'll not have that kind of talk at the supper table. Mr. Kelly, what does bring you to our state? I do believe you are the first man to come through here from out there. Our church helps support missionary work in the Indian Territory. Have you been there?"

"I'm proud to say I used to be a soldier, ma'am. I am going to Washington to renew old military acquaintances. And yes, I have been to the territory. What church do you belong to, if I may ask? There is much good work being done by the various missionaries there."

"We belong to the Cumberland Presbyterian Church, Mr. Kelly. Perhaps you haven't heard of us way out west. Not too many here have either. Our little congregation comes from miles around. The Baptists up near Sudley Springs are kind enough to share their church house with us. Some even stay to hear our preacher. One day we hope to have our own building."

Toomey, evidently feeling left out of the conversation, interrupted with an exasperated look on his face. "You mean to say, Mr. Kelly, that that's all you do? Visit friends? Surely you are engaged in some enterprise more than just visiting friends. After all, one must have some profitable endeavor to survive unless, of course, one is well-connected."

His expression left no doubt that he didn't consider that very likely. In truth I surely didn't look like a man of independent means. It suited my purposes for now, though, Toomey's assessment notwithstanding.

Before I could respond, he continued. "And I don't believe I've ever seen anyone in Texas with such strange clothes."

Louisa, sensing the brewing tension, announced that she had freshly baked rhubarb pie for dessert.

Apparently it was a treat because everyone enthusiastically endorsed the idea, and so Toomey's question was forgotten for the present. I wasn't really excited about anything with rhubarb in it, but the suggestion came at a good time. The last thing I needed was trouble before I had even been here a few hours.

The rest of the meal was without further unpleasantness. Toomey seemed to realize he had gotten on the wrong side of Louisa, so he made an effort to be cordial. He even joined in around the piano afterward while Louisa played some old standbys. Mary came out from the kitchen and added her voice. All in all it was a pleasant close of a most eventful day.

By the time we were finished, the summer day had ended, and with it, light enough to see without the lanterns and candles abundantly spread around the house. It was a homey setting, not without its appeal. No television or computers. No telephones ringing, just people interacting in the way that modern civilization had long forgotten. There was something to be said for it all.

Mary went back to the kitchen, and Toomey excused himself to go up to his room.

Louisa announced it was time for Tom to go to bed, to which he put up a fuss that would do a twentieth-century youngster proud. Some things transcended time. After telling him good night, I took the opportunity to pay her for two nights and told her that in case I needed to stay longer, if she was agreeable, I would pay at that time.

In the softening light and shadows, she seemed much younger, and her voice had a wistful quality that served to remind me that life couldn't be easy for a widow trying to manage in what was a male-dominated world.

"Mr. Kelly, you can stay as long as you need. I'm sorry for the late unpleasantness. Mr. Toomey meant no ill will, I'm sure, but I intend to inform him that I will not tolerate rudeness to a guest."

"You don't need to do that, Mrs. Biggers. I'm sure he didn't mean anything. He probably just had a difficult day."

"Well, we'll see," she said. "He has a nature that sometimes is quite pleasant and other times is somewhat fractious. We can always use the money, and he does pay in advance. However, he can be vexing.

"Listen to me gab," she continued. You must be tired, and here I am, burdening you with my troubles. Please pay me no mind."

"I'm pleased to talk with you, ma'am. I enjoyed the singing too. You must have taken lessons because you play the piano well. I'm afraid I don't have much of an ear for music. I enjoy it when I hear it, though."

Even in the dim parlor, I could see her flush with pleasure. "That's very kind of you, Mr. Kelly, but I know I don't play as well as I could. I just don't practice enough. Don't seem to have the time nowadays. I was going to teach Tom to play, but it just seems so impossible. Anyway, getting him to sit still for even five minutes is a chore, except at the supper table!"

I laughed. "He didn't seem to have any trouble there, that's for sure."

"No, he didn't," she said with a fond smile. "Now if you'll excuse me, Mr. Kelly. I have to straighten up before bed. Will you be having breakfast with us? We start early in the morning this time of year, but you are welcome to join us. And I can promise you Mr. Toomey won't be up at five o'clock."

She said the last with a scornful laugh. I wondered what he possibly could have done to get on her bad side. Not that he was all that pleasant a person.

"Ma'am, I would like to, but I just can't guarantee that I will be able to wake up on my own. Today has been tiring. So please don't go out of your way."

"If you're up, just come on down, and we will have something for you. Otherwise I'll save some bacon and cornbread for whenever you get up. You get a good night's sleep now. Well, good night again."

"Oh, before you go, ma'am, could I trouble you for a newspaper, if you have one? Traveling like I have, I've been out of touch with what's happening in the rest of the country."

I didn't care that much about what was happening; I just wanted to find out the date.

"I'm sorry to disappoint you, Mr. Kelly, but we don't even have an old one. You can probably find one down at the junction tomorrow, though."

"It's not that important. If anything has happened I need to know about, I'll find out in good time. Good night to you, Mrs. Biggers."

I decided to take a walk away from the house and grab a smoke. Fishing in my pocket, I pulled out my first cigarette of the day and lit it with my Zippo. I would need to keep things like lighters hidden.

God, the cigarette was good. I inhaled deeply, savoring the taste and sensation. Terrible habit, but one I was not likely to shed on my own. I might as well enjoy them while I could.

After slowly taking the last drag, I stripped it down and let the remains filter through my fingers to be picked up by the light breeze. Just as the wind carried away the bits of tobacco, so my worries about what to expect in the days to come lifted from my mind, at least momentarily. I turned back toward the house for my first night in this land of antiquity.

CHAPTER 8

I slept soundly that night, my first as an expatriate in my new century. And I awoke early enough for breakfast. I was famished, and although Louisa had promised she would save something for me, I didn't want to come down late. I recalled the disdain with which she had referred to Toomey's late-rising habits. Now there was a guy that it would be easy to underestimate.

I had left my window open. The early morning air was still cool but was already infused with the hint of the warm day to come. Most memorable was how clean and crisp it felt. I could smell the earth and grass and trees—sensations no longer available where I had come from. What price progress?

I lit the lamp and washed my face in cold water. Feeling my whiskers reminded me that if I were going to be here for any length of time, I would need a straight razor. Or grow a beard, which on me didn't look good at all. It made me look like Yasser Arafat.

Finishing up, I went downstairs and outside to the facilities. I would have to get used to outdoor plumbing too, but I didn't have to like it. I had used a lot worse, but that didn't make it any more enjoyable. After getting out of the army, I had sworn I would never rough it again. And here I was.

By the time I washed up and went back downstairs to the kitchen, Tom and Louisa were just sitting down to bowls of what looked like mush of some kind. I could smell bacon frying in the kitchen. Mary bustled in, bringing a bowl and a cup of steaming hot coffee. God, I was hungry. Even the mush smelled wonderful.

Louisa seemed more animated and cheerful than yesterday evening. Her cheeks, then devoid of makeup, now had a healthy glow, with just a touch of pink.

"Good morning, Mr. Kelly," Louisa said. "I heard you up and around. Did you get a good night's sleep?"

"Like a baby, Mrs. Biggers, like a baby. Good morning to you, and you, Tom. And Mary, I could smell your cooking all the way upstairs. A good morning to you too."

If it wasn't possible to see a flush of pleasure on her deep-chocolate face, I knew it was there, nevertheless. She practically beamed her reply to me.

"Morning, Mr. Kelly, sir. I done fixed you a whole mess of bacon and biscuits. I got the grits all sweetened up right nice for you too. You just sit down and fill yourself up. Traveling is hard on a man. You look like you need to be fattened up some."

"Mary, you scat and leave Mr. Kelly to his breakfast," Louisa said. Her words seemed to be an obligatory rebuff, probably for my benefit, but her tone was one of genuine affection. The black woman obviously knew it because she just chuckled to herself as she busied setting out platters of biscuits, gravy, bacon, and a big bowl of grits.

Louisa looked at me approvingly and said, "You've won Mary over now, Mr. Kelly. She is going to mother you as long as you're here. She's part of our family. We grew up together."

Her eyes flashed a challenge to me. It was pretty common-place in the South for close relationships to exist between slave and master. It seemed to have evolved in such a way so as to make the best of the situation. Not that it was an excusing factor for the condition the black race was in. Nor was it particularly elevating to be on such close terms with those who ruled over you.

"I feel right at home here, ma'am. And if Mary wants to mother me, well, I don't mind one little bit. Not when she feeds me such delectations as this."

Mary, who had been hovering just inside the kitchen door, smiled triumphantly. Louisa smiled at me and told me to eat as much as I wanted.

"That's one thing we have plenty of, Mr. Kelly."

Tom, who had been uncharacteristically silent, interjected, "You wanna go hunting with me today, Mr. Kelly? I'm going soon as I finish eating. I'll bet you're a good shot. What kind of musket did you use in the army?"

The boy must have been born with a question mark for a birthmark. Fortunately he asked so many questions that I could pick and choose which ones I was willing to answer. Not that he ever waited for one.

"I might go out with you today," I said between mouthfuls of biscuits. In fact, I intended to go back to where I entered into this world. I wanted to memorize the route and to mark the exact location while it was still fresh in my mind. It was my launchpad for a rocket ship ride back to Margaret.

"You take a rest from all your questions, Tom, and let Mr. Kelly finish breakfast," Louisa said, turning to me. "If you get tired answering all Tom's questions, just tell him to close his mouth for a while. Otherwise you'll never get anything done."

"Amen to that," said Mary, who had just come back in to bring a pitcher of milk. "Mr. Tom is going to grow up and be a lawyer man. I just knows it."

"No, I'm not! I'm going to be a soldier, and besides, I'm almost a man already. Momma, may I be excused now?"

"Make sure you go right up and brush your teeth. And don't forget your chores before you go traipsing off," his mother said, shaking her head with a smile.

Tom jumped up and hurried out of the room before stopping and, with a sheepish grin on his face, giving Louisa a peck on the cheek. "I'll finish all my chores, Mother. You'll see."

After he left, Louisa gave me an exasperated look and said, "I surely do appreciate you taking time to talk to Tom. He can be a mite tiring sometimes. Still, he's a good boy, if he would just not pester me so much."

After finishing my breakfast, I excused myself and went back up to my room to get ready for the day.

First, I took inventory of all my worldly possessions. Other than the clothes on my back, I had nothing else to wear, so I might need to expand my wardrobe. I couldn't see anyone buying my story about traveling without at least one change of clothes. My shoes were good brogans that weren't really too noticeably different from what was worn here.

I had a little over five hundred dollars in pre-1860 US coinage and state and commercial bank notes. I also had my wallet stuffed with worthless modern-day money. I might just as well burn that.

I had few other possessions. A wristwatch that was practically useless here. My valise contained little of value: a notepad, my reading glasses, my ballpoint pen, a penlight, a road map, and my reference book on Lee. Except for the pistol and pocketknife, the rest were just odds and ends. The contents of my wallet were equally useless: money, credit cards, identification, and pictures.

Only God could help me if I ever had to use the pistol. I thought of that aspect long and hard. The past had particular considerations that warranted special resolve. Everything I did here would play itself out sometime in the future, with unknown results.

My inventory didn't take long since I didn't have much to start with. Nevertheless, I knew from years of experience that it mattered little, because no matter how much or how little I had, I would eventually need something that I didn't have. I would just have to make do. That and my wits would be it.

Tom's voice at the door asking me if I was ready to go saved me from having to dwell on the prospect of an extended stay. It was a welcome diversion, but I knew I was going to have to knuckle down and devote time to the intractable problems of surviving until Margaret got me back home.

We set off at a slow pace, for which I was grateful. Tom was amply endowed with the enthusiasm of youth, and he was as interested in what went on around him as any young boy in the twentieth century. And right now I was the most interesting thing around. He peppered me with an apparently inexhaustible supply of questions and observations.

Fortunately I didn't have to suggest we go back in the direction where we had met yesterday. I supposed it was his favorite hunting area. Before long we were entering the wooded area close to the railroad tracks, and in just a few minutes more, we were crossing the stream we had crossed yesterday. It had seemed a much longer walk then, so I was surprised when he stopped in the very same place where I had exploded into his world.

He looked around and said, "This is where the wind liked to blowed me over, Mr. Kelly. And right over here is where you said you were sleeping. I still don't know how I didn't see you right before that storm hit, or whatever it was, 'cause I walked this very same way."

Sure enough, he would have had to see me if I had been there. However, I was only half paying attention to him. My primary interest was the marked limb I'd left behind yesterday. My disappointment at finding it still in the same place must have shown on my face because Tom asked me what was wrong.

I said somewhat lamely, "I don't know how you could have missed me, Tom. What do you reckon that big wind was all about? It sure woke me up."

"Beats all I ever saw," he said. "Well, we had better find us a place where we can watch for deer. If we don't see one, maybe I can get some squirrels."

"We might do better down at the stream. Have you had much luck with deer around here?"

"My mom just let me start hunting by myself when school let out," he said defensively, "or else I would have got one long ago. I shot some squirrels and a rabbit. Momma made some good stew too."

We started off down toward the stream. While we were walking, I mentally counted off my paces. Once there, we moved along the bank until we found a likely crossing place with some evidence of animal traffic.

After settling in a thicket about twenty feet from the stream, Tom asked me if I had ever shot a grizzly bear. I hated to disappoint him since I was beginning to see that he regarded me as a great frontiersman who daily tangled with mountain lions and bears. I was sure if I told him that I had single-handedly defeated the entire Sioux Nation, he would believe me and go tell everyone in the county.

"Never even saw one, Tom, but I wasn't in the business of hunting game. I was just a soldier who did those things that soldiers do. What are you going to be when you get older? Are you going to be a lawyer like Mary says? Or are you going to work your mom's farm? It's a right nice farm."

"I'm going to be a soldier, just like I said. I'll come home every year to help Momma get the crops in. Maybe I'll go to California and find a whole bunch of gold. Then I'll set her up in Richmond, where she won't ever have to work again, and so she'll never have to take in boarders either.

"You're different, though," he said quickly. "My mom likes you, and you treat her like a lady. That Mr. Toomey..." His voice trailed off, and he looked around furtively as if he half expected to see Toomey himself—or worse, his mom—behind a tree. "Momma doesn't like me to talk about people. She said it's for the LORD to do the judging, not me. But I don't care for the way he's always looking at her or the way he treats Mary either."

"Your mom is a real nice woman, a real lady, Tom. I'm sure Mr. Toomey doesn't mean anything."

He didn't respond other than a barely audible sound of resignation. One that clearly said adults didn't ever understand. With that, we settled in for a long wait.

Lost in thought in the morning heat, I started getting drowsy again. Just before drifting off, the horrendous ripping noise of mini-guns tearing through the overhead canopy tore me from sleep's sweet embrace. Sergeant Adams was screaming and shaking me urgently. We had incoming; we were sitting ducks here! The crew chief's anxious face looked down at me; his arm outstretched to pull me in the bird. If Adams would just stop shaking my shoulder, we could get moving to safety.

"Mr. Kelly! Mr. Kelly! Wake up! What's happening?"

The gunship and jungles of past battles faded away. It was a bad dream—a bad dream but comforting in its familiarity. I was reluctant to let go. The reality of the now would not be denied, though. Finally I gave it up and lurched into today. I was awake.

"I'm awake, Tom. What's going on? It sounds like a storm is coming through."

He just kept shaking my arm. I put my hand on his shoulder to stop him from yanking my arm out of its socket, and I realized he was shaking from fear. I wrapped my arm around him and pulled him close to my side. He kept pointing up the hill and mouthing something I couldn't hear for another explosion. I felt a chill settle in my bones. The temperature had dropped noticeably just in the few seconds I had been awake. It was as if we were sitting directly in the path of a blue norther.

Then it all abruptly stopped. All that was left was the rustling of things settling back in place and a branch falling in the distance. The natural sounds of the forest gradually resumed. Tom finally noticed my arm and pulled himself away as if he had shown a moment of weakness that he didn't know he had. The thought ran through my mind that before his life was over, he would know many such moments.

"Did you hear that? Did you hear that, Mr. Kelly? What happened? It ain't natural, what's been happening around here. What made it storm like that? Maybe we had better get on home now, Mr. Kelly."

It was weird coming and going so quickly and with no rain at all. A williwaw blowing down the Blue Ridge Mountains and through Thoroughfare Gap, just as Longstreet's divisions would on the way to Lee's great victory at Second Manassas. The sudden chill in the air—which seemed to be dissipating, even as we sat there—was something out of a gothic mystery novel. The only things missing were wisps of fog swirling around us and a few overturned tombstones. There was a whiff of an ozone smell in the air.

That must be it! No, it wasn't natural, just like yesterday wasn't natural either. The cold, now almost gone, was the same as yesterday. It was Margaret's machine again. She was coming after me. I was saved! I had to get back up the hill. Oh, why hadn't I been up there instead of down by the stream? I could've been on that cold journey home this very second. I had to get up there now. Maybe she would do it again. I had to get back. The hot bile of bitterness almost choked me at the lost opportunity. Maybe she would give up. I'd be stuck here in this godforsaken no-place forever.

I had to get up there now and without the boy. "Stay here, Tom."

I scrambled up the hill, stumbling through the underbrush clumsily, as desperation drove me to what I knew must be a fool's errand. The moment of escape had passed me by. It had been available, and I'd been found wanting. Down I went, on my face. Recklessly I plunged ahead, brambles catching my shirt and tearing my flesh. Finally, on my hands and knees, I reached the top.

Maybe I'd find the branch was gone this time, or maybe, just maybe, a message of some kind would be waiting for me.

But the branch was still there. There was nothing to indicate it had been anymore than a freak storm, except for a residual chill in the air to taunt me. I sat down on the ground with my head in my hands. I felt tears well up in my eyes from the despair of dashed hopes and lost opportunity. I'd been so close, but now I had nothing but the fate of a man lost in a world not his own. I was a man without a country, only infinitely worse. I was a man without a time, without a place. I possessed no history and no future. And my present was without hope. I was a prisoner starting the first day of an irrevocable sentence of life without parole. I didn't think I could resign myself to this cruel a fate.

I wanted to curse this place and century.

Tom, once again, pulled me out of myself and plunged me back into the present, or whatever now was. I could hear him moving up the hill with the same near panic I had felt, albeit for different reasons.

"Mr. Kelly! Mr. Kelly! Are you up there? Momma doesn't like me to be late for dinner."

I told him to go ahead and I'd be there later, but he wasn't too keen on that idea. He was as rattled as I had been. I doubted being punctual was his real motivation to get back home. I didn't blame him; I was still a little shaky myself. I'd just have to come back later today and comb the area alone.

Not that it would do any good now!

He picked up his musket and led the way toward home as I tried to memorize the terrain the best I could. My first order of business had to be making sure I had an escape route committed to memory. There could be no fumbling around, getting confused or lost, if the opportunity to leave ever came again.

"Hello. What's this?" Tom exclaimed. He kicked at an object that surely he had never seen before.

But I had, though! And hundreds just like it! The shiny, cylindrical tube, a little over a foot long, was my beacon of deliverance—a flare guiding the extraction chopper into the LZ to take me back to safety. It was that twentieth-century necessity of the hopelessly addicted coffee freak. A metal, quart-size thermos bottle!

Before Tom could pick it up, I pushed ahead of him and squatted down next to it. There would be a message inside. That would have been the reason she used it. It was relatively indestructible, and it would provide adequate protection from weather and from the turbulence of the voyage through space and time.

My hand trembled as I reached to pick it up. I longed to touch it, to caress the cold, smooth stainless steel, to feel its comforting twentieth-century modernity, its functionality. Relief and elation replaced the despair and hopelessness of just a few seconds ago. But how long had it been here? What if I was already supposed to have been here at a particular time? Had it come and gone and I already missed the boat? Had the sound and fury of a few minutes ago been my one and only port call?

And Tom. I had to see what was inside, but I couldn't do it with him standing there, peering over my shoulder. Already he was moving closer, and I could sense he was about to start with his questions.

"Tom, I've seen things like this before. I think it might be a bomb from a cannon. Take a look, if you want, but don't touch it. Have you ever seen anything like it?"

"No, sir, but it looks like one," he said, trying to sound knowledgeable about such things. "What do you think we should do? Will it blow up? Maybe we should leave it alone. We'd better get back before Mom gets mad."

"Tom, we sure don't want to leave it here where someone might stumble on it and get hurt, do we? Maybe if I try and disarm it, it'll be all right then. No sense both of us getting hurt either, is there? Since I know about these things more than you, it would probably be best if I took care of it."

"Do you think you can do it by yourself, Mr. Kelly? I should stay and help," he protested weakly.

Better men than him—or me, for that matter—had dared not go where angels too had feared to tread. Bombs, unexploded ones, possessed a mystique in a class all by itself. Something about a piece of ordnance that was waiting to detonate unnerved anyone with a bit of sense.

"Somebody's got to be able to go back and get help if it goes off, Tom. Why don't you stand back over there behind that big oak tree where the path turns?"

With that face-saving rationale, he left with as much haste as he could without seeming overly anxious. When he was well down the trail, I placed my body between the thermos and his retreating figure and quickly screwed off the cup and the cap. With my heart pounding and bated breath, I turned it upside down and shook.

And shook! For the briefest eternity, nothing happened. Then slipping easily out was a rolled sheet of that ubiquitous staple of offices around the world, computer paper, covered with modern-day type. A message from home!

"Mr. Kelly, what is it? Can I come back now? Are you all right?

I just stared at it, stricken with the paralysis of sheer gratitude. I would be going home. Margaret's letter would tell me what to do. I could stop worrying and just leave it to her. Unbidden tears misted my vision.

I stuffed the paper inside my shirt and screwed the lid back on the thermos before pushing it back under the bushes. I stood up and walked down the path toward him.

"Tom, it might be best for me to come back later to bury it before someone else finds it."

He evidently thought that was a good idea too because he stopped dead in his tracks quickly enough. Bombs have a way of causing that reaction. They were sort of like snakes in that regard. Fascination, but only from a distance!

With Margaret's letter burning against my chest, we started back home.

I must have been getting used to walking, because before I knew it, we were approaching the house. The field hands were walking back over to their cabin, so it looked like we weren't going to be late for dinner.

I suggested that we might not want to mention what we had found. I pointed out that his mom would probably not let him go back if there was a risk of getting hurt. He quickly saw the wisdom in that idea.

With obvious apprehension, he asked, "When are we going back to bury it, Mr. Kelly?"

To his barely-disguised relief, I told him I would take care of it this afternoon.

With a calmness that belied desperate anxiety, I went upstairs and ripped my shirt off. The letter was wilted a bit from the heat and humidity but was still intact. I opened it and began to read.

My dearest John,

By now you know what happened or at least some of it. You came in just as we were running another test. We knew right away that something had gone wrong because of the immediate power surge. At the instant of maximum power, I caught the briefest glimpse of something before it disappeared. That I now know was you, my darling. Since then (it's been three days here) we have been working around the clock to give you a chance.

Yes, my project has been time travel. You must already know that you have been transported not only miles from home but also years from now. You may have learned already exactly when. If so, you know more than we do. Our calculations tell us you are somewhere in Northern Virginia and sometime in the nineteenth century. That's what the tests have been about—to narrow the time and coordinates down.

My darling, I can't bring you back yet. It only goes one way now. We are working on it, but for now we don't have the capability to do it. I can't even effect two-way communication with you. I can send you things like this; however, I can't know if you received any of it, at least not directly.

I refuse to make things worse by allowing you more hope than is justified. So while what I've told you is grim enough, that's the worst of it. We are working on reversing the time flow, but it will take time.

That's where you can help. I have taken Paul Bindle into my confidence. He is a remarkable man. It took him the shortest imaginable time to assimilate all this and to come up with a plan of action. We must be able to identify your space/time so that when we have perfected returning to the present, we will know where and when to go to retrieve you there. To that end, you are to make a name for yourself in whatever endeavor you can devise. Nothing that will significantly alter events of the world, but something that would show up perhaps in newspaper archives or legal transactions that can be researched at this end. That will give us a starting point to reach you. From there it would be just a matter of locating where you live, knocking on the door, and taking you to a rendezvous point.

You might well ask, "Even if it takes weeks, months, even years of twentieth-century time, why can't she just set the machine to come back to say, the day after I got here?" That is a good question and one I can answer best by telling you that if someone shows up to retrieve you, say tomorrow, that means we were able to solve the problem of getting you back. If not, we weren't able to. Either way, we still need to know when and where you are.

What we have done is put together a package that should help you survive there. The contents are Paul's doings. Not only did he immediately grasp the situation of what happened here, but he also seemed to know just the things you would need there. By the time you read this, the trunk will already be there. In fact, it should have arrived before you did. You see, with only three elapsed days here since you were taken away, the variables of the warping inherent in time travel are slight enough that we can go either direction from your point of entry and still maintain sufficient accuracy to put it in reasonable proximity to where and when you are now. Even if we don't know where and when that where and when is. Do you remember your table knife analogy that was so helpful to me? This message was sent using the same criteria. Paul reasoned that you would do as he would do—that you would surely come back to your original entry place in the expectation we would come back to that same dot in time to retrieve you. Look for the trunk within maybe a quarter of a mile from where you arrived. That's the closest we can approximate.

Just know that I love you and I will never cease working to get you back home.

We will try to communicate until we are certain there is no longer any chance to get anything reasonably close to you. After that, my darling, it will be up to you to make a name for yourself.

I stared at the letter until I could bear it no longer. I was stuck here in this time passed. How long would depend on making my whereabouts known and on Margaret's ability to solve the technical problems. Assuming that hers was a solvable problem, everything depended on me.

The first thing was to find the trunk!

Later, at dinner, I mentioned the storm. Tom's face brightened as he told his mother about the lightning phenomenon and how it had scared away the game.

"Just as well because we would have had to skin it and bring it back. Next time, can I take Dad's hunting knife? Course it'll be hard to tote all the way back home."

I knew he wanted me to teach him how to dress his kill, which was something I wasn't too keen about. Not that I had anything against hunting. I just didn't have the heart for it. Moreover, the skinning and dressing down part was just too sad for me. Since there wasn't any likelihood of supermarkets around, I might have to get over my qualms about it, though.

Tom chattered throughout dinner about our adventures. Louisa said that she heard the storm too and thought we were going to get rain. From here it might have seemed like a summer storm, something probably not too unusual this time of the year.

In a break from Tom's excitement, I asked Louisa if she had any horses. I needed to spend some of my limited money supply and invest in a means of transportation. I wasn't hot about learning to ride, but better now than later. It took too long to get around by foot. It was just another aspect of this time that made me long for home.

"We just have two mules, Mr. Kelly. They're not much good for riding more than a few miles. If you want one, you might have some luck in Groveton or maybe Centerville. I just don't know. There are riders all the time on the Warrenton Turnpike, so you could probably find something in either of the two. Maybe even at the junction. Are you planning on leaving us soon?"

She asked the question casually, but her voice was wistful. Having a man around who took an interest in her son was probably a godsend to her. Moreover, the two bits a day were hard money to her.

"No, ma'am. In fact, I was hoping to pay you in advance for a couple of weeks. I plan on taking short trips for a day or so, and I need to have a place to come back to each time. Would that be all right with you? Of course, if you have the room already promised to some other traveler, I can make some other arrangements."

Her face brightened as she said, "Land's sakes, no. We never get that many travelers. I do believe that Mr. Toomey is our only repeat guest. Only one time did we have all three rooms filled. Goodness, that was a time too. The Gap broke down right before it got to the junction, and we had people two to a room for three days.

"And there's no need for you to pay in advance, Mr. Kelly. You just pay for the room as you need it. There will always be a welcome sign for you here."

All of a sudden, she seemed flustered. She cast her eyes down demurely for a brief second or two and then asked me if I wanted some more milk.

When we were through, I mentioned that I would probably walk up to Groveton and see if anyone had a horse they might be willing to sell. As I expected, Tom was eager to go with me. Fortunately his mother had some chores for him. She may have decided to give me a break. Actually I really cared for the boy and didn't mind having him around, but not today.

He fussed a little, but Louisa was firm, and he cheered up quick enough when I told him that if he wanted, he could ride the horse once I got it.

When I came back downstairs, Louisa called to me, "Oh, Mr. Kelly. I just remembered that over by the Henry house, there is a freeman who may have a horse to sell. I think I heard it at church. Now mind you, I can't vouch for it, but it might be worth a try. His name is Robinson. Do you know where old Mrs. Henry lives? It's east of Groveton, close to the turnpike. You might try there. You're welcome to take one of the mules over there, if you like."

"I do appreciate the advice and your kind offer, Mrs. Biggers. I think I'll just walk, though. It's only a couple of miles from here, and I need the exercise. I'm sure I can find it. I'll probably be gone most of the afternoon, but I'll make sure I'm back for supper. I surely do thank you too for the fine dinner. I hope you'll let me give you something for it, being as how I know it's not included with the room. Breakfasts too."

"You'll do no such thing, Mr. Kelly. You've earned your keep and more just by paying attention to my Tom. I'm afraid he's real taken with you. You just remember: if he gets to be too much, shoo him away for a while."

I laughed and assured her I would but that he was no trouble at all.

After crossing Flat Run, I hoofed it north on the Manassas-Sudley Road toward the Warrenton Turnpike. I knew by now where Louisa lived, generally, in relation to Manassas Junction, and if I knew any place in the United States like the back of my hand, it was the site of the first great battle of the war. The Henry house would be just about three miles from Louisa's and would be just a couple hundred yards from the macadam-sur-faced turnpike.

It was aligned with this country road connecting Sudley Ford with Manassas Junction that Colonel Burnside's brigade began the initial assault on the hastily thrown together left flank of the Confederate forces. General Irwin McDowell's soundly conceived, but poorly executed, turning movement succeeded in surprising the defending commander, General Beauregard. It was only a belated message from a Confederate signal tower warning of the turning movement, and Nathan "Shank" Evans's energetic and stout defense, that ultimately saved the day for the Southerners.

Off to my right front, Henry Hill was where an obscure commander named Thomas Jackson commanded a regiment of Virginia volunteers. General Bernard Bee would gallop from that hill back to his beleaguered command to rally them, and, in the process, the legend of Lee's most able general would be born. Bee wouldn't survive the battle, and Jackson would be fatally wounded two years hence. Nevertheless, in that short span, he would achieve immortal fame as the incomparable Stonewall.

As I walked along, I felt my usual sense of history when visiting battlefields. The times I had walked this same terrain, and the momentous events that had occurred here, had never failed to quicken my pulse and my Southern soul. This battle, small in comparison with the titanic struggles that followed, nevertheless would decide the direction and, ultimately, the outcome of the war. The South's triumph had masked its death knell; for a complacent and overly confident North it was a clarion call to arms. The sleeping giant roused itself and girded its loins for the long haul, one in which it held all the cards. Before, when I had walked this hallowed ground, it had all been a long past history. But now, now there was no history—just history to be made.

The free man was James Robinson, and he lived just a few hundred feet from Judith Henry's home. Robinson survived the war, but Henry, a bed-ridden old woman, would be killed by a federal cannon shot during the first battle to be fought here. The federal government would later rebuild the poor woman's death chamber as part of a memorial to the Union dead.

Robinson's home was straight ahead. Since it was on the turnpike, I cut across the Henry property to approach it from the front. I had no idea if Robinson would welcome visitors, especially white ones. Standing outside his property, I yelled out in the friendliest way I could.

"Hello? Hello in there? Is anybody home? Hello?"

There was no response. He could be reluctant to come out for a stranger, or he could be somewhere on his property. I had no idea how extensive his land was, and I didn't see anyone out in the field surrounding the house. The already-harvested cornfields could belong to anyone around here. There was some kind of crop growing around the houses. It could be forage crops or anything, as far as I knew. I wasn't much of a farmer.

The door finally opened, and a black man emerged from the house and asked, "Yes, suh, what all can I do for you?" He was friendly enough, but he had a wary look in his eyes, like he had had to prove his free status too many times and I was another one of those fugitive chasers. Who could blame him? I didn't know how he had gained his freedom, but I knew that no matter how he happened to be free, he really wasn't. And he knew it too. He had few protections under the law here. Or anywhere else in the United States, for that matter. He could very easily be forcibly dragged into another state and sold back into slavery in spite of papers proving he was a free man. There were any number of unscrupulous men that could take advantage of him, and there would be precious little he could do about it. Moreover, he knew the law wouldn't fall all over itself to protect him. He would always have to depend on the goodwill of white people.

I wondered if his family was inside.

"I'm just about dried out, and I'd like to trouble you for a cup of water. But what I really came to see you about is I heard you might have a horse to sell."

"Yes, sir. You do look like you could use a tall cup of cool water. That there is my well," he said, pointing to the back of the house. "You're welcome to as much as you want."

He had thawed a little, but he wasn't too anxious to turn his back to me to lead the way, as if he thought that as long as I was in his eyesight, he would be safe.

So I obliged him by starting off that way and let him tag along behind me. Only after I had drunk my fill did he answer me about his horse.

"I do have a horse to sell, Mister. She's not much, but she's got heart. You won't be using her for heavy duty or nuthin' like that though; she just ain't built for it. She'll carry you where you wanna go, though, as long as you feed her right. I'm asking twenty Spanish dollars for her."

I didn't have any idea what the going price for horseflesh was, but I figured he was asking more than he expected to get, especially if he figured me for a city boy that didn't know which way was up—which I was, of course.

"Well now, that's a mite pricey for a horse," I said, taking a chance on his willingness to dicker a bit. "Maybe I ought to take a look at her first. You got a harness for her?"

He nodded his agreement and took me back to a small copse of trees, where he had an old shed that opened on to his pastureland.

"There she is, Mister. I calls her Betsy."

She wasn't much to look at, for sure. However, she was well fed and appeared healthy enough. I walked over to her and tentatively rubbed her head and ears. She snorted appreciatively and whinnied softly, tossing her head back and forth to get the most out of the contact. I turned to Robinson and said, "I'll give you ten dollars for her and whatever harness you've got."

He grinned good-naturedly, and we commenced to haggle. We finally settled on fifteen dollars for the mare and bridle and, to my surprise, an old saddle and saddlebags.

I counted out the money in gold and silver coins, and we shook hands.

"My name is John Kelly, Mr. Robinson. I'm pleased to make your acquaintance. I'm a stranger in these parts, and it's nice to know that there are good folks around here."

He smiled and, for the first time, responded in a genuinely friendly way.

"I'm glad to know you, Mr. Kelly. If you want, I'll throw that saddle on her and get you rigged up. You want, you can sit under the tree in the shade while I get her ready."

I didn't mention it, but I wanted to see just how it was done so I could learn how to do it myself. I had probably already showed off my ignorance if for no other reason than venturing out in the summer sun without a hat. I hoped I could get on the damned horse without making more of a fool out of myself.

"You going far, Mr. Kelly? If you are, you might want to stay down the road at Centerville."

I told him I was staying for the time at the Biggers place over by the junction. He shook his head and opined that he heard that she was a right nice lady.

While he was putting the saddle on, I was playing back all the old cowboy movies I had ever seen as a kid. I remembered they always got on the horse's left side and placed their left foot into the stirrup. You had to hold the bridle with one hand and the pommel with the other while climbing aboard.

It was a daunting proposition, but when Robinson was through, I got on with no problem. I waved good-bye and coaxed my new wheels cross-country toward the hill where Tom had found me.

I managed to point her in the right direction, and to my pleasant surprise, she went where I directed her, so I didn't have much to do. I was mostly afraid that something would startle her and she would take off on a tear cross-country. She did have a tendency to stop and graze or just look around. Consequently it took almost as long to get to the Gap tracks as if I had been on foot.

The next challenge was to wend our way across the creek and up the slope of the hill. She responded pretty well to my increasing confidence in handling her, but she still stopped whenever the notion hit her. We finally got there, and I dismounted and tied her to a tree. I felt like a real cowboy now.

Now to find that trunk!

A thorough search yielded nothing except scratches on my arms and face and lots of frustration. I looked everywhere on the top of the hill and as far down as the creek. It could be anywhere or nowhere. Perhaps the time and space variables Margaret had alluded to had thrown their calculations off. The trunk could be in the next county or in the endless possibilities of time travel, it could be in another century. What a dismal and frightening thought. If she couldn't get the trunk here when the odds were optimal, how could she ever find me later when it counted?

Finally I gave it up for the day. It was getting on toward suppertime. I would come out first thing in the morning and start over. I just had to believe it was close by. To believe otherwise was too unpleasant to contemplate.

Somehow I was able to pull myself in the saddle again and start back down the hill. The mare, Betsy—it was as good a name as any—picked her way downhill without any prodding from me until we reached the creek. Once there, I nudged her east instead of west on the now-familiar path to home. It was then that she decided to take another one of her breaks. I just sat, waiting for her to finish.

A sudden breeze rustled the greenery on the edge of the tree line, whipping the sparse leaves to and fro in a choreographed

cadence that reminded me of parade-ground soldiers perform-
ing their intricate maneuvers. The formation moved as a mass in
perfect harmony, except for one squad of foliage a half step out
of sync with the rest. There was always someone out of step. The
ten percent that was never able to get it quite right. That seemed
so long ago now.

My musing was interrupted when the wind abruptly died
and the formation came to a halt. But the little band of wayward
soldiers continued their drill for a beat longer. That caught my
attention. It was indeed an artificial discontinuity on the hillside.
Unnatural! Maybe supernatural instead of unnatural!

I startled Betsy with a yell of discovery and anticipation.
Whinnying softly, she seemed caught up in my excitement and
obligingly carried me down to a small defile, where, upon closer
examination, I could see something had crushed and broken the
natural growth. It was as if an elephant had galloped down the
small depression.

And there it was! Upended in the saddle of a small ridge
running parallel to the path to Louisa's farm, the side of an old
army footlocker was plainly visible from here. I would have never
seen it from the trail or even from above, since the higher ground
would have masked its presence. As it was, the depression was a
natural leaf and debris catcher. Before long it would have been
buried by fall's annual shedding.

After tying Betsy to a bush close by, I clambered down the
depression. It was resting at an awkward angle but seemed to be
intact. It was heavy but moved easily when I pulled it right side
up. The top was securely fastened with leather strapping.

Its presence meant more than just what was inside, as valuable as that would undoubtedly be. The trunk represented a vali-
dation of Margaret's promise to get me back. It was a far cry from
a passage home, but it was proof I wasn't forgotten. It reminded

me of my Viet Nam days when I would wonder if anyone still remembered or cared. And then would come mail call, renewing faith and certainty that indeed they hadn't forgotten and would always be waiting and watching for your return.

I carefully noted my surroundings and covered the trunk with shrubbery, and then I headed back to borrow Louisa's wagon and mules so I could paw through my manna from the future in leisure.

CHAPTER 9

As had happened on previous trips, the mare sensed when we were a few miles from home. Strange to be thinking of Virginia as home, but that's what it had been for over a month now. I had no claim to anyplace else. On this trip, my third away from Louisa's place, I was experiencing a pang of homesickness.

I may have been a man without a home, but at least now I had a date. It was an anchor, a mooring, which provided a tangible connection to my past. Still, the thought of being in the year 1859 was enough to blow my mind.

The past three weeks or so had passed with an ever-increasing tempo. I was finally doing something positive to return home. Before, the days had fluctuated between syrupy slow periods of apprehension and frantic bursts of activity. It had been much like soldiering—hurry up and wait. Peaks of exhilarating optimism followed by valleys of despairing pessimism.

There had been no more letters from home. Only the trunk! I chuckled to myself, remembering how I had been like a child at Christmastime.

It had been well stocked with just the kind of things I needed for everyday living. Clothes, including an old slouch hat; more period gold and silver coins, totaling almost a thousand dollars;

a straight razor and strop; a reproduction army Colt, chambered for modern .44 caliber cartridges, which were also included; and various miscellaneous items. I detected Paul's hand in the variety of items sent. The most useful thing, though, had been pen and paper. That was what gave me the idea on how to make a name for myself, not to mention a means of support. The contents had all been utilitarian, except for a wallet-size picture of Margaret.

Her picture sustained my emotional self while the reality of taking care of my physical self kept me busy. Now I had the means to support myself, and I had clothes. The railroads were reliable enough, so I would be able to travel about the state easily. In addition, I had Betsy to get around closer to home. Things were looking up.

Betsy's pace picked up as we crossed the bridge over Bull Run. The clickety-clack of her hooves hearkened me forward to the sight this crossing, the Stone Bridge, would see in less than two years. Sherman's regiment would pause near here before moving north to a ford to paralyze the Confederate right while the main attack at Sudley's Ford drove the rebel defenders back across this very same road, the Warrenton Turnpike. And just a few short hours later, as the federal army struggled to escape east on the turnpike, a Confederate artillery battery, commanded by a future governor of Virginia, sent well-placed fire onto the bridge over Cub Run, a mile to the east on the turnpike. That volley caught part of the Northern forces in a near-fatal bottle-neck. But as exhausted as their federal counterparts were, the Southerners too were spent and failed to follow up their victory. Nevertheless, an otherwise orderly retreat turned into a rout that lasted until the last of the defeated invaders straggled into Washington the next day.

Ah, to have been there! To witness the end of an era and to take note of a seminal new order being ushered onto the world stage. The American century began here, although no one could foresee it at the time. It was here that the America of disunited states, little more than feuding principalities paying nominal homage to their central and distant government on the Potomac, took its first toddling steps toward becoming the giant of the next century. Truly the American colossus's birthing took place, not in the stately and elegant towers of great places, but at this obscure juncture of creek, railroad, and turnpike. The old union of states gave way to a true nation—the United States of America—here in the cauldron of fire and blood of the Manassas battlefield.

The casualties along the way were many, not the least being the lives lost and the limbs shattered. The death toll extended long past 1865. The abomination of human bondage heard its dirge amid the roar of cannon and the screams of the maimed. The fire and smoke of a thousand guns masked the beginning of the end of state sovereignties competing with the central government for hegemony in the conduct of their affairs. Finally, after all the fighting was over, it would be difficult to find the remains of constitutional federalism around the shell-pocked killing fields.

Unfortunately it would play itself out all over again. But was *again* the right word here? If I told someone about what I knew was to come, and even if he were to believe me, could he not say that my *again* was his *maybe again* and that, therefore, my events that had come and gone must be separate and different from his yet to occur?

If that were the case, it would mean my old and new worlds were two separate universes—worlds going their own way with no connection. Except me! I was the common denominator. Would the two equally valid realities of this *now* and that *then* be compatible? Would my alien presence here cause some kind of cosmic rupture in the fabric of time? Would the universe tolerate that kind of foreign meddling? Or would it, like the human body when infected with pathogens, rush its internal defenses to the rescue to eradicate the threat to its overall health? Was I to end up being the universe's deadly bacteria and fated to be destroyed by its antibodies? Maybe instead of being a common denominator, I was a wild card that would have to be dealt with.

Shaking my head at my whimsical frame of mind, I concluded it was pointless to try and analyze the unknowable like that. Still, there must be some kind of link, physical or otherwise, if there were two worlds. Or how else would I have gotten here?

A late start leaving the newspaper meant I would probably not make it home before dusk. I knew Mary would save something for me, no matter how late I came in, but I always made it a point to join them for supper. Not for the first time, I thanked fate for sending Tom to me that terrible day. I couldn't imagine plunging into such a strange world in any more accommodating circumstances than that. All three of them, and even Toomey, had been a godsend.

Crossing Young's Branch, I nudged Betsy forward a little faster. Maybe I could make it before nightfall. Straight ahead I could just make out James Robinson's place through the trees. I hadn't talked to him since buying his horse, but if he were home, I would at least stop and say hello.

I had already sold two serialized short stories to the *Washington Evening Star*. They were my version of Jules Verne, except while Verne wrote of things that had yet to happen, my stories were fantasy only to my readers. To me, it was everyday stuff— cars, telephones, and the like. The articles weren't making much money but hopefully were making a sufficient name for myself to allow Paul to find me. If the name *Kelly* weren't enough, the subject matter surely would be.

As I neared Robinson's house, Betsy decided to stop for a while, as she was prone to do. I could see he had company. The sun was just setting over his house and was shining almost directly in my eyes, making it difficult to see without squinting. Looked like a half dozen horses in back of his house.

I was less than a hundred yards away, when suddenly Robinson burst out the front door. Right behind him came two men, one white and one black. The first one out the door lunged at him, dragging him down to the ground. There was a scuffle, and then the other man—the white man—pitched in, quickly subduing him. They manhandled him back in the door, shutting it behind them.

I pulled Betsy into the tree line on the side of the turnpike. It was clear that those people meant Robinson harm. It didn't make any sense, though. From all appearances he wasn't well-off enough for a gang of men to bother with robbing him. Slave dealers would be on the prowl for freemen like Robinson. His letter of manumission would mean nothing to such men. Black men in on the scheme too? It didn't seem right. Anything was possible, though.

Whatever was going on, it wasn't going to happen on my watch.

I tied Betsy to a sapling and dug around in my saddlebag for the Colt. I had the Beretta in my jacket pocket, but I felt more comfortable with something a bit more substantial. Revolver in hand, I moved quickly through the trees, coming out just about twenty yards from the side of his house. Crouching down behind a woodpile, I saw my options were limited.

It probably wasn't a good idea to burst in and confront them. Judging by the horses, there were five men inside. Were they armed? I hadn't noticed weapons, but that didn't mean anything.

I could wait for them to come out, but that might be too late for Robinson.

The horses! If I could get from my position to the side of the house without anyone seeing me through the window, I could go around, untie their horses, and stampede them. The commotion would bring most of them out, and then I would have a chance to do something on a more even footing. I could hear them talking, and it sounded threatening. One voice was authoritative, and while I couldn't make out all the words, his intent was clear: he meant Robinson harm.

The sun inching down to the horizon was maddeningly slow. I would have preferred to wait until it was at least a little darker before running across the side to get to the rear of the house.

Once I made the decision, I wasted no time thinking about it. I was on my feet, running in a crouch almost before I knew it, and in less time than a heartbeat, I was at the side, under the window. Without pause, I skirted around to the horses. Other than a soft whinny, and a nervous shuffling of their hooves, they ignored me. Now closer to the house, I could plainly hear what was being said inside. As I fumbled with each mount's reins, the apparent leader of the gang was speaking to Robinson. His voice, harsh and uncompromising, belied his words.

"...And we meant you no harm, Mr. Robinson. I had hoped you would join us on our godly commission. Your reluctance is a great..."

There, I had the horses loose! They were snorting now and edging away from me. With my hat I shooed them away from the house and off to the west. Finally, giving the rearmost one a whack with my hat, I got them on the run. By now someone inside was bound to hear all the commotion. No time to lose now! I had to get out of sight in a hurry.

It was too late to run back to the east side of the house. I stepped around the other rear corner between the house and well. Already, alarmed yells and the pounding of footsteps meant I had to take a chance whoever came out would give chase to the horses without seeing me. Squatting down, I waited and prayed all of the men would come out.

They came out the backdoor, running, hell bent for leather, and yelling at each other to do something. I scrunched myself down to be as invisible as possible. *Too late!* I thought of the front door. If any of them came out the front, I was a sitting duck.

Four men, two whites and two blacks, ran by without looking my way. A loud, commanding voice at the door urged them on. I hoped the entire gang would have given chase and I could get in and get away with Robinson out the front door. It would have been only a short run to Betsy. It didn't happen that way, though. I had to decide! The horses, after scattering, stopped a couple of hundred yards away to graze. I didn't have much time to do something before they had the mounts and came back to the house. They wouldn't miss me. I was armed, but I didn't want to be shooting anyone.

I had to do it. I had to go around the corner and confront the man standing there. If I could surprise him and hustle him back into the house before he had time to warn the others and before they turned around, I had a chance.

I tensed my legs, ready to move when fate dealt the cards my way. A bumping noise and running footsteps at the front of the house gave me my chance. Robinson was trying to get away! Simultaneously the man giving the orders pounded through the house. There was a clatter and a hoarse yell of pain. He had fallen down.

I whirled back and ran around the way I had just come toward the front corner to see Robinson running for all he was worth away from the house in the direction of where Betsy was tethered. They had bound his arms to his torso, and the end of the rope was trailing along behind him. Just when it looked he might clear the open space and make the tree line, he stumbled and fell headfirst to the ground. As he struggled to get to his feet, the man chasing him burst out the door after him.

I had no more time. His men would have the horses in just a few seconds. They may even have heard the noise and already be running back. No thinking now; just move! As I cleared the corner of the house, I noticed a pick handle leaning against the house. In full stride I grabbed the handle and flung it at Robinson's pursuer. The impetus of my forward movement gave my throw just enough range. It caught him just below the knees and down he went.

By now I was just about used up. My breath was ragged and labored as I sprinted across the yard. He was just getting to his feet and turning to back to see what had happened when I knocked him down again. On his back now, I knelt over him with the Colt barrel pressed against his face.

In the dimness of the early evening, I could only see a face in the shadows. A prominent nose and beard provided its own penumbra of camouflage that softened but couldn't mask a raw-boned and austere countenance of about sixty years of age. But the eyes! Burning and intense, they bored into mine with a fervor that made me shiver. It was the look of killing eyes. Eyes contemptuous of death. I was looking at an avenging angel—a killer angel—supremely confident in a cause known only to him. He seemed faintly familiar, but that face would be difficult to forget.

Under that hypnotic gaze, my trigger finger tightened. The man's ferocity of purpose transfixed me.

Just then I heard the first of his gang running through the house and calling out for their ringleader. I relaxed my grip on the Colt and none too gently gouged the barrel into his face to avert that awful stare.

"Cap'n! Where are you? Cap'n! The freeman is gone. Cap'n?"

He easily saw us when he came out the door, and gesturing wildly he called for the rest of the men. In just seconds, they were all out, heading for me. One of the white men was armed with a musket and just bringing it up when the other white man pulled the barrel down. They stopped as I yanked my captive to his feet and shoved the Colt's barrel into his neck.

"Tell them to drop it or you're a dead man!

I turned Robinson's way and yelled, "James, the mare is down the turnpike. Wait for me there."

"If it be God's will for my blood to be shed in the cause of righteousness, so be it. It will be at his hand, not yours. So pull the trigger, if you will," my captive replied defiantly.

The man was a piece of work, but I had to hand it to him.

His men started forward again. I heard Robinson stumbling back toward Betsy.

"You may be ready for dying, old man, but are you ready for your friends to meet their maker as well?"

To show him I was serious, I snapped off a shot at his men. The report startled him and sent them scattering back toward the house, except the one with the musket. He was looking down at the shattered stock of his dropped weapon and wailing that he had been shot.

I was a pretty mediocre shot with a rifle. However, with a pistol, I was unusually good. Even in the near dusk of the late Virginia day, it was an easy shot.

"He's all right, Mister. Now call your men back, and tell them to sit down and nobody will be hurt."

In an absolutely unshaken and authoritative voice, he repeated my instructions to them. In under a minute, they all were less than ten yards away, sitting in a little huddle and looking at us fearfully.

He turned his head back to me and said, "You may take that revolver away from me, Mister. I can see you mean us no harm. My name is John Smith. Mr. Robinson has nothing to fear from us."

I relaxed the barrel's pressure against his face, but left it as a reminder, and told him, "Right, Mr. Smith. I guess that's why he was tied up and trying to escape. Where are you from? And why are you here?"

"We live in Maryland, Mister. We came to pay Mr. Robinson a visit. We just had a misunderstanding. What are your intentions for us? Are you a friend of Mr. Robinson's?" The last he said with something close to disbelief in his voice.

I was impressed. He was as cool as a cucumber, all right. He was calmer than anyone could possibly be under the circumstances. He had a pistol staring him full in the face, held by someone he could not fail to realize would use it. He had been caught in the act of committing mayhem, yet here he was, as calm and unafraid as if he were negotiating with a local farmer for grain. Sangfroid? Or insanity?

I didn't have many alternatives on what to do about them. I could scatter their horses and make them hoof it back to wherever they came from, which I doubted was Maryland. They would be on foot, though, and have reason to come back to retrieve their horses. Alternatively I could just let them go with the hope they would hightail it out of the area. The probability was high that they would consider coming back as not very profitable and that they had been lucky it hadn't turned any worse for them. My guess was that they had enough of Robinson and his friend.

I compromised. Pointing with the revolver, I said to one of the blacks, "You there, go back and bring your horses around over here. Don't do anything else but what I said. Do you understand?"

He looked to Smith, who gave the barest of nods, before running to the back of the house. At least one of them had enough sense to want to get away from here.

I knew without the slightest doubt that this man and his cohorts had murderous intentions in mind for Robinson and that it was a mistake to just let them go. Unfortunately, hauling them in to whatever law there was around here wasn't the best choice either. Assuming I could even find the authorities.

"Tie the one with the saddlebags to the house," I shouted as he came back with the horses in tow.

I pushed Smith forward and told him, "Here's the deal for you. You and your gang of cowards head back where you came from. I'd advise you to not even consider coming back this way again. Let me be blunt, Mr. Smith. If I ever see any of you again, you'll have reason to regret it. And if my friend ever comes to any harm by anyone's hand, I'm going to assume you are responsible. You may be able to run, but it will never be far enough or fast enough. I will find you, and I will kill you, you and your friends here. Are you clear on that?"

He spoke not a word but nodded his head.

"Get on your way then, old man. You have four horses between the five of you. If you really do live in Maryland, you should do just fine. The other horse stays with me. For my trouble, you might say."

It was dark by the time they disappeared, riding northwest across the fields of corn and wildflowers. I didn't think I'd be seeing them again. I hoped not anyway.

As soon as they were out of sight, Robinson came out of the tree line adjacent to the turnpike. He had gotten untied and was leading Betsy to meet me.

"Mr. Kelly, thank you, sir! Thank you! Them men aimed to kill me for certain. Oh, thank you so much. I prayed and prayed for deliverance in that house, but I didn't think the LORD was listening. But he was listening, and he answered my prayers. He sent you to me. Praise the LORD!"

There in the early moonlight, I saw his tear-streaked face. He was crying, not from fear, but from gratitude. He was still shaking as only a man will do who has looked at the merciless face of the reaper and been granted reprieve.

I offered him my hand, and there we stood, two men of different races and backgrounds, clasping hands and letting go of the emotions that had so consumed us both.

Finally, as we started back to his house, I asked him what the men had wanted with him.

He hesitated until we got to his doorway. He picked up a lantern hanging from the doorjamb and lit it before answering me. He turned, straightened his back, looked me directly in the eyes, and said, "Mr. Kelly, please don't ask me that question. I owe you my life. Nothing I can ever do for you will be enough to repay you for what you done for me. But please, please don't ask me to tell you what they wanted me to be doing."

His plea surprised me; it didn't make sense. But it was his business, not mine. I just wanted to get back to Louisa's with no more problems. "Suit yourself then, Mr. Robinson. Anyway you got yourself a horse out of the deal. Do you think you ought to stay here tonight? I truly don't believe you have anything to worry about from that bunch of scofflaws, but you might want to spend the night away from this house, just in case. I'm sure Mrs. Biggers wouldn't mind you staying the night there."

"No, sir, I won't be getting no sleep tonight, no matters where I stay. I believe I'd just as soon stay here and look after my belongings. I sure enough hope they don't come back, but if they do, they won't be sneaking up on me this time. I surely do appreciate the offer, Mr. Kelly. I reckon what I heard about Miss Louisa, she'd put me up all right. But I 'spects I'll stay here all the same. My family should be back from her folks tomorrow."

We shook hands again, and I got on Betsy to leave. Just as I turned her back toward the turnpike, he stopped me and said, "I won't be forgetting what you did for me tonight. You didn't have to do a thing 'cept just ride on by. But you didn't. If you ever in need of anything, Mr. Kelly, anything at all, I'm your man. All you gotta do is be asking."

I waved good-bye and gave Betsy the spur.

CHAPTER 10

Tom and I struggled sluggishly uphill, trying to make some headway against the brambles and bushes pulling at our clothes, but it wasn't doing much good. We were in a morass that kept slowing us down. I had his hand, pulling him along, but he kept stopping to ask questions about one thing or the other. Louisa was just a few yards in front of us, but she just kept moving away. She saw us but seemed strangely unconcerned at our efforts. She thought Tom was playing a game, so she just smiled and moved a little farther away whenever we got close to her. I yelled for her to stand still, but I was out of breath from exertion, and all I could manage was a hoarse whisper. I wished I had kept myself in better shape.

I could see Smith coming up the other side of the hill, but she couldn't. Spawned from some long past terrible time in mankind's bloody history, he was an unworldly avatar with a maniacal leer on his face. That same indefeasible fanaticism I had seen the day before! I could smell his putrid breath from here—a stench as vile as the crypt. He was wielding some kind of ax or sword. Bloodstained and gleaming in the moonlight, it was cutting effortlessly through the underbrush and tangles of the forest. No, it wasn't Smith after all. It was someone else. Someone

I had seen before. I was too exhausted to think clearly now. He kept getting closer and closer! I should have killed him when I had had the opportunity.

He was almost upon us. I could hear the terrible swish of his sword. There, I finally had her! But before we could get away, I tripped, dragging both of them with me. We were rolling back down the hill, and that awful sound of sword cutting through air kept getting closer and closer!

Syrupy slow, I pulled Louisa down the slope toward safety. But where was Tom? Then she slipped out of my grasp too. She called for me to hurry, to hurry back to her. I looked back one last time, but it wasn't her anymore. It was Margaret!

Tom, now in a panic, was calling from so far away, "Mr. Kelly, Mr. Kelly!"

Then I was alone, and the mad man was on me. I screamed for them to run as I weakly tried to fend him off. It was no use! The razor edge, hot and stinging, pressed against my bare palms. One final look at the monster—his mouth flecked with spittle, his eyes with a yellowish glow—and then the unspeakable slicing pain. Blood was everywhere. I was soaked with its wetness flowing from my arms and chest. Just as I felt my life slipping away, his features solidified into the well-known picture I had seen so often. Too late, I knew who he was. It was—

"Mr. Kelly, are you all right? Wake up! Oh, please wake up, Mr. Kelly."

He was safe. Where was his mom, though?

"Mr. Kelly, you've got to wake up. You've been dreaming, Mr. Kelly."

I wiped away the blood from my face. Only it wasn't blood. I was bathed in sweat. Tom was looking at me with a relieved expression on his young face. I was going to be all right. It had been just a dream. A terrible dream! But now I knew who Smith was. He was—

A light at the door and a tremulous voice asked, "Tom, what are you doing? Mr. Kelly, is everything all right?"

Each time so tantalizingly close, just out of reach.

I reassured her, "I'm all right now. I was just having a bad dream. I must have wakened everybody in the house. I'm sorry for all the commotion."

Wraithlike, she was at the door with a lantern casting its soft-yellow light in front of her and clutching her robe to her throat. I shuddered; the glow of the lantern reminded me of those Charles Manson eyes—eyes with an insane inner mirth shining through opaque glass. Then she turned toward me and thrust the lantern forward; the light attenuated and took on a warm, silvery ripple across the bed's linen.

I sat up in the bed, bare-chested. She gasped, and Tom drew back as the light played across my body.

"Why, you're soaking wet, Mr. Kelly. You must be coming down with a fever. Tom, go downstairs and bring some clean linen from the closet. Hurry now, and bring water too!

"You're shivering too. Please lie down and cover up before you get a chill. You were shouting awful loud a while ago. As soon as Tom gets back, I need to sponge you down. Now I don't want to hear any argument from you. Do you hear me?"

Weakly protesting that I was all right, I succumbed to her admonitions and let her have her way. I wondered if I had called her name aloud a few minutes before. I had been trying to save them from that madman. It was on the tip of my tongue, just at the edge of memory. I couldn't pull it up, though; each time I reached for it, it slipped a little further away.

Louisa turning into Margaret! What did that mean? And what did that crazy old man have to do with them?

Tom came bursting into the room with a handful of cotton cloths. He was full of questions, but his mother quickly shushed him and told him to go back to bed. He put up a fuss, but she wouldn't have any of it.

"Mr. Kelly, I've nursed my husband and Tom, and now I'm going to tend to you. If you put up a fuss, I'll call Mary, and you can argue with her. You can take your pick. Who's it to be?"

I gave it up. In truth I didn't feel so steady. Maybe I was getting sick. The dream had unnerved me. What did it mean? There was something about it I needed to remember, something terrible that I had to know. The night phantoms bore down on me with a fearful crushing weight.

Mercifully, Louisa's comforting insistence lulled the immediate urgency into the background. I knew what it was. I was alone and isolated, and she was a woman: someone to relax with, to be able to let my guard down for a change. I relaxed and turned myself over to her competent ministrations.

As she sponged my chest and face, I began to feel the tension drift away and my eyelids getting heavy. I started to apologize for using her first name, but I hardly noticed it when she felt my forehead and gently drew the sheet up to my neck.

I awoke to a late morning's light shining through the shutters and curtains. Louisa had left sometime during the night, but part of her was still here in the room with me. Her feminine scent and the memory of her soft touch lingered.

Before I could completely rouse myself, Mary came bustling in with a tray. Instead of my usual fare of biscuits, gravy, grits, and ham, all I could see was a bowl. And instead of coffee, there was a tall glass of milk. She jabbed a spoon sloshing over with some kind of broth in my mouth before I knew what hit me. I ceased being my own boss. There wasn't any sense in putting up a fight. She was in charge.

"Now then, Mr. Kelly. How you be feeling this morning? Heard tell you was all a mess last night. Looks like my Louisa doctored you up good. You need to be taking care of yourself today. Stay around the house and relax some."

"Thanks, Mary. Actually I'm feeling pretty good this morning."

"That's Miss Louisa's doing. She's right fair at tending to folks that need looking after. I 'spects you be needing quite a bit of looking after. Yessuh, Mr. Kelly. I reckons you do."

I needed something for sure. Mostly a one-way ticket back home!

With that, she left me to my own devices. I was glad she hadn't tried to make me stay in bed for the day. I really felt pretty good this morning in spite of that hideous nightmare. I did as I was told, though, and other than visiting the stable to rub Betsy down, I took it easy.

We had the house to ourselves: Louisa, Mary, and I. Tom was off most of the day at school up at Sudley Springs. The day was pleasant, so I spent most of the morning on the spacious front porch, reading the Washington papers I had brought back with me. My second story was there. I felt no little bit of pride seeing my name in print. Pride, but most of all hope; hope that at this very instant, Paul was reading and noting dates and times.

Only in the early afternoon, when the sun was in the western sky, did I go into the cool of the parlor.

Mid-afternoon, Louisa came in and asked me how I was getting on and if I needed anything. I told her I was doing fine and that I really appreciated her efforts the night before. I felt like I owed her more than just a cursory thanks, but I was at a loss at what else to say.

She blushed, and then hesitating, asked to join me for a few minutes. She obviously had something on her mind. I hoped she wasn't too upset about last night.

After a few pleasantries, she finally got around to it. "Mr. Kelly, your stay with us has been a godsend to me, and Tom too. I want you to know that. You've been more than just another boarder to us. Not to say that the steady money hasn't helped. It has. But you've almost become part of our family. Just for being a man in the house and for the attention and time you give to my son, if for no other reason. And Mary adores you."

She looked up, smiled a little, and went on. "But I know you won't be here long, and that's what I wanted to talk with you about. Tom, he's all I have. When you go, he will too. Oh, I don't mean he'll leave with you—nothing like that. It's just that you've brought the outside world to him, and now he'll never be satisfied with life here on the farm. It would have been difficult enough anyway, but you're all he talks about now: you, the places you've been, and the things you've done.

"Mr. Kelly, I'm sure you're from Texas, just as you say. But I believe you are also, somehow, from farther away than that. And I know one day you'll be going back where you came from—you'll be leaving suddenly, just like you came. When you do, we will never see you again. I'm worried about what that will do to my Tom."

I acknowledged her concern. "Mrs. Biggers, I know Tom thinks a lot of me. The last thing I would ever want is to hurt him or let him down. I don't want to cause you any distress either. Surely you must know I'm fond of him too."

I flushed with sudden guilt. She was right. I would be leaving sometime, and I hadn't given a thought about what it might mean to everyone here. She had hit the nail flush on the head. I would leave, and she would have to explain it to the boy. I hated to admit it, but all I had been concerned about was myself.

I was duly chastened, and it was time to do the right thing!

"But I must concede the point. You are absolutely correct. One day I will be leaving, and the likelihood is that it will be a sudden departure, just as you said. Selfishly, I had not given due consideration to the impact on Tom, and you and Mary too. I truly thank you for talking to me about your worries.

"So I'm sorry to say that I believe it will be best for Tom that I plan to leave here as soon as it's convenient for everyone. I recognize the wisdom and the most admirable maternal instinct of your concerns. I care too much about all of you to be the cause of any distress. I've enjoyed my stay here, and it will be with the most reluctance that I will leave you all. You have accepted me, a total stranger, into your home and made me feel part of your family. I must say that the hospitality you have given me has been most rewarding and memorable."

"Yes, well, I only wish—" With a resigned look, she continued. "Very well. We'll just try our best to prepare him for when that time comes. I don't want you to leave until you're ready, Mr. Kelly. The manly virtues you represent for him are sadly lacking with no man around. His father," she faltered, "passed when he was too young to know. And now you've come into our life. It's been a blessing for him, for all of us. I'm quite sure it's more of a responsibility than you bargained for."

"I've gotten much out of knowing all of you, so don't worry yourself about that," I said.

"On a different subject, Mrs. Biggers, I must apologize for all the noise and bother last night. I had a difficult day yesterday, and it must have stayed with me when I retired. I hope I won't do it again, but I can't promise."

She responded by taking a deep breath and squaring her shoulders. With a slow flush reddening her neck and face, she looked straight at me and said, "If you prefer, you may call me by my given name, Mr. Kelly. It would please me. And please don't worry yourself about last night. A man like you must carry many terrible memories around. Last night was your worst night since you've been with us, but your sleep has often been a struggle for you. I was glad to have been able to comfort you."

Aware that she was blushing, she looked demurely to the floor and said, "Oh dear. Will you listen to me? I've embarrassed myself with my boldness."

"Not at all." I hesitated for a second. "Louisa, and I hope you will dispense with the formalities too. I'm sure you heard me use your name last night. I was fearful that I had offended you."

"It was not unpleasant to hear you use my name. But you use many names, John, when your sleep is troubled. And you speak of many places you've been, places I've never heard of. I hope that someday you will find what you are looking for.

"I've enjoyed our conversation, and now, if we are to have supper tonight, I had better get back into the kitchen. You continue to rest. Tom will be home shortly."

The source of that nightmare was no mystery. My run-in with that crazy old man and his cohorts had been an experience. A man willing to die for unknown reasons was unnerving enough; to find myself in the middle of it was another thing entirely. Since leaving the army, and after Caroline's death, I had settled into a life without anything more exciting than campus politics—until I met Margaret! Then the incident on the highway, the hurricane, our relationship, and finally, being catapulted into a science-fiction nightmare.

Then last night at Robinson's place. I had reacted almost instinctively to a situation fraught with danger. Everything had slipped into place. The very violence inherent in what was going on with those men had keyed something in me long forgotten. Luck, good or bad, had put me in that place at that time, but everything that came after was as if I had pressed a switch designed to activate a long, dormant set of semi-conductors and circuitry. The only thing missing had been my physical condition. Years of soft living had taken the edge off. Still, I got out in one piece.

It was disturbing to be sucked into those kinds of situations, and it wasn't exactly the notoriety I needed either. I had to admit, though, I harbored a bit of satisfaction at my prowess. I wondered, though, what would be happening next.

Who was that man, the man in reality, and the very same man of dreams? He was definitely someone I should know, but how? We were of different times. Maybe he was a historical character. If only I could have gotten a better look at him. Anyway, what historical person would be visiting the house of a poor, free black man, and why?

What was my dream trying to tell me? Had I been just a few nods of tormented sleep from learning whom he was? Or was that just a tantalizing illusion too? A "dream within a dream," as Poe would say.

But what was really and truly real anyway? Back in my own century, I was not only real in the memories of those who knew me, but I had physical substance there too. There was a paper trail from birth attesting to a life lived. Except for my newspaper articles, there was none here. No one here would ever find a record, a mention, or even a memory of my existence in this world before a month ago. However, here—unlike there—was where my physical being existed. Once I left here, though, would there be any thought of me residing in the minds of Louisa and Tom? Or would I be like a wax impression, substance and reality only in the coolness of the present but quick enough to melt away from the friction of time's passage from the now?

Thoughts like those were best not dwelled on. There were never answers, only more questions. And it never failed to depress me to think that here, in this place and time, I could only end up like the John of dreams: transient atoms dissipating always with the flight of time—the only real thing left to me.

Getting up, I decided a little fresh air would clear my thoughts and invigorate me with the things of the here and now. I wandered outside and watched the workers in the fields. Workers! They were slaves, I reminded myself. Men they may be but just a commodity here in Virginia and throughout the South—and even in the North. The only difference was that, shanghaied and transported from their homeland in Yankee slave ships, their income potential was more immediately realized there than here. Now they were merely the medium of exchange for the increasingly bitter cultural war waged against the Southern slaveholding interests. It was not only a brutalizing existence for the blacks but also a slow corruption of the soul for their masters and traders alike. In that regard, I had to hand it to Mr. Lincoln, whose denunciation of slavery was visionary and compelling.

I strolled around to the back of the house and into the woods. It had not been such a long time since Margaret and I had had our picnic in woods not too unlike here. What was she doing now? How much time had passed there? Was it the same measure as my life here or somehow different? It was senseless to think about stuff like that. I couldn't know. Just the same, my thoughts seemed to always turn to the imponderables of a dual existence.

Then there were the practical things, like my job and house. The electricity and other bills left unpaid, not to mention mortgage payments. Thank God I didn't have any pets. Those were things I would have as my first concerns if I were back home, say laid up in the hospital.

My loved ones were a different matter, though. Robert and Darla were real-life, feeling people. They cared about me, and they would worry. My guess was that they wouldn't know anything. To them I would have just disappeared. No trace or clues as to my fate. Margaret would know, but it might even be worse on her knowing and unable to do anything about it. On the other hand, perhaps I was a public issue, a subject of debate. What did the scientific world think about it? There would be skeptics, of course! I could see the supermarket tabloids now. Did debates ensue on the morality or immorality of such projects? Or more likely, was I a subject to be swept under the scientific rug as a mistake? My head reeled. No wonder Louisa said my sleep was often disturbed.

Heading back out of the woods, I saw a rider heading our way along the Gap tracks.

As I went in the backdoor, I chanced to overhear Louisa and Mary carrying on an animated conversation. Mary's rich voice was scolding as she admonished Louisa about something. They certainly had a strange relationship. From where I was, it would have been hard to tell who the slave was and who the mistress of the house was.

As I started upstairs, Louisa came around from the dining area. She was less composed than she had been earlier, maybe from whatever she and Mary had been arguing about.

"Mr. Kelly, I forgot to mention that Mr. Toomey will be with us for a few days. He should be arriving soon, so we'll be having another guest for dinner tonight. Have you seen Tom yet? He should have been home an hour ago. He's usually not this late."

"I haven't seen him, Louisa. Why don't I hitch up Betsy and ride out that way. He probably just found something or the other he'd rather be doing than hurrying home. I saw a rider coming up from the junction. That might be Mr. Toomey. Oh, and are we to resume the formalities now? I was so much looking forward to hearing the welcome music of my given name from such a fair hostess."

It was my first attempt at Southern manners since coming here. I thought it was pretty good too. Instead, it must have been ludicrous because she broke out in laughter.

"Why, John, that's the first time I've heard you speak in our way here. I think I like your Texas manners better. Still, it was very nice, and I'm flattered. But it's not you. You are always such a gentleman just the way you are."

I was saddling up Betsy when Toomey led his horse into the little stable. He didn't appear overjoyed to see me, but he was pleasant enough.

"Good afternoon, Mr. Kelly. The stationmaster said he thought you were still here, but I assumed you would be off on your travels by now. I trust you are well, sir. It will be a pleasure to share your company for a few days."

"Welcome back, Mr. Toomey. Mrs. Biggers said you'd be staying a few days. More business, I assume. Where do your travels take you, if I may ask?"

"Mostly here in the Old Dominion, Mr. Kelly. Occasionally I visit Washington, and I have toured many of the Northern states. I must say that in spite of their barbaric ways, the Yankee does know how to run his railroads. Much better than us, I'm afraid. The insanity of each line doing whatever it wants will some day be the ruin of our region."

He was right about that. While the Confederacy would be the first to move troops from one area of operations to another by rail to successfully change the outcome of a battle, Northern efficiency in moving men and material by rail would soon surpass and overwhelm them. At its core, the South's failure to establish a country of its own was simply a result of the very same political ideology that drove it to secede from the Union in the first place. The fierce independence of each state, and the identification of its citizens with that state, precluded the cooperation that modern warfare demanded. Railroads were as good an example of that fact as any aspect of Southern life.

He continued with a sigh of long-suffering frustration. "Incompatible scheduling, a veritable patchwork of gauges to complicate shipments from one line to another, rolling stock of every imaginable design, criminal neglect of beds and tracks—all will doom our systems to obsolescence before the turn of the century. Mark my words on that, Mr. Kelly; mark my words. Not that either of us will be around to appreciate that observation."

I smiled to myself at that. I would! Or to be more precise, I already had.

"I'm sure you've pointed out those shortcomings, Mr. Toomey, because you are most certainly correct in your observations. Do your employers appreciate the potential problems, or are they like so many others—too shortsighted to look further than the monthly profits?"

He looked at me with those shrewd eyes as if a reappraisal was in order. "Very astutely put, Mr. Kelly. One day, when the ship leaves port, they will be standing there, waiting, and wondering how they could have missed it. In this case, though, I should say they would be standing at the station, watching someone else's engine pulling out without them. The world is filled with simplistic men with simplistic solutions. One day, perforce, they will mend their ways. But I fear it will be far too late for our Southern states."

He made to leave and then, with a flourish, produced an envelope. "I almost forgot," he said. "The stationmaster had a letter for you. I trust it is not bad news; looks like it came from the capital."

I noticed that it did indeed come from Washington. It was from Wallach, the *Star*'s editor. It was probably some last-minute details on my literary arrangements with the paper. I tucked it away in my pocket.

As I rode off to find Tom, I thought about the petty little differences Toomey and I had had that first night, and it dawned on me that he probably saw me as a rival for Louisa's attention. Thinking back on those first few days, he was overly attentive and flattering around her. That she had paid little mind to his efforts never seemed to have bothered him. I wondered if she even noticed. Tom sure did.

Supper that evening turned out to be exceptionally pleasant. Toomey was all charm and less unctuous than was his custom. He even indulged in a little friendly repartee with Mary, who eventually responded with a wide smile. Louisa had dressed a little more formally than usual, and she seemed to have more color in her cheeks. Tom was in a bright and cheerful mood and not at all his usual defensive self around Toomey.

Conversation was a hodgepodge of lighthearted and trivial matters until the inevitable matter of politics reared its head. I had made it a point to avoid the topic. When my thoughts and opinions were sought, I tried to be as noncommittal as I politely could get away with. Toomey and Louisa were under no such restraints and engaged in a lively discussion. She didn't seem to be that well informed on current events, but she had definite opinions and expressed them freely. No doubt she was typical of Southern womanhood.

Abraham Lincoln's fame—or notoriety, as it was here in the South—had faded with time since the last of his debates with Stephen Douglas last year. Apparently though, his name could still be counted on to liven up dinner conversation at any Southern table, and tonight was no exception. Then young Tom uncharacteristically interjected something his teacher had said at school that day.

I didn't pick up on it right away because I had been observing Louisa out of the corner of my eye. Her interplay with Toomey was so markedly different from his previous visit that I couldn't help but notice. Then she had presented a studied, polite indifference to his attempts at charm. Tonight she responded animatedly to his gambits and even seemed to encourage him on with an enchanting combination of naivety and coquetry. The lively dinner conversation seemed to bring out the best in her. Maybe it was her dress, a soft-pink dress with a cameo brooch at her bodice, or maybe her lightly applied makeup. Perhaps it was just the stimulating conversation, but she was a different woman tonight—very attractive and vivacious, with a most winsome smile! I hadn't noticed just how attractive she was until now, nor had I previously found any occasion to speculate about the womanly figure underneath her nineteenth-century fashions.

"...that killer from Kansas on the turnpike," finished Tom.

That caught everybody's attention, including Mary's, who had been coming in and out with plates of biscuits and honey.

"I'm sorry, Tom," Toomey responded, "What was that you said about Brown? He's not coming around here, is he? Last I heard he was hiding out somewhere around Boston."

It slammed into my gut with the impact of a battering ram.

That old man with fanatical eyes and messianic references to blood being shed! Some Civil War historian I was. John Brown! His murderous raid in a little more than a month would become a catalyst for the abolitionists' crusade to destroy the South and its "peculiar institution." The odious practice of human bondage would cease to exist, all right, but that wasn't all; along with it, the Southern way of life would forever be different. In its place would come decades of subservience to the industrial and financial interests of New England and to the midwestern radicals' rabid hatred of all things Southern.

And it explained Robinson's refusal to tell me what Brown had wanted of him. *Insurrection!* The word struck fear in the hearts of all Southerners, whites and blacks alike. For whites, it was a tender box waiting to consume them and their way of life. For blacks, it meant indiscriminate lynchings and worse.

Brown had only hastened the inevitable. He was just the spark that ignited the long, simmering sectionalism that had plagued the American experiment in democracy. The North and the South: both American, but both with radically diverse ideas about the Constitution that had bound them together in 1789. One side now tended to view the central government as the embodiment of all the states and supreme in all matters—a more national government. The other saw Washington as the child of the states that had created it—federalism in its purest form. It was one America with common language, laws, currency, and the shared tradition and pride of being part of the only self-governing federal democracy in the world. They were two factions with wildly disparate views on just about everything else, though. One was essentially rural, agrarian, and parochial, desperately clinging to their ancient way of life. The other was always looking outward and always dynamically pursuing progress.

The Southern ideal of tradition, refinement, and chivalry were fated to perish in the coming generations, in any event. The Northern eminence in industry, finance, and trade, fueled by massive immigration and expansion into the western territories, was destined to rule this continent, even without the terrible conflict to come. It was Seward's "irrepressible conflict," indeed. But did it have to be so?

"...in your travels, Mr. Kelly."

Toomey was looking at me impatiently. "I'm sorry, Mr. Toomey. I was lost in thought. Yes, I know of John Brown, but only by reputation, or infamy, in his case. He is indeed a murderer. There is plenty of that going on in Kansas and plenty of guilt to go around on both sides of that ugly little dispute. I wouldn't be at all surprised to find he would be passing through here since financial support for his terrorism comes from New York and New England. Hopefully he will be gone from Virginia by now."

"That may be so, sir," Toomey replied, "but his presence here can only mean trouble for our region. It wouldn't surprise me if we were soon to become like poor, bleeding Kansas. His backers—Howe and Parker, among several—are fanatics on the subject of abolitionism, just as he is. The only difference between them is one does the other's dirty work. One only cares about destroying our system of labor, while the other will not be content until our people are made over into their image. That alone is a frightening enough thought."

I wondered how he could possibly know of Brown's co-conspirators. That he knew at least two of their names was quite remarkable. As if reading my mind, he answered my unspoken question.

Directing his comment to me, he said, "It's the talk of the tracks, especially the western lines. Apparently there is big money involved in his financing."

Louisa responded, "It so angers me that that man, a fugitive from justice, is mollycoddled and allowed to go free, to go on killing. Those people would not be so remiss if he were killing their own. But as we are only Southerners, killing us is quite acceptable. I do wish they would simply remember common courtesy and mind their own affairs instead of meddling in ours. We certainly don't interfere in how they choose to govern themselves."

Maybe I had made a mistake in not turning him in to the authorities. It would have been a lot of trouble, but...

What had I almost done? Worse, ever so worse, what might I still do, even as unknowingly as yesterday? If I had turned him in, his reign of terror would end. That wouldn't be all that would be over, though. No John Brown. No John Brown, no Harpers Ferry raid. No raid, no martyrdom, no abolitionism's *cause célèbre*. War probably, but maybe later and maybe a different outcome.

History changed, but not just changed. Significantly altered! Even minor changes filtered down through generations of events and personalities would affect the world I had left behind. I was only dimly aware and concerned about its import to the world, per se. But I was acutely aware of its impact on me personally. Everything would be different. Different to what degree for Margaret and those connected to the time machine, I didn't know, and I didn't want to find out. All I could think of was that a different world back home might make it impossible for me to get back. If that were the case, what then? There were so many facets of time and its endless possibilities. I was a time bomb here. I was a danger to everyone and everything back home, as well as to myself here. A cold chill swept over me.

How could I ever relax? I would have to watch everything I did from this day on. But how could I ever know what seemingly inconsequential event or situation might turn out to be a history breaker? The answer was self-evident: I couldn't. Hell, I might have already made some small impression on someone that wouldn't bear fruit for years in this time, but that had already evolved into some different outcomes on Margaret's time-machine project. I shivered with the dark possibilities that thought raised.

We were spared further discussion on the subject when Mary brought in a delicious-smelling apple pie and directed us to the parlor for pie and tea. She stared at me with an arch look on her brown face, like we were privy to some inside story.

In the parlor Louisa served the pie and prepared tea off a lovely teacart that Mary had wheeled into the room. Spooning the tea out of a unique little tea caddy that reminded me of one my grandmother had used, Louisa seemed to be in her element. The teapot was gleaming silver, and unless I missed my guess, the cups and saucers were of good quality china. All the while, she engaged the whole company in conversation. Mary was standing on the periphery of our little group and looking at me expectantly. I wondered what was going on with her tonight.

It was clear that Toomey, responding to Louisa's attention, had decided the best way to catch the fly was with honey. He was so gracious tonight as to be almost likable. *Well, good for him,* I thought. He sure hadn't made any friends here before. Maybe Louisa had had a change of heart.

The pie was hot and sweet, and the tea complemented it perfectly. Everyone seemed to have forgotten the discussion about John Brown, which was fine with me. Toomey plied us with all the latest gossip from Richmond and news from around the state. Louisa was particularly interested in the latest fashions, and Tom, while trying to maintain his disdain for Toomey, was intrigued enough about all the Richmond happenings to let his guard down.

As we were finishing, Mary came in to retrieve the dishes. Before leaving, she turned to me and, with a perfectly innocent look on her face, asked if I had a wife waiting on me back in Texas. Louisa made an exasperated little sigh and said, "Mary, my goodness. Leave poor Mr. Kelly some privacy."

I was thoroughly discombobulated. Toomey, as well as Mary, was watching me intently. Louisa was blushing and glaring at Mary. Tom was as clueless as I was.

"I must say that I lost my beloved a number of years ago, Mary. I have never remarried and instead have embarked on my journeys around the world. I'm afraid I'm too far removed from the civilized world now for the gentle nature and felicitous disposition of the fairer gender."

Toomey relaxed. Louisa looked like she was ready to bolt out of the room, and Tom was nonplused. I was too, for that matter. I felt like a ninny; everyone knew what the subject matter was, except poor Tom and me.

Nevertheless, Mary was completely unabashed. "Oh no, sir. There's a good woman for every man in this world. And don't need to look far either. You be wanting to settle down sometime."

Finally Louisa managed to retake charge of the conversation, and it got to safer ground. Mary had evidently said what she had on her mind. She triumphantly exited the room in a swirl of petticoats.

By the time our little tea party was done, I was just about ready for my room. Tom too was ready for bed, or at least his mother thought so. I excused myself and left to say good night to Mary. Toomey looked pleased with the way things had turned out and wished me a good night's sleep. I surely hoped for one. Now, with another guest in the house, I didn't want to go through all that nightmare stuff and wake everyone up again.

As I burrowed into my pillow that night, that old man filled my thoughts. He most certainly had gone to Robinson's place for the purpose of recruitment. Robinson, being a freeman, would be more accessible than any slave would. He could travel with less difficulty, and he would be a real asset for support of Brown's murderous intentions. And it definitely explained his reluctance to tell me what Brown wanted of him. Slave revolts were all too fearsome a possibility in this plantation-owner society. And any black man—free or not—implicated in such a plot wouldn't last very long before he would be hanging from the nearest tree.

Just as I was drifting off, I remembered Wallach's letter.

CHAPTER 11

Ahead, the old steam engine spewed out clouds of black smoke and embers as it toiled the last miles into Alexandria. On the curves, if the wind was blowing right, the pollution blew away from the one passenger car and out into the countryside. Otherwise, one arrived with lungs full of noxious fumes. Along the tracks and the paralleling turnpike, workers in fields and youngsters at roadside doffed their hats and waved as we chugged by. It was an experience I normally would have savored simply for its uniqueness, but the anticipation of seeing Bindle and setting our course for home was heady competition.

I pulled Wallach's letter out of my coat pocket one more time. I knew it by heart, but I had to read it again anyway. I caught myself nodding at the well-remembered words of the editor of the *Star*. It was a short note but, for me, one with all the importance of any document in the National Archives.

Yes, Wallach had it about right. Bindle was a queer duck, even in his own time. How much more so here? The pertinent part of the note was clear enough. The visitor was extremely anxious to see me, and he had identified himself to Wallach as "Peter Binder." His presence here meant only one thing: I would at last be going home.

Now that my deliverance was so near, I could afford to relish just what I had accomplished. I was the one who would forever be known as the first time traveler! Like Neil Armstrong, I would always be in the public mind: the man who had gone where no man had ever gone before. Too bad, though, that I had had no opportunity to deliver the kind of pronouncement that confers instant immortality and is forever associated with its deliverer—a Churchillian "blood, sweat, and tears."

A sudden jar and shrieking of iron against iron brought me back to the present. The train announced its arrival with a long blast of its whistle while pulling into the station. The score or so other passengers began fidgeting with their bags and gathering in their children. The conductor announced the end of the line just as the car shuddered to a stop. It wasn't inconceivable that in a couple of hours I would see Paul—my first contact with someone from my own world.

A fussy, authoritative voice penetrated my reverie. "Hurry it along, Mister. You can't just sit there. This is Alexandria. We don't go any farther. Haven't you ever been on a train before? God help us for you westerners. The big city's gonna eat you alive." He said the last with pity, and just a little kindness, in his voice. He handed my hat to me and ushered me out onto the platform and into the fresh air.

Finding a hack was no problem, and soon I was bouncing down Patrick Street north and out of town toward the Long Bridge. I could sense rather than see the broad expanse of the Potomac off to my right as it flowed southward into the Chesapeake. Arlington loomed up to my left front. It had been at the edge of my vision since we left the confines of Alexandria, but now it assumed a prominence more associated with my musings than its proximity. The Lee mansion. Robert E. Lee. Soon to be the man of the hour, he was now just an upper mid-level, although highly regarded, officer in the service of the United States Army.

The clatter of hooves and wheels on the bridge reminded me that it would in time be replaced by the ill-fated Fourteenth Street Bridge. Even now it was the most convenient way into the city from Northern Virginia.

The capitol as yet offered only a promise of what its founders intended. The river, on the other hand, was the finished product of a far-superior architect. I marveled at the changes the Washington of today would have undergone before the century ended. For lack of a better word, it was just plain ugly now. To my left was the partially finished monument to our first president, and to my right were the bizarre spires of the Smithsonian, and in the distance the capitol with its unfinished dome. It smelled terrible too. The canal straight ahead would one day be filled in and become Constitution Avenue. Today, though, it served as the city's sewage system and the natural dividing line between the more affluent Northern suburbs and the slums, prisons, and insane asylums of the Anacostia area.

I had the cabbie drop me off at Twelfth and Pennsylvania, between the *Washington Star* and the Kirkwood Hotel. I had stayed at the Kirkwood before, and now Paul was there. Just the thought of it made me almost giddy. I let go with a barely subdued "all right" that earned me a disapproving glower and sniff of disdain from a young dandy. Probably another Washington bureaucrat looking down his nose at the people he served. I was in a charitable mood now, so I just gave him a friendly nod and a tip of my hat as I crossed over to the hotel.

I decided to get the best room in the house. I could afford it, and I definitely wouldn't need nineteenth-century money much longer.

As I approached the desk, the hotel clerk's face lit up with that professional smile that I knew masked a cool assessment of would-be guests. That his smile became a little more genuine only meant that he recognized my face as a previous guest.

"Welcome back to the Kirkwood, sir. Do you have a reservation today?"

It was the beginning of the political season. Congressmen and their families would be descending on the district, bringing with them the underside of democratic capitalism: various office seekers, supplicants for a share of the federal largess, land speculators, and others endeavoring to parlay their connections into something profitable. In addition, the inevitable swarm of prostitutes and procurers following the money would soon be amply evident in hotel lobbies across the city.

"I'm afraid the circumstances bringing me to the capital on business were unanticipated," I said.

"I believe we have something for one of our favorite guests, Mister—?"

"Kelly, John Kelly. I hope you have a suitable room for me."

"Oh yes, sir, Mr. Kelly. Indeed, we do. In fact, sir, your friend, Mr. Binder, has reserved our very best room for you across the hall from him," he said as he rang for a servant to take my bag. "Wonderful man, Mr. Binder. He's such a gentleman. We are truly honored to have him as a guest. Will you be staying long, sir? Of course, the room is yours as long as you need it."

Upstairs, I opened the door to what had to be the most luxurious suite in America. Richly appointed in velvets and brocades, and with the gas lamps that were beginning to show up in the most fashionable homes, it was quite a room. A little ostentatious for me, but what the hell. I might as well enjoy it. It was on Bindle's nickel. For some reason I found that thought humorous.

Shaking my head at such foolishness, I crossed the hall to Bindle's room and knocked on the door.

The door opened to only my first shock of the day!

"Come in, John," the stooped and balding old man said. "Don't just stand there staring, if you please. Do come in, and close the door behind you."

It had been a whimsical fantasy, our meeting.

Instead of the exuberant sights and sounds of joyful reunion, there was only the dull, gray silence of shock and disbelief.

It wouldn't take Ann Landers long to denounce me for being altogether a boorish lout. I couldn't take my eyes off the man looking back at me so impatiently. The tall, fit professor of history I had come to know so well was long gone. He might as well have never existed. In his place stood what appeared to be a representative of a subterranean ghetto, a gnome from another world.

Paul's patrician bearing may have disappeared, but not his Ivy League aplomb. Or his acerbic wit! This was Paul all right, just as bilious as ever.

"Come, come now," he drawled. "If it's drawing attention to the both of us that you are after, perhaps I could manage to make myself even more grotesque for your amusement. I'm not a revenant or a ghost. I'm just an old man. Haven't you ever seen an old man, John?"

With his hand at my elbow, he firmly guided me to a straight-backed chair. I felt like I was the subject of a Star Chamber inquisition. He sat down in its match directly across from me.

"Have you had quite enough of how I look? If so, then perhaps we can talk about your future, and maybe mine while we're at it."

I tore my eyes away. Besides being unforgivably rude, I was being no friend to a man who had traveled far to come save me—at no small cost to himself.

"What can I say, Paul? I'm sorry for staring so. It's just that your appearance is so drastically changed from just little more than a month ago. When I got Wallach's letter, he had mentioned that you didn't look well, but I had no idea—no idea at all—that the trip took that much out of you."

"Oh, spare me," he snapped irascibly. "Get a life, John. I didn't age on the trip, although it was a turbulent ride. I didn't risk a damned thing to save you. Your Margaret assured me that blasted machine would work fine, and as you can see, it did."

"But, I don't—"

"You're being tedious, John," he interrupted. "Is that one of the effects of going back in time—diminishing ability to think and reason? Good God, man! Think it through for a minute!"

Smarting from his criticism, I winced and responded defensively. "You needn't be insulting about it. What am I supposed to think, that you aged naturally in such a short—"

The light came on! It must have shown in my face.

"That's more like the quick graduate student I once knew, John. Now quickly! What is the first question to come to mind?"

"How many of your years have expired, and is that what it took to perfect the return function on Margaret's machine? But that's not it, is it? It is relevant, though, and what I'm most interested in. How soon do we get back home?"

He was annoyed with me. He wanted something else.

"Margaret's machine can come and go with sufficient degree of accuracy," I ventured. "Is that it?"

He sadly shook his head and said, "I can see that I've expected too much. Not of you, John. Of anyone caught in the situation you are in. What applies to you applies to me just as much. The difference is that I knew it coming in. You are only half correct about time travel's efficacy, my friend. Only half, though; no more."

Damn it! There was no pleasing the man. What did he want from me? Only half right. What on earth did that mean?

"Paul, I'm sorry, but I don't get it. What do you want me to say, to see, and know? Granted it is self-evident that the damned thing can go to any point it wants now. But what else you want from me, I don't know."

Paul Bindle only looked at me with a trace of speculation in his eyes; maybe a little sadness and regret too. He leaned back and crossed his leg. It was a typical Bindle pose: right leg crossed over left, with ankle resting on the knee and right hand grasping ankle. It seemed faintly British, and it suited him to a T.

"Are you hungry, John? You've been here enough times to suggest where we can get a repast suitable for the occasion."

"There are any number of places, Paul," I told him, "but I must say, I haven't had the feeling that the occasion has been as pleasant as it should be, given the circumstances. We can eat downstairs or several places within walking distance. Are you up to a short walk over to Willards?"

I instantly felt contrite asking him if he could stand a short walk. He let me know he didn't appreciate it by snorting contemptuously and remarking that he was just old, not puny.

Willards' reputation in modern times couldn't hold a candle to that which it held in nineteenth-century Washington. It was the place to be seen and heard. When Congress was in session, which it would be shortly, it would really be jumping. Even now it would have its fair share of government bureaucrats, embassy staffers, and various other wielders or seekers of power and influence lined up at the bar or gorging themselves at their dinner tables. During the war, Willards' clientele would also include that blight of all armies—military officers of the flagpole variety, and the various contractors and suppliers seeking to do business with them. They, like so many of the detritus of war and misery, all would wine and dine in splendor and luxury. Rarely would Washington establishments, in marked contrast to their Richmond counterparts, suffer from the shortages of war.

We left the Kirkwood and turned right on Pennsylvania Avenue, or simply "the Avenue," as the locals were wont to refer to it. Willards was about three blocks up toward what would only later be called the White House.

Willards was the preeminent hotel and dining establishment in Washington. The Kirkwood had its devoted fans, as did the National and Browns, but none could compare with Willards, at least for the status conscious. All boasted some of the finest food on the continent. Present-day Washington, for the most part, bore little resemblance to the capital cities of the Old World, or even of South and Central America. Rough-hewn, with very little pretense at grandeur, the capital was definitely the backwaters of world cities. The food here was in a class by itself, though. Americans of the day had simple tastes, but Washington was just as different from the rest of the country now as it would be more than a century later. Meals here were monstrous affairs. As best as I could tell, Washingtonians ate five meals a day.

The food police were nowhere evident—they would have to wait their time in the sun—but if they were, they would be in an absolute frenzy. Breakfasts of steaks and eggs were warm-ups for noon meals of equally huge proportions. Dinner was served in the late afternoon, only to be followed in the early evening by a kind of happy hour of drinks and finger food. Rounding off the day would be supper at about nine. The sheer bulk of the food consumed by the citizens of the capital only marginally exceeded the amount of alcoholic beverages used to wash it down; champagnes, beer, toddies, and juleps all swilled down in gargantuan quantities. The gusto, with which the city unapologetically satisfied its voracious appetites, somehow seemed appropriate for this new country, with its borders still to expand outward and its oceans still to master and rule.

Like high-dollar hookers spotting a couple of marks, two doormen, resplendent in their uniformed finery, descended on us as we turned toward the entranceway of the rather-large building. Their manner had the off-putting quality of being both haughty and ingratiating at the same time. Since the business of government, as well as the business of Willards, wouldn't begin until the Congress convened, they undoubtedly were lowering their standards by deigning to treat with us. Even at that I had the distinct impression that if Paul hadn't been with me, I wouldn't rate much attention. He possessed a sort of refulgence, a style I could never attain. Probably that upper-class finishing school he had surely attended and just some plain old good breeding.

Inside, and seated with whiskeys in hand and our orders placed, my curiosity finally got the best of me.

"Paul, just how much time has elapsed since I left?" It couldn't have been a terribly long time if for no other reason than Paul, if not really well, was certainly alive.

His eyes probed mine as he peered at me. It was as if he was assessing my capacity to cope with what he had to say.

Finally he said, "Almost three years, John. Three long years and a round of chemotherapy for cancer, pancreatic cancer. That's the reason for my appearance. I'm seventy-nine now, and the cancer is still there."

Cancer! Chemotherapy! Terrible news for anyone, especially a friend and colleague. But sadly, all I really heard was "three years."

I started to offer my concerns for his cancer, but he just waved it off.

My first thought that it couldn't possibly be three years was quickly supplanted by the realization and acceptance that it could very easily be. Why not?

Hell it could just as well have been a hundred years.

If Paul had aged three years in the same period that I had aged less than two months, that would mean time traveled at different speeds in our two eras; ergo, we were in different universes. No wonder it had been so traumatic a landing in Manassas—I had stepped off one world, streaking along onto another barely moving.

On the other hand, if there had been only one universe, then time's passage was uniform, and Margaret could have simply aimed Bindle back to when only little more than a month or so had elapsed here, no matter how much time had passed at her end. She could just have as easily sent him to before I had even shown up here, as she had the trunk. That seemed more plausible than two or more universes and had the added virtue of being aesthetically more pleasing. Moreover it would explain how my making a name for myself here could show up as a matter of record in her later time.

The important thing was that everything back there was three years later. Three years later simply because three years had passed. It wasn't going to be home to me at all. I would be going back to a place that wasn't mine anymore—except in the most metaphysical sense of the word.

I think he must have known that right then was the best time to tell me. To tell me when my mind was still trying to grasp the significance of those years.

"John, old friend; it's just as well."

It was as if he could see into my mind. Where I had been lost in thought, I now jerked my head and eyes to him. I had that peculiar sensation of my lens to the world being narrowed, of a reduced field of vision. My pulse was a drumbeat of retreat from reality into never-never land.

"What do you mean?" I managed to ask.

"I brought no golden cord to bring you in out of the cold, if I can jumble a few analogies. I'm not George Smiley, and I'm definitely not Ariadne. There's no going back for you. Not for you, and, for that matter, not for me either. Not that it matters anymore for me."

I could feel a stupid grin plastered all over my face. "Don't be silly, Paul. Of course it matters for you, even more than for me. Back home, you'll be able to continue your treatment. For me, maybe it is no longer home. You just left, though; nothing will have changed for you. Yes, I understand that my world is changed, but it will still be the physical world where I was born. I'll rediscover it, that's all."

He looked at me with the saddest expression on his face and said, "It only goes one way. That's it. No round-trip ticket. A one-way street, get it?"

"That has been the problem," he hurriedly continued, as if afraid I might just get up and leave before he could finish driving the last nail in place. "That and narrowing down the entry window, as Margaret puts it. That's the part you guessed right on, John. She can now place someone—me, in fact—to precise coordinates and within a fraction of a second in time. However, it only pushes backward. It apparently can't pull forward. I don't understand it all. She did tell me she had some other possibilities to investigate, but essentially the problem is akin to the fact that objects can only go to what has already happened. That's how you and I got here. The transporter sent us back to a time that had already occurred. But things can't be pulled to what has yet to happen."

His words thudded into my gut in that sickening way that only absolute, undeniable truth can do. Disbelief, or even doubt, would never be an option when uttered by a Paul Bindle in circumstances such as these. It was as final as anything could be. What time I had left was to be breathed right here.

With a steadiness in my voice that surprised me, I noted, "This must be the highest price anyone ever paid for eternal fame. The most famous man in the universe, and I'm not even around to enjoy it. Most people have to die to achieve this level of immortality. I appreciate the fact I haven't had to die to be this famous, but it is damned difficult to bask in the glory from here.

"How sad for Robert and Darla to know their dad has gone off to instant fame, but they can only share in it in the abstract, so to speak. Did you have a chance to speak with them, Paul? And Margaret. How is she? Has she gotten married?"

I couldn't have expected her to be waiting for me after all those years.

He started to reply when our waiter brought our order. With a look of relief on his face, Paul sent him back for a bottle of champagne and hushed me quiet. It wasn't until he was back, and our glasses filled, that the old warrior shook the very foundation of my existence.

"This has got to be the saddest duty a friend can ever have."

"What do you mean? Nothing has happened to them, has it? Are they all right?"

"They're fine. Both of your children are well, and Margaret too. No, she hasn't married. That's not it. What I must tell you now is this: not only does the world not think of you as a hero, John, it doesn't think of you at all. Robert and Darla do, but only as a father they loved and now miss. Ambrose and Mary miss you too. But only Margaret, a very few others, and I know."

"What do you mean?" I was sounding like a broken record.

His voice was soft and comforting. "John, there were no encomiums for you, no posthumous awards, no nothing. To the extent anyone thought of you at all, you just didn't show up for work one day; you turned up missing, and after an appropriate wait, you were presumed dead. Like other victims of political expediency, you're not famous—you are just forgotten. Expunged from the records, one might say."

"But why?" I was getting better at this. "To what purpose, Paul? Margaret's machine has got to be the biggest thing since the moon landing. Hell, more so. Okay, I understand the need for secrecy. But why am I not part of it? This doesn't make any sense at all."

"The public knows nothing of time travel, except as science-fiction tales. The Manhattan Project was nothing compared to this, John. This is the best-kept secret I have ever witnessed. And I've been privy to quite a few. To tell the truth, no one should want to know about this little gem. A little knowledge can be a dangerous thing. Maybe I should say a deadly thing."

"You mean...? How can that be? And why, for God's sake?"

He just shook his head, as if I had failed a test he expected me to ace. "Just think about it for a minute. You came back to this time, and so far you have done next to nothing to alter what would otherwise have happened in the natural scheme of things. You have left a record in a now-defunct newspaper that managed to show up in some old, musty archival records. But no offense intended, they are not literary works of art that are likely to affect the cosmos in any significant way. For that, the twentieth century thanks you. But what about others, say someone willing to change things around just a bit, or maybe just an honest mistake by a well-intentioned but clumsy time explorer? Consider a disgruntled nation with the ability to alter history more to their liking, or maybe worse: a lunatic with reasons known only to a twisted mind. Surely you see the potential for world disaster!"

"Well, yes. Of course I see that. However, just what exactly do you mean by dangerous deadly knowledge? Sounds like you're saying the government will go to extreme measures against its own citizens to retain this exclusive knowledge. So who gets to decide the uses Margaret's machine is put to?"

We'd been picking at our food, talking more than eating. The dining room was filling up, and it wouldn't be long before the waiters would begin to covet our tables. I was no longer very hungry and mentioned that maybe we should just go. But he said we should get our fill while we could. Since he didn't seem inclined to answer any more questions, or elaborate on what we had been discussing, I managed to force down what was on my plate.

When we were finished, he settled up with a gold coin. I mentioned that I had found it strange paying for things exclusively with coins.

He laughed. "I made my money the old-fashioned way, John. I copied paper money on one of the university copying machines. Old bank notes duplicate rather easily and are surprisingly redeemable in coin. You might be interested to know that I'm very wealthy now. Of course, when they are presented to the bank in question, it won't take them long to realize they have been snookered. By then it won't matter anyway. And I would give most of it for a decent bottle of gin."

He seemed to find the idea amusing. I only saw it as a further example of the finality of my status in this world. I had made the transition from a green-card holder to a naturalized citizen!

We left the hotel to the early evening shadows of not-quite dark streets. The gaslights flickered bravely against the impending dusk. We walked together, him and me, but we were in two different worlds. Here I was, lost in thought about this latest turn of events and the new challenges I would face, and he was whistling the theme from Star Wars. While mulling it all over, I gave some thought to Paul coming, knowing he had no chance of ever returning home, especially given the need for continuing his cancer treatment. Why would he do that? What would be the purpose? To caution me about meddling in the past and to experience history firsthand. Maybe, but it must be more than just that. It defied logic that he—or anyone, for that matter— would give up the rest of his life for those reasons. I certainly wouldn't. But what else could it be?

As if he were eavesdropping on my very thoughts, he spoke for the first time since leaving Willards. "Who gets to decide the uses, you ask. Well, Benjamin Clay does! It is arrogance, John. But, that's not important to you now. What is important to you is why they would send anyone here to tell you things you surely would have figured out on your own. More to the point is why was it me who came and not someone else? Perhaps you've thought about that finally."

So that was it. That was what he had been so insistent I figure out. That it didn't make sense for him to come was obvious now. What still wasn't so apparent was why he came anyway.

What had he said about messing with time? Time travel was a big secret because it was just too dangerous for people to be going back to the past. Okay. That made sense. Coming back to get me out of here so I could do no harm would be the thing to do if it were possible to go back. But it wasn't possible. Nevertheless, Paul came anyway. Of course! He would be the ideal choice to...

To what?

He was watching me intently.

My confusion probably showed because he started to say something.

I furrowed my brow and held up my hand to silence him. Despite the balmy Washington weather, a sudden chill settled in my bones.

More for my benefit than his, I spoke out loud, "Given that return is impossible, it would be difficult to get anyone to come back just to let me know I was to be forever marooned here. Now back at the Kirkwood, you asked me what the first observation to come to mind was. That was right after you told me your age and about your cancer treatment. But it was before I knew there was no going back, that the machine only went one way."

"And so, what is your conclusion now?" he interjected.

"So in that context, my observation—had I been astute enough to make it—would have been this: why send a man your age on that rather difficult trip when a younger man could make it so much easier?"

He prompted me again. "So why do you think they send me instead of some young jock, John?"

I replied, "I'm not sure how it would go after that, but it must finally lead me to the conclusion that there was no going forward in time, only backward, and that was the reason you came instead of a younger man. No one with his life to live out in his own time would consign himself to living far away—eternally far away—from his own time. So send a man with not much longer to live anyway. And who better to send than a colleague, a fellow historian? Someone who knew me, someone I would trust. It still begs the big question, though: under the circumstances, why send anyone at all?"

"Someone you would trust," he repeated.

Someone I could trust.

"Was it to alert me that I must be very careful lest I screw the future world up? That doesn't make sense. Certainly anyone could easily conclude that I would be aware of that fact. After all, I'm not a grade-school dropout. I'm a scholar of history. If anyone would be aware of the consequences of his acts, it would be an historian, wouldn't it? And by sending someone, there would then be two of us here; two of us with twice as many chances to foul up history."

We had not headed directly back to the Kirkwood. It was as if an unseen hand had steered us north on Fifteenth, adjacent to the White House and around the corner from Willards. Off to our left front was Lafayette Square, on the other side of Pennsylvania Avenue. At that corner, New York Avenue was interrupted by the White House grounds, and Pennsylvania jogged back to the west before angling northwest.

Just as our circuitous route was winding us around historical Washington, so too were my ruminations, taking me through the labyrinth of human machinations. Just as I was being prompted and led to a final conclusion, so too we were being led on a tortured path back to the Kirkwood.

Paul wasn't content just to let me ramble on. Whenever I would come to a stumbling block, he adroitly guided me back to more productive reasoning.

"Right, why come at all?"

I couldn't afford to be anything but brutally honest at this stage of my forensic discussion with myself. "If someone must come back here to reason with me, then far better it be that that person not have much time left. An older man like you; a man who would: one, be more willing to come; and two, who could be counted on to conveniently die, leaving only me."

Still thinking out loud, I said, "But then we would be back to square one: I would still be here in the vulnerable past. Unless..."

In spite of the dim light, I sensed a sudden change in his demeanor.

At the corner of Fifteenth and H Street, we turned around and started back to the Kirkwood.

Behind us and to the rear of Lafayette Square were the homes of the ardent secessionist Kate Greenhow; Slidell, the Confederate emissary soon to gain fame as a *cause célèbre*; and the late Daniel Webster. Across Sixteenth from there was the venerable and impressive Saint John's Episcopal Church.

Acting as a buffer around the presidential mansion behind us were the executive buildings of the Treasury, State, War, and Navy departments. The Treasury Department building was arguably the stateliest building in Washington. It was large enough to house its poor cousin: the State Department.

By mutual—if unspoken—consent, we turned east on G Street and began the short walk back to the Kirkwood. The sun had finally disappeared, and in this part of Washington, no streetlights penetrated the night. In the dark, Paul stumbled against me. We saw few pedestrians until turning right on Tenth Street, where the lighted and still well traveled avenue pointed the way to the Kirkwood.

I still couldn't make a connection, though. There was something else to it, but it was just out of reach. I waited for another question or prompting to get me started again when he pointed out a building to our left front.

"Look, John. The Dealey Plaza of 1865! The war that Lincoln won against your rebellious states will be lost inside that building. There he will pay the piper for that war, and there any hope of ever putting it behind us will die too. And should it all turn out different, where would we be now?"

It would have to be someone I would trust! Someone I could let my guard down with?

It was Ford Theater, a few years hence to be the most infamous theater in the country. The home we were passing on our right was where they carried the president after the assassin's bullet struck him down and where he breathed his last.

And then finally it came to me. This site of death brought me to the logical conclusion that Paul had been leading me ever so patiently. Had he steered me here deliberately? Did he know I knew finally? That I was far too dangerous to let live? Why go through this elaborate question and answer period when it was far more propitious to just take me back in the darkness we were emerging from? He could have done it easily—I had been totally unsuspecting. A muffled shot or a discreet plunging of a blade and the future world could rest easy! Draconian measures to be sure. But necessary and expedient!

"So! Now you know. And what do you make of it?" he said so softly, I found myself leaning toward him to hear his words.

He was staring at me with eyes as calculating as any politician. Yes, he saw I had figured it out—that he was my assassin and that the circle was soon to be complete.

I gasped and started to pull away, but in leaning forward to hear him, I was off balance. My sudden jerk exacerbated my awkward stance; it was all that my old friend needed.

With barely a discernible motion on his part, I found myself nudged backward and on my butt on the hard walkway. He made no sound and hardly seemed to have moved a muscle, and here I was, looking up at him as helpless as a newborn babe.

I tensed myself for a rolling sweep of my legs to bring him down. Leaning back as I was made it impossible to reach the Beretta in my jacket pocket. Before I even set myself for the attempt, he leisurely stepped back out of harm's way while, at the same time, gently admonishing me with a shake of the finger.

"Bang! Bang! You're dead. You're out of the exercise, Colonel Kelly. Report your name, rank, and unit to the umpire."

What the hell was going on here?

"John, get up. Surely you can see I mean you no harm. By the way, you may want this back."

He reached into his pocket and pulled out the Beretta and proffered it to me, butt first. He had nicked it a couple blocks back when he fell against me! What an easy mark I turned out to be.

Chagrined at how easily and completely I had been taken, I got to my feet and dusted myself off. Attempting to muster what dignity I had left, I ignored the Beretta and glowered at him in indignation.

We were standing at the intersection of Tenth and E, a long block from Pennsylvania and then around the corner to our hotel.

The tableau unfolded with an inevitable slowness.

"Oh my word!" The shrill feminine voice was followed by a booming masculine objection.

"You there, sir! Step aside, my dear."

They had come around the corner just as I was getting off the ground. The man, weighted down by his considerable girth, moved surprisingly fast with his walking stick brandished as a weapon. Behind him I caught a fleeting picture of a slight woman with her hand covering her mouth and her eyes widening in fear.

Paul was just turning around when the man's cane came down with a sickening thud on his shoulder. The sheer force of the blow knocked Paul to his knees. Even at that, he managed to maintain his grip on the pistol and was starting to roll away to escape the next blow and to bring the pistol to bear when I finally was able to react to the assault on us.

With the best move I had in me, I stepped forward and inside the cane's already-descending arc and, with my left hand, grabbed the assailant's wrist. At the same time, rotating my body to my left, I was able to throw my body into his and pull his arm in front of me. At that point he no longer controlled the direction or speed of his forward momentum. Putting just enough body english into it, I rolled him sideways instead of over my shoulder.

"Humph," and a clatter of cane on the street, followed by the beginning of a wail of panic and fright from the woman looking down on her escort, now on his back! Paul quickly got to his feet but with a grimace and a low grunt of pain! A horse and buggy turned off Pennsylvania a block away onto our street! Disparate images gradually came together as Paul, ever poised, bowed to the woman and offered his apologies for frightening her. The Beretta had disappeared God only knew where.

Paul's assailant scrambled to his feet, protesting vigorously all the while.

"My good man, what on earth is going on here?" he harrumphed. "This man was attempting to dispatch you. Have you no sense of gratitude? I save your skin, and this is what I get in return. Our fair city is in a sorry state of affairs with footpads and thieves, and now a good man is attacked for trying to prevent another robbery, or worse."

I hastened to assure him everything was just fine and that it had all been a misunderstanding. The buggy was just reaching us when I stepped into the street to retrieve the man's cane. The driver steered his horse well clear of our little imbroglio. It was the nineteenth-century equivalent of not getting involved.

I bowed to our Good Samaritan and handed him his cane. Paul, all the while, was assuring them we were actors, the best of friends, and that we had been merely rehearsing a scene. Finally his feelings assuaged somewhat; they left with the man muttering imprecations down the street. His lady was less than mollified, however. She berated him for his impetuosity and for putting her in danger.

Poor guy. For trying to do the right thing, his reward was getting roughed up, losing his dignity, and now being harped at.

I watched them go with relief and then turned to Paul just in time to see his eyes hood over as, with a hoarse moan, he reached out toward me and collapsed in my arms.

Ever so slowly our poor engine puffed up and down the slight grades. The occasional span over creeks and gullies morphed the subdued rhythmic beat into a cacophonous clatter, much like the furious whirling of wings and protesting exclamations of dispossessed mourning doves when imposed upon. Then the sonorous tempo lulled the unsuspecting passenger until the next intrusion of sound and vibration.

I hardly noticed the terrain alternating between heavily forested tracts and open fields and pastures. Both would one day disappear into the ravenous maws of a soon enough to come modern world. It would be a world dazzling with technological achievements, nurtured by America's unique legacy of liberty and free enterprise. However, all would not be well there. The lights that had, for generations, so brightly burned across the land were to be dimmed by changes in the relationship between the individual and the state.

Here among this unspoiled setting, the festering sores of rebellion denied would be merely the harbingers of bitterer times to come. The war to sweep through these Southern states, even with all its attendant horrors, would inflict lasting damage to the national character. The war would reverse the trend of less government and begin the pendulum swing that would culminate in a Benjamin Clay assuming the reins of power in America.

Still, even a Benjamin Clay couldn't have overcome the institutional safeguards of American democracy without the introduction on the world scene of two powerful phenomena: international terrorism and Islamic extremism.

Paul was only able to relate the barest outline of the events that had transpired after I left.

After massive attacks against American diplomatic and economic interests abroad, and the indiscriminate destruction of the revered symbols of American nationhood at home, Islamic terrorism became the bubonic plague of the world order. All countries were affected, but none more so than the United States. Devastating attacks on the nation's infrastructure forever shattered the American people's once-complacent sense of security.

I knew only that General Clay and his Union Party swept into power by exploiting those external threats and internal fears. Promising deliverance, he was elected president with a working majority in Congress. True to his word, terrorism against the homeland was eliminated through an aggressive policy of rigid controls on American society and international force applied against the faceless and stateless bands that had threatened the American way of life. He had been efficient; the trains ran on time again.

While President Clay was busy protecting their shores, Americans hardly noticed the insidious dilution of their constitutional safeguards into a tepid concoction of feel-good palliatives. Clay and his Unionist Congress suspended habeas corpus requirements and prohibitions against ex post facto laws for the duration of the terrorist crisis. Second and Fifth Amendment protections were the first to go, and other protections were routinely violated with little or no opposition. The few outcries were quickly nullified by intimidation, character assassination, and blackmail. Those voices that remained simply disappeared into a legal system, unencumbered by a now-impotent Bill of Rights. The American people had forfeited their birthright for security.

Paul was only able to tell me that much before he succumbed to the ravages of age, disease, and the vagaries of circumstance. That much and how he came to be my intended killer. Margaret's time machine had been a research project funded by the Department of Defense. When I disappeared, Margaret immediately made it known to her research superiors. That brought in military control of the project within a few days. Benjamin Clay, as the chairman of the Joint Chiefs at the time, soon assumed a personal, day-to-day interest in the project. For years work continued at an expanded pace on perfecting the machine's accuracy and developing the ability to retrieve people.

Margaret and her colleagues' best efforts were unable to find a way to get me back, so a by now President Clay determined that the potential threat of a maverick bumbling about in the past was simply too risky. Even with the discovery that time variations weren't a constant factor, the research teams had narrowed the machine's accuracy down to an acceptable level, and I had conveniently provided them with my when and where. Therefore, the decision was that the world's safety demanded my removal from the continuum of influence as my here and now came to be known. Finding the right man, though—a man who could do the job but was psychologically stable enough to disappear into the past—wasn't that easy. Paul, with his government connections, soon became aware of the need for a volunteer.

He convinced the decision makers that at his age he hadn't that much time left and that, as a historian, he would rather spend that time in the past that had been his life for so long. He also convinced them he still had the ability and the will to carry out one last sanction, one last assignment for his country. Paul had never acknowledged his exact past exploits to me, but he hadn't had to. It was one of those situations understood by both parties to need no elaboration.

Margaret had earned the lead role perfecting the transporter, and despite the failure to reverse the process, she proved indispensable in narrowing down the space/time window.

In the end Paul had proven the consummate double agent. Disgusted by the excesses and cynicism of the Clay era, he had come to this world on a twofold final mission: to satisfy his love of history with the ultimate experience, a fantastic voyage to the past, and, at the same time, to take a stand against the despot's heel wedged upon freedom's throat.

We both agreed; the situation there in America's future was intolerable. And we agreed that our presence here in America's past offered us a unique opportunity to influence that future. Who could be better than two historians with the knowledge of foresight and the tools of hindsight? It went without saying that the tool was the great conflict two years hence. Together we would save America!

Now it was left to me!

As our train began the last miles into Alexandria, I mentally revised my plan of action. Instead of first finding suitable lodgings as I had planned, I decided to go to the cemetery first. I knew what it was. Thinking about Paul and the past had changed my mood. It somehow seemed more fitting—before setting things in motion—to go to the place where rested the symbol of my old self.

Paul slept there in the Episcopal cemetery, but he didn't sleep alone. The world's most awesome secret shared that warm, moist earth with him. It wasn't some weapon of mass destruction or a formula for eternal life resting by his side, though. Instead, nestled there was the promise of renewal—a rebirth of America's covenant with her citizens. It needed only to be nourished and replenished.

It needed a Robert E. Lee.

The shrieking and hissing of the engine pulling into the station snapped me out of my musings. Unlike the first time Alexandria greeted me, I now had my wits together. The conductor—maybe the same one who had ushered me off before—just nodded as I swung my bag down from the overhead and disembarked before the engine shuddered to a stop.

I was out on Henry Street and flagging down a buggy before the rest of the passengers had emptied onto the station platform.

The ride to the cemetery seemed inordinately slow. The clouds overhead were ominously dark and promised a downpour before the remains of the day. Maybe the cemetery idea was a poor one. I almost told the cabby to turn back and take me to the nearest inn or boarding house here in Alexandria. Instead I decided to chance the quick visit and find a room afterward.

The clouds couldn't wait, though. Even before we rumbled across the bridge, they opened up with a vengeance. The crackling of early autumn lightning and the deep-throated crash of thunder was an unwelcome herald of tumultuous times ahead. Paul had perhaps meant it to be this way. He certainly couldn't have come here only for a historical indulgence or in a fit of pique against the status quo. To be sure, he didn't have time to elaborate on the historical possibilities. Nevertheless, I had to believe he would not have just let it sit there, that he could have the tools at hand and not use them.

The cabby skillfully maneuvered down side streets to escape the river of mud from the major avenues. The cemetery was in far eastern D.C., adjacent to the Marine Hospital fronting the Anacostia. I had chosen the Episcopal cemetery, not because Paul was an Episcopalian, but because he wasn't and I was. I picked that particular cemetery because it was the lesser known of the several graveyards in the area. Moreover, because of its location, I was sure time and progress would render it overgrown and abandoned. It was what I wanted! Flesh and bones DNA lost to time, but church records preserved for posterity.

Finally the cabby reined in at the corner of G and Eighteenth. The rain had begrudgingly stopped, and the late afternoon sun was just peeking through the clouds. Fortunately the cemetery had weathered the storm pretty well, and only a few fresh graves were partially washed away. From where I sat, I could see the marker.

I slipped the driver a dollar and told him I would only be a few minutes. If he thought I was crazy, he opted not to show it. Tomorrow Tom would be bringing Betsy on the train so I wouldn't have to worry so much about transportation.

I picked my way through the mud and around the eternal resting places of the not so recently expired citizens of the capital. Paul's still-fresh grave was bare of the flowers I had placed there last week. The deluge had washed most everything into the gullies wending their inevitable way back to the Anacostia. A few flowers with long, faded petals strewn about the immediate area by the force of the storm were a reminder of the futility of man's efforts to leave his mark on his surroundings.

Unmindful of the mud, I knelt next to the purposively modest stone. Even so, it stood in stark contrast to the surrounding worn and washed steles and crypts. I could read the inscription quite easily by the last rays of a fading sunlight. It was a simple epitaph for future eyes to read. Unabashedly I allowed a tear of melancholic loss to make its way down my face. I wept for Paul all right, but my tears were for another life too, a life now gone full circle.

I squinted one last time at the marker and the grave. I stood up and lifted a farewell salute to Paul—to Paul and to myself. With a silent mumbled good-bye, I turned away and made my way back to the hack with the image of the inscribed letters— *John Kelly, Died October* 3, 1859—burned forever into my mind.

BOOK THREE

CHAPTER 12

After leaving Lee to absorb my unbelievable tale of time travel, I crossed the Potomac into Washington to do a little sightseeing before returning to my inn. I had been here many times during two lives lived, but now I needed a bit of unwind time.

What had I just done?

Washington was a sleepy town of less than sixty thousand souls not yet aware of the dramatic events two years hence that would transform it into a vast bureaucratic center and the capital city of a great nation. Soon it would be swarming with soldiers from every state left in the Union. Young men who had hardly been out of their own barnyard would come of age here. For many it would be the last stop on their way to eternal anonymity in lonely, unmarked graves. The looming "irrepressible conflict" would also bring those less-noble souls to the city gates too. Office seekers, contractors, prostitutes, politicians, and hustlers would swell the population until the town was bursting at the seams.

And it would never look back.

It was essentially a Southern town without the charm of those places. It was a sprawling community with only the potential of the grandeur yet to come. The planners of Washington had not reckoned with stingy federal outlays. Government buildings, in various stages of completion, were spread all over town. The capitol dome was but half completed, with derricks and cranes clinging to its frame. Masonry and equipment littered the grounds. The Washington Monument looked like an explosion had broken it in half. The debris of unfinished construction lay at the base of the obelisk—a tribute to lagging public donations to complete the project.

The place, by any standard, was squalid and dirty. Gone now was the clear air of the Northern Virginia countryside. The clinging, cloying odor of open sewage was pervasive. September's oppressive heat and humidity had faded somewhat, and with it much of the stench, but it was still odiferous. In spite of the temperate weather, wood fires for cooking cast a gloomy spell throughout the area. Looking back to the southwest, I could see Arlington House with its powerful columns and pastoral grounds. It stood like a beacon midst the rocks and shoals of Washington.

I had offered Robert E. Lee a glimpse into his future.

By the time I finished my tour, I was depressed and disheartened. Certainly there was no comparison of today's Washington and the city I had visited so often in my previous time. Nevertheless, some things remained the same. Crime was clearly a problem, even in Lee's time. Poverty was just as visible now as then, as was the smoggy, unhealthy air. When the influx of federal troops descended on the city, it would be even worse. Their presence would be just another pathology the terrible war ahead would visit on America—unless Lee would treat with me.

So, what would he do with the opportunity to know God's plan for his life?

On the way to my lodging, I had ample time to reflect on today's events. I had done what historians could only dream of doing. I had not only gone back to view history in the making; I had actually had a conversation with a true history maker. Under any other circumstances, I would have been exhilaratingly happy. But the specter of failure loomed large ahead.

It was a little after eight o'clock before I came down for a late supper. It was late for me anyway. Folks here usually ate very late; ten o'clock seemed to be the most popular time.

Who knew? I may have done nothing more than mystify, but I didn't think so! He could not ignore the Beretta and the other things I had shown him nor could he ignore my foreknowledge of his future. No, a man like Lee would have to know more. Assuming he would be receptive to my suggestions, what then? Would it be enough to change the future?

I was just finishing when my waiter came over and whispered in my ear that Colonel Lee was in the lobby. Would I do him the honor of speaking with him? The waiter's manner, always respectful, was now deferential. It wasn't at all surprising. Lee was well known, not only as a rising star in the Army, but also because his family had a long and illustrious record of service to the republic and to Virginia. His father, Light Horse Harry Lee, had been a cavalry commander in the Revolutionary War and a trusted confidante of George Washington. His wife, Mary, was the great-granddaughter of Martha Washington.

Or, would it be too much?

"Please ask the colonel to join me for coffee," I told the waiter.

As he scurried off, I thought back to just a few hours earlier. After finishing my sales pitch, Lee had taken less than a minute to politely but firmly show me the door. I had anticipated his reaction, but when it came I had been beset by doubts that I would ever hear from him. Fortunately I had the foresight to write where I was staying on the back of my card.

So he was here! I had hoped that I knew enough about him—his personality and temperament—that he would be unable to resist coming. What I had told him were the things of dreams and fantasy. Who could blame him for wanting to see if the man he had met with had need of shelter and food, the same as any human? Perhaps he had simply come expecting and hoping to find that no one of my name was or ever had been registered here. If so, he would have perhaps wondered about his experience for a few days and then forgotten it all in the rush of events that would soon overtake him and the nation. Pessimistically I had expected to have to check out of my hotel tomorrow and make my plans to try and see him at Harpers Ferry, as busy as I knew he would be.

Now he was striding purposely toward my table with the waiter hurrying behind him.

I stood up as he approached, smiled, and stuck out my hand in what I hoped was the right mix of deference and confidence. "Colonel Lee, what an unexpected pleasure. Please join me for coffee."

He took my hand and, looking me straight in the eye, said, "Colonel Kelly, I apologize for intruding upon your supper. Thank you for taking the time to visit with me at such a late hour."

He was taking my measure, not in an overtly calculating way, but as a man will do to ascertain just how far to go toward establishing a relationship. That in itself was somewhat surprising. If Robert E. Lee had a fault, it was being too trusting. He ascribed to others the same exemplary qualities he possessed in such abundance. That otherwise commendable character trait would cost him and his cause dearly in the years to come. As for me, I already knew his character. He had always been the noblest of men, and nothing I had seen of the real-life Lee had dispelled that image. I only hoped I would not be found wanting in his eyes.

"Colonel, it is my pleasure to see you again. I rarely eat this late, but I have had a long and personally rewarding and fulfilling day. Please, sir, sit down. I hope you didn't have any trouble on the way here."

The entire capital area was burdened by a criminal element that came out after dark. The Potomac thankfully kept the worst of the problem in Washington proper.

"No, I didn't, but you are right. Washington is a dangerous place after dark. The ruffians and scoundrels from all over this country seem to have come here to torment our citizens."

"They certainly do that, Colonel Lee. But it is no different where I come from; in fact it is decidedly worse. I haven't spent much time here, but it didn't take me long to become acquainted with the underside of our capital."

I signaled the waiter, who was hovering nearby, to bring a pot of coffee and another cup for Lee. After he had moved out of hearing range, I looked at my guest expectantly. We both knew who had to broach the subject matter at hand—why I was here and what I wanted from him. I didn't desire to make it particularly hard for him to open the conversation, but he had come to me. It was his serve. He would ask the questions. And like a good salesman, I hoped to turn each question to my advantage!

We talked for a while about the social problems of the area and sectional differences looming ever larger on the national scene.

Then he asked, "Would you, by any chance, be the same John Kelly that has until recently been writing stories for the *Star*? I didn't connect your name until now."

"Yes, I am the same. It has been a way for me to make a living."

"You certainly have a rich imagination. But then perhaps for you it is more a reporting of the facts than imagination," he observed dryly.

I was encouraged. He had just acknowledged my origins, however, tacitly.

Lee finally broke the ice by reaching into his coat and bringing out the pen I had left behind. It was a gold-plated ballpoint pen: common enough a hundred or so years from now but undoubtedly a bit of magic to him. I didn't have to ask if he had tried it out.

"You left your pen behind. It is a beautiful writing instrument, and I knew you would want it back. I must admit that I tried it, and it baffles me as to how it works. Just how long does it last before needing refilling? That small tube inside doesn't seem to hold much ink. I suppose, Colonel Kelly, that you will tell me that it never needs refreshing. And how on earth would one get the ink in the tube to start with?"

When I left his home earlier today, I had left the pen on his desk. It was an old trick to have an excuse to return; I had used it on more than one occasion in the past. Lee probably knew why I had left it behind, but he was gracious enough not to say so.

"Please keep it, Colonel Lee," I said, laughing, "as a memento of our first meeting. It, as well as some of the other items I have, would be hard to explain if used in public, so I suggest you use it only at home. In any event I have other pens that are just as functional and not nearly as conspicuous. In answer to your question, that ink tube, under normal usage, will last more than a year. And when it is empty, one discards the old tube and buys another. For obvious reasons you will have just that one tube to enjoy."

With a chuckle and a nod of understanding, he thanked me and quickly tucked it away in his coat pocket. Before he could say anything further, the waiter returned to freshen our coffee and asked if there would be anything else. I dismissed him with a silver dollar to pay for my meal and our coffee, as well as a generous tip.

The waiter's departure gave Lee the opening he apparently needed, for he said "Yes, there is much I have to ask you. Considering the fact that you sought me out, I don't believe I am too presumptuous in expecting answers. In any event I imagine you are willing—even eager—to answer all my questions. Yours is a story that is beyond my ken. Yet my senses compel me to give your unbelievable tale credence.

"I remain doubtful. Not of you, Colonel, but of my own faculties. This may not be the best place to conduct our business, though. There are far too many prying eyes and ears. Therefore, I hope to have answers to just two questions here tonight. How did you get here, and what is your purpose in seeking me out? Then, if you are willing, I suggest we find a more suitable place and time for further conversation.

"I beseech you to use all the powers of your intellect to convince me that the impossible is, in fact, possible. Show me no more tricks or gimcracks, though. Persuade me with the force of logic—logic beyond dispute. Force my mind to accept what you say as fact."

"Colonel, I accept your challenge. As to your first question, I cannot begin to tell you how it was possible for me to get here; indeed I don't know myself. Nevertheless, if the notion of traveling through time is unimaginable to you now, please consider this: a mere one hundred forty years ago—about the difference between my time and yours—it would have been difficult to convince anyone that it would be possible to send messages hundreds of miles in a blink of an eye. The telegraph you now take for granted. The railroads: could you ever explain to

George Washington that railroads would enable him to move vast armies hundreds of miles overnight? To try and explain how those things worked would only make you appear the more ludicrous. If I am unable to tell you how my conveyance—let's call it a time machine—works, I am quite able to convince you beyond any doubt that it did work and that I did come from the future. The reality is what's essential here, not the process. If you are willing to unfetter your mind, you will come to believe that I did travel back in time. I do have other gadgets, but I brought no tricks with me.

"As to your second question, please let me be clear: I came here to see you—you and only you. In my estimation you represent history's *sine qua non*. I am here to present you with the particulars, as I see them, of my world. It is my belief that they merit changing and that you offer the best hope of meeting those ends. Yes, as you have noted, I am eager to answer your questions."

I was somewhat uncomfortable in inferring I had come to the past purposely and with an agenda. It was stretching the truth a bit, and I was guilty, at the very least, of the sin of omission.

I put that thought aside. I was just as committed as if I had come with the premeditated intent to change the future. What did it matter why or when I decided anyway? History would only record the fact of it. The thought—an unbidden thought it was too—crossed my mind that rationalization was only the first step toward expediency.

Oh well. In for a penny, in for a pound.

I plunged ahead. "I pledge to you now that every answer I give to your questions will be true. I further give my word that our association will end at the time of your choosing. You will be presented with no devil's bargain, Colonel Lee. I intend to give freely the information I have, and you are just as free to do with it as you will."

He considered me thoughtfully for several seconds before replying. "Somehow you have managed to answer my questions, though I must confess your answers leave me even more mystified. Do you have any idea how incredulous all this sounds? I must be losing my senses even to be listening to you, let alone giving any credence to your pronouncements. I find myself hoping this is all the game of a skilled and unscrupulous charlatan, if you will please not take offense.

"I apprehend the concept readily enough, Colonel Kelly. Please feel free to correct me as I stumble along. I am to do—or perhaps not do—certain things that will change the present in some way that will ameliorate conditions in your time. It is your understanding, through prior knowledge of my time, that I will be in a position to affect these changes. It only follows that, by virtue of this historical knowledge you possess, you intend to guide me to this proper course. Proper by your lights only, I might add. I understand, as far as my limited resources will allow, this is why you are here: to change history?"

"Well put, Colonel Lee," I said. What else could I say? He was right on with his brutal assessment of my intentions. It was an uncomfortable reminder of my recent righteous indignation over Clay's efforts to control the world's future. Arrogance? Willful pride?

He went on. "So while I am inclined to believe—in spite of its violation of good common sense—you are who and what you say you are, you must convince me as well of the justness of your cause."

"Colonel, I will present the facts as I see them. Yes, I hope you will see that my cause is just. It will, however, be your decision. Yours and yours alone! Based on your considered judgment as the best course of action to take, you may elect to advance or hinder the outcome I deem in the best interest of our country.

Or you can simply make the decision to do nothing. In that instance, I will have failed.

"I am satisfied you will eventually conclude that I am who I say I am. The only thing I don't know is what you will do with the information I have for you. In my own time, I am considered an expert on you. Still, even with all the information that history has to tell me, I cannot know what your decision will ultimately be. I am confident of my ability to show you what the facts are and that you will come to believe them. But what you will ultimately do with what I have to tell you, I can only await the judgment of Him who works all things to His will."

With that, we both seemed to realize there was nothing further to discuss tonight. As he pulled his watch out of his waistcoat, he asked when we could continue our conversation. I casually mentioned that we would be unable to meet for a few days. What a mistake that was!

A perplexed look briefly crossed his face. His expression didn't signify annoyance exactly; it was more like consternation. I had overplayed my hand by my cryptic response. I hastened to mollify him before my blunder caused a rift in our newfound relationship. As calmly as I could, I said, "Sir, I have spoken in a manner ill-suited to the matter at hand, as well as to one who has done me the honor of hearing me out. May I explain myself?"

Before he could answer, I said, "Since coming to your time, I've tried to avoid unnecessarily influencing events here. Every second I am here, I make some changes to what would have gone on if I hadn't come. That would include my knowledge of where you will be a few days hence. And that is why I spoke as I did."

He interrupted me with an impatient wave of his hand. "Surely you will admit that even this conversation has impacted your time and mine in some way. Do you think my life will ever be the same now? What little things will I do differently just by having heard you out and nothing more? With half my mind, I urge you to go back to where you came. But my other half is too curious about you and the possibilities your presence raises. Surely if you have come here from another time, with all the devices you have shown me, our country has prospered. So what is it you would change, and why? What do you answer to that, sir?"

I replied, "Prospering isn't the only measure of success, Colonel. One may prosper by robbing others. The science that created the time machine is a modern marvel, but it may turn out to be a bane to society. In fact, by coming here, I may have already so altered events that it may no longer exist."

He shot back, "As for that possibility, that would indeed be fortuitous, insomuch as we both would be spared the present moment. Instead of being unable to return, you would never have left. You would still be in your own time, and I, I would be going about my business without the aggravation your presence has visited on me.

"Actually, using your logic, the same could happen if I were to carry out your grand plan. Have you considered that possibility?" he concluded.

Touché! I hadn't thought of that.

"You are entirely correct," I replied hastily. "Already I may have forever changed the outcomes of tomorrow. What effect will this conversation, by itself, have on the future? I, of course, don't have an answer. However, I do hope it is minimal. That same principle pertains to my dealings with all whom I come in contact. I acknowledge to you now that I came to you with the ultimate goal in mind of affecting change, but until the time comes, it would be reckless to cause unintended changes in the here and now. Colonel, my response was poorly constructed, but my intention is to let a sequence of events play out with no interference from me. My knowledge of days and years to come is a burden, as well as a benefit."

Before I could continue, he again stopped me. "I accept what you have said, but it seems to me that mere arrangements to meet at a time and place would be no more than you would have had to know would take place during your stay. A stay—I would be less than forthright if I didn't point out—was uninvited. I say to you now, Colonel Kelly: You have come into my life, wanting something from me. You have asked me to believe a preposterous tale. You inform me that I am to be blessed with success and recognition beyond any that I ever imagined. Yet you seem little inclined to repose any particular trust in my discretion. I find that inconsiderate and most insulting."

I sighed. I had painted myself into a corner. I had intended to keep some things to myself until the right time. Would he do something out of character with what I might tell him? I would inevitably lose some degree of control of events whenever I revealed what was to come, but I wanted the time and place to be of my choosing. Still, there was nothing to do for it now.

"Very well, Colonel Lee. Tomorrow, at this time, you will be on your way to Harpers Ferry. Lieutenant Stuart will deliver a message with orders to that end at about ten o'clock tomorrow morning. Further, while you will consider your mission routine and easily resolved, what is happening there now, even as we speak, will have profound and ominous consequences that will be long remembered."

His normally somewhat florid face turned pasty and ashen with that pronouncement. As he struggled to regain his composure, I thought about his physical health. He was a robust and healthy man used to the rigors of an active outdoors life. However, I also knew that he would ultimately die at the relatively young age of sixty-three. Was he in the throes of a heart attack or maybe a stroke? I watched him carefully as his complexion slowly turned back to normal. Breathing a silent sigh of relief, I resolved to be more careful in the future.

"Forgive me," he said, "but for some reason, despite all the astonishing things you have already told me, what you just informed me of is even more astonishing. Not for the fact of it but simply because of its proximity in time. Suddenly it has become a more personal thing. I don't even question for a minute that what you just told me of will happen, just as you say."

I had him! That same proud facet of his character that I had to consider in my dealings with him had, in fact, facilitated his conversion. He was a believer now. No more wasted time attempting to convince him of my origins. It would still be necessary to persuade him of the rightness of nipping the impending and calamitous war in the bud. But the first hurdle was now out of the way.

"In that regard," he continued, "I do not need to be told to do anything other than what I had planned for the day. It will find me! In the remote possibility that you intended to tell me more about tomorrow and subsequent days and events, please do not."

"Colonel Lee, thank you for your understanding. For my part I will take heed of your admonition."

I continued, "It is getting late, and I am sorry to say that we are attracting some small bit of attention. May I suggest that we conclude tonight's meeting with plans to resume at your convenience?"

He nodded and casually glanced around the room. Off to my right, two men were engaged in what could have been just innocent conversation—maybe a business discussion or the politics of the day. Unlike earlier, though, they were studiously ignoring us now. Apparently Lee shared my thoughts.

"Yes, I noticed them earlier. They seem to have had an uncommon curiosity in the two of us. What do you make of it?"

"I am a bit of a peculiarity, Colonel," I said, "in spite of my efforts to blend in. And forgive me for saying so, but you are not exactly an anonymous figure in this area. You will be noticed wherever you go."

Lee pushed his chair away and said with a rare smile, "Yes, you do seem a bit out of place, as indeed you are. In any event I will contact you when I am able. I suppose you know exactly when that will be far more than I. I will try to devise a plan that will allow us to meet in more privacy. You are more than welcome in my home, but as a frequent visitor, you may start tongues wagging."

We both stood up and left the table. I noticed that the two eavesdroppers were studiously avoiding meeting our eyes. One was young—maybe about thirty-five. He was well dressed, but slightly overweight, and seemed to be a bit of a fop. The other one was a different story altogether. Closer to my age and also well dressed, although not quite as elegantly as his companion, he had the air of a self-made man. He had a full head of jet-black hair. He was strongly built with a resolute-looking jaw and the piercing eyes of a bird of prey. He had a somewhat raffish appearance, but he looked competent and self-assured. I shuddered as I pictured him circling before the final swoop for the kill. Like a hawk!

I said good-bye to Lee in the small lobby and wished him well, which seemed a little phony considering that I knew, and he knew that I knew, that he would be just fine. As I headed to the stairwell to go to my room, I glanced out of the corner of my eye to see what our two friends were doing. They were still talking away and didn't seem to be paying any attention to me.

I slept that night the sleep of the righteous. I was satisfied with the progress I had made with Lee, and no black clouds as yet had dampened my enthusiasm. My last thought before passing into a deep slumber was how much I would give to see Lee's face tomorrow when he received orders to put down an insurrection in Harpers Ferry led by the zealot John Brown.

CHAPTER 13

"So now that you understand my position, what do you propose to tell me?" Robert E. Lee challenged.

"Very little, I'm afraid," I retorted with a touch of exasperation in my voice.

It was late, and I wasn't in the best of moods. The stubbornness of the man on whose shoulders so much of the future of two histories depended was derailing my carefully laid plans. As we had agreed to do after his return from Harpers Ferry, we were meeting again. It hadn't gone well almost from the beginning. He wanted no part of foreknowledge. That was the first thing he said when we finally met over coffee. He made it clear. By that, though, I found he only meant foreknowledge of those events that would put him in a position of choosing between opposing courses of action.

We were in the same dining room we had visited just a few days before. Since then, though, everything had changed, and America would never be the same. The powder keg's fuse had been lit. John Brown was a household name throughout the United States, North and South, and soon would be the rallying cry of the abolitionist movement—a movement that would elect a president and that would propel an embittered South to sever the ties of Union. And now that Lee had decided to be uncooperative, all things would come to pass just as written. The slow but inevitable demise of federalism would continue on to its preordained path—a path leading to the Odets and Clays of my old world.

"We are all destined to make our way in life with imperfect knowledge," he said. "Surely that is the way it should be. The evolution from time past to our time now would have necessarily taken us to a different present state of affairs if you had gone to a past more distant than this and found someone there willing to make a different decision than they otherwise did. What consequences would that have had for me or my family? My country? What changes to society as now exists? Who would gain and who would suffer here for decisions changed back then?

"How, with those questions in front of me as to how they would affect me personally in that instance, could I presume to decide them for future generations in the other instance? I cannot match, nor do I wish to try, the ends as fashioned by our Creator—one who most certainly jealously guards such powers for his own use."

I hadn't anticipated such a reaction. I had had every confidence that he would at least hear me out. I had been sure that natural curiosity about what lay ahead would ensure me a fair hearing.

Robert E. Lee had other notions about that.

"Just as I told you before that I wanted to know no more of the events of the next day; therefore, now may I elaborate so you will be under no misapprehension about my wishes? I desire to know nothing of my fate; indeed you have told me too much as it is. I expressly and emphatically adjure you that I want no part of advance information designed to place me in a position or, once naturally in that position, to influence me in any decision I would make or not make.

"I respectfully request, as from one gentleman to another, that you honor my wishes and refrain from any more revelations about me or what lies ahead for me," he finished.

He caught me flat-footed and without a ready reply.

"So," he repeated, "what do you have to tell me?"

I gathered my thoughts together as well as I could before answering.

"Colonel Lee, your instructions are unequivocal and difficult to honor. I should say 'difficult to honor' if I am to tell you anything at all. I gather that you are willing to hear some of what I have come to tell you. Please inform me precisely of your expectations."

"Colonel Kelly, I realize I have made it difficult for you, just as you have for me. You may only surmise how much more complicated my life is now that you have entered it. No, I do not wish to send you forever away from me. I am curious, just as you might expect, about what my world might become." He paused and, with a speculative and contemplative look in his eyes, continued. "But perhaps it would be more accurate to say what your world is rather than what mine will become, would you not agree? After all, the two may not be the same.

"No, my visitor friend from Texas." He smiled, emphasizing the state. "I hope you don't decide to return home before we have had an opportunity to learn from one another. I will continue to ask of you to be discriminating in what you reveal, though. I am certain we can have a mutually-rewarding dialogue under those restrictions."

Yes, he was intuitive and direct. He knew, even by limiting what I could tell him, I would nevertheless be desirous of continuing the discussion. The scholar in me couldn't resist that opportunity.

"Well, Colonel Lee," I ventured, "my best-laid plans have gone awry. But one thing seems to be resolved: you are satisfied I am who I say I am."

"Yes, yes. But I was certain of that the day you came to my home. By that evening I knew. I've wasted no more time questioning your origins. And I am under no illusions concerning the subject matter that brought you here. Presumably, and most regrettably, it must still be an issue of contention in your day and age. I have wished it were not so, but I am saddened to say that I expect desperate times for our country. We seem to have lost our common purpose. I would that no African had ever been brought to this land. Slavery brutalizes us all—black and white together—and will continue to threaten, it seems, to tear us asunder.

"If the people of New England would cease meddling in our affairs, we of necessity will resolve this particular domestic problem—if for no other reason than to avoid history's harsh judgment. Just as Virginia has no business in the affairs of the New Englander, they have none in ours. I'm sure your history of these times recorded the answer to this very simple question: by whose authority did those people up there appoint themselves as the custodian of our affairs and supervisors of how we govern ourselves?"

His rhetorical question gave me the opening I was looking for. "Yes, you are right. The impending crisis! There will be a war, but it will be a war the likes of which the world has never seen, Colonel Lee. Armies will possess and use the means to kill their fellow countrymen at an unprecedented rate. And when it is at last over, when the victor stands unchallenged, the America you know today will be no more."

"You are suggesting disunion, sir—a civil war," he retorted. "But that has been predicted for years, and it has been avoided. Avoided at terrible cost to our national harmony, but avoided, it has been. The naysayers cannot be right. No rebellion could survive in the face of the country's disapproval."

"History may judge it a civil war, but it will possess few of the characteristics of that sad state," I replied. "And yes, the common man will disapprove of the separation. But he will step into the breach with a dedication and ferocity that will astonish the world and sow the seeds of discord and acrimony that will plague both sides for generations."

"Death," he interjected, "is the way of war. Even one is a tragedy. The more so when it places in opposition those whose heritage springs from the common fount of liberty and democracy and whose forefathers shared the same battlefield for the same cause. But surely you exaggerate."

"I'm afraid the reality is a bit more serious than you currently contemplate," I countered. "It does not surprise me! Few Americans today are able to apprehend just how serious and how bloody it will all turn out to be. Even fewer are able to imagine the world they will inhabit after the last shot is fired."

He didn't blink an eye.

"Colonel, you have again alluded to carnage and slaughter to come," he said impatiently. "Please be more specific. Just exactly what do you mean?"

I took a second to respond, wondering just how much to tell him. We had already discussed more than I first thought he would tolerate. I decided to demur. I would hold for later the dreadful statistics of man's ability to wage a fratricidal war.

"You place me in an awkward position, sir. You have requested I refrain from placing information before you that may compromise your independence."

"Yes, of course. I did. Please accept my apologies, Colonel. I'm beginning to see that there is no halfway in revelations. It's either all or none, it seems. One gets a taste for that kind of knowledge. If you will overlook my impatience, I will place in your capable hands sole discretion in these matters. I am confident I can rely upon your good judgment."

I didn't quite share his esteem for my competence or my perspicacity!

I looked around the room as the guests began to arrive for supper. There were no suspicious faces tonight. No surreptitious glances our way; no sudden lowering of the eyes or any evidence of anyone paying undue attention to either of us. Still, we soon would be attracting attention if for no other reason than we would be the only ones not eating.

I mentioned that it was getting late and asked him if he would mind us continuing our conversation on horseback. He readily assented, and I motioned for our waiter to arrange for our mounts to be readied. He was pleased when I suggested accompanying him back to Arlington.

It was a pleasant evening, and our horses seemed eager to be stepping out. I was glad to get out of the confines of the hotel, and I knew Lee would be anxious to get back to Arlington. He would know, as I did, that he was to be leaving in a couple of days for a board of officers meeting to discuss parades and ceremonies. He was a family man; his time with Mary and their children was preciously husbanded when he wasn't engaged in the business of his country.

Finally I could avoid it no longer.

I knew what I had to do, and I had figured out a way to do it.

"Colonel Lee, I am desirous of honoring your wishes, but I know of no way I can do that while answering your questions. Therefore, I'm going to talk about the one thing I know the most about. You will be interested because of the subject matter. Soldiering! Almost three decades of service to America. Most of those years you will be familiar with: the humdrum existence of the peacetime army. You know all too well of the remote postings, the crushing boredom, the never-ending drill and ceremonies, the quiet desperation of loneliness and frustration, the failed marriages and ruined families. The life of a soldier is the same today as it was for the legions of Rome, and it will be the same for tomorrow's soldier.

"Ah, but those other years. The years at the ramparts! The destiny of a nation and way of life validated by blood and tears, fears conquered and manhood proven, horrible waste, and noble salvation. Witnessing the destructive power that only war provides, enjoying the sublime camaraderie found only in danger shared, being a part of events that are bigger than self! The emotions I need not explain. They will be the same no matter the century or the cause."

The night was still as the flickering lights and sounds of the city lost their frail hold on us. The road ahead faded away as the evening's darkness closed in behind us. Lee made no comment, but I knew he was intently hanging on to my words.

Now ease off for a beat or two.

"Our worlds are, literally, worlds apart. We share the same planet—you and I—yet the one is not one-hundredth of the other. It would not be the slightest hyperbole to declare it not even one-thousandth. The stars overhead will one day soon share the heavens with celestial orbs fashioned by man himself. Distant probes to other planets and other universes! Man himself standing on a cold, dead, yellow moon. Closer to home, I could talk to friends in Texas—or on the other side of the globe, for that matter—as easily as I'm talking to you now. The time it would take us to ride to Baltimore, Colonel, I would be able to very nearly travel the far points of this continent. With the turn of a switch, Americans can see and enjoy events taking place hundreds and thousands of miles away.

"Those afflicted, like Mrs. Lee, with constant pain and crippling infirmities will find relief. The plague and the pox wiped off the face of the globe, along with those childhood diseases that take away so many of your children today. Damaged or flawed parts—hearts and lungs, eyes and flesh—replaced or made new. Life spans and, more importantly, life quality drastically improved. Miracles will abound in all facets of life."

So far, so good!

The wide Potomac off to our right was a yellow road greedily glistening in the moonlight as it flowed restlessly onto its salty end. Ahead, Arlington House beckoned. Faint lights twinkling silver in the upstairs windows. The Lee-Custis Mansion: not yet an empty mausoleum standing sentinel over its garden of death, not yet opaque windows staring down with sightless eyes at the magnificent but jaded city of power and privilege, not yet presiding at the gilded sepulcher of twentieth-century Washington. Now it stood as a shining house on the hill, looking down on the hope—the fading hope perhaps of American federalism.

I couldn't fool myself. I was thrilled and intrigued by the possibilities. In the great drama of history—at least this instance of passing moments—I could become the *deus ex machina* that determines the outcome of the most vexing issues of American culture. Paul's description of an America under the thrall of Benjamin Clay and his minions loomed large in my resolve, too.

I was here with America's most noble practitioner of the military arts. And ironically Benjamin Clay, the antithesis of Robert Lee, had himself unknowingly sanctioned this mission.

Lee's polite cough brought me back to the present, which just happened to be a past I was aiming to change. The man was proving to be so obstinate, though. His determined proscription had thwarted me in a way no other person could have done. I wondered if he knew or sensed the near-reverent awe I held for him and if he was above using that knowledge to bend me to his will.

No matter now. I was committed!

I continued. "All of these things—and so many, many more—are what the future holds for this country and the world. And the one area needing no such improvements will end up getting the most. Man's propensity to kill his fellow man will at last be equaled by his ability to do so. Death on a scale truly obscene awaits the next few generations. The only difference, besides the sheer numbers, between now and then will be the abstraction of it all; soldiers may never see the enemies they destroy. The trigger pullers can be miles, even hundreds or thousand of miles, from their target. War will have lost its personal touch, and lost with it will be the horrors and repugnance of decent man for slaughter. The grotesquely inhuman concept of war with no limits will only dehumanize us. Gone will be the soldier's code of decency toward his foe. All will be the legitimate target of the policy makers in their council rooms, far apart from the killing fields."

Not much time. High diddle-diddle, straight up the middle!

"Colonel, in little more than a man's lifetime—just about eighty-six years from now—America will detonate a bomb on an arch enemy of our country. That hostile country, the Empire of Japan, will have been the perpetrator nation of crimes against humanity, the likes of which are unimaginable to your time. Yet Japan was only a student in the horrors of genocide. Their allies in Europe were even more adept at systematic murder.

"That bomb—that one device—in the time it takes you to blink your eyes will incinerate and reduce to vapor more than one hundred thousand human beings and utterly level a modern city of more than a quarter of a million souls. By the time the final obituary is written, most of the remaining Japanese civilians of that unfortunate city will die as a result of that one bomb. One bomb! Men, women, and children! It matters only to history that the use of that fearsome weapon was entirely justified.

"Listen to me, Colonel Lee. That number is only a fraction of our countrymen soon to perish in the coming war of rebellion, not to mention a million or so to be horribly maimed, the families shattered and—"

Lee pulled up, and his horse shied away as if it had spotted a coiled rattler. A superb horseman, Lee struggled to control his mount. Betsy stirred uneasily but kept her composure.

Lee finally controlled the horse and turned to face me. Darkness hid his face from me, but it couldn't mask the intensity of his gaze or the impression of potential, quivering energy emanating from him. For a man famous for self-control, he was fairly hovering with the emotions of one faced with the inconceivable.

Once again his natural stoicism quickly reasserted itself, and the image he presented to me as the prancing of our horses brought his face in and out of the moon's glow was of the imperturbable Lee. He slowly shook his head and wondered aloud simply, "How can it be? How can it possibly be? Even Camillus waged his wars under 'certain laws which good and brave men will respect.' What happened to us?"

I wasn't too sure who Camillus was, but I got the point. The opening I was looking for was now.

"The seeds yielding that bitter crop, and even more sorrowful harvests than that, will be sown right here in our native land, Colonel Lee. Here is where the threshold was crossed. You will live to see the birth and nurturing of concepts so loathsome that only those whose delicate sensibilities have led them to avoid direct contact with it could possibly recommend it to those whose job it is to implement it.

"The canker on my country—and on my army—started right here in this place and in this time. And you have the means to prevent it."

I stopped then. The call had to be his. "Shall I go on, Colonel?"

I would be wrong again. How many times in dealing with the man had I misjudged what he would do?

"You have gone too far, sir," he barked out as if on a parade field. "I know what you are about. I told you it cannot be. Don't you realize, my dear visitor from another place, the solutions you want can only be if the hand of God moves it so? Presumably he is satisfied with what he will have wrought or with what he will allow to occur. What I do know is that your world has already happened. It cannot be undone! The history you are asking me to change has nothing to do with the world you came from. Can you not see that simple truth?"

I started to answer when, with a peremptory wave of his gloved hand, he silenced me. "Those events have already happened. Your very existence proves that. Surely you know that. Surely you realize that if you want an outcome changed, it will have to be from what might be, not what has already been."

Once again the doughty warrior demonstrated the intellectual agility and uncanny intuition he would be known for in arenas not too far hence.

On the other hand, maybe he was wrong. I didn't share his conviction that there was no connection between the two possible worlds. If, as Lee believed, that I was proof that my world had already occurred and that, therefore, no changing after the fact could ever alter all the already occurred events there, then it must also be true that my being here meant that somehow, in some way, what happened on one world impacted the other. That was to say, something happened in my old world—me getting transported—that changed at least one thing here, those things being anything and everything associated with my presence!

As a matter of fact, I myself had done things here that had changed things back home. Before I left my old century, there had been no archival record of the old *Washington Star* publishing science-fiction tales, and now there was! There was because I had done something here that caused them to show up there. Granted it wasn't much of a history-changing occurrence, but it did alter events here and there.

Still, I hadn't even considered the implicit argument of his assertion that occurrences couldn't be undone. The unchangeable aspect of happenings—that is to say, the utter inability of any force to undo an action once completed—was the touchstone of philosophical thought on the subject.

Yet one couldn't discount the possibility either. Clay's regime obviously feared change was possible. I couldn't afford to stand on academic certainty, as Lee seemed able to do. He had never seen, and would never see, the future I came from. I had family, friends, and memories there; he didn't. It was my country Clay was stealing, not his.

I was aware that Lee was staring at me, awaiting my answer. Before I could respond, he began to speak so softly I had to lean forward to hear him. As if imploring for divine interpretation, he looked out into the darkness and intoned, "If an event occurs and I subsequently manage to return to before that occurrence and prevent its happening, I still haven't changed the fact of its once occurrence. I have done nothing but stop it from occurring the second time. Likewise, if I died and God brought me back to life—which, being God, He could do—it still would only just mean that I was now alive where once I had been dead. When something occurs, nothing on this earth—or even the heavens—can change that fact. The resulting situation from that point on may change, but the fact of the occurrence itself can never change."

He turned to me with consternation written on his face. "I confess, that is the limit of my understanding, and I'm not even sure about that. After all, the events of my now have already occurred for you and your world. You weren't here then, but now you are. If you purchased real property here, for which a public record will be made, will it suddenly show up in court-house records where it wasn't before? On the other hand, maybe it would have been there all along and only awaited someone to find it! I fear I am making no sense now. The reasoning, which begins in a logical way, soon collapses under the weight of its own contradictions. Can you enlighten me?

"Did you flow backward through time, or did your machine propel you across time?"

I tried to answer him the best I could.

"Colonel, that's a remarkable analysis considering the probability you never gave it much thought until now. I, on the other hand, have spent quite a bit of time on the subject and have yet to resolve much to my satisfaction. Moreover I can assure you that the best minds of my century have not managed to do much better. I hadn't ever thought of it in terms of traveling through or traveling across time, although I'm sure others have. It is an interesting notion, though.

"But there are some things I can tell you and that you should know. The first thing is that my even being in your century was an accident. Because of my willful nature and my stupidity, I stumbled into a scientific experiment in progress. It's as simple as that. No other reason except sheer stupidity. My sole effort this past two months has been to get back, to facilitate my return.

However, it's not to be! I have come to know that I am to live out my life here, and there is nothing I can do about it. It has only been since arriving here that I have concluded your time's future and my time's past warrant changing.

"I can't tell you that you are wrong about the immutability of events. Who knows for sure? Only God! Admittedly it certainly does defy human logic. But what I can tell you for sure is that certain people in my world are convinced that previously happened events can be altered. They believe that so fervently that they have expended considerable resources to bring me back. To them I am a loose cannon—a cannon on the deck of a rolling ship firing wildly with neither plan nor purpose. They want me back very nearly as much as I want to accommodate them."

"You are remarkably well informed, Colonel Kelly," he interjected, not unkindly. "How is it you know these things? You can't be sure there is no hope for your return, especially given your people's quite natural desire to avoid disruptions of their history with all that that entails."

He paused, and, with a thoughtful look that I could just make out by the light of the silvery stars overhead, he said, "Oh yes, they would want you back very badly. Yes, very badly, indeed. How many of them would be willing to forfeit their known present for an unknown future? A future in which the 'haves' may become the 'have-nots.'"

Lee surprised me again. Still puzzling out loud, he nudged his horse up the short pathway to the front steps of Arlington House.

"Your presence here portends such troubles for your generation, Colonel Kelly, that they cannot fail to view you as any less than the most dangerous man alive—at least as long as you are here."

"Marse Robert, is that you, suh?"

Lee nodded to the black woman in the doorway. The dim light from the hallway briefly illuminated his features as he turned to me and said, "You must be very careful."

An involuntary chill seized me and settled into my bones. Where had I heard a similar warning before?

BOOK FOUR

CHAPTER 14

I was bone tired that evening, and I paid little attention to the distant sound of a single gunshot. The Yankee patrols had been especially aggressive recently. Usually we were able to avoid them. Even so, it was getting harder and harder to move about. I hadn't reckoned on the extent of interdiction by partisans throughout the state, especially in those areas served by the railways and macadam turnpikes. In response, the federals increased not only the number of patrols and outposts but also the harshness of their occupation.

The rolling thunder of hoof beats ahead alerted me to a fairly large patrol coming my way. Betsy well knew the drill by now. She whinnied and, anticipating my lead, made for a break in the forest to our left front. By the sound of it, this was no ordinary patrol. It was coming too fast and was too large.

We were returning home on the Manassas-Sudley Road from a visit with James Robinson. The battle here had pretty well ruined him. His small home had been only slightly damaged, but his land had taken a beating. Wars are much like hurricanes or other natural disasters. They don't discriminate. There need be no intent or malignity, only to be in the wrong place at the wrong time. In James's case, it was the tens of thousands of soldiers advancing and retreating over and through his crops that had done it, just as it had done to Louisa's farm.

Equally destructive was the month's stay of both armies. Robinson's race didn't serve him any better with the Yankees than it had with the Southern armies. He was still an innocent victim of circumstance.

It was not quite yet dusk this early spring evening, so I edged Betsy well back into the wood line and out of sight.

And not a minute too soon! About two-dozen federals rounded the curve in the road ahead just as we backed into the underbrush.

I nervously patted the mare, hoping she wouldn't pick this time to get skittish and bolt as she occasionally did. Just when it seemed they would come crashing through the thicket and flush us out, they galloped past and around the bend.

The beat of their hooves faded in the distance as the sun's last rays disappeared beyond the western mountains. I waited a few seconds and nudged her back out toward home.

Suddenly she stopped in her tracks and, shaking her head back and forth, snorted in protest.

Impatiently I started to give her a tap with the crop when I realized it had gotten quiet—too quiet and too soon. The horsemen had stopped! Why?

I froze!

Several voices arguing, but about what wasn't the important thing.

One of the voices was familiar. I'd heard it before. Maybe one of the federal officers posted around Manassas I'd had contact with lately.

Then it hit me with a horrible, sickening sensation.

It wasn't a voice I recognized. It was the where—or rather the when—the voice came from that I recognized. It wasn't a voice from here. Not this place and not this generation. The speech pattern, its cadence, and inflection were foreign to what I had been hearing the past two and a half years. It was straight from the next century, and under any other circumstances, it would have been music to my ears.

But what it meant now was that Lee's prediction had come true. It was what Paul had been sent to take care of. Me, the loose cannon! Not only were they probably looking for me, but they also wore the uniform of the United States government. With all that that entailed.

Instead of worrying only about rogue assassins, I would be contending with the full weight and power of the federal government. Instead of spending what was left of my existence worrying about who was waiting around every corner, I stood every chance of being on the run from every soldier and agent of that regime.

What to do now, though? Run or hide? Brazening it out was out of the question! I couldn't fight—there were too many of them, and, in any case, I wasn't armed.

The decision was being made for me, though!

Scuffling, louder and louder imprecations, and finally a shot shattered the still evening.

"Stand back or you'll get it too!" It was the modern voice. I placed it from New England. And I knew that particular voice. I had heard him speak before somewhere!

I wouldn't have a better opportunity to get a look at his face, so I quickly dismounted and secured Betsy to the nearest branch.

I moved through the brush as quickly and quietly as I could, all the while cursing myself for not carrying the Colt. It had always seemed to not be worth the time and effort to take it along. Plus, it would be difficult to explain if I were ever stopped by any of the increasingly more aggressive and hostile Union patrols.

I crept up as close as I dared and was just pulling the foliage aside to get a good look when the rest of the party that had thundered past me returned. That was too much for my would-be bounty hunter. With a thoroughly twentieth-century oath, he turned and galloped away.

I just caught a glimpse of him, but it was enough. I had seen him before! The black hair, the raptor eyes, and, even on the run from his erstwhile accomplices, the quietly competent look.

As soon as I could, I headed back home. But even before fording Flat Run, I knew something was wrong. Betsy felt it too. We broke into a quick trot, then into a wild gallop. Splashing across the stream and up the slight rise, I was possessed with a terrible feeling of dread—Louisa. I think I knew it even before bounding across the tracks and, at last, up to the doorsteps.

Sitting on the porch, her neck arched back, staring sightlessly at the dark sky overhead was Mary. Even in the sparse light from the lanterns glowing through the window, her face glistened with tears of anguish. Her lips could only mutter the quiet wails and moans that would never go away, for cradled in her arms was her beloved mistress. Tom's mother. My confidant and friend.

"*No!*" It was my voice now. It couldn't be happening. I couldn't bear it to be so. Not this good, sweet woman who had taken me into her home, her family, and her heart.

I was off the mare and onto the porch before she had trembled to a panting and frothy halt. But there was to be no use. I knew too well the peculiar laxness, the utter quietness of eternal sleep. Kneeling down at her side and into a pitifully small puddle of drying blood, I knew her life was already over—over even before I had eluded Benjamin Clay's hired gun.

I gently lifted her from Mary's grasp and pulled her to me, only barely conscious of the tears blurring what was left of my life. All that I had touched seemed to be destined to pass from my world. Louisa now gone, Caroline so long gone, and Margaret just as forever past.

Holding her as I was, I could feel the raw flesh under her shoulder blade where the bullet had exited. Her breast was almost pristine, showing only a small hole barely visible in the fold of her dress.

"She didn't tell him nothing, Mr. Kelly. She didn't let on nothing. Said she never heard of you and that he had no business terrorizing poor widows and children. And I done tucked your bag underneath that old cookin' pot, just like she told me to do if ever there was any trouble."

"Who, Mary? Who?"

But even before she opened her mouth, I already knew.

"When she asked him who he was and why Mr. Lincoln was employing such trash as him, he turned terrible mad. That was when he...he..."

She bowed her head and began crying soundless tears; her body shook for a few seconds before she once again regained control of her emotions.

She looked at me with eyes now strangely bright in her dark face and said, "I don't know his name, Mr. Kelly. But he looks as mean as one of them hawks flying around here all the time."

I didn't say anything. I didn't have to.

A body in the repose of death is rarely pleasant to look upon and is even less so when the cause is violence. Louisa was no exception. Her body, already cooling now, showed the effect of the violence visited upon her by a large bore weapon at close range. As evidenced by the paucity of blood and the location of the wound, she had mercifully died instantly. But her killer, with his choice of weapon, had brutalized her body. He had shot her with a modern weapon by the looks of it. Perhaps a magnum or even the effective .45 automatic! The hydrostatic shock of such weapons savages the human body internally, as well as externally. Mr. Hawkface had robbed her of her final dignity. Blood was now dried around her nose and mouth, as well as her ears. The impact had loosened her hair from its bun once held together by the ribbon I had bought her months ago and that she had prized so highly. Belatedly, I noticed her feet were bare. He had literally knocked her out of her shoes. The effect was obscene. I rearranged her dress in an attempt to grant her some semblance of decorum.

It had been more than two years ago when I first had seen the man who had committed this foul deed. It was at the inn when Lee had come to continue the conversation we had begun in his home. Louisa's killer was one of the two men we had suspected of eavesdropping.

So long ago, it was. I had not thought of those men since—until now. And one of them was a killer of innocent women!

Thank God Tom wasn't here. His mother had sent him to his uncle in Richmond because of the Union troops all around. Tom had the impetuousness of youth and had already taunted the federal soldiers to the point where he endangered himself and put the farm in serious risk for retribution. The slaves, except for Mary, had taken the first opportunity to head north soon after Johnston retreated south.

But now what did it matter? Louisa was dead, leaving him and Mary behind. The war would draw to its inevitable conclusion. The farm was done for. Mary had no place to go, not that I knew of anyway. Tom couldn't tend to the farm, even if there was no war going on with enemy troops occupying and confiscating everything in sight. Not that he would be interested in any case. He had already made a determined effort to join the Army of

Northern Virginia and had been deterred only by his mother's promise that she wouldn't stand in his way, if he would only wait until he was seventeen.

And now I had to face the unpleasant fact that it was because of me and my secret that his mother was dead—shot down by a killer, a hit man, in the employ of Benjamin Clay. A man looking to take care of me and not too fastidious about how he went about it.

"Mr. Kelly, the farm is 'bout done for. With the way they do things, them Yankees will just about kill us all. They going to make us folks belong to 'em, no matter what they have to do.

"You all needs to be getting along. You got some settlin' up to do. I'll take care of Missy here, and then I'll be getting on down to Richmond to be with Tom. He'll need someone to tend to him 'fore he goes off and gets hisself killed, just like Miss Louisa here."

She broke down again. The enormity of her loss and her uncertain future were just settling in.

Regardless of what she was saying, I knew I couldn't abandon her—her or Louisa.

Although she had put words to what was whirling around in my confused state of mind, I had to take care of first things first. And the first thing was to close out here and get Mary to Richmond, where she would be with Tom and hopefully have a home with Louisa's brother.

Closing out here meant burying Louisa—burying her in her good Virginia earth. I would bury her properly with a Christian preacher saying the proper words, if I could find one. Her minister, the Cumberland Presbyterian preacher, had gone off to fight for his home state, Arkansas.

Revenge would come later.

And it would be revenge far beyond settling up with Louisa's murderer.

CHAPTER 15

Betsy didn't like it any better than I did. Her breath billowed gray in the still air as she softly neighed and snorted in subdued protest. Steaming ground fog, clinging and pulling, misted around us as we picked our way up the slope.

Her measured pace was terribly loud in the still early hours as each step announced our unwelcome intrusion into history's backwaters—this past with its documented record of destined events. Soon she and I would be wiping that slate clean.

A "brave new world" was waiting not so far past this known now. However, it wouldn't be a paternalistic, centralized national government eager to satisfy every indulgence and placate every rebellious spirit. Instead it would be an America with the founders' intentions still intact—a nation of shared powers and responsibilities among its constituent parts—a central government, the many states, and, finally and ultimately, the people.

Betsy stopped suddenly, throwing me off balance. I gently patted her neck to soothe her, but it was only the movement of troops—soldiers in gray moving into position and into the history books. Like a drop of oil introduced into a bowl of water, the air around us shifted and folded. A bright moon glistened on the moist leaves and branches like a Christmas tree with glittery, silvery tinsel.

I maneuvered Betsy into the small glade off to the left and slightly below the bluff overlooking the river bottoms. Sheltered from the faint rays of an early dawn, and out of sight from the bluff above, I dismounted and tethered the mare loosely to a small sapling. From here, I would be able to command practically the same view as the general commanding the Army of Northern Virginia would from the small promontory above me.

I knew what the battles soon to rage over the peninsula would bring. It was an outcome I intended to change!

The question was: Would Robert E. Lee maintain his resolve to not treat with me on the subject of a future America? Or would he, faced with the possibility of his country's defeat, turn to me for answers? Would he choose expediency to further ends he thought worthy, or would he continue to stand on principle and rely only on his God-given talents to achieve his purposes?

The tramping of thousands of boots, the harsh sounds of soldiers coughing and spitting, the faint but endless jingle of martial accoutrements were all familiar sounds for me. More alien were those occasional noises from horses pulling supply wagons, ambulances, and artillery pieces and their caissons. It took me back to that moment on a late autumn evening when Colonel Lee had bid me farewell and issued his final enjoinder.

"And now, my friend, I must once more be guilty of discomfiting you. I do believe you are scrupulously motivated solely by noble intentions—intentions that are, I suspect, not so inimical to my own. But I must prove stubbornly resistant to the temptations you offer.

"Yes, I am curious about the marvels of your world. The power of future weapons is more than enough to pique my interest and my repugnance as well. I'm fascinated as much by the science that could produce such weapons as by a world that required their employment. I'm sickened by the possibility that it all started here—here in this age."

I could almost hear now the longing in his voice as he had acknowledged the opportunity he was rejecting.

"No," he continued. "I cannot possibly deny my curiosity about the knowledge you alone in this world possess. Your mention of medicines—medicines that could give my Mary relief from her constant pain and deformities—is the most tempting of all the possibilities you represent. But I cannot let it be. Our history is destined to unfold as God wills, not as mortal man intrigues. So I must not see you again lest the siren song of omniscience seduces me."

He dismounted and gave the reins of his horse to a servant appearing out of the night.

Turning to face me, he had raised his right hand in a military salute and said, "Farewell, and may God be with you and protect you."

He had climbed the steps and left me. I had not seen him since.

I had honored his wishes to the fullest. Two and a half years had passed since that night. Although I had briefly toyed with the idea of trying to convince someone less principled than Lee, I soon gave it up. Besides, why should I care how a future America might turn out? If there were a connection, a cause and effect, between this *here* and that *there*, what did it really matter? I couldn't go back to that *there* anyway.

All that had changed in the time it took for one person to die and two more to become homeless. My implacable rage wouldn't serve me well in the long run, but it kept me going—for now. I would find and I would kill Mr. Hawkface, or whatever his name was. Like me, he wouldn't be going anywhere anytime soon. I would tend to the orphan maker in good time.

For now, though, the business at hand would demand all that I had. And, if needed, I would do it with or without General Robert E. Lee's participation.

Today was 26 June 1862, the second day of the series of battles known as the *Seven Days Campaign*. Major General George McClellan's Army of the Potomac was at the gates of Richmond. Hastily put together, the Confederate army, commanded by a newly appointed Robert E. Lee, was all that stood between McClellan and immortality as the savior of the Union. In McClellan's view, he would crush the rebellion. A staunch Democrat, he had little use for the Republicans and their agenda. He, like the majority of Americans, generally disapproved of slavery but wasn't keen on the notion of equality with white men or of blacks' competition for wages in the highly industrialized ghettos of Northern cities.

In most circles, there was little doubt McClellan would decisively defeat the Confederate army. He had the means. The affairs of the Confederacy had suffered dramatically since Manassas. In the west, the Southern forces had seen calamity after calamity befall them, culminating with the surrender of New Orleans to Admiral Farragut.

Here in the east, Lee's predecessor had retreated and retreated until there was no place left to run. In the end, Joe Johnston had to fight and, in so doing, he prepared the way for a continuation of the war long past the opportunity for the two sides to put aside their differences. By getting himself grievously wounded, he had had the command of his army turned over to one who did not have it in himself to concede the field to the enemy. And so—instead of a war-ending capture of the Confederate capital and restoration of the Union to its *status quo ante bellum*—under Lee's generalship, the war would grind on for three more years.

My original plan to intervene in the war had been predicated on my conviction that the ultimate Union triumph had provided the opportunities and motives for breaking down the constitutional safeguards of shared powers and on the understanding that Lee was key to the prolongation of the war. Paul and I had been in agreement on the effects the long war had on the republic and that Lee was the indispensible man. Without his services, the Confederacy would fall in this very campaign instead of three blood-soaked years later. Without Lee, the results of the conflict would be so limited that the Southern states would quickly rejoin the Union, slavery would be abolished peacefully and Reconstruction avoided. No Lee, no long, bloody war; no long, bloody war, no Reconstruction; no Reconstruction, no federalism-killing amendments to the Constitution; and, finally, no Clay.

It all seemed so simple. It might not unfold so neatly and cleanly, but it would be a start. Lee would be desirous of saving the Union and would easily perceive what was best for Virginia. Together, he and I would preserve the Union and change the world. He had obstinately not followed my script, though. So like Plato's wise man living in a wicked age, I had determined to withdraw from events of import and to just live out my life as an observer.

But even that was not to be my lot. Lee's prediction had proved to be terribly on target.

Little had I considered the zeal with which I would be pursued or the ruthlessness of my pursuer. Louisa's death changed everything for me. No longer was a happy return of the Southern states to the bosom of the Washington government good enough. No longer was simply saving federalism worthy enough a goal.

Instead I was going to make it all turn out differently!

A shaft of light poking its way through the foliage gently nudged me out of my brown study. The panorama below slowly unfolded as the sun freed itself once again from darkness's grasp. The river was just visible as it worked its sluggish way eastward. I stretched myself and settled in for the long wait ahead.

Lee's battle plan for defeating McClellan was ambitious but destined to fall apart early. In fact, unbeknownst to him, it had already done so.

Jackson was the linchpin to Lee's vision of the campaign. But Stonewall would uncharacteristically fail him, not once, but several times in the next five days. To be sure, Lee's operational plan suffered as much from lack of detail and command and staff oversight as it did from Jackson's failures. In any event the result would be less than the complete, war-ending victory Lee counted on.

The Confederate capital would be saved, and McClellan would be expelled from the peninsula, but not in the decisive way Lee had in mind.

Even now, not yet seven in the morning, Jackson was to have been moving to turn McClellan's right flank—Major General Porter's Fifth Corps—spread along the hellish bastion of Beaver Dam Creek north of the Chickahominy River. His approach would alert the assault force Lee had assembled to flush Porter from his stronghold.

Fitz-John Porter, General McClellan's most trusted and perhaps most able corps commander, was separated from the remainder of McClellan's huge army by the Chickahominy. His placement there, by none other than Abraham Lincoln, had been intended to facilitate General McDowell's movement south from Fredericksburg. It was a linkup destined to never material-ize. Lincoln, reacting to Jackson's earlier Valley campaign, had changed his mind and denied McClellan the promised McDow-ell forces. Now Porter's thirty-five thousand soldiers served little strategic purpose to further McClellan's plan to invest Richmond and to pound it into submission with his large-bore siege guns.

But they did serve as an inviting target for Lee. Outnum-bered to the tune of more than one hundred fifteen thousand Union troops to his somewhat fewer than ninety thousand men, and with a pronounced disparity in heavy artillery, Lee knew that the battle of posts that McClellan clearly intended to wage would inevitably result in a federal victory. McClellan would move toward Richmond by successive bounds, each time employing his overwhelming superiority in artillery to batter the rebel lines into retreat until only the Confederate capital remained! Lee knew he had to carry the battle to his enemy, not wait for the enemy to come to him.

Therefore, he devised a strategy entailing a bold but cal-culated risk. He would split his already-inferior force into two parts: one to fix McClellan's main force of seventy-five thou-sand men and the bulk of his siege train south of the Chick-ahominy, and the other to force Porter to retreat along a line paralleling the river. Facing the Northern main force south of the river, and directly in front of Richmond, was Magruder's wing of only about twenty-three thousand soldiers in butternut gray. Magruder's performance here in the suburbs of Richmond would be the highlight of his career. Falling apart even before the campaign was finished, he would quickly fade into obscurity. But here he would do his job with flair and fanfare.

While Magruder was employing his theatrical moves and countermoves to freeze McClellan into a state of indecision and paranoia, Lee would expel Porter from his positions along the swampy and gloomy feed into the Chickahominy. Lee felt that Jackson's sudden appearance, coupled with the rest of the assault force's forward movement, would be enough to convince Porter his stronghold was untenable. McClellan would have no choice but to reunite his split command, and Lee would be able to engage him on terrain of his own choosing. With the initiative decidedly wrested from his grasp, and with his advantage in artillery nullified by the hurried move, McClellan's prospects would be dim. Lee, for his part, had no doubts he could best his opponent in the open field.

The crucial backdrop to this dramatic ballet was White House Landing, the Union logistical base several miles to the east. There, the largess of an industrial and agricultural giant was concentrated to maintain McClellan's force. Protected by the Union navy, the landing on the Pamunkey River was the heart of McClellan's effort on the peninsula. And if the depot was the throbbing heartbeat of the operation, the Richmond and York Railroad was the aorta carrying its lifeblood. Without that railroad, the Army of the Potomac would fall over three hundred thousand meals a day short of its needs, not to mention the paramount necessities of war: ammunition, medical supplies, forage for over ten thousand mounts, and the other essentials of invasion. Equally as important to McClellan's grand plan was the railroad's singular ability to move his biggest siege guns to the front.

The Richmond and York's tracks traversed the peninsula from the apex of the Pamunkey and Mattaponi rivers at West Point, where those rivers formed the York River all the way to the Confederate capital on the James River. In doing so it crossed the Pamunkey and the Chickahominy rivers before reaching McClellan's forward-supply points.

Lee's target was that area between those two rivers. If he could interdict that line of communication, McClellan would have to come out and fight. And Lee need not even interdict; he had only to threaten to in order to ensure McClellan's cooperation. Lee's advance through Porter's stronghold would be that threat!

Robert E. Lee, the man McClellan earlier in the month had derided as "timid and irresolute in action," intended to give battle with no less an objective than the total destruction of the Army of the Potomac.

But it was an outcome history never recorded. Lee's elaborate plan depended on a synchronization of effort rare even in modern warfare. In 1862, it was near an impossible feat to bring together the disparate parts of an army in any kind of coordinated attack, especially when the pivotal command was miles away and spread out over the countryside. And the renowned Stonewall Jackson of the lightning marches proved utterly incapable of getting his divisions in position to turn Porter's flank that morning.

History recorded the attack by Lee's forces north of the Chickahominy as much as seven hours later than intended. And at that, it was finally initiated, not by Jackson, but by Ambrose Powell Hill in a spontaneous act of nervous impatience. It was well he did too because Jackson would do nothing that day. If Hill had not impetuously crossed the Chickahominy at Meadow Bridge and forced the federal pickets into their lines at Beaver Dam Creek, there would have been no battle and no salvation for Richmond and the Confederate cause. With only Magruder's small force between McClellan and Richmond, even George McClellan would have found it difficult to not use his considerable advantages in manpower and artillery to carry Richmond by assault, and Lee would only have been able to helplessly stand by and watch from north of the river.

But Hill did launch his attack! He showed his fighting mettle that day and paid dearly for it. His command would be decimated in fruitless attacks against a well-trained and well-led enemy in near impregnable fortifications. Porter's artillery, supported by longer-range cannons south of the river, would quickly out duel the inferior Southern guns and then turn their fire on Hill's hapless regiments as they courageously but futilely assailed the federal bastions. All the while, Stonewall's divisions would be in bivouac only a couple of miles away. They would provide no succor for Hill's Light Division.

It wasn't only Jackson that would fail the Southern cause today, though. Lee himself would be unable to bring the remainder of his command to bear. Of the fifty-six thousand men Lee intended to commit to evict Porter, by the end of the day, less than fifteen thousand would fire their weapons. And so it would be. Unless I could somehow change the calculus!

At the close of the day, Porter would suffer only minimal losses and, as he reported to McClellan, would be able to maintain their positions indefinitely against all the rebels could throw at him. But if Porter hadn't lost much, McClellan had lost plenty.

What was left of his nerve deserted him completely in the early morning hours of the third day of the campaign. He would issue the orders to move his army and logistical base on the Pamunkey to Harrison's Landing on the James all the way across the peninsula. In a way, an inert and bewildered Jackson proved to be the decisive factor in the day's hostilities. Once he discovered Stonewall's divisions were still uncommitted, McClellan—always fearful of every boogeyman—succumbed to the specter of Stonewall Jackson out there: always out there somewhere—everywhere. In the end it was the man's near-mystic reputation as a general who could materialize out of nowhere, defeat forces larger than his own, and then disappear, only to pop up again somewhere else that saved the campaign for Lee.

Before the day's fighting was even done, McClellan would be preparing himself for the worst. Beginning with ordering Porter's retreat to the vicinity of Gaines Mill, he would repeat the same pattern: retreat and retreat until his command would finally be rendered ineffective. In every instance of protracted combat, McClellan would concede the field to his foe, even where his army had prevailed. But in so doing, the Army of the Potomac would survive to fight another day, and Lee would be stymied in his grand campaign to destroy McClellan. The war would thus play out to its forlorn conclusion.

The morning shadows were shortening, and it was already becoming uncomfortably warm.

I hadn't quite decided how and when the next four days I would intervene. If only I had made this campaign the focal point of my graduate work instead of Manassas.

Since Jackson's divisions were meant to play the key role, it only made sense to somehow get him to the right place at the right time in order to carry out his part of Lee's concept of the operation. But that was easier said than done!

Stonewall Jackson was brilliant as a commander, but he was very strange. Of his plans, even his division commanders were clueless. His secretive nature definitely contributed to his battlefield successes, but in this day's engagement, it turned out to be disastrous for the Confederate cause.

He was also a deeply religious man with a superstitious nature. Because they had become used to being winners on the battlefield, and even though he was somewhat a martinet, his men adored him and accepted that strange aura of eccentricities peculiar to genius and dynamic leadership. It became part of the

Stonewall legend. But those same qualities would make it even more difficult to gain his confidence, even if I could get near enough to talk to him. I really didn't think Jackson would be as amenable to the notion of a man from another time appearing before him as Lee had been.

In any event I had zero idea of where he was.

So I was left with Lee himself. That very same Lee who wanted no part of my help! I needed to figure out a way to not only approach him—no small task in itself—but also to convince him to rethink his convictions. I didn't relish the prospect. When a man declines the opportunity to know the future because of his reliance on God's will, now that is character.

My speculation was interrupted on a jarring note. "What ya'll doing down there? You hear me? Yeah, you! What you doing sneaking around like that?"

He was slightly above me and to my left, facing up the slope to the bluff. His eyes were friendly enough, or at least what I could see of them over the long barrel of a musket with the biggest bore I had ever seen.

Betsy was a couple of long strides away, but she may as well have been a couple of miles downriver. That rifle never wavered. Nor did his eyes. They anticipated my quick glance to the bushes straight below where I possibly could have rolled downhill and lost myself in the dense undergrowth. He didn't seem a bit perturbed that I might try to get away.

"It's up to you, friend. You can head up that there path, or you can go ahead and pert near start off my day on a sorry note."

I had no choice. I nodded, and he motioned me up past him. From somewhere behind me, there was a snicker as another trooper materialized out of the bushes. So I not only had been caught off guard but had let them get above and below me as well. Some kind of old hand I was.

We came up and around the same cut in the sheer face of the bluff that I had guided Betsy down earlier this morning. As we crested the bluff, all my options disappeared, for there in front of me was none other than the now-bearded face of Robert E. Lee. It was the first time I had seen him in uniform, now Confederate silver-gray.

"I must apologize to you, Colonel Kelly. After all, I did ask you to forbear from contacting me, and here I have initiated a meeting. I know you were doing all you could to avoid meeting me here today, were you not?"

CHAPTER 16

By two in the afternoon, waves of heat were shimmering up from the marshes below us. Lee's usually florid face had an unhealthy tawny pallor. He was distraught over Stonewall's tardiness, and that, as well as the heat, made him look slightly rumpled. He bore little resemblance to the legendary impresario of the battle-field who would soon capture the imagination of his country-men, as well as the attentions of Lincoln and his war managers. Even his headquarters flag hung limply from its guidon pole as if it had already conceded the battle.

Widely regarded before the war as the best soldier on the continent by friend and foe alike, he had turned in a stalwart but hardly sterling performance as Jefferson Davis's military advisor. Many in the Confederacy felt he possessed insufficient ardor for the offense, as evidenced by his sobriquet "the king of spades," so given for his advocacy of well-constructed defensive positions. Even after christening his new command the Army of Northern Virginia, clearly announcing where he intended to engage the enemy, the Richmond press savaged him for timidity and faint-ness of heart. Before this week had run its bloody course, they would sing a different tune.

After thanking and releasing the troopers who had so neatly bagged me, Lee asked me to remain at his side during what I alone knew would be a long wait. We didn't speak much other than to exchange initial pleasantries and for him to explain, with a chuckle, how it had been so easy to capture me. He had been here the previous day; the same as me, except that he had been a trifle more observant—he had watched me locate my hiding place. After that, surmising what I was up to, he had the two soldiers spend the night nearby. He had set me up rather easily, and it was evident he found it amusing.

But his amusement didn't last long. By noon he began to show the strain. Hell, I wasn't doing much better, and I knew what the day would bring and why. The man's resolve was unbelievable! He knew all he had to do was to ask, but there was nary a peep from him.

Here I was, in his presence, and I didn't have a clue how to proceed. Ironically Lee himself had solved the first of my problems by apprehending me. But his demeanor suggested he wouldn't look too kindly on like initiatives from me.

But why leave me here at all? Why not just have me escorted out of the area? Was I missing a bet here? Was I letting preconceived notions of his character deter me? Certainly he was pragmatic, but was he pragmatic enough? Did he possess that same worldliness that afflicted those of a more cynical and practical nature?

When another courier headed our way, I nudged Betsy down the turnpike a couple of hundred yards as I had done whenever someone joined him. We had a tacit understanding that I would not disappear on him, but I wouldn't have anyway. This was where I needed to be. I certainly didn't know any better place. Anyway, I had long since recognized that I wouldn't be doing anything to discredit myself in his eyes.

I reined up and looked back in his direction. He was still conferring with the courier. Close by were gatherings of staffs and general officers. Longstreet was in their midst, holding forth on the long wait. His penchant for a defensive campaign was well known, and he was not hesitant about speaking his mind. Off by himself was the man I considered to be one of the true, unsung heroes of the war. Harvey Hill was a brave and resourceful general. Unrelated to Powell Hill, but related to Jackson by marriage, he never quite gained Lee's full confidence. He too, like Powell Hill, would see his command suffer horrendous casualties in the coming days.

I came abreast of a pantheon of Confederate notables with President Davis and several of his cabinet members all huddled together in gloomy silence. Davis, with a worried look on his gaunt face, nodded as I cantered by. I had seen Jefferson Davis on several occasions during the past year or so. He was a historical figure about whom much controversy would consume historians for more than a century.

A hundred yards farther down toward the capital, thousands of soldiers were lined up and camped out alongside the turnpike. Ammunition wagons were still moving toward the front. Artillery emplacements were scattered all around with their crews going through all the same nervous routines that troops throughout history had acted out prior to combat. Off in the direction of Magruder's lines, the scattered rumblings of his artillery and the deeper sounds of the federal siege guns were a reminder that Lee's desperate gamble was held together by the shaky nerves of generals John Magruder and George McClellan. Both men still had their critical parts to play, and then both would disappear into history's long list of also-rans.

I kept my eye on Lee, but my mind wandered. Concern for Tom and Mary was always close to mind. I knew they would be fine for the immediate future. Louisa had had her hands full keeping the boy from heading off to war, especially after the war's first battle practically wiped her out. He would be even more determined to put on a uniform and avenge his mother's death.

It was only when General Johnston retreated that Louisa's real troubles began—troubles that ended with her murder. Lee's prescient admonition had been on target. I hadn't listened! Bindle himself had told me straight on that I was a threat to the existing order back home, but I hadn't heeded his warning either. I had carelessly assumed that Bindle would be the only one to be sent after me. It was sweet, innocent Louisa who had paid the price for my negligence, though, not me.

If I could find a way to alter the outcome of this pivotal week of combat, if I could somehow derail the passage of events, it would ennoble her death and achieve the ultimate revenge. Hopefully some measure of atonement would come with it.

Since bidding farewell to Lee that strange night in Arlington, I had pretty well divided my time between living and working at the farm and traveling. I witnessed John Brown's trial and hanging, and I saw the future assassin John Wilkes Booth there, perhaps even then fascinated with death. I saw the fiery bombardment of Fort Sumter and the wild jubilation of the firebrands of Charleston, little suspecting they had played into Mr. Lincoln's hands. And it had all happened just as it had been written.

The battle at Manassas! The clouds of battlefield smoke had not been enough to obscure the dreadful personal nature of the struggle. Modern warfare, for all its savagery, was a sterile sandbox campaign compared to the killing grounds on Henry Hill. The frantic and doomed charges, the killing face to face, the terrible shrieks of maimed horses, and the mournful wails of dying men left me shaken in a way I wouldn't have thought possible. There were no medics with their red-crossed armbands rushing about, offering aid and comfort to the wounded. No battalion-aid stations with their plasma, penicillin, and morphine. Only limbs scattered about the arena or piled up around the surgeons' grisly tables. The fate of the animals was a heinous aspect of the battlefield. The terrified brutes were floundering around with legs blown off or racing to nowhere with their entrails trailing behind them and making unearthly bellows of protest. It was enough to shake even the most battle-hardened. The warriors all knew why they were there and were, for the most part, there of their own volition. But the animals' grotesque fate somehow seemed more obscene. They didn't know why they were being slaughtered.

The dangerously addictive "lust of the eye" had pulled me closer and closer until I risked getting swept up into the maelstrom. It was close enough to last a lifetime! I wondered how such horror could exist with God's knowledge.

Months after the Union defeat there, Johnston at last succumbed to his fears of decisive engagement and started his long withdrawal. The federals were quick to fill the void. At first their occupation wasn't particularly punitive, and relations between the civilians and the authorities were friendly enough and respecting of the common courtesies of the time. But as days lengthened into weeks and months, and Lincoln's efforts to neutralize support of the war effort in the occupied territories failed to bear fruit, the "heavy hand of war" began to get harsher and harsher.

Roaming bands of renegade soldiers, often with their commander's approval, confiscated or indiscriminately slaughtered livestock. Crops were burned, and the contents of smokehouses and granaries were confiscated. They vandalized and looted even the humblest of abodes. Families were uprooted from home and hearth as scavenging and outright theft took the place of civil order. Southern families were getting a preview of the horrors to come. Unlike McClellan and Lincoln himself, the Republicans in the Congress and administration had no desire for an early end to the war. Those men, wallowing in the Augean stable of abolitionist Washington, intended nothing less than the total destruction of the Southern way of life and the subjugation of its inhabitants. A long war was made to order for that purpose.

Betsy's ears pricked up as the short, quick rattle of small arms fire arrested my thoughts. Powell Hill's patience had at last run out, and the day's bloody events had begun!

I rejoined Lee just as he was giving the order to cross the river for the long awaited assault on General Porter's lines. He beckoned me to join him as he rode to join his divisions on the river's far side. His small staff followed closely behind us. I suspected they weren't enamored with the notion of a civilian on the battlefield and one so obviously in the confidence of their boss at that.

Porter's pickets were making an orderly retreat through Mechanicsville and leaving the field clear for his artillery to begin playing on Hill's rapidly advancing soldiers. This should have been the first clue for Lee to realize that not only had his operation been delayed but also that not all the parts in his intricate plan were working properly. I didn't know if he yet suspected Jackson hadn't arrived, but in any event, as soon as he met with Powell Hill, he would find out the hero of the Valley campaign was missing.

As we crossed the hastily repaired bridge to the plains facing Mechanicsville, he turned to me and remarked wryly that things weren't happening as he had hoped. The look on his face said everything. The thundering of Porter's heavy guns pounded the reverberating message home: not one soldier in gray could be out on Porter's right flank, and that not only had time run out for Lee but so had his options. However, as he would later write, he felt he had no choice but to continue the attack. To do otherwise would hand over to his opponent the tactical initiative, and that he was not prepared to do and couldn't do with Richmond's stripped defenses easy prey to McClellan's divisions.

Waves of oleaginous smoke, as thick as the accompanying sounds of killing, drifted down over us. As if the bilious puffs were the plague, the cohesive phalanx that was Powell Hill's advancing division began to dissolve into formless and mindless clots of vulnerable troopers. It was the bane of battlefield commanders the world over. It was the primordial urge to cling together, the herd instinct, and it was the very thing that always attracted the attention of enemy gunners. Still, the assault carried forward. Its destiny lay in the swamp waters of death ahead.

The closer we came to the battle area, the more animated Lee became. His customary ruddy and robust demeanor now replaced the earlier pasty and drawn look that had seemed to enervate him. It was as if he were saying to the world, "I may not be in complete control of events taking place, but I am back in command of myself." As the buzz of random shots began to whistle by, I could only marvel at his aplomb. He would be increasingly aware that if his audacious plan was to succeed, he would have to raise the stakes even higher and continue to press the attack far beyond the limits of an acceptable strategic risk.

We had entered that area of combat I always thought of as purgatory, where the best one could do is breakeven. It was that compressed unit of time and space where random death seemed anything but random. It was where you felt every enemy gun was aiming only at you.

The whole situation had become more than I bargained for, maybe more than I could deal with. For the first time since Louisa's murder, I forced myself to take stock of the obstacles facing me.

My understanding of the battlefield and the opposing forces' dispositions were only of a most general nature. I knew the approximate location of most of the major commands, but I had only anecdotal knowledge of the deployments of the various components of each command. Moreover, my familiarity with the terrain was of the most limited nature. I had no recall whatsoever of what the coming days' weather would bring. I couldn't remember any details of the general orders of the two opposing commanders. I had to conclude that I was grossly unprepared.

Jackson was lost somewhere off Lee's left flank. I had the advantage of knowing he wouldn't be linking up with Lee this day, and I even knew he was close enough that Lee could use him in a decisive way, if only anyone knew where he was. At one time I knew, but that was too long ago. Now I hadn't the foggiest. So even if Lee gave me the opportunity, I couldn't tell him where Jackson might be.

Here I was, being dragged along as a spectator of events just when something needed to be done. And all I really knew to do, if given the chance, would be to advise Lee to find Jackson. Find him at all costs; find him or the game would be up!

Lee had wandered off some distance from me with his staff in tow. No doubt he felt the burden of keeping the momentum going and putting a brave face on for his subordinates in spite of the near-total failure of his operational plan. He was busy now talking to one of Powell Hill's commanders, who had behind him a dispirited band of men in Union blue guarded rather casually by a dozen or so Confederates.

It was a strange sight. Not that there was anything at all standard about uniforms this early in the war. Later, the Union forces would achieve a more standardized look in keeping with a traditional military force. The Confederates too would achieve uniformity as the war progressed. Except theirs would be one of deficiency—almost all would eventually become the tattered and shoeless, ragtag remnants of once proud and near-invincible legions.

But for now the extravagant and gaudy military attire lent a comic air to the otherwise deadly business at hand. I could hear a band playing a popular ballad, and above the battlefield murmurs, I could even hear the skirl of bagpipes.

These men were wearing floppy field hats adorned with what looked to be deer tails. As they passed by, I asked the nearest man, a sergeant by the chevrons on his sleeve, what unit they were and what had happened.

"We are the Bucktails, Johnny. The Thirteenth Pennsylvania, and I'm sorry to say our captain put us in this mess we're in now. He got plumb away too. No matter, though. Little Mac will be here to get us pretty quick now. Say there, you wouldn't happen to have a plug on you, would you now, sir?"

I hadn't any tobacco to share. My smoking habits had changed quite a bit. Now I rolled my own like everyone else. Tobacco was easy to get for Southerners. Yankees would go to almost any lengths to trade for it. As would their rebel counterparts for one of the commodities already in short supply: coffee.

I just laughed and waved him on. The war was over for those guys, at least for a little while. Not much glory left for them. If they were lucky enough, they would get an early exchange for Southerners in a like predicament. If not, they would be spending time in a military prison, where their circumstances would be anything but glorious. By the war's end, some twenty-five thousand Union soldiers would die in Confederate prisoner-of-war camps. As appalling as that statistic most certainly was, the federal record was even worse. More than twenty-nine thousand

Southern captives died in Northern military prisons. It would be an especially sorry record since the Union had the means to feed and clothe their prisoners better, whereas the Confederacy was reduced by war's end to near starvation just for its own soldiers and civilian population.

By now the smoke and noise had made its way toward the low hills and murky swamps of Beaver Dam Creek. Already trickling out of that contested area was the inevitable residue of war. The battle-dazed were the first out. Those men had, for the first time in their lives, experienced that sublime awareness of life's fragility and the casual capriciousness of unannounced death. Mingling with those broken in spirit from both armies stumbled the left-behinds—those blue-jacketed unfortunates who just hadn't moved in time. Once bypassed by Powell Hill's rapidly moving soldiers, they had no place else to go except into their captors' waiting arms. And as on every battlefield came the skulkers and cowards. Gone was the splendor going in; only exhaustion, fear, and gratitude were left coming out. Such were always the early casualties of battle. High expectations and low fears lost in the reality of god-awful moments of bedlam and mayhem.

We had been slowly moving closer to the river where Harvey Hill's regiments were going into action when General Lee made toward me. His troubled face, already lined with the heavy responsibilities of his nation's survival, nevertheless seemed still hopeful and determined.

I felt nothing but frustration. Nothing had gone right since this morning for me either. My best intentions had gotten me nowhere.

Such was my detachment from the furies and wastage all around that I found myself in a peculiar state of heightened awareness. Every observation made and every sound heard only served to attune my senses. Instead of encumbering my reactions with the baggage of reasoning, it allowed me to react simply and smoothly. I knew exactly what it was, where it came from, and where it would land.

The shell shrieked overhead, and at what seemed like the exact same instant, a muffled explosion rocked the ground. Screams of rage and agony quickly filled the void left by the detonation.

But I had already swung Betsy over to the right and toward Lee. Like an image frozen in the brilliance of a flashing strobe light, his face told the story that I already knew. Somehow some Yankee gunners had avoided Hill's advancing columns and were now taking aim at the general commanding the Southern army.

I went past him at a dead gallop for all that my poor mare was worth. This was it. Now was the time; there wouldn't be another chance. This was all I would ever have. If I failed here, I would fail at each and every subsequent chance for redemption until there was nothing left—no chances and no propitiation. The war lost, Louisa unavenged, my soul damned. I rode on.

Another round—the ranging one—flew over. Its burst was even closer than the registration round. There was no time for looking back. Ahead, farther and faster was all there was. Already, Betsy's pace was beginning to lose its rhythm, its steady tempo. It was still so far away. But I could see them now. They were at the edge of a small cluster of bushes. Little stick figures clustered around two belching furnaces maybe two hundred yards away. How had the gray columns ever missed them? I pushed Betsy harder still.

I reached for the Colt. Its familiar heft was warm and comforting to my touch. Its soothing perfume of oil and powder lent strength and purpose for the killing to come. We were going so slowly, but somehow we had shortened the distance; I could see their faces now. Another crashing roar! The scorched air blasted against my face. I tasted the acid saltiness of blood.

Desperate men up ahead. The gun on the right—its gunner bringing his hand down to the breech, launching an instant sheet of fire and light and noise and thunder—looked downfield. The other gun stared straight ahead, confusion around the muzzle.

Betsy—God bless her—didn't fail me. One final burst, and we were there! An impact and a scream cut short as a heartbeat. A small, frail popping noise pulsed in cadence with a strange bucking in my hand. Another man, this one in dirty trousers and a stained, faded red shirt, down on the wet, crimson Virginia earth. With a bubbling snort of protest, Betsy shuddered to a dusty stop over his twitching body behind the gun trails.

A cracking sound and a "Goddamn you, rebel traitor. You went and killed old Arch."

He was running straight at me, swinging his still-smoking ramrod like a baseball bat. Over his shoulder another artillery-man's face scrunched up in indecision: run, fight, or surrender. I made his mind up for him, or rather the Colt did. The charging man stumbled and then fell to his knees, still snarling defiance. Then he too gave it up and joined his crewmate in that last reunion of old soldiers who just knew to do their duty.

There remained only the last of the gun crew to contend with: him and the other crew behind me.

I wasn't given time to worry about either. The soldier in front of me flung down his artilleryman's short sword and threw up his hands in surrender. But he was looking over my shoulder, even as he blubbered for mercy.

"Don't shoot me, please," he cried. It was the voice of man far from home and wishing he were there now.

"Run," I said, flicking my revolver toward the Confederate lines. "Run like you've never run before. Run, and always remember this moment, you son of a bitch. Think long and hard about it. Remember that your life was spared by those you were sent to kill."

He hesitated a moment, glanced again briefly beyond me, and took off, headed for the advancing gray lines, wildly waving his red kerchief while screaming like a banshee.

I started to turn to deal with the other gun crew, but I never got the chance!

A quiet, silky voice cut through the crashing sounds of conflict. "Dead still now, Professor Kelly. No, don't turn around."

It was a voice belied by what I knew was its owner's predator-like face.

"Looks like you won't be making it to the church on time," he said, laughing.

A chill settled over me, even as the post-adrenalin surge left me shaky and short of breath. Betsy snorted and trembled under me. There was a lull in the firecrackers of rifle fire in the distance. From somewhere I could hear the jingling and clatter of an artillery piece making for its firing position.

CHAPTER 17

I could feel his exact presence behind me and slightly to my left about ten yards away. The Colt dangled heavily in my right hand against Betsy's flank. Might as well have been on Mars!

"Ah, Colonel! I've been looking for you a very long time. I am here to stop you, and since you so kindly presented yourself today, I will take the opportunity to take care of you for good. I won't be taking too much of your time, little as it is."

I couldn't let him get away with it.

"But first, I want to tell you just how much I enjoyed killing your little rebel slut. I'm just sorry I didn't fuck her first. How was she in the sack, Kelly? Did she give good—"

With the pent-up frustration of revenge denied and this life lived for nothing, I pulled the trigger of the Colt, sending a round between Betsy's legs. Even with the noise of the battle-field, the explosion was incredibly loud. She lurched to the left, and at the same time, I spurred her cruelly, turning and twisting both of us farther leftward. She followed my lead perfectly. The effect was to leave me off balance but facing my adversary. As I swung the still-smoking pistol around, I saw he was wearing the uniform of a Union army officer.

Mr. Hawkface was even more off balance and facing slightly away from me. He was desperately trying to reorient himself and his aim as I brought the Colt to bear.

It was a race in which I had the advantage. My move had forced him to bring his gun arm around across his body—an awkward firing position, even for the best of shooters. And his mount wasn't cooperating as it pawed the ground in excitement. I had to give it to him, though. He never hesitated. Still intent on me—his prey—his arm completed its pendulum swing across his body and toward me. I could see the whiteness of his gripped fist as he tightened his pull on the trigger. But he would be too late. With not a twinge of remorse, I squeezed the grip of the Colt, anticipating the sweet satisfaction of a roaring pistol fired in a righteous cause.

Click!

It all happened at once: the firing pin hit a spent cartridge, Hawkface's triumphant grin, and a faraway cannon roar followed almost immediately by the ground heaving around our arena of mortal combat.

Civil War-era artillery was a work in progress, especially on the Confederate side. Seldom able to match their federal counterparts in the quantity or the quality of ordnance, as well as in gunnery skills, Southern gunners had to contend with more than their share of dud rounds and poorly synchronized fuses. With the most rudimentary technology, it was fortunate indeed when artillery rounds actually performed as intended.

I wasn't sure whose gun it was or even what type of round. What I did know was that I was on my back, looking up into a graying Southern sky with no air in my lungs. The smell of burning flesh and the hideous bellowing of tortured animal propelled me to my knees, retching out my innards.

Throwing aside the empty pistol, I scrabbled on my hands and knees over to the lately-departed Arch for the short sword he no longer needed. Weapon in hand, I struggled to my feet and cast about for my adversary. He was crawling toward his bellowing horse. Betsy was nowhere to be seen.

More fire was incoming now. The noises of combat were more immediate and louder, and time was getting shorter. All that mattered now was Louisa's murderer. He reached the poor flailing animal and somehow managed to unsheathe his cavalryman's carbine.

I was in the open with only the artillery sword, which was little more than a long knife. He swung the carbine around my way as I flung myself to the ground. The sharp crack was followed by a low cry and the sound of a falling body. I leapt up to charge him, hoping it was only a single shot carbine. I intended to hack the sorry son of a bitch to pieces before he was able to get in another shot. I had never had to use a knife—let alone a sword—in any kind of fight, but it was all I had.

Throwing his spent carbine aside, he took off running past me. It was actually a fast limp. It looked like he had pretty sizable wound in his leg. Before I could react, he reached a horse whose hapless owner was writhing on the ground. A few seconds later, he was on the steed, and with a last malevolent look at me, he spurred the horse up the road past Mechanicsville.

He was getting away, and I couldn't do much about it. So far, I wasn't faring so well in my efforts to thwart Clay or to avenge Louisa's death. On the plus side, I was alive, which, considering my prospects a few minutes earlier, was quite an achievement.

The reason he was in such a big hurry became immediately apparent with the cloud-of-dust arrival of a squad of troopers headed by a young lieutenant—a staff officer by the looks of his spiffy clean uniform.

"Suh, General Lee's compliments! That was quite a bit of derring-do! You might near whipped them boys all your own self. Can't say the major fared so well, though. He appears to be *hors de combat*."

He barked out a quick order, sending several of his men to tend to the unfortunate officer. I hoped he would be all right. He, after all, had taken the bullet intended for me.

"General Lee said to provide any assistance you might need, Colonel Kelly."

I looked over to the other Yankee gun. The tube was pointing impotently up at the cloudless sky. Probably the same battery that had damned near put me out of action had rendered it ineffective.

I made a quick decision. Hawkface was just rounding a curve and out of sight.

I pointed that way and said, "Lieutenant, that man must be stopped. Can you help me?"

"What are your orders, Colonel?"

"I need a man that knows this area and is willing to go with me behind the Yankee lines. And I need the rest of your men to go after that man. He is dangerous, so take no chances. But he must be stopped, one way or the other."

In less than a minute, I was on Betsy heading northeast on Old Church Road out of Mechanicsville. My guide was a young fellow named Priestley. His family's home was north of Richmond, close to Hanover courthouse. He claimed to know the area well, and it appeared he did.

The lieutenant had taken the rest of his men north on the turnpike after Hawkface. I didn't have much hope they would be able to run him down.

While reloading the Colt, I had time to reflect on Hawkface's presence. It was obvious why he was here. Me! Was he

Paul's backup? Probably! That made sense at least. But why it had turned into a grudge on his part didn't.

Young Priestley was pointing out a potential problem ahead. A unit was moving at the double-quick north of the road and into the open field to our left. It was a company of gray-clad Southern boys. It was part of a larger unit, probably a regiment, which was deploying to the northeast. A rider had separated himself from what looked to be the command element and was headed our way.

The battle sounds had been diminishing the farther we traveled from Mechanicsville but were now picking up quite a bit as Powell Hill began moving his brigades forward to test the federal lines firmly entrenched above Beaver Dam Creek. Hill, sometimes more familiarly known as A. P. Hill, was attempting to turn the right of Porter's lines and probably still hoping Jackson would finally show up. But it would not be today.

The rider pulled up in a cloud of dust and bluster. "Who are you men? What is your unit? What business do you have here?" he demanded.

It was a fair enough question. We were in the rear of units being roughly handled by an army invading their homeland. There would be many a Southern family mourning their fallen husbands, fathers, and sons as a result of this day's work. It would be the rare or incompetent commander who wouldn't demand to know the identity of two strangers in the midst of his deployment, especially when one wasn't in uniform.

Fortunately, young Priestley was in uniform and possessed a quick mind.

"Cap'n, I'm Corporal Del Priestley, attached to General Lee's headquarters. I'm escorting Colonel Kelly at the order of the general commanding this army, General Lee himself."

I was impressed and the captain was too, at least momentarily.

"That's easy to say, Corporal, but maybe not so easy to prove. Far as I can see, you could be a deserter, and unless your friend here has papers to prove his bona fides, he just might be one of those spies we've been told to watch for."

He made a move toward the pistol at his side, but it was tentative and halfhearted. He was out of his depth and didn't quite know what to do. I could almost feel sorry for him.

Priestley had shot his best shot. Now he looked at me with that classic enlisted man's expression that shouted out, "Okay, sir, you got us into this, now show us how smart you are and get us out of it."

Although it had been years since I'd had to use it, some things one doesn't forget, and the voice of command was one of them.

"Captain, it looks like we're going to need safe passage through your lines. Can you arrange that, or will we need to talk to your commander? By the way, just what unit are you with, and who is your commander?"

To his credit, he made a fast decision and cut his losses.

"I reckon you don't look like no damn Yankees. Don't sound like 'em none either. You can get going now. Just mind you stay clear of the fighting."

He turned to go, but now that I had the upper hand, he wasn't about to get off that easy. Besides, we might need a little assistance getting through the lines ahead. And the best way to do that was to make a lasting impression and to find out the unit and commander.

He interrupted his turn only when he saw I wasn't taking him up on his dismissal. He started to fidget and look for a way to extricate himself from what had turned out to be a no-win situation.

I waited until he made the first move. It didn't take long.

With a barely audible sigh, he turned back, saluted, and snapped out a parade ground report. "Captain Jenks, sir. Adjutant, Fourteenth Georgia, General Anderson's brigade. As you can see, Colonel, our orders are to root those blue-coated bastards out of the creek area. Do you want to meet our regimental commander? He's kind of busy now—maybe after we get the companies on line. If you would like to wait back—"

What he really wanted was for us to get out of his hair with the least commotion possible. And what I wanted was safe passage through the rapidly-forming lines ahead.

It was getting late. "Captain Jenks, I really don't have time to visit with your commander, and as you say, he has plenty to do for the time being. My respects, and please ask him to see to it that my corporal and I get through your lines up toward Hundley's Corner."

Young Priestley was smiling from ear to ear. I could do no wrong in his eyes now.

Five minutes later, we were on our way past the deploying Southerners off to our right. We were traveling on a line roughly parallel with the headwaters of Beaver Dam Creek. According to Priestley, we were about two miles from Hundley's Corner, which lay at the intersection of Pole Green Church Road and Shady Grove Church Road.

It was there, or in that vicinity, that we would find Jackson's command, if we didn't wind up getting ourselves shot first!

As we crossed a feeder stream at a rundown farmhouse, I mused on the irony of how the man sent to stop me from changing the world was to be the instrument of me doing just that.

"Sir?"

I was laughing out loud at the sheer justice of it all.

"Corporal, have you ever wondered why things turn out like they do?"

"Sir?"

I couldn't blame him. Here we were, slipping between thousands of the bitterest enemies trying their damnedest to kill one another, just so we could get to an obscure country church—for what reason, he couldn't possibly figure—and I was laughing and asking goofy questions. In the eyes of an enlisted man, typical officer behavior.

But it was funny. I hadn't had the vaguest notion where Jackson was until Louisa's murderer showed up. He had the drop on me, but he had to gloat; he had to rub my face in it before doing the job he was there to do. That was the part I didn't understand: his needless and costly injection of personalities into his mission. Why the offensive and hateful remarks about Louisa? Why kill her at all? It was as if he were exacting revenge for something I had done to him.

I could think about that later. What was important for now was his little joke about "not getting to the church on time." That remark did it. It was the catalyst that took me back to Clifford Dowdey's study of the Seven Days campaign that I had read decades before. I only wished I remembered more of it. It would come in handy right about now.

Now that would be a paradox for sure! If I remembered enough of it to know exactly when and where to concentrate on changing the outcome—and was successful in doing so—then Dowdey's book, as written, would not have been. And if that were the case, then there would be no reference to a church for me to be reminded of. Maybe I wouldn't even be here trying to alter the results. But if I weren't here to change the battle, then the book would have been written: round and round reasoning, *ad infinitum*.

What I did know now, courtesy of Hawkface, was this: Jackson had made his premature camp for the day in the vicinity of

Hundley's Corner, not far from Pole Green Church. And there was where we were heading. Priestley knew right where it was and exactly how to get there.

I still didn't have the faintest idea what I was going to do when I got there. No matter! I had to feel lucky to have gotten this far.

And something else significant had occurred too. Lee, by sending his troopers to render me all possible assistance, had tacitly acquiesced to my intentions to influence the day's events. Or so it seemed.

There was plenty of activity off to our right front. The ever-present rattle of small arms, punctuated by an occasional pounding of cannon fire, waxed and waned as we so slowly distanced ourselves from the battle area. But as that danger receded, we were increasingly at risk from cavalry units screening Porter's extended flanks.

I should have paid more attention to what I was doing and less to what I had no control over.

We hadn't any warning. One second we were safely negotiating the wooded terrain toward the road just appearing through the greenery ahead, and the next we were in the midst of a squad of blue-coated mounted troopers.

"Bejabbers, now! What do we have here? And who might you gentlemen be? Look here, Aloysius, as I live and breathe, if it ain't one of them there non-combatants!"

With the exception of the Irishman, a burly sergeant, the rest were young. Young and nervous, and, I prayed, not too jumpy with their trigger fingers. Every last one of them was pointing his rifle straight at poor Priestley, who seemed not at all concerned.

I was, though!

One thing I couldn't do was to let it play out. They had the upper hand, and it would only get stronger the longer we were at the disadvantage. The best chance to make an escape was as soon after capture as possible. The capturing soldiers were themselves the weakest link in the chain of events that would take us farther and farther back behind their lines. The farther back we were taken, the more the herding of prisoners would become organized and institutionalized. Plus, unfamiliarity with the area and the sheer distance to travel all made escape from the enemy's interior lines less and less likely.

"Let's have your rifle now, laddy, like a good fellow," the sergeant growled. He was the one I would tend to first.

We did have a small advantage. The young troopers were concentrating almost exclusively on Priestley. The sergeant, though, never took his squinted eyes off me, even as he ordered the corporal to un-sling his carbine. He was to my left front, directly in front of Priestley, with his men arrayed to my front and right. The Irishman couldn't see my right arm dangling against my leg, where I could feel the bulk of the Colt in my coat pocket, but he was straining his neck around to see what I was about.

The trick was going to be to move at just the time when I hoped everyone would be focusing their attention away from me.

Time to make that happen!

"Give it to him, Corporal," I said. "They caught us fair and square."

As I intended, when Priestley obediently extended his arm with his carbine, the sergeant's eyes momentarily shifted to the proffered weapon. As I casually as I could, I slipped my hand into my coat pocket and pulled out the Colt.

I pulled it out, firing. This wasn't the time for squeamishness.

The .44 caliber slug lifted the big Irishman out of his saddle and upside down with his left boot caught in his stirrup. With a frightening shriek, his horse bolted past us, dragging the poor man behind him and knocking Priestley from his mount.

I had tightened my grip on the reins, so I had Betsy under control, even before shooting. The remaining soldiers were desperately trying to bring their weapons around to bear while struggling to cope with their startled horses. One of the youngsters was careening northward, either running away or simply at the mercy of a horse he couldn't manage. I silently thanked the fact that until much later in the war, the federal cavalry was terribly inept.

That made five of them left. The Colt barked out its lethal staccato twice more, and now there were three. Two had steadied their horses and were attempting to bring their weapons to bear. The third man had had enough; he threw his carbine down and raised his hands in surrender. The other two may have been young and scared, but they were gutsy all the same. It was a shame too because it would just be more wasted lives. I shoved those emotions aside and hardened my heart. They were in the wrong place, namely in a land their masters were determined to conquer. And they were here to compel free men to submit to a government not of their own choosing—to demand allegiance at the point of a gun. They deserved not an instant of regrets.

Tightening my grip on the revolver, my next victim's face leapt out with a heartrending surreal clarity. He was crying! Salty furrows lined a dusty face. I was killing a teenager, a pimply kid, crying over having to kill his first man. Well, I was just going to have to save him the trouble. He was about to shed his last tear. He was a dead man—a dead *boy*. Another dead boy, one after another! I tensed my grip in anticipation of the recoil.

A shot rang out.

Priestley, leaning against a tree, was pointing his still smoking revolver at the three soldiers. A shattered weapon lay on the ground in front of them.

"Throw 'em down," he commanded, with a threatening wave of his pistol.

They'd had enough. With their sergeant dead and two pistols trained on them, they really had no choice. The two boys dropped their carbines and raised their hands. Was that relief on their young faces? Was it relief for young lives spared, or was it for the brief respite from the demands of adulthood?

I slowly lowered my arm, aghast. What had I almost done? What had I already done? With no compunction at all, I had killed three men and was set to kill three more. Except for the sergeant, they were youngsters a little older than Tom. I had given it no thought, except to justify it in a way I had never done before. It had been so easy to pull the trigger and so easy to excuse. Vietnam hadn't affected me that way. It was this place. No, it wasn't the place. It was the time! Except it wasn't that either. It had to do with me—the change in me.

But in changing, what had I given up? Had I, like so many men at war, simply regressed back to barbarism? What would be next?

"What do we do with them, Colonel? We can't stay here long. There are probably more just like this bunch between here and the church. They're thicker than fleas around here. The one that got away is sure to be bringing more of those blue-bellied bastards this way."

Priestley was right. This was a hot area. And we were tantalizingly close now to Stonewall. Too close to be tarrying here any longer, and too dangerous to be saddled with prisoners. There was nothing else for it.

"You men skedaddle back to where you came from. I'd suggest you make it all the way back to your hometown, if you can, because if I ever see you again, you'll be joining your friends in hell instead. And on your way, you might spend a little time thinking about the motives of those who sent you here.

"And you there. Yes, you, with the chicken hanging from your saddle. So you are nothing more than a pack of common thieves stealing food from the starving mouths of Southern women and children. Or is it that you are just liberating chickens from the clutches of evil rebels? Is that what father Abraham sent you here for?"

Half a minute later, they were out of sight, and we were on our way again. They would have to explain to their commander how they had managed to lose their weapons and their sergeant, all at the same time. I hoped that most soldiers' natural propensity to avoid having to tell superiors bad news would give us a few extra minutes to vacate the area.

As it turned out, we didn't need the time. No sooner had we reached the road to Hundley's Corner—Shady Grove Church Road—than, once again, we found ourselves surrounded and looking at the business ends of rifle barrels.

Only this time, gray-uniformed troopers wielded them.

We had found Jackson!

CHAPTER 18

"Let me get this straight. You claim to come from General Lee, and you need to talk to General Jackson. You have important information, but you have no dispatch and no proof of who you say you are. You are not in uniform, and you have strange mannerisms. Yet you want me to rouse the general to meet with you about certain information you possess."

The man in front of me didn't know it yet, but he had a rendezvous with destiny far beyond his most ambitious dreams. Instead of a sometimes-deserved reputation as a self-serving officer, and instead of an ignominious and early death in a Yankee prisoner-of-war camp, Brigadier General Chase Whiting would, this very night, reverse the fortunes of a beleaguered Confederacy and pave the way for his inclusion in the pantheon of Southern patriots.

"Your corporal is authentic enough, and he does seem to know the area," he continued. "Maybe he can help us tomorrow. But you, sir, you are an enigma. You have the air of a soldier, an officer, but with what army? And where did you find such a pistol, an army Colt, with a quality of construction too sophisticated, even for Yankee manufacturers?"

We were sitting on campstools alongside a dilapidated rail fence close to the juncture of Pole Green Church and Shady Grove Church roads. The summer sun was casting longer shadows now as the day faded into a tomorrow of fruitless slaughter. But it wasn't going to be. I was determined to end it tonight, and this rather intemperate soldier was going to make the decision to believe the unbelievable. Even more so, he was going to do the unthinkable: he was going to defy the volatile and occasionally-vindictive Stonewall Jackson. While the exhausted Jackson would be sleeping the early morning hours away, General Whiting was going to lead his division on to Porter's withdrawing corps.

"Can you satisfy my doubts, Colonel Kelly?" he demanded.

He began idly replacing the cartridges in my pistol as he studied me with melancholy eyes. He looked like a less dissipated Edgar Allen Poe, but I knew him to be far more than that. He was a complex and gifted man with the attendant flaws those such as he always seemed to possess in abundance. He was brilliant and fearless too.

What I needed now were his ambition, impatience, and impetuosity. That, and his courage.

I glanced over to the small knots of soldiers twenty or thirty feet distant. Priestley was laughing with the men who had brought us to Jackson's lines. Another smaller group, staff and command officers, was just out of earshot but watching us closely. The towering giant of a man, John Bell Hood of Texas, easily stood out.

I shifted my body slightly to reach into my coat pocket for the same Beretta and plastic calendar I had used almost three years earlier.

We were moving easily through a night punctuated by bursts of musket fire and occasional thuds of distant artillery. As the starlit night parted for our lead column, it just as rapidly closed behind us. Our guides—including young Priestley, just back from his mission deep into the enemy's rear—were just a few yards ahead but barely visible in the gloom. Whiting seemed oblivious to the potential difficulties that lay ahead.

And they were tremendous difficulties, indeed! Not only were we attempting a complicated military maneuver, a movement-to-contact at night, we were traveling over terrain that lay well behind our foe's positions—behind them and square in the middle of their interior lines of communication. None of us, except for Priestley, had even seen the area of operations before. And we intended to engage a superbly trained and equipped force fresh from an impressive trouncing of Hill's attacking division. On top of all those disadvantages, our target was a force maybe eight times larger than our own.

Our one advantage, the element of surprise, was wholly dependent on our ability to move undetected into the enemy's rear—that and my imperfect memory of when Porter would begin his withdrawal to the high ground south of Dr. Gaines's mill.

Whiting, the engineer, had quickly realized the items I carried couldn't possibly have come from this century. He had bought into my tale of time travel with an alacrity and eagerness bordering on recklessness. He accepted me exactly as I presented myself. Whiting, the general, hadn't bothered with philosophical imponderables, either. Fighting generals met opportunity decisively, and my appearance here represented a combat opportunity to be exploited. If he had been able to articulate it in modern army doctrine, he would have thought of me as the ultimate force multiplier. He readily grasped the situation and the opportunities it afforded, and he presented not one whit of concern for his boss's vaunted temper and sometimes spiteful pettiness. In fact, he was almost openly contemptuous of the Valley hero.

I couldn't have asked for a better response.

After absorbing my wild tale and my knowledge of Porter's movement tonight, he had quickly summoned his staff and brigade commanders. He had introduced me only as an envoy from Lee carrying vital intelligence on enemy movements. With only token objections from the slender and ramrod erect Evander Law about the impropriety of acting without informing Stonewall, there was a buzz of excitement about finally facing an enemy most hadn't seen since Manassas.

Next, he had sent advance parties from both brigades to scout the two likely routes—Old Cold Harbor Road and River Road—the federal forces would have to use in withdrawing from Beaver Dam Creek. Corporal Priestley was in his element here, so he led the way. After reaching the point where the road we were presently traveling crossed Old Church Road, the detachment from Law's brigade was to continue for another mile or so and reconnoiter the area around the junction of Old Cold Harbor Road and Telegraph Road for the best blocking positions. Hood's advance party was to continue on Telegraph Road to New Bridge Road and then on toward the Chickahominy to River Road. Theirs would be the more difficult task. They not only had to determine the best blocking positions, but they also would need to consider the potential threat from across the river.

After establishing the best locations, they were to be prepared to guide their respective brigades into position. It was up to Priestley to marry us up with those guides.

There hadn't been difficulty getting away from the rest of Jackson's command. Jackson himself had been no problem—he was sound asleep. His factotum and confidant, Reverend Dabney, would have been the biggest concern, but Whiting, with the decisiveness of a man accustomed to dealing with such lesser mortals, had one of his staff officers contrive to distract him until we were well on our way.

The other division commanders may or may not have known we were leaving the bivouac site, but they chose not to interfere or question our departure. This may have been due to Stonewall's well-known propensity for secrecy. They would have every reason to believe the man himself had ordered our movement and predictably neglected to inform anyone else. With his volatile nature, it was doubtful if either could imagine any Jackson subordinate acting on his own.

Thus Jackson's greatest strength and weakness—his penchant for secrecy and speed and his intimidating temperament—were already dominating today's events. Although the campaign's demands on his physical health had rendered him incompetent to command, his reputation would work to his cause's advantage this morning.

Jackson's phantom presence off on his right flank, and his inherent distaste for decisive engagement, gave McClellan all the excuses he needed to suspend Porter's successful defense of Beaver Dam Creek and to order tonight's anabasis to Gaines Mill.

I couldn't help but feel buoyed by the way things were turning out.

After finding Jackson's army, I fell into the hands of the one Confederate general officer with the imagination, courage, opportunism, and disdain for the fearsome Stonewall to put his career and reputation on the line.

In the interest of noise security, General Whiting had opted for leaving his artillery batteries and our mounts behind. There were no supply trains; every man was loaded with all the water and ammunition he could carry and only one meal. Commanders had issued warnings on the importance of stealth and had even taken the extraordinary measure of ordering weapons to be left unloaded or unprimed. Regardless of those most rigorous efforts, though, thousands of men moving in the still of the night make a lot of noise. It seemed inconceivable we could remain undetected.

Whiting also left his staff chief behind. His most unenviable job was to explain to Jackson where one of his divisions was. I wouldn't want to be in his shoes.

One thing I knew for sure: either General Chase Whiting would end up a true hero of the Confederate nation or he would be arrested and court-martialed. He could end up dead too, which might be preferable considering the alternative if tonight's action turned belly up on us. I had no doubt he knew exactly what to expect if the die rolled bad, and I was just as sure that understanding would make his efforts tonight all the more energetic. It was beyond imagining what my fate might be.

It was getting close on to midnight, and we were just starting up a gentle slope after a sharp bend in the road to the southeast, when out of nowhere, a light magically appeared dead ahead. Before I could do more than register that fact on an increasingly fatigued mind and body, the low murmur of conspiratorial voices, all regional, reassured me there was no danger to our cause here. We were at the intersection of our narrow road and a wider, more traveled road—Old Church Road!

A few seconds later, Priestley appeared at our side and saluted. "Sir, Mr. Richardson says there've been some Yankees along Old Cold Harbor Road ahead. His boy just got back and told him a party of five soldiers on horseback passed the church going down Telegraph just about an hour ago. He said it would have been a snap to waylay them and what a shame it was to let them bunch of looters go. He hasn't heard anything from his oldest out at River Road."

Whiting returned his salute. "Good work, Corporal. Thank Mr. Richardson, would you please? Tell him we will make sure his son gets back safely. How much farther do you figure to the road to Old Cold Harbor? We need to get Colonel Law's regiments in place before too long."

"Yes, sir, it's just about a mile ahead. Our lead element will pass Walnut Grove Church in just a few minutes, and General Hood will have another two miles to get to the Hogan place. Mr. Richardson says to tell you Major Coles is ready for you and Colonel Law and that he's got some good positions picked out. Should be able to give them Yankees you know what!"

Whiting sent the word back to close ranks and step up the pace. The night closed in on us again as the cloudy skies gained ascendancy over a golden moon.

I was getting too old for this business, and increasing the pace didn't help. While the last three years had toughened me, I was also three years older and that much worse for wear. Moreover, I had been up since before dawn, ridden hell for leather into battle, confronted my arch foe, and, in the process of all that, killed several men. I could feel the shakes gathering in exhaustion's wake, even though the night's dealings were only just starting. God help me if I fell apart now. I couldn't let that happen now. Not now when everything was at stake.

A deep breath and a supreme effort kept me going for a while, one foot placed in front of the other—a jittery psyche willing a reluctant body to maintain that simple repetitive motion. I couldn't see how it would be enough, though. I was burned out. I willed myself to take just one more step and then another. Again and again! Physical pain now accompanied every torturous step. I couldn't do it—I had used too much up. Just a few more steps now, and then I was going to have to give it up, to admit I couldn't hack it. I was going to fall out of a march. I was sick with self-loathing, but I was past caring. I could go no farther.

Now silvery stars cast a tree's waving shadow on the road ahead. I angled toward it pretending I was only stopping long enough to relieve myself. Kelly the malingerer!

Then the shadows turned into men, then several more came out of the underbrush. Just to the right was the unmistakable silhouette of a church against the dusty backdrop of Old Cold Harbor Road.

We had reached our first phase line with no problems, which was quite an achievement for upward of four thousand men marching through enemy territory in the middle of the night.

Just like that, the wounded nerves and the wobbly legs got a shot of adrenaline. I knew it would be only a temporary fix, but it would get me a little farther down the road and through the night's work.

As planned, General Whiting peeled off with Law's columns, while ours continued on ahead. I was going with Hood to the southernmost of our blocking positions. With a fresh burst of energy and resolve, I surged abreast with Priestley. Hood's long strides ate up the dusty road ahead as he set the pace, leaving the two of us to play catch up. He was a big man in every way. It was just as it had always been: me taking twice as many steps as the big guys.

At this pace, we would be getting to our positions in thirty minutes or so. I was going to make it fine now, but it was still an effort. When we got there, I was going to chill out. Catch up on some sleep, I hoped. It had to be getting on to one o'clock or well past a murky midnight anyway.

McClellan would spend some time at Beaver Dam Creek tonight before departing for the other side of the Chickahominy. I didn't know exactly when that would be, but I did remember that Porter would begin his withdrawal sometime early this morning and that it would be largely completed by seven o'clock. All in all, the movement would be a stunning success. In a masterpiece of deception, most of his command would safely reach the high ground near Gaines Mill. Those men and guns would inflict grievous casualties on the rebels before retreating again for Lee's first win of the campaign.

But lost would be his grand plan to force McClellan into battle. It would die with the wasted day fighting at Gaines Mill. In fact, it will have already succumbed to McClellan's fears for his logistical lifeline. Soon after arriving back at his headquarters this morning, he would direct Porter's withdrawal and give the order to move the massive supply base at White House Landing. Instead of a climactic, war-ending struggle somewhere between the Chickahominy and the Pamunkey rivers, Lee would end up chasing McClellan across the peninsula. After terrible losses at Malvern Hill overlooking the James River, Lee's efforts to destroy the invading army would finally be over.

Whiting had proved to be a quick study. I outlined the troop dispositions as best as I could recall and reiterated the overview of Lee's vision for seizing the initiative from McClellan. I didn't have to elaborate much on Porter's withdrawal to Gaines Mill—his soldier's mind saw the inevitability of McClellan's decision to vacate Beaver Dam Creek to a more easily-supported stronghold. He had no trouble grasping the tactical situation or the strategic implications of squandering a day of fighting at Gaines

Mill, either. The potential for a dramatic reversal in the fortunes of war had been more than evident to him.

This strange man, whose wartime achievements rarely lived up to his pre-war credentials, had wasted no time dithering over the best course of action. His was not to seek safe havens. He put his trust in even a stranger man than himself—namely me—and then quickly satisfied himself that Priestley did, in fact, know the area well. Afterward, it was just a matter of having his staff work out the details of getting a division on the move.

The situation was this: if we could impede Porter's withdrawal to Gaines Mill, a day of battle might be averted. Porter, his corps in extended march order, would be at his most vulnerable. Unable to deploy his artillery, and ambushed by a force of unknown size in the hours of darkness, he would have few options. He couldn't know we were a rogue division of only modest size. And he couldn't know that ours was not part of a coordinated attack. He would have to assume Lee was poised to strike his exposed rear as we blocked his movement to the high ground of Gaines Mill. And to seal his fate, the wily Jackson would probably be waiting to pounce just as he became decisively engaged.

If he decided to fight through us, we had the advantage of position and surprise. After our first volleys, confusion would reign within the federal leadership, but only up to a point. Porter had over thirty thousand men. Sheer numbers ultimately must prevail. The veterans of Porter's Fifth Corps could well-abandon their equipment and supplies and easily move through our lines.

If that happened—the worst-case scenario for us—he would almost certainly be without his one edge over Lee: his artillery. Without that advantage, and with his formations broken up by our ambush, he would be unlikely to consider defending Gaines

Mill. Instead, he would be forced to cross the Chickahominy and rejoin the main body of McClellan's invasion army.

If there were no battle tomorrow, Lee would gain that essential day in his grand plan to flush McClellan out in the open. As soon as McClellan heard the sounds of battle here, if he hadn't already done so, he would issue orders to make his change of base to the James. In the world already passed, Lee would always be one step behind in his attempts to engage the Army of the Potomac as it retreated across the peninsula. In this world, the one day saved at Gaines Mill might just give Lee his chance to force McClellan to fight.

Of course, with his army largely intact, McClellan could always strike toward Richmond—his original objective. A massive and coordinated attack could overwhelm Magruder's holding force, and the Confederate plum would be easy pickings for the Little Napoleon. The fearful residents of the capital should have little cause to worry, though. While the always-cautious general might be able to overcome his reluctance to attack what he still considered a superior force, his very real and legitimate concern would be his overextended lines of communication. Taking Richmond might be a symbolic victory of some significance to Lincoln and the Northern public, but it would doom his army, and he would know it. In spite of his manifold shortcomings as a combat leader, he was an astute student of the maxims of war. With near one hundred twenty thousand men and thousands of horses wholly dependent on a secure railroad line stretching from White House Landing across the Chickahominy into his positions, he would instinctively understand its vulnerability to an opportunistic opponent.

That was the worst case for us, but perhaps the best for General Lee. On the other hand, if we managed to stop Porter, there was always the chance he might just repair back to Beaver Dam Creek. It was certainly a possibility, given his enthusiasm for staying and his confidence in defending that position against Hill's hapless Light Division. By staying, though, his command—however formidable their defense might be—would be isolated and surrounded. The bulk of the Army of Northern Virginia would be arrayed against him with his back to the Chickahominy. There could be no escape. McClellan then would truly face a Hobson's choice: he could sally forth to relieve what constituted more than one-third of his army, or he could secure his base. As long as General Magruder kept his nerve and blocked the approaches into the Confederate capital, and as long as McClellan remained convinced of his own numerical inferiority, his very own nature and the demands of protecting his lifeline would dictate his response. He would abandon Richmond and his Fifth Corps to save the remainder of his army and his logistical base.

Then, Lee would have a bird in the hand. He would have an entire corps with all their artillery at his mercy. With McClellan running with what was left of his tattered reputation, Lee would have the luxury of simply waiting for Porter's inevitable capitulation. Or he could fix him in place with a portion of his force and then pursue McClellan with the rest, including Magruder's twenty-three thousand men.

If it came to it, I figured he would go for the war-ending prize. But that was in the unknowable future.

After passing Old Cold Harbor Road, we broke out of wooded areas and into shrubby terrain. With satisfaction, I noted that Priestley was breathing heavier and had fallen silent. Indeed, Hood's pace seemed a little slower and more irregular too. Suited me just fine!

"Halt! Is that y'all? You pert near making enough racket. We heard you coming a mile away."

Out of the dim shadows appeared a lanky Texan. His East Texas twang was as distinctive now as it would be more than a century later. He was quickly joined by several more of his comrades all gathering around their commander.

We had reached New Bridge Road!

"General Hood, you made it in fine time, sir, but it's getting on. If you don't mind following Clem here, we can get to our positions directly. It's down the road a bit more than a mile or so on the other side of the creek," said a short, balding officer. "Are we going to leave any of our boys here, or are Colonel Law's people going to be able to keep them off our right? We're pretty much dangling here—makes me right nervous, stuck back here like we are—especially with the entire Yankee nation sitting at our backdoor only a couple of miles away on our left."

Hood snagged a staff officer and instructed him to have Colonel Marshall leave a company of the Fourth Texas forward of the intersection at the tree line and to be prepared to stop any wagons or guns getting past Law, at least until he could get some reinforcements to him. We continued on the road to New Bridge and the intersection with River Road.

We had upwards of two thousand Southern boys to defend a line of more than a half mile. That was pretty thin, but surprise, darkness, and terrain would offset much of that disadvantage. Since the tree line stretched about a hundred yards forward of the New Bridge Road and Hood intended to set his lines there, we would also have the advantage of the road to facilitate moving our infantrymen to where most needed.

We all figured Porter would have to use the two main roads coming out of the Beaver Dam Creek area to move his command. That was pretty well a certainty, given the terrain and the darkness. Those two main roads—Old Cold Harbor Road to Telegraph Road, where Law's men were laying in ambush, and River Road—were roughly parallel with the Chickahominy. They both led to the general vicinity of the high ground southeast of Gaines Mill, where Porter intended to make a stand. Telegraph Road was in better condition for Porter's guns and supply trains and had the additional advantage of being a straighter route.

River Road couldn't be ignored either. Porter would almost have to make use of that route, if for no other reason than the sheer numbers he had to move. Del Priestley was our ace in the hole here. He enabled us to supplement our rudimentary maps and drawings with detailed knowledge of the terrain and the condition of the roads.

We all agreed that Porter would more than likely use the southern route for his infantry. That was us. We had a marginally larger force than Law's brigade, which was tasked with stopping the heavy guns and material movement. There would be some combat units guarding that precious supply line, but, for the most part, Law would probably be facing non-combatants. His task might be less hazardous than ours but was infinitely more important. Without his big guns and the supplies to sustain his force, Porter Fifth Corps would turn into a colossal liability for McClellan.

For us, Hood's Texas Brigade, we would be contending with the bulk of Porter's battle-hardened infantry. And to add to the mix, as Hood's staff officer had noted, only the Chickahominy protected us from the remaining eighty thousand men of McClellan's invasion force. The river was a formidable obstacle, but the Northerners boasted the finest engineering units on the continent. Priestley knew of some of the fording points and the New Bridge, but he was uninformed about any other bridges the Yankees might have erected. Certainly one, and maybe two, would be in the vicinity of tomorrow's battlefield near Gaines Mill.

My ruminations came to an end with the terminus of our midnight march. We had reached River Road.

CHAPTER 19

The faint rumble of faraway weaponry hadn't prepared us for what was at hand. We couldn't see them yet. But we could see the fearsome, yellow glow of their lanterns weaving and flickering like feral eyes looming from blackened caves, and we could hear the dreadful cadence of thousands of booted feet. I felt the dread pulsating up and down our fragile lines. The notion that this pitifully-small band of men could challenge the approaching juggernaut now seemed obscenely criminal.

What could I have been thinking?

Yet we would have to now. We were where they were going. There would be no reprieve for us!

We had intercepted two parties from Porter's corps: one an engineering team, and the other a command element of some rank replete with all the gear to establish a command post. It was a rare coup, but one with little immediate tactical significance. It had to be an additional worry for him, but one that he could do little about. Like a mighty locomotive, an army has a ponderous momentum all its own. Going back to Beaver Dam Creek was no longer a viable option—not now. Neither was staying in place. He had crossed his Rubicon; he had to keep going.

I wondered what he thought of the gunfire going on to their rear. Could he ever imagine it was anything more than the last feeble spasms of yesterday's failed rebel offensive? Was he beginning to wonder and worry?

Yes, General Porter had a lot of worries right about now. Good! It was what he got paid for. I had enough troubles of my own now. In spite of a short nap, I was bone tired; I was hungry, and I was scared.

The only thing that mattered to me now was what was happening right here. Like most soldiers facing the imminence of combat, I was only slightly ashamed to admit that all I really cared about at the moment was what was about to consume us. Law's men and their fate, as well as the fate of the Confederate nation, was only an abstract. This was real, it was personal, and it was immediate!

I was at the extreme left of our ragged line, a couple hundred yards or so from the river's edge with my feet ankle deep in its mucky swamplands. In the parlance of the day, our left flank was badly dangling. There was little danger of it getting turned, however, and certainly not in this darkness and not in this muddy terrain. Hood was somewhere off to my right, probably straddling River Road, where the bulk of the advancing bluecoats were heading. He hadn't included me in his plans, but it was a good place for the doughty Texan. I hoped he was a good night fighter. What I wouldn't give for a pair of night-vision sights!

They were closer now. We could hear exasperated calls for this company or that regiment and men swearing at every little misfortune and inconvenience. Shouted commands by overwhelmed sergeants and company-grade officers added to the mix. It was all too familiar.

They were so near I could smell the sour sweat of their effort and their fears. Or was that us I smelled? As if in answer, the young soldier next to me silently vomited, his slender frame heaving with the effort to avoid giving us away. I felt like throwing up myself!

Then suddenly a crashing volley of musketry off to our right! Hood had struck.

A second round of firing almost immediately followed the first. Even more confusion and noise now filled our front. The lanterns that had guided the swarm of bluecoats through the night were now targets for Hood's Texans. It was obvious from the visible streaks of fire that Hood had moved some of his men off to the side of River Road, flanking the Yankee corps and at right angle to us. From the volume of fire, it looked to be about two of his regiments. We held our fire.

It would be soon now. Fear of the unknown was always the worst. Once battle is joined, though, training and leadership sweep away much of the nameless and amorphous dreads of combat. And this intrepid band of farm boys and city clerks was settling into a posture of avenging determination. They silently awaited their turn to fire into their enemy's ranks. The young soldier who had spilled his sparse rations just seconds ago now grimly peered down the long barrel of his rifle.

The Northerners began to return fire the best they could but to not much effect. Like any spooked and ambushed force, they were firing wildly off in any direction at all—anywhere just to be fighting back. If I was any judge of Hood's battlefield acumen, he had already started his men back to our main lines.

To make matters even worse for the federals, fires from hastily-discarded lanterns began to break out in their lines. And as their lead elements foundered in the night, the following regiments began to pile up and break out of the close formations needed for night movements. It looked like a scene from a hideous nightmare or a drunken hallucination. For us, it was a mesmerizing attraction. They were still too far away to engage effectively, but it did seem a shame not to be able to add to their travails. It would be nice to have a battery of twelve-pounders firing canister into the mix.

The developing situation was encouraging. If their artillery was in the process of being neutralized, as seemed likely, and their main body here stayed immobilized for a couple more hours, maybe that would be enough to annul today's incipient battle at Gaines Mill. A force to his rear with his artillery maybe lost, and now an attack on his flank while in extended column would be enough to unnerve any commander. Porter would have to assume his cannons were now in Lee's hands and that the only prudent thing to do was to save the remainder of his command. In that event, Lee could fix Porter's corps in place and then have a clear line of march to McClellan's logistical lifeline. Little Mac would have no choice but to debouch and fight.

Unfortunately, that scenario placed us square in Porter's sights. *So be it*, I thought. I couldn't picture Hood stealing off into the night.

As their commanders struggled to regain control, I sensed a gradual thickening of our lines. Hood was back. Not that it would make much difference. We were still outnumbered fifteen to one. Still, it was a reassuring presence—kind of like seeking protection from a driving rainstorm with nothing but a folded newspaper over your head. You took what you could get.

Just as I was considering Porter's options, the massive force in front of me began to uncoil itself. Porter was wasting no time. He had quickly enough calculated his possible courses of action. It wouldn't be long now.

"Colonel Kelly. General Hood's compliments, sir. The general would like to discuss the situation with you. Is your corporal close by? I do believe he knows this area well."

It was one of Hood's staff officers.

I motioned for Priestley to follow us.

These guys must be like cats the way they could see in the dark. I stumbled several times, following the sure-footed young officer past the long, gray lines to Hood's command post, such as it was. Looming out of the bottomland's diaphanous mist, the hulk of the Texan was indeed an impressive figure. His rather dour features lent a tragic cast to an already dismal scenario.

The greeting I received only partially dispelled that feeling.

"Kelly, Colonel Kelly! What have you gotten us into here? General Lee was on target with Porter coming this way, and it does look like we've got him right where he wants us, so to speak."

A bit of subtle irony from a man such as this one was more than incongruous—it was almost comical. But as I saw next, there was nothing laughable about what he had in mind.

"It is my estimation that our cause, our crusade, hinges on what happens here this morn. If Law has been as successful as it sounds, he will have done his part, and those big guns will never again be used on our boys. It is now our sacred responsibility to finish our part."

I didn't like the sound of this.

"Porter will be on us soon, within the hour—as soon as he can line up a few regiments to our front. He has no choice. You can see our situation as well as I can. We can make a stand and slow him here, but not for long. He is bound to prevail. If he gets through us and onto the high ground behind us, he will have a formidable defense—guns or not. McClellan will have to save his command. Every man and gun he owns will be at Porter's disposal. The Old Flag engineers are the world's finest. If there is no bridge there, little George will have a half dozen in place before sundown."

That wasn't exactly how I'd envisaged it turning out. I had taken it as a given that Porter's artillery was the crucial factor here, and that without it, he wouldn't even attempt making a stand any place this side of the river. But what if Hood was right and McClellan ordered Porter to defend this dominant terrain feature?

I just nodded my head wisely.

"Therefore, I have determined that instead we will defend in a different way. We will interdict them as long as we can and then move to occupy the plateau ourselves and defend it for as long as possible. I am hopeful too that being there will offer my men a route to rejoin the army when we are no longer able to slow Fitz-John down. I have already given the orders."

What a quirk of fate! In the Gaines Mill battle already fought, it is Hood responding to Lee's request who carries the federal positions, forever endearing himself to Lee. In the battle to come, only now defending that very same terrain, he possibly could end up with accolades for his defensive prowess. Ah, Kismet! I wondered if that same fate would destine him to suffer the terrible injuries he endured later in the war. What would he say if I told him I had attended John Bell Hood High School as a young fellow?

It wasn't a bad idea actually. We would have a better chance there than here, if we could get there before daylight. And there would be more than enough routes to safety. Unfortunately, as I was about to learn, that didn't include me!

"I understand you are General Lee's personal emissary, and as such, I believe I can exercise no authority over you. But you are the best suited to get word to him that his orders have been carried out with no small success so far and that, if he can bring a sufficient force to bear on Porter's rear in quick time, he could well have a Yankee corps in the bag. The exigent circumstances,

circumstances that I'm satisfied you can well appreciate, compel me to request your cooperation for our cause."

When would I ever learn? I was way too old for this crap. Well, he could just kiss my ass. There was no way I had it in me to do what he was asking. I barely knew where I was, let alone where Lee was. I was near twenty years older than Hood. He could just damned well go himself!

"Colonel Kelly," he continued, "I believe it is my lot to make no dramatic contribution to our struggle. But you, sir, can."

If he had said one word more, I could've blown him off with my tattered honor still intact. But he didn't, and I was left with no choice.

Left to me, we would have been back somewhere along River Road or wading through the Chickahominy's backwaters, trying to avoid being shot by Porter's men. Instead, our only worry was running into ill-tempered vanguard elements of Hill's Light Division looking to settle scores or being caught up in a headlong rush of hundreds of fleeing Union soldiers.

Priestley had provided a soldier's practical solution to an officer's inevitable complication of things. And he did it like a good NCO, discreetly. He simply led us to a local family who graciously provided us with mounts and some bacon and cornbread with cool buttermilk to wash it down, and then north along Powhite Creek to Telegraph Road, and finally west toward the junction with Old Cold Harbor Road. That was where we were, along the same stretch of road over which we had labored so much earlier this morning.

The new day's early light cast a sparkled gleam on the morning's dew. It was faint but light enough to begin to see evidence of Law's ambush as we rode west. The place was a shambles. Abandoned equipment, overturned wagons and caissons, and the gruesome human debris of battles fought littered the landscape. Here and there, the occasional artillery piece with tube pointing skyward wagged accusing fingers at us.

Sporadic crescendos of rifle fire off in the distance had before heartened us that Hood was still holding out. But now, as we drew nearer to Walnut Grove Church, it seemed that the muffled crackle of those guns had fallen silent. Had his valiant effort failed? Was Porter even now scaling the heights and preparing to fight, with all that that boded for Lee and for all my efforts? And where were Whiting and Law? They had engaged the enemy, of course. But successfully enough? I was worrying myself about that when around the bend ahead came a bevy of horsemen.

Before we could do more than draw our steeds up, the lead equestrian raised his hand in greeting.

CHAPTER 20

It was the man himself. It was General Robert E. Lee!

"You have been quite busy, quite busy indeed," he said as he approached us. "It seems that I owe you a great deal. Possibly my life. And now it appears that perhaps my country is equally in your debt."

"That may be so about your life, General. If it is, then I will have earned the undying gratitude of every patriot in the land, and that will be reward enough. As for our country, only time will tell. And time is now of the essence. If I may have a word with you in private please."

The always courteous Lee ignored me. He turned to a member of his party and asked, "Is this the man, major?"

"Yes, sir, that sure enough is Colonel Kelly." It was Whiting's left-behind staff officer.

Oh, my aching ass! Jackson was going to be pissed!

It was only then that I took notice of Lee's other traveling companions. What a shock, for there was the legendary Stonewall Jackson himself, as well as Powell Hill, arrayed before me. An old soldier's dream team! Jackson, with his scruffy forage cap, and Hill, in his red battle undershirt. Together, they presented quite a picture!

I again heard the distant battle raging for the heights at Gaines Mill. That meant Hood was still holding out, so there was still time. I needed to get Lee's ear, and I no longer cared who heard what I had to say.

I turned to him. "General, you must hear me out. There is no time to waste. General Hood is holding—"

An outraged Jackson interrupted me. "General Lee, this man must be court-martialed or, at the very least, face a board of inquiry. Yes, he has managed to gather intimate knowledge of our foe's intentions and to contribute significantly to our cause. But no man is above the law. He and General Whiting, as well as any who colluded with them, must answer for their actions. I insist he be arrested."

"Where," he demanded, "is Hood, and where is the rest of my division?"

This was vintage Stonewall! Always a stickler for the proprieties. General Hill prudently said nothing. He too would face Jackson's wrath and indeed would soon find himself placed under arrest by the oftentimes prickly and demanding general.

Before I could respond, Lee turned to him and said, "Colonel Kelly and General Whiting will be dealt with in an appropriate fashion at the appropriate time, General. For now, though, I desire that you have General Ewell bring up the remainder of your wing with all due speed. I expect you to exploit Porter's withdrawal from Ellerson's Mill as early as possible. We must take advantage of Providence's generous offering. Do you understand?"

Without waiting for Jackson's reply, he looked me directly in the eye and commanded, "Colonel Kelly, your presence on this battlefield is no longer helpful. You are to report to General Whiting at the church. I am sure the two of you will have much to discuss on your way to Richmond."

"General Lee, if I may take—"

"Do as I say, Colonel. That will be all!"

As he turned away, another summer storm parted the clouds over his shoulder to the southwest. Its angry claps and lightning streaks seemed appropriate for the occasion, matching Lee's uncharacteristic anger. I could even detect the shorted-out wiring odor of ozone over the too familiar stench of cordite and rotting flesh.

I waited for a second or two, but he had no further time for me. I had been summarily and professionally dismissed and given my walking papers. Hill gave me a pitying look before turning back to receive Lee's orders.

It took Priestley to gather up my bridle and lead us down the road to break the spell. I was being denied my rightful place here. I had done all that a man could do to bring success to Lee and the Southern cause, and now, at the crucial hour, the moment of decision, in spite of it all, I was being sent away.

It was clear that Lee was moving to take advantage of the opportunity my meddling had afforded him. Whether he understood the need for speed well enough was the question. But he was moving. That had been my entire focus this, so I should be happy. But I wasn't. I needed to be a part of the end game. Instead, I was being sent away!

I couldn't stay depressed for long, though. The sun was out in full now and quickly drying the last of the early morning humidity. It was going to be a beautiful day.

The storm that had been brewing off toward Richmond was disappearing as quickly as it had come, and with it, taking away my despondency. After all, I had done all I could do. It was certain the outcome of today's event would end up better than it would have otherwise been. Whiting's force had apparently captured the federal artillery. If Hood could continue to hold out,

Lee could count on inflicting terrible losses on Porter's force. And probably bag the lot. It was even well within the realm of possibility that the rest of McClellan's Army of the Potomac could fall into Lee's hands.

In any event, I was out of it for good now.

Whiting was jubilant. He was carrying a dispatch from Lee to be handed personally to President Davis, and even though his superior, the fabled Stonewall, was probably still insisting he be arrested, he had the certain knowledge nothing would come of it. He would be the toast of Richmond once his role in the liberation of Richmond became public knowledge. And he would genuinely deserve the recognition. Besides his personal bravery and his willingness to risk all on a long shot, it was no small thing to incur Jackson's wrath. Whiting was destined to be a central figure in Southern politics.

My future was not near as rosy. I had no home, no friends, and no role to play. I could never go back to my time and to Margaret. Louisa was dead. Tom would make a place for himself in the New South. And Mary—well, I would need to provide for her. Perhaps even find someway to obtain her manumission. Eventually I might travel west. I just didn't know.

At least I had my faithful mare. A grateful Whiting had made sure I got Betsy back. It was comforting to have her with me. And I was satisfied to have made a difference in this world. The South would be free, and federalism would be granted a reprieve. Who could know about these things, though? Perhaps one day the two sides could rejoin with safeguards against the climate that produced the likes of the Odets and Clays of the world.

Probably the worst feeling I had, though, was one of estrangement. The man I had always idolized had found me wanting and had made it clear he wanted no more to do with me. Maybe I was just a reminder of a crack in his own value system, his personal code of honor. He was more the successful general now and perhaps no longer the chivalric man of arms he had always been, at least in my eyes.

Not that millions of Southerners would care at all. What an idealistic fool I was. I had wanted a winner, and now I had one. The whole idea had been for him to use me for his ends, and now he had—sort of. The only thing he was guilty of was simply responding in a tactically sound way to the opening my interference had provided him. To do otherwise would have been irresponsible to the point of criminal negligence.

Whiting and I didn't know how the day's events would play out, but neither of us doubted McClellan's fate. Even if Porter escaped to the other side of the Chickahominy, the way would then be clear for Lee to interdict McClellan's logistical lifeline. Without that, McClellan's splendid Army of the Potomac would wither and die, and capitulation would be inevitable. He would have to fight—fight or quit.

Little Mac had long been convinced he was outnumbered anyway, and with the loss of his artillery, he might very well just concede defeat and surrender his army. If he chose to fight, the end of his army was equally as certain. At his best, McClellan was no match for Lee, especially in the open field. He had already lost his nerve, given up the initiative, and seen much of his artillery fall into Southern hands. There wouldn't be much generalship left in the man. He and his army were finished, one way or another. It was only left to see how: honorable defeat on the field of battle or disgraced but humane surrender.

With the loss of his army, Lincoln would have few options. England and France were looking for any excuse to offer recognition to the Confederacy. The American people, tiring already of some of the wartime measures, would be appalled that the magnificent army they had outfitted and supported was lost so quickly. They already were getting squeamish at the mounting losses of men and material anyway. The midterm elections were coming up, and the mood of the people was surly. Lincoln was looking at the real possibility of losing his majority to the Democratic Party—the Peace Party. Newspapers, those not already shut down by the administration, would be howling for the heads of the radical Republicans—the War Party. The only historical event that had saved the Republican Party in real history was the bloody stalemate at Antietam. That event now could never occur with the Army of the Potomac in the process of being captured or destroyed.

But most grievous of all to Lincoln, Washington would be left defenseless. The few garrison and green troops protecting the capital were totally inadequate to deal with a victorious and unimpeded Confederate army commanded by a General Robert E. Lee. Pope's Army of Virginia was only in the planning stage. So armies would have to be shifted from the west to protect the capital, conceding the western theater once again to the Army of the Tennessee. New Orleans would become a great liability to the occupying Union garrison. Ulysses Grant's nascent effort to take Vicksburg would wither on the vine, and the Confederacy would remain a contiguous nation. Grant himself would have to find his road to fame and the presidency by a different battle.

Yes, independence was near certain. Who would lead the nation after Davis left the scene also seemed certain. Davis was an American patriot, sacrificing much, both for his land of birth and now his infant country. He was never comfortable in the presidency, though. He would be a transitional figure and go on to serve in some other capacity.

So Lee was the man of the hour, or soon would be. The Southern people, accustomed to a long streak of military misfortunes, had found in him its George Washington. Lee could have the helm of the new nation if he wanted it. I felt that he would be a reluctant politician, though willing enough to serve if needed. I knew, and perhaps Lee did too, that eventually the fledgling nation would have to deal with the social issue of the century: slavery. He might be the only man with the stature and public esteem to convince Southerners to give up their odious reliance on slave labor.

As we neared the outskirts of the Confederate capital, anxious citizens were gathering for news of the military situation. They surrounded and questioned anyone coming from the direction of the front, and we were no exception, especially when one was a general officer.

"General, can you tell us what is going on out there?"

"Is McClellan on the run?"

"Is it true that Lee resigned and turned the army over to Longstreet?"

"Sir, could you take a message to my husband? He's in the Eighth Virginia."

We answered such questions the best we could and continued to plow our way through the crowds without trampling over some poor citizen. Finally, Whiting requested help from a passing cavalry detail in getting us through the crowds and on our way to the Confederate Executive Mansion.

My part in the great struggle was over, and my role could never be acknowledged. Nor did I want it to be. I already had enough of visitors from a fretful future. I didn't need to draw any more attention to myself than I already had. And Hawkface was still a loose end. I wondered what happened to him. Had the young lieutenant been able to run him to ground? Somehow I doubted it. Maybe he would simply become an unintended casualty of war. If so, he would be out of my reach, and vengeance would never be mine. In any event, as long as his fate was unknown, I really had no life.

For now, though, I had to find young Tom and make sure he and Mary were provided for. Once that was taken care of, then I would worry about Hawkface.

Betsy softly neighed. We were there. Later known as the Confederate White House, it really wasn't a Southern version of its better known counterpart. Because of its more than off-white color, it was simply known as the Gray House. Or even as the Davis House. The whole world would know it soon enough as the home of the other American president.

President Jefferson Davis was descending the steps with as close as he ever came to a smile on his face. He couldn't possibly know yet how well things were turning out. But, know he did! Victory was in the air, and a new nation was taking wing. Davis was far too astute a politician to not sense the seismic shift in geopolitical power now taking place on the American continent. The nineteenth century would still be an American century, but it would be one with two centers of gravity. It was too momentous an occasion to ask myself just what I had wrought on a lifetime of love and fealty to the "Old Flag."

As Whiting dismounted, I faded into the crowd, and I hoped into obscurity.

BOOK FIVE

CHAPTER 21

It hadn't quite worked out that way, though. Only Lee and Whiting knew the details of my contributions, but I had been at the physical center of events, and many had taken notice. Lee's mysterious emissary was the talk of Richmond. Even Northern newspapers were speculating on the wild man who had single-handedly silenced two cannons and saved the commanding general of the rebel army.

Whiting was getting plenty of favorable press himself, as well as Hood, who had held firm against Porter's seasoned troops just long enough. Jackson struck Porter's extended and defenseless flank while the remainder of the Confederate army north of the Chickahominy hit him to his rear. His artillery gone, and attacked on three sides, Porter had done all a general could do. With no succor in sight, he surrendered his corps to Lee.

Poor McClellan would be getting a lot of media attention back home too, but he wouldn't be enjoying it near so much.

It was three days after General Lee had ordered me away from the field of battle. It was from this distant outpost that I was reduced to following the operational situation the same as everyone else. From rumors and newspapers, which were little more than founts of more rumors and ever more lurid tales. I was mentioned often enough for it to be discomfiting, not to mention hearing my name used by the matronly proprietress of the rooming house I had been fortunate to find. Even though I was using an alias, it was only a matter of time before someone discovered my true identity.

I hadn't made any progress in finding young Tom and Mary in the now-bustling Confederate city either. There were a lot of people here doing the same—looking for lost family and friends. I felt it necessary to be somewhat discreet too. I had briefly considered placing ads in the Richmond papers but thought better of that idea once I remembered that had been the way my past had caught up with me once before. So I was using a pseudonym for now.

I was just finishing my breakfast of grits, honey, and bacon while catching up with the latest news in yesterday's newspapers when a cannon shot shattered the morning calm. Everyone in the dining room flinched, but Richmond wasn't under attack again; there was no foreign army threatening the capital. The shot stood alone.

Around the corner, outside my window, a large crowd surged into view. It was a happy crowd—a joyful throng pulsing with unconstrained enthusiasm. It had to be good news, something from the front. I had been expecting something for the last twenty-four hours, and now it seemed to have arrived. What was it to be? Had McClellan surrendered, or had there been a decisive engagement?

Lee had returned to the capital twice in the past two days, both times radiating the quiet air of a winner. I had seen him myself. Even surrounded by an entourage of staff officers and an unusually large troop of cavalrymen, it was plain to see. I knew a victorious general when I saw one. And so did thousands of Southerners who turned out whenever he showed up. Long lines of dispirited federal prisoners further testified to the failed fortunes of the once-invincible Army of the Potomac.

I had to see for myself, but before I could arise from my chair, our landlady burst into the dining room, her plump face now swollen even more with emotion.

"We're saved. It's over at last," she gushed through her tears and holding her hands to her ample breast. "God bless our Southland. Cheers for old Jeff and General Lee. Praise the LORD. Oh how the wicked have succumbed. The righteous have devoured the wolf at long last! Our sufferings and travails have not been in vain. We are saved. We are saved."

Hers and the crowd's enthusiasm was infectious. Sure, there might be many months of campaigning ahead, but it was bound to be just a matter of time. If there had been a decisive battle, Lee would need time to replenish and rest before resuming the offensive. If McClellan had capitulated outright, he would still need to secure his prize before moving north. Either way, Washington would now be the target that could end the war on favorable terms for the Confederacy.

Lincoln had always obsessed on protecting the seat of government, so he probably would not relish having to rely on an untested Army of Virginia to save his capital. He had his successful western armies he could transport to Washington in relatively short order. But then, if the Army of the Tennessee only mounted the feeblest of offensives, the great breadbasket of the Union war effort would be ripe for the picking. A war-weary Yankee public, already chafing at the terrible costs in dead and maimed, and by now thoroughly disenchanted with the administration's management of the war effort, would not stand for it. Illinois was already near revolt from the army's incessant demands for young men to replenish its decimated ranks, and Indiana was not much happier. All the Southern states had wanted was to be left alone, and now Mr. Lincoln's capital was to be at risk!

Along with the other diners, I jumped up to join the bandwagon. As I brushed past the excited woman, she clutched at me, exclaiming, "What's happened Mr. Kirby? Is General Lee on the road back from Cold Harbor? Has he captured McClellan? Oh please, sir, please tell me what's happened!"

I hoped the poor woman wasn't going to have a stroke.

Stepping outside my rooming house off Broad Street and into an unusually warm and humid Richmond, I was immediately swept up in the roiling current flowing toward the president's mansion. What was it to be, more months of war and deprivation, or only weeks before peace returned to the American continent? I grabbed the shoulder of the nearest man and shouted my questions at him in rapid order. He winced in pain, and it was only then I noticed the empty sleeve and his youth.

I yanked my hand back, and before I could manage embarrassed apologies, he answered over the din, "Mister, I don't know for sure, but it's gotta be good from the way everyone's carrying on so. Maybe the war is done and they will finally just let us be. God, please, God, make it be over soon. They can have my other arm and my legs too, but just leave us alone."

As the mob brushed by us, he pointed his empty sleeve past me and continued, "See, even the niggers want it all to end."

And sure enough, there were a sprinkling of blacks clapping and yelling with the rest of us. They probably, at this point, didn't care who won. The deprivations of war fell on black and white alike.

By the time I turned back to him, he was gone—swept away in the rush. Soon we were at the Davis home. I was pinned into place well to the rear of the swaying and chanting crowd. "Jeff, Jeff! Come out, Jeff! Come out, Je—"

I was caught up in the excitement, rocking with the beat, and straining to catch a glimpse of the president, just like the rest of the crowd. Would he come out to greet us, to give us the latest *communiqué*? Where was General Lee?

I strained to see over the crowd, turning this way and that to gain a better vantage point. There were probably several hundred excited citizens by now crowding up to the steps of the Executive Mansion, with more coming. Mostly they were men, but here and there, the occasional woman could be seen. It was their country too, and they had sacrificed much. There was one up ahead of me with a little different look about her. Her hair was done up differently from what I had been accustomed to the last three years, a style reminiscent of...No! No, it couldn't be. Could it?

"Jeff, Jeff! Come out old, Jeff! General Lee, where are you Bobby Lee?"

"My fellow Americans. Thank you for gathering here today. It is a historical time for our country, for our continent, and for the world we live in. Our people have endured much these terrible months of suffering and loss. But your countrymen have not sacrificed in vain. Indeed, you and they have prevailed in the cruelest war ever waged on this continent. God willing, you will have your freedom."

The president was speaking. What was it to be?

With the crowd shifting and swaying with Davis's every word, I could only catch tantalizing glimpses of the woman here and there. She, like me, seemed to be looking for someone—a husband or perhaps a son. Or was she searching for a fellow time traveler? It was just too impossible to believe. It couldn't be her, could it? Could it possibly be her looking for a familiar face? My face! Could it be Margaret, here in this time?

There was good news from the front. But was it decisive news? Was the president going to announce a capitulation with thousands of Yankee prisoners now in Southern hands? Had there been a great battle with equally horrific numbers of casualties? Was the war to end, or was it destined to drag on forevermore?

The answer was on the way, but the woman ahead competed for my attention!

Desperately trying to keep her in sight, I began to claw my way toward her in a near panic. What if I lost her? Not now, not after all these years. Oh, please let it be her. Please, please don't lose her now. It had to be my Margaret looking for me here, where she knew I would be, in the heart of a victorious Confederacy. All around me, the surging and clinging citizens of Richmond impeded my every step. There, there. She turned my way!

"Yesterday evening, at General Lee's headquarters, the general commanding the Army of the Potomac, General McClellan, offered his surrender to our forces. I have directed General Lee to accept that surrender, but only on our terms. General McClellan is awaiting approval of those terms from Mr. Lincoln. Dispatches from General Lee confirm what has become increasingly apparent these past days: our army, under the command of America's greatest living general, has out maneuvered and out-fought the largest army ever assembled on this continent."

The crowd roared its approval!

"*No! No!*" I screamed. It wasn't her. For a glorious moment, I'd thought the impossible. The mind plays such tricks. But it wasn't her. Margaret was much, much younger. This woman was too old, too old by far. She was closer to my age. And her hair was different; it wasn't the same color at all. The woman was handsome, though, and bore a striking resemblance to Margaret, but not enough.

A last look before the crowd pulled her away and, for a brief moment, our eyes met. Was that an instant of recognition and disappointment on her face too before, like me, she realized I wasn't the loved one she was looking for? Hope indeed springs eternal, for the both of us perhaps. The poor woman was nothing like Margaret. And certainly not a fellow time traveler!

Next, I would be hallucinating that my kids were dropping in for a quick visit. I needed to get a grip.

"Colonel Kelly," a voice said.

I stiffened, but it was a pleasant voice, vaguely familiar. I looked up into a face I had seen recently. It was a young officer in uniform. I couldn't place who he was until he leaned over and softly reminded me that I was still under the thrall of my hero.

"The general asks if you will join him to discuss the man from Mechanicsville."

It was the young officer Lee had dispatched to help me the first day's battle. And who went after the "man from Mechanicsville." From the looks of him, he had not fared so well. His uniform had lost its parade-ground crispness, and his cap looked even worse. As did the young fellow himself. He was different now. I wondered how much killing it took to turn the boy into a man.

I looked back at the woman, but she had disappeared. It was just as well.

Since there was nothing else to do for it, I turned and followed the lieutenant around the corner and away from the chanting crowd.

In just a minute or two, he ushered me into the presidential mansion's rear courtyard, where graceful columns stood tall in the early Southern sunshine. I could still hear the crowd, and even Davis's stentorian oration. Nevertheless, a curious stillness permeated the morning's heat. I had passed out of one dimension and into another, for there standing before me was a much changed General Robert E. Lee!

CHAPTER 22

Lee, the general, was exactly as one would expect. He was no longer just the officer brought in to replace the critically injured Joseph Johnston. Now he was the victorious Lee. Not just victorious, but triumphant—wildly triumphant. He stood before me as the savior of a nation and of a people grown pessimistically accustomed to failure on the field of battle. The world was now his oyster, and even the ever humble and self-effacing Lee could hardly be unaware of his new standing.

His uniform was immaculate, clean, and freshly pressed. The morning's sunlight filtering through the courtyard foliage sparkled silver on his lustrous boots. His hair and beard appeared freshly trimmed.

He was every inch the conquering titan of the battlefield.

I felt shabby and insignificant.

But Lee, the man, was here too. I was quick to find out it was the man, not the general, whom I was here to see. In this sublime instance of one man's achievement and vindication, it was Lee the man—Lee the family man—who stepped forward to offer his hand. But I was not to bask, even for the briefest of moments, in the reflected glory of his military triumphs.

"Colonel Kelly," he declared. "Thank you for meeting with me on such short notice."

His manner was not encouraging, but I bowed slightly, and, in the Prussian fashion, even managed a click of the heels as I replied, "I am pleased for the opportunity to congratulate you in person, General Lee. Like all of Richmond, I know of your successes but have precious few details. In any event, from one soldier to another, I offer my congratulations."

With no answer forthcoming, I lamely continued. "I understand from the lieutenant that you have news of the man of such interest to me. I realize this is a critical time for you and the Confederacy, so I especially appreciate you taking time to inform me of the disposition of the matter."

I suddenly felt queasiness in the pit of my stomach.

With a nod of dismissal to the young officer, he said, "I'm afraid I have no resolution of the problem to report, my friend-from-whenever. In fact, your interest in him is now my interest. And the problem has been compounded immeasurably in the past twenty-four hours. May I assume he is a man of your time? And do you know him?"

There was an edge to his voice and a hard glint in his eyes. Suddenly, I wished I were back at the inn, finishing my breakfast.

"I believe he is, General. No, I do not know him. But I have every reason to believe he is the fulfillment of your prediction almost three years ago. If so, given the circumstances of the day, I am hopeful he will cease to be whatever problem he has become to you."

Without a word, he pulled a folded and stained piece of paper from a well-worn field dispatch case and handed it to me. The gesture seemed pregnant with reproach.

My excitement over the day's events suddenly evaporated.

What had happened? *Oh please, God*, I silently prayed.

With trembling hands and trepidation, I carefully unfolded the paper. The coppery stains leapt out at me, screaming bitter recriminations. Something had gone terribly wrong. It was going to be Hawkface again. He had, once again, seized the initiative. What had he done this time? Had he threatened Lee in some way?

Of course, his family! I had no notion where they all were. His sons were off to war. Custis was here in Richmond, young Robert was a private somewhere in Virginia. Rooney, I didn't know. But it was unlikely they would be targets. That left Mrs. Lee and their daughters. That had to be it. Yes, that was it. I must tell him just how dangerous the man was.

I started to speak, to tell him the danger his family was in. But his glare froze the words in my mouth and directed my eyes down to the paper in my hand.

I had to force my eyes to the bloodstained page. Every faculty I possessed screamed a silent wail: throw down this doomsday letter and run! This *communiqué* from hell with the Beast's Mark indelibly emblazoned on it.

I read, "Your daughter is safe, for now. I will exchange the rest of her for the traitor, Kelly. Place a personal ad in the *Richmond Examiner* when you are able to turn him over. You have until the tenth of July. I will instruct you at that time. Otherwise, I will put her to good use as a common camp follower—as long as she lasts, that is. You'll get the chance to visit her in a few weeks anyway."

That was it. Was it Mildred, the apple of Lee's eye? Or poor Annie, destined to die early. Which one of the Lee daughters? Agnes or Mary? The cowardly bastard! And the bloodstains cruelly calculated to horrify and terrorize! I didn't want to think about what he meant by the "rest of her" and "camp follower" comments.

The message's meaning was unequivocal. I suppressed the urge to look around for an escape route. Did he have the court-yard surrounded? Had he already placed the ad in the paper?

I dared look up into the accusing eyes. I had wronged this man in the worst of ways. Rage! Homeric rage and prideful wrath had done this thing. By arrogating to myself privileges reserved only for the gods, this man was suffering in the one way designed to bring the most pain.

What had I wrought? Oh, the horror of it all. I wanted to be already dead and presented to the misbegotten monster from hell.

I told him, "You will have no problem from me, General. Place the ad. I will cooperate. I place myself in your hands. But verify that she is alive and well before turning me over. That man is capable of the most heinous acts, and he can be counted on to use every expediency to accomplish his aims. I am what he wants. If you take every safeguard in turning me over, you will have your daughter back safely."

I was not done in this world yet, though!

It wasn't Lee the father who answered me. Nor was it the general. It was Lee the man who exclaimed, "You who claim to know my life so well, you know it not near well enough. Perhaps it is that history has recorded me thusly. Regrettable, if so.

"It is true that without your presence here, my daughter would not be in that man's hands now. That is where your part in these evil doings end, though. I wish you had never come here, and I wish that, having come, you had heeded my wishes. But just as turning you over to that fiend would dishonor me, you, having been thrust here, could do no less than what you have done. If our natures were different, our actions would be different.

"I had thought that your time would send someone to neutralize you as a force of history. I no longer believe that is so, at least not this man. Not now. This man, by seeking no military advantage for his cause and by kidnapping an innocent young girl just to harm you, it seems obvious, is here for personal reasons. Can you think why, and would knowing why help in finding him before he carries out—"

He was unable to complete the thought, but I knew just what savagery Hawkface was capable of committing. Although I hadn't previously given it due consideration, it did seem Louisa's murder may have been more than a casual act of wanton violence. Was it simply to exact a measure of vengeance? And why?

The ransom note made no strategic demands of Lee, and there was no attempt to marginalize him or his victorious armies. When Hawkface had shown up on the field at Mechanicsville, at considerable risk to himself, he had confirmed his mission was to stop me. But, he had made those hateful personal remarks, too.

The son of a bitch wanted me dead for personal reasons, it seemed. And he would have had me too, if he hadn't had to gloat first. I had wondered about it at the time. It had been there in front of me, but I had been unable to imagine the unimaginable. Who from my time could possibly hate me that much? I had made plenty of enemies in the course of a career of violence and strong personalities. But there were few, if any, with enough of a grudge to kill innocents out of hateful spite, and fewer still willing to squander their lives pursuing me here.

I shook my head at his question and said, "No, sir. I can't imagine anyone coming here to do violence to me unless to remove me as a force of change. He may have originally been sent for that purpose. I don't know. I may yet have to contend with that some other time. But not now!

"You may recall that night at my lodging when you visited me that there were two men who were showing inordinate interest in us? This monster is one of those men. The other one, I don't know, but this one is a truly evil man."

I looked at the note again. There was nothing there. On the face were the message and the bloodstains. The back was blank, except where the blood had seeped through. The paper itself was unexceptional—just ordinary unlined, rough paper of the era. The printed letters were not of this time's style. But that was all. There was nothing to glean from the note that I could see.

I handed it back and asked, "How was this delivered to you? When did you get it? Was there anything with it?"

He answered, "It was placed in my hands this morning. Someone delivered it to the War Department last evening. It remained there unopened until just two hours ago. A telegraph message alerting me she was missing came to my headquarters yesterday afternoon. I have no other details, except what is in this note. And yes, I do remember that night and that man. He had the appearance of a predator, as I recall."

A hawk!

I hated to ask which of the girls. I just knew it was going to be Mildred, his Precious Life. I wasn't wrong.

"It was my youngest, my Mildred. She's just a child. No one could find it in his heart to harm her."

I chose not to mention the cold-blooded killing of innocent Louisa. Instead, I asked, "Where was she, General?"

"Jones Springs, North Carolina," he answered. "Near Warren Plains, just across the border. She and the other girls have been there for a couple of weeks. Until the situation here is ameliorated, I think. But it doesn't seem likely she would be held in the vicinity there. He would have taken her somewhere else."

"And Mrs. Lee, where is she?" I asked.

"She's here," he answered.

"General, have you brought the others home? You need to get them here all in one place. Don't think he will be satisfied with only one bargaining chip. Bring them here with Mrs. Lee, and place ample security around them. It wouldn't be a bad idea to do the same for yourself and, for that matter, President Davis as well.

"I don't believe this man has any desire to alter what seems to be a *fait accompli* concerning hostilities. Nevertheless, protecting the president and yourself may be the prudent thing to do."

"I have already attended to the safety of my family. As for President Davis, I will discuss it with him. I doubt he will agree to that. I had enough trouble keeping him out of harm's way a few days ago. He tends to follow the action. For now, though, I need your help to find my Precious Life. Even if I could blanket the countryside with troops, I wouldn't know where to start. Would it do more harm than good, though? Would it alert him?"

Something about that! What was it? "What do you mean, sir?" I asked. "Say that again, what you said about following the action. No, no. Never mind. I've got it. Let me see the note again."

He quickly handed it to me, asking hopefully, "What is it? Have you thought of something? Tell me, please."

I scanned the note. Maybe that was it. For there to be camp followers, there had to be camps! And his mention of Lee's future opportunity to "visit" her soon, what did that mean? "Are there any federal units anywhere close to where the girls are? That was Jones Station you said. Where is the closest concentration of federal troops from there?"

My brain was in overdrive now. The questions were tumbling out faster and faster. I had to keep it going. Keep asking before it all got away from me.

"Could they have gotten through your lines to McClellan's positions? Where else could they have gone to be near soldiers? Where? South? Surely not! West? Maybe, but he would have to travel to Tennessee. That's just not accessible enough for him. Remember, he needs to have access to the Richmond papers. Maybe east, but what's there in the way of federals? New Bern, but I think he wouldn't have been able to make his way there. Plus, it is a small force, lightly defended. He would need to be closer to concentrations of friendly units. So where else but—"

"North," he completed the question, picking up on where I was going. "North! Already Lincoln is filling the vacuum in Northern Virginia with troops. Word is he is forming a new army, probably commanded by the braggart Pope. That's Halleck's doing. He would have to be near a rail line. They have to be north, fairly close, near enemy troops, and close enough to have access to newspapers."

"Go on, General. What else? Where could he have gotten to with a hostage in tow? When did the kidnapping happen? How far could he have gotten since then, especially with a hostage? How far could he have gotten by rail and then on to wherever by whatever means? Assume it is only as far as he needs to be. Where then?"

"They could have made it north up through the Shenandoah Valley, but probably not much newspaper circulation there or adequate rail service," he answered. "That leaves railway to maybe Gordonsville or even on to Culpeper. But not farther than that surely. I don't know exactly the circumstances of the abduction or the train schedules. I need my rail man here. He possibly could have traveled by train from Jones Station. From there, wherever there is, to someplace else via horseback. It's too much, too many unknowns, too many possibilities."

"No, no. Forget about how," I ordered. "That man is amazingly resourceful. Think about where. Where, other than McClellan's army are troops encamped in garrison or in the field? A place where he would know about, a place he would believe secure! Where, General, where? Think, man. Think!"

There was no way he would ever tolerate someone speaking to him in such a way. But this was the here and now. Focus his mind. Keep the flow going! I knew where I wanted to go with it all, but I needed him to get there on his own. It was so perfectly right; it just had to there. Where it all started!

And he did!

"You seem to know already, Colonel. But north of Fredericksburg, I would say. With the situation now moving in our favor, he would need to get closer to Manassas for security. He may have gotten as far as Culpeper by rail and by horseback the rest of the way. May take time for Richmond newspapers to get that far, but with an accomplice, he could speed things up. And he has to consider a rendezvous point to make the trade. Someplace both parties can get to safely. If I am to suggest the best location, I will have to say Manassas. It is the junction for two lines, the Gap and the Orange and Alexandria lines. And there are enough federals reorganizing there now. They will have to be attended to eventually."

"I agree, General. It must be Manassas. In any event, it's our best chance," I agreed.

"What are you saying, Colonel Kelly?" he demanded. "To move in that direction for a rescue operation will require a significant cavalry force—a cavalry force formed for the defense of the republic, not as my own personal Praetorian guard. Any movement that direction will of necessity be dictated by the enemy, not my personal needs. My duty is here. I had hoped you knew of something, somewhere close by. I agree it was an unrealistic hope. Regrettably, for the time being, there is nothing more to do here. I will continue to pray for some degree of humanity in that man."

Offering his hand, he turned to me and said, "I thank you for your time, your concerns, and for your service to the Confederacy. For now, though, it is time for me to direct my efforts to that same Confederacy. We are at a critical juncture in our history. Good day, sir."

Ignoring his outstretched hand, I said with more conviction than I felt, "I know where he has her."

"Yes, yes," he said with a touch of irritation. "We have already determined that it quite possibly is Manassas. But that knowledge does us little good. First, where in the Manassas area, and secondly, what difference does it make? It may as well be on the moon. Now if you will excuse me, I have business to attend to."

"They are in a farmhouse, Louisa Biggers's farm, just about a mile from the station house. I know exactly where she is. I will get your daughter. I will return your Precious Life to you alive, or I will not return at all."

For a long moment, this great judge of men plumbed the depths of my character. Then, finally he said, "I don't doubt your resolve, my friend, and you have already proven your courage and commitment to our cause. But in the event you do know where they are, the odds are decidedly against you. You will be deep in enemy territory, if you can even get that far. It will be on terrain chosen by him, and you will stand out in an area where able-bodied men of military age are scarce. Which, I hesitate to mention, is something you might want to consider. I don't think you have mentioned your age, but this would be a physically arduous undertaking.

"And," he concluded, "I hold you not one iota responsible. I thank you for your willingness, but, nonetheless, I cannot encourage you on this undertaking."

"I'm sorry, General Lee, but I am responsible. I'm also responsible for the cold-blooded murder of a young woman and the orphaning of her son there on that farm. He shot her at point-blank range in anger at her refusal to divulge information about me. That beautiful woman was my friend. Her son is somewhere in this city. I have two things left to do in this century. I intend to find and provide for young Tom Biggers, and I'm going to find and return your Mildred.

I didn't mention that, in the process, I was going to kill Hawkface.

"This morning, at breakfast, I was pondering, wondering just how I was going to go about finding them. Well, now I know where one of them is. And I'm going there. Today!"

I turned to go. I had a full head of steam behind me, but I had one more thing on my mind. So I turned back to Lee and said, "One more thing, sir. As you might gather, I no longer have much to offer in the way of unwanted military advice. Almost all that I knew would happen has happened, was thwarted from happening, or was overtaken by events. It's a clean slate for me now as regards to the tactical situation. I can tell you this, though: the man in Washington is not finished, and he still packs a powerful punch. My admiration for President Davis is unqualified. He is a great patriot schooled in the military arts and proven in the arena of combat. But he is no match for Lincoln.

"Lincoln has an uncanny grasp of strategy. He is ruthless in the pursuit of that strategy, and he is absolutely dedicated to preserving the Union. He knows exactly the disparity in the resources of our two countries, and he will relentlessly exploit that to the fullest. He will not hesitate ordering a scorched-earth campaign of war without limits against civilians, of naval bombardment of our coastal cities, of the most Machiavellian contrivances, all to undermine our war efforts. He will stop at nothing.

"You can count on this, General. The telegraph lines are already humming with messages to state capitals demanding more troop levies and messages to the western armies to move units to the eastern theater. I expect that his railroad czar will be marshalling rolling stock and moving to protect the lines. Lincoln may yet end up having to negotiate, but he will be doing everything he can to bargain from a position of strength."

I had his undivided attention now, and I didn't intend to waste it. "General Lee, it is in your power to maintain the tactical momentum of the past couple of days. Without a continuation of offensive operations, the United States may well gain the strategic advantage for years and decades to come, even if they are compelled to concede our independence, which is far from certain. Lincoln is looking at the fall congressional races and facing the prospect of losing control of Congress. He will be doing everything he can to alter the geopolitical situation. Just imagine what the radical Republicans will be demanding of him."

Finally, I turned to go. I had much to do in the next couple of days, and I had said everything there was to say. I didn't really know what Lee would do with his time and his army. I hoped both would be used to secure what had been gained at such cost. I was tired, and I had stuff to do.

"General, I wish you good fortune and Godspeed for your tasks ahead. I have my own way to make. Perhaps our paths will cross again, perhaps not."

With that pronouncement, I snapped him my best parade ground salute and walked out of the courtyard into an overcast day.

CHAPTER 23

Even as I meandered about the city, I reckoned speed would be my best ally. Today was the last day of June. I had until the tenth of July. If young Mildred was taken sometime yesterday, or even the day before, under the best of circumstances, Hawkface would barely be settling into his hideaway and would be the most vulnerable.

It had been his cryptic comment at the end of the ransom note that had clinched it. All the other factors pointing toward a flight north to Manassas were valid. But they weren't enough to commit to a long and hazardous trip, especially with the time deadline. By horse, it would be a day—a full day of avoiding enemy patrols and of finding my way off the main roads. Just getting there was a problem in itself.

Lee hadn't seemed to notice the spiteful remark "get the chance to visit her," but I had. Presumably, Hawkface would know of the second battle fought at Manassas, so he would figure Lee would be heading that way shortly. And while that battle had occurred in the 1862 of my past, the General Pope of today's 1862 would soon be forming his army in the Manassas area—the army Lee might well have to deal with. In fact, if Hawkface was in Manassas, he would most likely be witness to the new army's activities. So yes, he would be certain Lee would soon be in the vicinity!

And if they were there, where else could they be but at Louisa's? Where else but the scene of her murder and her grave? It would be perfect for his twisted purposes. I could almost visualize the horrifying scenario now. Just as he had taken pleasure gloating at killing Louisa, he would do so again. He would want my last thoughts to be of helpless rage and agonizing defeat. The farm had to be it. Where else to exact such delightful pain but the site where he had only delayed the ultimate retribution?

And young Mildred; she would be kept alive only as long as she was useful. When she had served her purpose as a bargaining chip, she would be quickly disposed of. Yes, she would die. How and when was the only question. He would want to derive the maximum pleasure out of that too.

Yes, it had told me, if it hadn't told Lee, that he had no intention of returning her, alive or dead. But it had also told me where Lee would find her.

Lee, bargaining in the good faith that only men of honor understood, would trust whatever terms were offered him. Expecting his daughter, he would get her corpse. That the monster's perverted mind could relish the thought of a heartbroken father visiting his daughter's grave only hardened my resolve.

I arrived at my boarding house and managed to slip upstairs without notice. Pausing at the top of the narrow stairway, I resolved to make right the wrongs I had caused. Hawkface would be waiting for Lee's response. Instead, he would have mine!

In the meantime, I had much to do. I didn't have the slightest notion of how far I could get on a train, if there were even any running that direction. Would military authorities already have commandeered all the available rolling stock? Would the tactical situation limit my mobility?

Or would it be up to loyal Betsy to get me there? What about fords over the Rappahannock, and maybe the Rapidan? Or the York, if I tried an easterly route? Once again, I was grossly unprepared.

So what's new, I thought as I turned the key and walked into yet one more surprise for the day.

"Good morning, Colonel Kelly. Or should I say, Mr. Kirby?"

The years had changed him but for the better. Gone was the seediness and softness that I remembered from our last meeting. But not gone was the sharp look and shrewd, inquisitive eyes. It really hadn't been that long since we last met, but it had been a light year in world-changing events.

Toomey! It was, of all people, probably the last person I would have expected to ever see again. And in my room at that! Using the name I had taken such pains to hide. What next? Mr. Spock beamed down to invite me to a reception at the Vulcan embassy?

Since I didn't spot any pointy-eared aliens in the room, I just sputtered indignantly and demanded to know how he got in my room.

"My apologies, sir, for dropping in uninvited. I expected you sooner, and I was beginning to attract unwanted attention from your landlady. Formidable woman! So I put some of my more dubious skills to use and let myself in. Please, let me explain. Time is, as they say, of the essence. We don't have much of it to spare. Ten days, to be exact."

He was sitting in the only chair in my tiny room, so I sat down on the still unmade bed. Collapsed was more like it. It was too much for one day, and the day was only half gone.

"I am General Lee's advisor and facilitator on rail matters," he began. "He realized early on that our thousands of miles of borders and our considerable disadvantage in manpower and other resources mandated efficient utilization of the means to move our armies. So while he was the president's military advisor, he sought out those who were familiar with not only Southern railroads but also those of our adversaries. I am honored to have gained his confidence and to have played some part in our successes, rare as they might be.

"As you will have deduced by now, the general kept track of your whereabouts after returning from your recent endeavors. You might imagine my surprise when I learned today that the Kelly he wanted me to assist was not only the very same Kelly I had the pleasure to be acquainted with previously, but also the subject of so many rumors and articles. And you will be pleased to know he has requested of the president to locate Tom and Mary. I have little doubt they will soon be found and well taken care of. Someday I hope we will have occasion to discuss Mrs. Biggers's—Louisa's—death. She was a good woman."

He left it at that, for which I was glad. He could not have failed to have known of our relationship, just as I knew of his unrequited affection for her. I wondered how he knew of her death. I couldn't see how it would serve any purpose to tell him the details, so I just nodded.

It turned out we had a couple of less-than-ideal rail options. Both offered some advantages, and both entailed a considerable risk of discovery. That was to be expected. Even though Lincoln's men had fared poorly in this preeminent state of a victorious Southland, for now much of it was still enemy territory. But both were less risky than traveling the entire way by horseback, and both afforded the one thing I wanted—an abundance of time.

One was traveling as far as possible by train and making the rest of the way to Manassas overland. The tactical situation ruled out rail to Fredericksburg, so that left the Central line to

Gordonsville and then the good old Orange and Alexandria toward Manassas. Toomey felt he could guarantee passage as far as Gordonsville, and perhaps even to Culpeper. From there, I would be on my own. The big advantage was that Betsy could be transported too. I would have more mobility and wouldn't be as vulnerable to capture. Plus, I would have the means to return poor Mildred to her father in the event I could effect a rescue.

My earlier certainty had already begun to evaporate. What had I been thinking?

The disadvantages were finding my way to Manassas after disembarking the train, and the federal presence in the area.

And finally, how quickly could Toomey find an engine and car? Lee had made it clear to him, as well as me earlier today, that the war effort took priority.

The other option was far more risky and did not allow for Betsy to accompany me. It entailed far more exposure to interception by federal authorities and far less options for getting the child back to her family. But it would get me there tonight!

If only the roar of the tracks could drown out their ordeal. It was brutal and exhausting for those suffering in body and spirit. I had long ago experienced war's sordid side, and there was no glory and no glamour riding these rails. Every mile or so, a lurch of the engine brought extra urgency to the tormented cries of agony. Were they crying for relief, or were they pleading for deliverance?

It was to be only a seven hour or so trip, but already it was an eternity for these unfortunates, especially after changing trains in Gordonsville. It was a mixed blessing for many of them.

They were going home but to an uncertain future. They were the worst of the wounded still given a chance to live. They were the amputees with gangrenous stumps, young men with terribly disfiguring burns, and gut-shot soldiers going back for treatment in better facilities. Slight chance for many perhaps, but blind hopefulness was the one constant—the one gift of the gods—held close, even unto the foreboding hours of death.

I wondered how many hoped only for quick, merciful death.

It was a prisoner exchange. Both sides used the hiatus in the killing for advantage of some kind, but this was a humanitarian mission, pure and simple. The surrender negotiations included provisions that good faith efforts be made to save the lives of wounded prisoners, to return those in serious condition who had some hope for survival, and to provide palliative care for those who didn't. Hard to fathom! Grotesque carnage followed by gentle ministrations. Well, we were all Americans. As if that made any sense.

President Davis had acceded to the suggestion but with the stipulation that it be our trains used to transfer the wounded back and forth. He was ever mindful of President Lincoln's propensity for diplomatic deceit. The failed Confederate effort to negotiate Fort Sumter's fate after secession but before hostilities was only the first instance of Lincoln's skillful use of words and time to achieve a desired outcome.

So it was that I was creeping along on a Southern train surrounded by Northern cavalry into Southern lands occupied by Northern intruders. I meant to liberate a Southern woman from a Northern murderer and to celebrate a Southern victory over Northern aggression. I was nearing the culmination of my effort to exalt and validate the Southern way of life.

A Southern way of life that excluded almost half of its citizens from its benefits! What to make of a Lee blessed with aristocratic birth matched by unsurpassed nobility of character defending a failing and despicable social order, and a Lincoln of mean circumstances adept in the use of sophistry and treachery promoting the abolition of that same odious institution? Not for the first time, I was uncomfortable with the thought.

I was acting as a medical officer for the first three passenger cars of six. Another medical officer, whom I hoped was better qualified, attended to the other three coaches. I could move relatively easy among the cars, looking after my wards—not that I was able to do that much. About all I could do was make them as comfortable as possible, bring water to those who weren't gut shot, and spend a little time offering words of solace and encouragement to as many as I could.

The cars had long since been stripped of cushions by thousands of gray-clad soldiers ferried from one grim battleground to another. Still, the Richmond hospital authorities had made it as comfortable as possible for their former patients. Many of the benches were converted into rough beds for the more seriously wounded, while the few ambulatory amputees used what coach seats there were. All of it would get good use carting wounded Confederates back to Richmond for the return trip. Not that I would be coming back with them!

The ancient locomotive struggled along, pulling its pitiful cargo to whatever fate lie ahead. For some, it was a race with time. For two, the chase was already over—they had died fitful deaths only an hour out of Richmond. One more, perhaps two, appeared unlikely to make it much farther.

For me, I just needed the sun to beat us there. Instead of accompanying my charges all the way to the junction, I intended to jump ship, and I wanted as much darkness as possible. They could make what they wanted at the other end about it. Hopefully the other medico would be enough for the authorities there, but I didn't care about them. The only one I really needed to fool was Hawkface and any of his henchmen, and the best way to do that was to disembark before arriving.

I figured he probably needed an intermediary, if not an outright co-conspirator, to carry the whole thing off. Perhaps nothing more than a local hire to pick up the Richmond papers as they filtered up from the victorious capital. He probably wouldn't expect a response this soon, but I couldn't count on that. I couldn't count on him failing to anticipate a rescue effort either. He was far too resourceful to assume any advantage.

And now bad weather seemed destined to add its two cents to the muddle. Maybe that was to the good, if rain served to mask my movement. More than likely, it would add just another factor to my misery index.

Leaning out the doorway, and watching the ground rush by, I suddenly wasn't so sanguine about my prospects for even getting off the old train in one piece, especially at night. For an old paratrooper, it was a short enough jump, all right, but the operative word here was *old*. And old bones break easily, which would definitely be a mission-ender. Fortunately, track conditions and curves mandated frequent slow downs, so I should be able to find a flat enough patch to jump with nothing more than a few bumps and scrapes.

More troublesome was exiting the train at a point close enough to make it safely to Louisa's farm. I would be on foot, in enemy territory, and it would be dark. There was a way station fairly close to the farm, where I intended to disembark. Toomey and I had pored over his maps, and we both agreed Bristoe Station offered the best opportunity to get in place tonight. A tall order maybe, but it would give me all morning to finish my business.

I hadn't thought through any of this past killing Hawkface and rescuing young Mildred. As for getting her home, I had sort of a plan but very little beyond stealing a couple of horses and somehow making it back to Richmond. What a Mickey Mouse operation this was. Still, I had made it this far. Not too bad for an old soldier.

Old! Suddenly, old seemed to fit, maybe for the first time. Old and alone. It struck me, though, that everyone back home would have caught up with me by now.

Even Margaret would be...

Another mournful chorus of wails brought me back to the present. I hurried over to the closest of the young wounded with a cup of water. He was a slight fellow, and as I knelt down next to him, I could see he was a little more than a youngster—a child who had done all the growing up he would ever need. And from the looks of him, perhaps all the growing up he was destined to get. A filthy bandage covered one eye and half of a pimpled face. I held the cup up to his parched and cracked lips and reached for his hand to steady the cup, only to grab a bandaged stump of a hand.

Then the bloody lips parted, and with a bitter and heart-rending grimace, he said, "I wish to God you had shot me dead when you had the chance, Mister. Look at all that's left of me. Not going to be much of a farmer now, am I?"

Shocked, I barely recognized him. It was one of the young boys I had almost killed. He was no longer a boy, though. And how long ago had that been? Just a few days, and look at him now! A hand and half a face sacrificed to Lincoln's cause. Hope and a youthful life lost. But if survival was the criteria after duty performed, then this lad had indeed done better than many.

I forced a smile and let the water slowly trickle past his lips as I asked him his name and hometown.

"Don't imagine Becky Sue is going to want much to do with what's left of me either," he said, ignoring my question. "Is it true we done got ourselves whipped? So here I am, with no face and no fingers, all for nothing. And you up to no good," he concluded, his voice rising ominously.

I had to stifle the urge to clamp my hand over his mouth.

He went on. "From what I seen of you shooting poor old Moran plumb off his horse, I reckon you ain't no doctor. I don't know much about wars and the like, but we was giving you boys a thumping, and then everything went plumb to hell. Just about the time you showed up. Now what? Is Jeff Davis going to take Maryland away from the Union? While they were patching me up, one of our boys said he'd heard tell Lincoln had resigned and sailed to England. Do you know where they are going to take me? Will I ever get to go home? My mother will be glad, I guess. Sergeant Moran, hell of a mean bastard. Good riddance, I say! Justice has to be done, though."

The more he talked, the louder he got. I felt like throttling him, wounded or not.

He was rambling now, and his voice faded away. His head was hot to the touch, which probably meant infection had begun to have its way with him. Possibly they would be able to nurse him back to health, but it didn't seem likely. I started to turn away, but his good hand shot out frantically to grab my arm with the strength of the desperately doomed. His eyes burned the bright-gold color of a new penny.

"You're up to some more mischief, I 'spect. Don't care much, at least not anymore. All the killing for nothing. It ought to count for something, though."

His grip loosened, and his arm fell away, exhausted by the effort. But even as the fires in his eyes dimmed, he muttered one last imprecation, "I'll be telling somebody about old Moran.

Don't imagine it will do much good, if I make it that far, that is. There's no escape when the time done come near, and I feel it close by..."

He could go no further. His voice trailed away, and he seemed to shrivel into something not quite lifelike.

I moved quickly through the cars, giving only minimal attention to the wounded. The exchange had shaken me. If he started talking, who knew where it would go. By the time I was a mile away from Bristoe Station, the train would be in Manassas, and he could be blabbing to God knew whom. Best casing it, once alerted to the presence of a rebel provocateur, the authorities would at least increase their presence in the area. I didn't need that, and I sure didn't need anything to alert Hawkface.

As I moved down to the next car, I reasoned that it just might turn into a non-problem. He was clearly on the endangered list. Even if he survived to Manassas, he might not be able to tell a credible tale. Would anyone ever have the time to listen to one more poor soul's demented ravings?

There was no meaningful life ahead for him anyway! A farm boy with no hand wasn't exactly going to be in demand. Just another ward of the government he had given his all for. And with a scarred and disfigured face, his Becky Sue would find someone else, if she hadn't already done so.

"Yes," I muttered to no one but myself, as if the uttered word trumped unspeakable thoughts.

He would be just a droplet in a downpour of death if he were to not make it to the junction. Another name forgotten in the national angst of lost military campaigns and doomed manifest destinies. He would just be one more soldier fated to breathe his last before making it home. That's all—just one more! No one would know or care where, when, or how he died.

I found myself back in his car but avoiding where he lay propped up in the corner. *It will be easy*, I thought. Easy and merciful. He couldn't be allowed to deny the hero his reunion with his daughter. Not now! A daughter's father, a nation's liberator, a soldier's soldier.

The sun was slowly granting my wish for darkness. It was barely light inside the swaying old cars now, and my patient had become just a shadow—a shadow with no name and no future. As if I was the one with the shattered body and psyche, I stumbled toward him. His one eye was hooded over, but I felt his presence with me, nevertheless. It summoned me and mocked me, surrendered to me and condemned me. I could see no sign of life in the wasted body, but he possessed a burning energy that drew us together.

I knelt by his side with my hand on his shoulder just inches from his throat. I could see the slight pulse of his carotid artery and hear his labored respiration. His face already had death's chalky pallor. Surrounded by maybe forty other shattered bodies, we were alone, he and I. *Look at me!* I silently screamed. *Look at your killer angel, I willed him! Look, look at me, damn you. Look!*

Was that a smile on his pimpled face? Was he laughing at me? I couldn't breathe here in the fetid confines of this hellish ambulance, this filthy ferry of Charon.

This was no time to wax philosophic and no time for squeamishness.

The locomotive's somnolent tempo suddenly changed, and I could feel our human cargo shift with the slight deceleration. We were pulling into what had to be Bristoe Station at last. At long last!

It was now—now or never. I reached over to cup his jaw with my right hand and to anchor his head with my left. A sudden twisting shove, and it would be over. First, a quick prayer for his soul, and then one for mine!

Not a minute to lose now!

The train lurched again, and I lost my balance for a moment. Steadying myself, I glanced down at a small red puddle spreading around his shattered fingers. In just that instant, everything changed. My charge—not my victim now—was bleeding to death. No wonder the clammy pastiness and shallow breath. No time to think!

Within seconds, I had the boy on his back with his feet elevated to treat for hemorrhagic-induced shock and his hand up and re-bandaged to staunch the flow of blood. I bathed his now-cool forehead with a bit of water and thought I saw a hint of flush on his face, although it was difficult to tell in the gloom of a rapidly approaching night.

There was hope for him, if not for me.

With the frightening recognition of what I had turned into, I walked away from the precipice and out, tumbling down a steep embankment. Just before coming to a rough stop at the bottom of a wet ravine, I saw the train slowly pick up steam again as it passed a wooden building with a sign. *Bristoe Station*! I had arrived.

CHAPTER 24

What had I been thinking? What had started out as a short five-mile or so trek following the tracks to just south of the Gap line had turned into an amateurish thrashing around in the middle of the night. I was hopelessly lost.

It had all seemed so simple. Admittedly, both Lee and Toomey had been skeptical, but I had let passion rule reason and had brushed aside their reservations. So now the former jungle fighter was lost in a little stretch of lightly-wooded countryside in what had been his own backyard for two years. Apparently I had forgotten all I had ever learned about land navigation. The first of which was to not rely on man-made landmarks. And the second was to have brought a compass and map along.

I had gotten off to a rocky start. Almost immediately after jumping from the train, I realized I should have waited until it had crossed the small creek at the station. I had moved upstream to find a place to ford it, and I hadn't seen the tracks since. It was dark as coal, and I couldn't see the time on my pocket watch, so I had only the vaguest notion of how long I had been stumbling along. My sense of direction had completely let me down. The tracks were someplace nearby, but I no longer trusted my judgment on that either. Twice already, alerted by the rumblings of locomotives, I had headed in the direction of where I thought the tracks were, only to become even more disoriented.

I had had to avoid several mounted patrols but had had little difficulty. This area was, and had been for several months, firmly in Union hands. Other than infrequent forays by irregulars and sympathizers, they had had little reason to rigorously patrol this part of Northern Virginia. Now, with the war possibly winding down and political solutions imminent, there was little stomach for conducting pointless operations. No one wanted to be the last to die for a lost cause. It was a feeling I remembered all too well.

I was going to have to find a place to stop until daylight before I found myself even farther away from Louisa's. Which meant the whole operation would be delayed a day. Not a show-stopper, but more risky. Who was I kidding—the whole thing was a risky, madcap adventure not very well thought out. I was hungry, I was lost, my feet hurt, and time was running out.

My nature was to keep moving toward my goal, but fatigue and what little sense I had left finally won out. I angled toward a small break in the terrain that might be able to afford some modicum of cover and concealment and gratefully lowered myself to the ground. As I lay back against a fallen tree, I had just time to reflect on what a day it had been before drifting off to an exhausted but fitful sleep.

It was nothing I could identify, but something roused me. What was it? Trees rustling in the light breeze and faint background noises were still there. Something changed the rhythm of the countryside, though. A tempo that hadn't been there a minute earlier. Different sounds barely unidentifiable. Familiar noises, a crackle, and smells in the early morning air. I'd been part of its life before, but when? Where? What was it?

Slowly, so slowly, waves of recognition tantalizingly out of reach nudged me back to my feet again. Old bones creaked, and aching muscles protested. Whatever it was drew me irresistibly up a gentle slope. With dawn's anticipation, the firmament above receded as the earth below rumbled, and suddenly, I knew.

Topping the rise, I instinctively crouched and moved down to the opposite side's military crest. There below, thousands of twinkling fireflies illuminated the waking giant as it stretched its limbs to every point of the compass. It was a sight to see—an awesome and fearsome sight.

And it changed everything!

It was a field army slowly rousing itself from its slumbers. It was more than just an army, though. It was an intact army— intact and where one was not supposed to be. Not yet anyway. Not here, and not now! President Lincoln formed Pope's short-lived Army of Virginia toward the end of June 1862—a little over a week ago. But its component parts were spread all over the state. Jackson had bloodied two of its three corps in his famous Valley campaign just prior to his reappearance on Porter's right flank last week.

Is that all it had been, a mere week ago?

There just wasn't any way. Banks and Fremont's corps were still licking their wounds and were not yet up to strength. The other corps, McDowell's divisions, was a viable fighting force, but it was back in Fredericksburg. Porter's corps would have eventually been added to the mix, but that wouldn't be happening now. Not in this time.

So whose army was this, and where did it come from? It was Pope's, obviously. But one vastly different from the one he had fielded in the previous lifetime. Judging from the orderly rows of campfires, artillery, and tents, this was no defeated force dragging ass back from the Shenandoah Valley. Nor was it a hastily put together assortment of disparate support units and ragtag garrison troops. From what I could see, it appeared to be a top of the line, combat-proven, disciplined army. It was huge and growing bigger.

I was looking down on a vast cantonment area of tens of thousands of troops on the Plains of Manassas at the junction of the Orange and Alexandria and the Manassas Gap Railroads. I had no notion of how I got to where I was, but I had ended up less than a mile from Louisa's and my final rendezvous with Hawkface. Which proved that even a blind pig could uncover a truffle once in a while!

From what I could tell in the dawn's early light, there were maybe a hundred regimental flags arranged in tidy ranks and echelons below me. Just a quick guess put the numbers at forty or fifty thousand pairs of boots on the ground. And more arriving as I watched—from both rail lines: the Gap from the west, and the Orange from the direction of Washington. Lincoln had indeed wasted no time.

They had to be coming from the western theater of operations, from Tennessee, largely. Pope would soon have a huge army, a formidable fighting command, to lead deep into the heart of the Confederacy! These were men not used to defeat. They had been successful more often than not. Prior to Lincoln summoning him to lead his latest army, Pope himself had been a victorious western general. He may have been successful there, but Lee had made pretty short work of him here.

That was then, though. This was now, and the now was a different situation.

Back then, Pope had to use valuable time preparing his force for combat operations. He was also obliged to wait for McClellan's extraction from the peninsula so he could add Porter's corps to his army. By the time he was ready to commence offensive operations, McClellan's departure freed Lee to head north to confront the new threat in the Second Manassas battle. And right here in this very place, where this tremendous army was being born, Lee had administered the *coup de grâce* to Lincoln's stillborn Army of Virginia.

True, in this world, General Lee has inflicted a stunning and decisive strategic defeat on the pride of the Union war effort. Nevertheless, he was still obliged to maintain his position near Richmond until Lincoln agreed to the terms of McClellan's surrender. From the looks of this force, those terms were not going to be approved anytime soon. This was classic Lincoln. Once again, I had cause to marvel at the political and military acumen of the man in Washington.

Would it be straight toward the capital of the Confederacy and Lee's Army of Northern Virginia? Or would he go for the fertile Shenandoah Valley and lay waste the south's breadbasket before proceeding on to Richmond? Either way, the new nation was in mortal danger. Unless Lee could elicit McClellan's total surrender with all its means of waging war in the next day or so, he would have two huge armies: one to his front, and one to his rear. Not even a Lee could prevail in such a scenario.

So now Lee is held in place by Lincoln's stalling tactic, while Pope, no longer needing to reorganize, is free to launch his attack. Lee had to be warned! He had to somehow disengage from McClellan's front and move his victorious but worn force to the north to confront this new threat, not to mention McDowell's corps in Fredericksburg. All the while he had to be mindful that a not-yet-surrendered McClellan was still a potent force. Suddenly, what had seemed so exhilaratingly certain a few short hours ago now was collapsing literally before my eyes.

And pitifully, there was little I could do about it. It would be next to impossible to get back to Richmond and warn Lee. And even if I could, what could he do about it with a reenergized and resurgent McClellan to his rear? And what about unfortunate Mildred's fate at the hands of Hawkface? Was she just plain expendable?

I resolved not. I had pledged to bring her home.

And Hawkface? Well, he was where Mildred was.

Lee and the new republic would have to fend for themselves.

With that, I pulled myself together and started the short trip to Louisa's place. At least I knew how to get there, now!

It took almost thirty minutes to make the ten minute walk.

In the dawn's early light, I couldn't see what I was looking for yet, but I could smell it. The accusing stench of corruption faithfully guided me. It was palpable now. He was there. Only a few more steps to finish what had been denied me at Mechanicsville, and to deliver to Lee his Precious Life.

It was just beginning to be light enough for me to discern individual trees from the gloom of the forest. I had taken the time to circle around and come in from well north of the farmhouse. I was approaching from the direction young Tom and I had come that day so many heartaches ago, past the long-deserted slave quarters, toward the back of the house.

There it was. The only home I had known here. Now it was a derelict—a casualty of war, like hundreds of others throughout the South. But this was no house abandoned to warring regiments. Its owner had yielded not one handful of Virginia earth to its conquerors. Instead, she had stood her ground, and for that, she had been murdered.

Despite its appearance of abandoned seediness, the ravages of time and circumstances inadequately signified the putrefaction lurking inside.

Finally, I settled in between the well and outhouse along the tree line. Either way he went, I intended to waylay him when he came out to begin his morning ablutions. I double-checked the Colt and the Beretta. Both were ready to exact vengeance— vengeance masquerading as justice, maybe. I didn't care! Others could call it whatever they wanted. I just called it long overdue.

I was satisfied he would be coming out at some point fairly soon. I didn't have any problems with the morality of taking him out straight away. If he came out with Mildred in tow, that was another matter. How it would play out would depend on the scenario presented. I would just have to wait and see.

Ominous darkening clouds, a smattering of rain, and louder and louder winds lent a surreal urgency to it all.

I didn't have long to wait, but instead of Hawkface, it was a lone rider coming down Sudley Road, heading this way. That had to spell trouble of some kind. Why would someone be coming here? Something else to worry about! Anything out of the ordinary was potentially a problem. I could wait it out if I had to, but I damned sure wasn't keen about hanging around in the middle of the Union army.

As he approached, I couldn't help but notice something familiar about him.

He passed out of sight in the front of the farmhouse. If Hawkface came out now, I would have to let him pass until the stranger left. What about Mildred, though? She would need to have her morning needs tended to also. Sooner or later, they both had to come this way. The crapper was here, and the well was here. It was just a matter of time.

It looked like we were going to get a storm too. The wind seemed to have taken on a life of its own. Now it was more of a roar—a roar that kept building in volume and intensity. Why were things always difficult?

As was usually the case for me nowadays, events answered my questions and dictated my actions.

A man's voice called out from the front of the house, "Y'all home in there?"

A sudden stillness for a moment, and then the backdoor crashed open, and, with a streak of blurred motion, a young boy in shorts flew off the small porch and hit the ground in full stride. He was running for all he was worth and heading straight for me. But it wasn't a boy. It was a young woman, with her dress gathered immodestly above her knees, doing a very credible one hundred-meter dash. Immediately, another figure burst through the screen door after her. Mildred and Hawkface!

Meticulously laid out plans were legion; plans actually followed were chimeras.

The daughter I was here to rescue, and the man I was here to kill, both in front of me. I leapt to my feet with Colt raised, and all thoughts of using the much quieter automatic were gone with the wind. It all moved forward in fits and starts: Mildred, her bodice torn and her left hand bandaged, momentarily swerved away as she saw me rising from the bushes; Hawkface, his visage contorting with savage recognition, came to a stop and fumbled for his pistol. And around the corner of the house, a familiar figure loomed large in the unfolding drama.

Just as before, I had the advantage. He was reaching for his sidearm, and I had mine in hand. He was off balance from running, and I was steady as a rock. I wasted not even a heartbeat of hesitation. Like Orestes, I had come to shed blood—blood for blood shed! Like the executioner's final stroke, my arm chopped down for the shot. It wasn't one that I would have chosen but easily doable. Again, he never faltered but dropped to one knee and, with single-minded purposefulness, finally pulled his pistol free. In that strobe-light clarity of frozen and fateful time, I saw it was a modern large-bore pistol.

Dead perfect axis down the forearm to the evil heart and the trigger's abrupt release of built-up energy. A last look before the familiar report and recoil.

A grasping, desperate collision! The Colt, unused and uselessly pointed nowhere. Hawkface, the phoenix rising. Thunder off to my right.

An abused Mildred was sobbing and clinging to my shoulder. Her headlong, panicked flight had knocked me off balance. The tables were turned now. My nemesis was aiming his pistol as I shoved her away in a vain attempt to bring mine to bear. Too late!

Then, out of nowhere, the thunderous rumble of a cloud's shadow enveloped me, and then was gone. Panting exertions and muttered curses followed as I rolled away from the hysterical young woman.

Where was she? I yelled for her to run, as much to save her as to distract him long enough to do something brilliant. My momentum carried me close to the corner of the house, but I had about run out of roll. I steeled myself for the shot—the shot and the impact.

But nothing! No shot, no impact. No nothing. Even as my fingers curled around the revolver's grip, I wondered if it was but a split-second dream before the merciless noose snapped taut.

I pulled myself to my hands and knees, still holding the pistol. With all the effort I could muster, I struggled to my feet and stumbled toward a curiously-misshapen Hawkface thrashing around in a paroxysm on the ground. I lifted my pistol to send this two-headed monster to hell.

What! Two-headed? It wasn't Hawkface anymore. Somehow he had changed into—

"Reckon us about even now, Mr. Kelly. Yep, reckon so."

"James!"

It was Robinson! It was James Robinson picking himself up and straddling a now-motionless Hawkface. Such was the insanity of the day. James Robinson, the man John Brown had almost killed. And the man I had saved.

"James," I repeated. "What are you doing here? What's going on, James? Why are you here?"

"I been keeping an eye on Mrs. Louisa's place after she died, and when I noticed folks fooling around here yesterday, I determined to come by. Looks like a good thing I did too. You don't look so good, but don't see any holes in you."

He punctuated his observation by handing me Hawkface's pistol. It was a Ruger Blackhawk, a .44 magnum. Hell of a pistol. Dirty Harry would have been happy with it.

A quick look around revealed an apprehensive Mildred tentatively making her way toward us. She had lowered her dress to a more modest length and was clutching her bodice. She was no longer the precocious young girl admonishing a doting dad. She had seen a hell that no young woman of a privileged class could ever have imagined, and yet she had come through it.

"Colonel Kelly, is that you? How did you get here? How did you know where we were? What has happened to our world? That man," she said, pointing to where Hawkface was now moaning and trying to get up, "wants to kill you. He's crazy, demented. He wants to do terrible things to you, things I never heard of. He is a fiend, a devil on this earth. Here in Virginia. What could you have done to him to hate you so?"

If she only knew how many times I had wondered that very same thing. Several times I had come tantalizingly close to making some kind of connection, but it had always slipped away.

This Lee daughter was of the same stock as her famous father. She never mentioned what the beast might have done to her, only her concern for me. Her bloodied hand confirmed my worst fears: that he had maimed her to impress Lee to do his bidding.

"I wish I knew, Miss Mildred. But it doesn't matter now. It's going to be all right for you. We will get you back to your parents as soon as possible."

I turned to James and asked, "Will you help me, James? I need to get this young woman back to Richmond."

"Yessir, I surely will if I can, Mr. Kelly. There are two horses behind the stable. Reckon the livery is back there somewhere. Who is this...?"

Just then, the pounding of steam engine pistons and several shrill whistle blasts announced an approaching train. It was the Manassas Gap coming from the northwest toward the junction. More troops for Pope's army.

Just one more problem! Wind howling, steam engines pounding, whistles shrieking. And now rain adding to the mix. I could hardly think! We were right in the middle of all the Yankees in the entire universe, and now this complication. It was just too much.

The track ended at the junction just about a mile away, and anyone looking our way might very well consider all this worthy enough to report to the authorities there. That was the last thing we needed, so I grabbed Mildred by the arm and pushed her closer to the side of the house and yelled for James to bring our prisoner. Before the train, I had been contemplating just how I was going to kill Hawkface. I couldn't shoot him in front of

Robinson and Mildred, but I had been denied too many times. He had to die, and it had to be me that did the killing. They could just judge me as they wished. I had already been judged—by a higher authority anyway.

After all, just a few short hours ago, I had been within a train lurch of murdering a defenseless boy for nothing short of expediency. Well, a few minutes more thought on Hawkface's fate wouldn't hurt.

I didn't get even a few seconds!

Everything happened at once: another loud shriek from the engine's whistle, Robinson's mount bolted, Mildred grabbed my arm in surprise, the train puffed in view, and Hawkface bowled by James and disappeared around the opposite corner of the house. Just like that, everything was topsy-turvy.

Then there was the wind. Louder and louder! Blacker and blacker!

With the engine pounding and screaming behind me, I tore out around my side of the house to see him clear the other side. He was running for the tracks in an ungainly lope, trying to put the train between us. Because of his limp, I quickly gained on him. It was an uneven race, though.

He could afford to wait until the last minute to commit to crossing over. I couldn't! If I hesitated, I would lose my opportunity to the passing train, and he could get across to safety on the other side. If I jumped the tracks, he could just stay on this side, and I would have wait until the train passed before I could get back.

The deafening cacophony of iron brakes and howling whistles left no time for rational thought, just instinctive reactions. Instinct trumped reason in one final explosion of revenge.

At a dead run, I raised the Colt one last time and took the shot. I took it, and a whirling hell engulfed us all.

EPILOGUE

It was really all I could have done. I had imagined and fantasized for months how I would kill the sorry son of a bitch, and finally all I had left was a snap shot. I may have hit him; I thought I had. It would never be enough, though. I had wanted to feel the killing, to know I had pulled the trigger that had sent him to hell. But now I would never get to know. He had just disappeared. Present for duty, and in a blink of an eye, AWOL.

In a roaring and rising crescendo of rage and violence, the cyclonic maelstrom had smashed into the train just as I fired. The engine shuddered, and Hawkface had disappeared as I went flying through the air. The passenger cars lifted themselves and the engine off the tracks. It had been all sound and commotion. And wind. Wind that had sucked the air out of my lungs as it flung me against the tree nearest the tracks.

I remembered that I couldn't move. That all I had been able to do was hang on to the base of that tree—a tree that with each torturous second seemed as if it would lose its fragile connection with this world.

Now, a little more than a week later, it was all a fading memory. I was out of action and out of the picture. What had started in Margaret's lab continued to unfold, though. Just as man-made killing machines leave behind consequences, nature's weapons of mayhem are no different. Natural disasters may be indiscriminately purposeless. But, like their man-made counterparts, their application seems brutally discriminate. If it had been a Confederate army bivouacking that history altering day, the result would have been just as catastrophic for their cause of self-determination as it was now being for Lincoln's efforts to preserve the Union. And some would have seen the hand of God in that, just as they were now seeing it in Washington's overplayed hand.

Actually, our tornado was short-lived and wreaked little destruction other than the Gap line. It tore the engine from its tracks like a plastic toy being tossed around by an unruly child. The smash up of its following passenger and freight cars was a spectacular sight, I was told. How the twister could have ripped hundreds of tons of locomotive and rolling stock apart and yet spared Mildred, James, and me was impossible to fathom. It did, though, just as tornados have done throughout history!

But our little acre of disaster was nothing compared to what struck the junction and the marshaling yards of Pope's army. Local accounts varied, but all agreed that several twisters set down in about a three-mile radius there. The casualty count was significant, but not more than several hundred dead, injured, and missing. With what it could have done, one could make the argument the tornado was mercifully benign.

But what it did to the army's vast staging area was anything but. Thousands of tons of supplies, rations, ammunitions, artillery pieces, forage, and more were destroyed or scattered across the countryside. In less than five minutes, most of the divisions and regimental headquarters ceased to exist as operational elements. The means of keeping an army in the field and on the move—the rail system, supplies, wagon trains, and organizational structures—were totally lost or rendered unusable. Time had suddenly become very short for President Lincoln.

Perhaps mindful of my parting warnings, Lee had convinced President Davis to order a redeployment of one wing of Lee's worn and depleted army north toward Fredericksburg. Under the command of Richmond's newest hero, Major General Chase Whiting, those Confederate divisions served as a blocking force to McDowell's federal divisions. He also sent a now fully-recovered Stonewall Jackson back to the Shenandoah Valley, where he had been so successful before.

About the time the tornado tore into Pope's embryonic command.

At that point, President Lincoln, as shrewd a president who ever held the office, saw it was useless to continue the fight—that the Union lay sundered. He may have very well seen Jackson's and Whiting's redeployment as a threat to Washington. And as he had stripped his western forces to create Pope's now aborted Army of Virginia, he had to watch helplessly as Confederate forces moved to fill the void left by the departed federal divisions.

In any event, that afternoon, he ordered his field commanders to cease all offensive operations, and he instructed Secretary of State Seward to establish contact with his Confederate counterpart to discuss cessation of hostilities and to ask the British Embassy to use their good offices to mediate a truce between the two sides. Jefferson Davis, with one federal army captured by General Lee and another left in shambles by the forces of nature, agreed to negotiate. But he agreed only to a temporary truce until Union armies withdrew from all territories of the seceded states, including New Orleans and the breakaway state of West Virginia.

Davis had the upper hand for now, but he realized it wouldn't last. The population and the industrial capacity disparity of the two sides were too great. It was incumbent to gain every advantage in strategic positioning of his forces in the occupied Confederate states, as well as to secure every political concession as quickly as possible. He also moved to seek recognition of the Confederate States of America by the major European powers. Most were glad to see the CSA as a counterweight to the growing strategic threat a unified America meant to their hegemony in world affairs.

Davis did have a few powerful hole cards, though: he had thousands of newly-inspired soldiers heading north, led by generals who knew how to win; he had a surrendered Union army with its vast logistical base; and he had good reason to believe European powers would recognize the new nation with the expectation their navies would soon break the blockade that had strangled the South's commerce.

And most important of all, he had the sure knowledge Northern public opinion was shifting dramatically against the war. They were getting tired of the endless levies for troops and the growing casualty lists. The Democrats were gaining ground for the midterm congressional election. Davis knew that Lincoln's short-term options were very few.

I was in Lee's Richmond home, tended to and recovering under the care of three of the Lee daughters, with Mary Lee supervising. My broken left leg was not healing as fast as everyone had hoped, probably because of the long, rough ride back to Richmond, which I only vaguely remembered. Besides the broken leg, I had a couple of cracked ribs and various lacerations and bruises, all of which were healing nicely.

Each evening, General Lee would look in on me to ask how I was doing. I had asked that Tom and Mary be found and taken care of and that some provisions be made for getting Robinson back to his home near Manassas. He had assured me that James had been escorted back home on one of the casualty trains and that he had been rewarded handsomely in appreciation for his part in rescuing Mildred. He was also making every effort to locate Tom and Mary.

Last night, Lee very graciously brought me up to speed on all the current affairs, which was how I was so informed, probably more so than all but a couple dozen high-ranking officials and generals. He assured me negotiations were proceeding briskly and that adequate safeguards were in place to protect the homeland from further encroachment on Confederate territory. He added, though, that it appeared President Davis would end up conceding the breakaway western section of Virginia to the US. In turn, President Lincoln agreed to promptly remove the federal garrison from New Orleans. It seemed a fair trade-off.

I could hobble around a bit with crutches, but mostly I was confined to my bed and the ministrations of the Lee women. To them, as well as to all the household, I was a hero of the first order. I had been treated like a king by everyone, including the staff. This morning, though, everyone was acting a little strange. Not unfriendly by any means, maybe just more reserved than before. Reserved and a bit mysterious. It was so out of character. I had found the Lee home to be a house of warmth and love, and now everyone seemed enigmatic, even somewhat Delphic, in their dialogue with me.

I was just getting up to practice with my new crutches when I heard the gentle notes of the opening movement of Beethoven's "Moonlight Sonata." As always, I was intrigued by the slow, even tentative, melody so different from the traditional sonata form. One of the girls, I supposed, was practicing. Since being confined to bed for the past few days, I was always eager for a break from the boredom, so I limped toward the parlor to show my appreciation.

Then, in a dramatic switch, the sweet melody was replaced by the discordant notes of a very familiar tune—one that I knew but couldn't quite place. It didn't belong here, in this place, or in this—

Seated at the piano was a woman, a stranger with her back to me. Then I noticed Robert E. Lee standing next to her. Strange, it was midday, and he wasn't in the habit of coming home for lunch. Finally, I saw the rest of the family gathered around behind him, and the staff assembled at the large entryway into the parlor. All were looking at me with expectant smiles on their faces, the Lees and the household staff. Black and white!

What is going on? The rhythmic notes gelled, and I finally picked the tune out of my past. It was "Chopsticks!" And the last time I heard it was the night of Hurricane Clyde at Margaret's apartment when we—

She finished the piece and turned to me and said, "Hello, John."

It was the woman in the crowd at Davis's mansion when he had announced McClellan's capitulation. The woman who I had mistook for Margaret. Wait a minute, how could she know my name? What was she doing here in the Lee house anyway?

The Lees and the staff broke into applause and cheers. What was happening?

It was her. It was a much, much older Margaret. How could that be? And then I knew! What had I been thinking that his-tory-making day? Margaret had been frozen in time for me; I had compared that woman to the Margaret I had left behind. It had been her all along. Just like Paul, she had aged too. She had grown older.

"Margaret," I asked?

She stepped into my arms, and suddenly, we were alone in the room.

"Yes, dear John, it is me. You've been waiting almost three years for me, but I've been waiting much longer for you," she responded.

It was only later that Margaret told me about the disappearance of her ex-boyfriend, the project's Director of Security. So finally, I knew who Hawkface was and why he came to my world.